I0606736

This was the banking world, jobs here were not supposed to be dangerous…

"The incident at McBride's place worries me and, yes, I've run into this sort of thing in the past with a money laundering scheme at a bank in New York," Carenza said. "It can get nasty, which is why I want you to be careful. If you suspect something, say something. Don't try to *do* something. I intend to give this same speech to Campbell."

"Tony, I appreciate your frankness," Jim said. "You haven't said anything to Ed yet?"

"No, I decided to go after you first, and I'll get Ed later. I have to go back to Newark anyway and, besides, I'm convinced Ed is in the same place I am on this, only he understands the potential for manipulation more than I do. I think he also understands the risk and where the loose cannons might be."

"Do you really think we might be in danger?"

"Can't say, but given the way the guy at McBride's acted…well, all I can say is that it's better to be safe than sorry.

It is 1993, the banking world is in turmoil, and in New Jersey, there is outright panic. The big New York banks and emerging regionals are gobbling up everything in the state. Every financial institution is now both predator and prey. The Fed has opened the floodgates, and traditional banking ethics are disappearing. At a used book sale, Jim Fairmont, a career banker having worked for First State Bank for more than twenty-five years, finds a blank, signed invoice belonging to an auto parts supplier. The document is contained in a box of books donated by Larry McBride, a new-breed, brash, thirty-three-year-old former New York banker. McBride had been hired by First State Bank to give it credibility in its defensive entry into international banking and who, like Jim, is an avid book collector. Alerted by McBride's strange behavior at the book sale as he searched for something, which Jim suspects was the invoice, Jim begins to investigate McBride's relationships with some of First State's customers. What he uncovers is much bigger than he ever imagined, involving clearly unethical conduct and questionable international asset movements. His discoveries put him in the sights of New Jersey's underworld who are determined to protect McBride and his clients, putting not only Jim's life in danger, but those of his close associates' as well.

KUDOS for *What the Mirror Doesn't See*

In *What the Mirror Doesn't See* by Tim Holland, Jim Fairmont is a big-city banker who thinks he has discovered something illegal going on in his bank by the person in charge of the international banking department. The problem is that he doesn't know if what he suspects is actually going on, or if the person in question just has an unusual way of doing things. When Jim goes to his coworker, Ed Campbell, and explains his concerns, Ed, who has a lot of experience in international banking, confirms Jim's fears, and together they begin to investigate. But there is a lot more going on than they realize, and soon they are in over their heads. Now, not only their careers are at risk, but their lives too. Not being one who has much experience in high finance, I wasn't sure what to expect, but I soon found myself drawn into the mystery and the lives of the characters as they dig for the truth. Well written and intriguing, this is one you will want to read more than once so you can get what you missed before. A really good read. *~ Taylor Jones, The Review Team of Taylor Jones & Regan Murphy*

What the Mirror Doesn't See by Tim Holland is the story of man trying to do the right thing in a world where that is not always appreciated or even helpful to your career. Long-time banker, Jim Fairmont, goes to a book sale, where he sees a coworker from his bank acting strangely. Since Jim knows that both he and his coworker, Larry McBride, collect rare books, Jim isn't surprised to see Larry there. But when Larry starts frantically digging through the boxes of books that he donated to the book sale, Jim can't help but wonder what he's looking for. When Larry rushes out of the sale, Jim goes over to the boxes of Larry's books and finds a blank, signed invoice from a customer at the bank where they both work. Normally, he would have thought nothing of it, but considering the way Larry was behaving, Jim is concerned that something illegal is going that might hurt the bank. He takes the problem to another coworker, Ed Campbell, and the two of them begin to investigate, uncovering much more than either of them bargained for, especially when they find out that the bank might use the two of them as fall guys should any bad publicity touch the bank. But what nobody realizes is that there are other players involved who have a lot more to lose than reputations, and they don't even pretend to play by the rules. Holland's background in international banking is clearly evident as the story unfolds, weaving mystery and suspense with excellent character development and a solid plot, to create a tale of high-finance, intrigue, and two honest men who only want to do the right thing, no matter the cost. I found it educational, entertaining, and hard to put down. ~ *Regan Murphy, The Review Team of Taylor Jones & Regan Murphy*

ALSO BY TIM HOLLAND

The Sidney Lake Mystery Series

The Rising Tide ~
A Sidney Lake Lowcountry Mystery

WHAT THE MIRROR DOESN'T SEE

TIM HOLLAND

A Black Opal Books Publication

GENRE: FINANCIAL THRILLER/MYSTERY/AMATEUR SLEUTHS

This is a work of fiction. Names, places, characters and incidents are either the product of the author's imagination or are used fictitiously, and any resemblance to any actual persons, living or dead, businesses, organizations, events or locales is entirely coincidental. All trademarks, service marks, registered trademarks, and registered service marks are the property of their respective owners and are used herein for identification purposes only. The publisher does not have any control over or assume any responsibility for author or third-party websites or their contents.

WHAT THE MIRROR DOESN'T SEE
Copyright © 2018 by Tim Holland
Cover Design by Jackson Cover Designs
All cover art copyright © 2018
All Rights Reserved
Print ISBN: 978-1-626948-71-6

First Publication: FEBRUARY 2018

All rights reserved under the International and Pan-American Copyright Conventions. No part of this book may be reproduced or transmitted in any form or by any means, electronic or mechanical, including photocopying, recording, or by any information storage and retrieval system, without permission in writing from the publisher.

WARNING: The unauthorized reproduction or distribution of this copyrighted work is illegal. Criminal copyright infringement, including infringement without monetary gain, is investigated by the FBI and is punishable by up to 5 years in federal prison and a fine of $250,000. Anyone pirating our ebooks will be prosecuted to the fullest extent of the law and may be liable for each individual download resulting therefrom.

ABOUT THE PRINT VERSION: If you purchased a print version of this book without a cover, you should be aware that the book is stolen property. It was reported as "unsold and destroyed" to the publisher, and neither the author nor the publisher has received any payment for this "stripped book."

IF YOU FIND AN EBOOK OR PRINT VERSION OF THIS BOOK BEING SOLD OR SHARED ILLEGALLY, PLEASE REPORT IT TO: lpn@blackopalbooks.com

Published by Black Opal Books **http://www.blackopalbooks.com**

DEDICATION

Carol Kent Holland

*My wife, whose love, friendship, and guidance
makes it all worthwhile.*

I saluted a nobody.
I saw him in a looking glass.
He smiled—so did I.
He crumbled the skin on his forehead,
Frowning—so did I
Everything I did he did.
I said, "Hello, I know you."
And I was a liar to say so.

~ Carl Sandburg
from "Chicago Poet,"
Cornhuskers

CHAPTER 1

The Book Sale

1993:

Had a strange experience at the book sale this morning," Jim Fairmont reported, while making a pot of coffee.

"Not mystical, I hope. Wouldn't want to lose you to some cult in New Mexico and have to suffer here all winter by myself," Marian Fairmont replied to her husband's thoughtful observation in her usual quick-witted way.

It was how her mind worked, strange responses just seemed to jump to her lips as though certain words triggered a spring-loaded, verbal slingshot that released a storehouse of retorts awaiting the right words to release them.

Jim smiled. "No chance of that. It was McBride. Very curious behavior."

"In what way?"

"Well, you know how he and I are usually the first ones at the sale on Saturdays?"

"Oh, yes. We wouldn't want anything to get away from us, would we?"

"Now, now, you know I've done very well at that sale. I've picked up some pretty good first editions. Anyway, that's not what I was saying. It was McBride. He really acted strange. You know, I thought for sure I would be ahead of him this morning, with the rain and everything."

As he began to outline the events of the morning, Marian thumbed through the contents of the Saturday mail and concentrated on her sorting. Jim, on the other hand, continued the process of making a pot of coffee as he talked and reviewed his book sale experience…

❦

The rain fell gently, barely more than a mist, as Jim walked along the cracked and worn sidewalk. He looked appreciatively at the old tree in front of the Oak Street School. The tree's thick girth and bulging root structure caused the sidewalk to be laid around it in a neat semi-circle. It should have been cut down, the new residents claimed. It should have been cut down, some members of the town counsel claimed, fearing a potential law suit from one of the new residents whose daydreaming youngster might accidentally walk into it. Calmer heads prevailed and the tree—which happened to be the old oak in the school name—was grandfathered, having reached its maturity long before the construction of the school. So now it stood as a sentinel watching over generation after generation of promising young minds in the historic center of Liberty Corner, New Jersey.

His black umbrella held upright in his right hand, he made his way to the entrance that would lead him to the now designated "multipurpose" room, using the four steps instead of the newly built ramp for the handicapped. Opening the door, he deftly avoided being impaled on the tip of an umbrella being thrust out in front of a young woman in an obvious rush.

"Whoa!" he said as he jumped to the side, brushed against the sign announcing the *AAUW 1993 Book Sale*, and knocked it off the tape holding it to the inside of the door's window.

"Oh, I'm terribly sorry. Did I hit you?"

"No, I'm fine. Good reflexes." He reached over to retrieve the sign.

"I am sorry."

"It's perfectly all right. I probably should have seen you coming. My own umbrella you see." He indicated that he had been holding it partially in front of his face. "Okay if I replace this?" he asked, referring to the sign.

"Oh, sure, but we're not open yet."

"Excuse me?"

"The book sale. You're here for the book sale, aren't you? We're not open yet."

"Oh, yes. I expected that. I was trying to be first."

"I'm afraid you're not."

"Really? You mean there's someone here ahead of me?

Wouldn't happen to be a dark-haired fellow in his mid-thirties, about five foot eight?"

"That's him."

"They still won't let him in until they officially open, will they?"

"Oh, no. We're still setting up. I have to bring in some more of the signs."

"Ah, well, don't let me keep you. I'll just head on in and keep the other fellow company. Here let me hold the door for you as you get that umbrella up."

Jim held the door open as the harried-looking American Association of University Women volunteer put up her umbrella and started out into the mist.

"Hope you find something you like," she said in parting.

"So do I. Thank you."

Jim watched the woman head down the stairs, then he let go of the door, turned quickly, and stepped into the vestibule, which was about ten feet square. Directly across from him was another set of doors, but on these were some hand-lettered signs and arrows on white poster paper which pointed the way to the used book sale. Although the old Labor Day Fair was gone, a victim of liability insurance rates that devoured the proceeds that would have gone to charity, the book sale continued, as it had become a major money-raising event for the AAUW. Books were collected all the yearlong so that by the sale weekend there were thousands of titles to choose from. It was difficult to go anywhere in town and not find a book-barrel: supermarkets, banks, town hall. They were everywhere, and they were always full.

As he opened the second set of doors, he immediately spotted the short, slim silhouette of Larry McBride standing at a table that blocked the entrance to the room, apparently talking intensely with someone just in front of him.

"Well, look who's up bright and early this morning. Hello, Larry." Jim offered the greeting as he stepped through the doorway. McBride turned and, seeing the speaker, said nothing in response. Not even a flicker of recognition crossed his small, bespeckled face, but he immediately turned and addressed the woman at the table.

"Told you he wouldn't be far behind me," Larry said and then continued talking to the woman as though no one had come along. "Would you happen to know from which estates the major donations have come?"

"Well, they're not all from estates."

"Oh, I'm sure he knows that," Jim cut in, and then, in a flippant tone, added, "But if you could point him in a direction where he might find something of rare value, but as yet undiscovered, I'm sure he would be most appreciative."

"Fairmont, I don't need your help," McBride snapped, exasperated.

The poor woman at the desk was beginning to look nervous. This being her first year as a volunteer at the sale—it wasn't what she had anticipated.

"Just being helpful."

"Now, miss," Larry continued. "Why don't you just tell me how the room is set up this year?"

"Well, as I started to say, not many of the books are from estates this year." As she spoke, the attendant stood up behind the desk and began pointing out sections of the room—a cavernous area that was filled with rectangular folding tables, upon which were stacked boxes and boxes of books. Some of the tables had identifying signs on them, such as *FICTION, BIOGRAPHY, RELIGION, HISTORY*, etc., while others had merely letters of the alphabet.

"And the 'special donation' section?" pursued McBride.

"We haven't set up that area this year."

"What do you mean you haven't set up that area?" McBride was obviously agitated, and his voice rose as he continued speaking. "Will it be set up later?"

"Well, as I said before, we haven't had many estate or special donors this year and, quite frankly, we've been somewhat short on volunteers, so that we just didn't have the time to set up two alphabetical groupings. I hope it's not going to be too inconvenient?"

He snapped his response at the unsuspecting volunteer, "Well, it is! When people make special donations, you should at least recognize them. Are you telling me everything is all mixed together out there? How the hell do you expect people to find the quality stuff? How do you people expect to make any money?"

"We do very well," said the woman, getting her back up. "Besides, this is a charity event. No one here is paid."

"Yes, yes, I know. What time can I go in?"

"It's still five minutes to eight, but I suppose there's no reason why you can't go in now."

"Good." Larry immediately turned and headed inside and could be heard mumbling, "You get what you pay for."

"I'm sorry," said Jim as he moved in front of the desk. "Didn't mean to start a row. Larry's usually a pretty good guy. A little down to earth sometimes but a pretty good guy, nonetheless. Not sure what's bugging him today."

"He certainly is rude," she said while getting a good look at her second customer of the day, as he moved from the hallway to her desk front.

"Well, I'm certainly not going to defend him. Is this your first time working the door?"

"Yes, it is."

"Well, look, I'm Jim Fairmont," he said, extending his hand. "And I do appreciate all you're doing. Volunteering your time, and all."

"Jean Slattery," she said, taking his hand. As she looked at him, the word *brown* came to mind as that's what she saw: brown hair, brown eyes, brown coat, brown sweater. Even the frames of his glasses were brown. "He is rather intense, isn't he?"

McBride came into view heading for the *BIOGRAPHY* section.

"A collector of books. But then so am I. He obviously has something on his mind today."

"Have you known one another long?"

"I suppose you could say we really don't know one another at all, even though we work for the same company." Fairmont spotted McBride moving toward the *FICTION* section. "Do you mind if I go in as well? Wouldn't want Mr. Rude to find something valuable and make his day."

"Sure," she said, cracking a smile. "Good luck," she offered as he started to move away from the desk. "By the way, the prices are posted above the books on each of the walls."

"Thank you. See you in a few hours."

Giving a short wave of his hand, Jim headed for the *FICTION* section to see what he could find. Books were everywhere. For the most part, they were arranged lying on their ends so that the spine was parallel to the table, making it easier to read the titles.

The selection was definitely smaller than in years past, although to a new browser it would be difficult to tell. Then he recalled that the woman said the estate and special donations were down this year. That, in itself though, was not significant, as it was all in the luck of the draw. Sometimes he had done well in small shops, so he knew volume was not always a critical factor. There was that time in Trenton when he had spent almost four hours in a used bookstore in The Commons. They had an enormous selection, but virtually every work by an author that interested him he already had. For all that time, he ended up with only one volume. Being the senior corporate officer of the commercial banking division of a bank had certain advantages, as it enabled Jim to travel around the state. He knew where most of the good used bookshops were, and he did his best to frequent them during his designated lunchtime—as long as he didn't have to entertain a customer. In fact, there had been a number of times when he specifically avoided a customer lunch in order to provide more time to pursue his hobby. Besides, over the years, many of his best contemporary account contacts—presidents, vice presidents, and treasurers—had many of the same interests as he did in history and literature. Although the group continued to diminish of late, as more and more of the old guard retired and were replaced by youngsters with a variety of advanced university degrees but lacking an actual education. The twenty-first century loomed just around the corner, and Jim didn't look upon it as a particularly inviting prospect given the emerging business leaders he had thus far come across.

Time passed quickly, and the room was beginning to fill. This was a favorite place for people to pick up their annual reading material inexpensively. Many of the books were best sellers only a few years ago. Not a bad bargain when you thought of it: eighteen and twenty dollar books going for one and two dollars. The big bargain hunters came on the final day when, in order to get rid of the leftovers, a bag of books went for two dollars. His own search was not going too well thus far, as all he had to show for his efforts was the original hard cover edition of *Number One* by John Dos Passos.

As he excused himself around a rather large, stern looking woman with a bulging shopping bag, he spotted a volume under the table and immediately squatted down, reaching for it. *The*

Breaking Strain by John Masters. This would make seventeen of Masters' books he now had in the original hardcover edition. Then, as he thumbed through the pages, checking the binding and the jacket, he saw, peripherally, a very intense Larry McBride looking through a box of books across from him. Jim had to admit he really did not know the man, had never engaged him in a serious non-business conversation. Jim began to consider what it was about McBride that bothered him. His appearance was pleasant enough—slightly below average height, mid-thirties, dark hair, clean shaven, neatly dressed. But there was that something in his manner. He usually had a quick smile and an engaging way about him that undoubtedly worked well with customers—that salesman's way of making pleasing small talk: remembering names of wives, children, dogs, common events of interest. But there was always something Jim felt in the background—something he didn't trust. When McBride smiled, Jim felt like grabbing for his wallet or double checking to see if there wasn't something sticking out of his back. To those who didn't know him well, McBride always appeared as a "good guy," smiling, joking, kidding, and pleasant. *But if you worked for him, what then?* Jim wondered.

McBride managed the international group at First State which, for a moderate sized emerging regional bank, meant working with local companies interested in importing and exporting and some foreign corporations located in the state. Jim covered the domestic corporations so that their paths did occasionally cross when one of Jim's customers needed some international help. They were usually civil in a business setting, but Jim just didn't know what to make of him. He remembered being invited to McBride's house in July for a cocktail party. Anyone perceived important was there, something he learned was a characteristic of a McBride gathering. The parties were always entertaining, probably the best given in a town of six thousand suburbanites. Everything was first class: the food, the conversation, the entertainment. But there always existed an edge to everything McBride did, which distracted from his efforts—usually involving trying to impress an acquaintance with his superior sense of culture. To attend the opera was not enough. McBride would make sure you knew he had season tickets, classical music was always playing in the background whenever you attended one of his gatherings, and he always served the in-fashion food and drink properly provided by the "in-caterer." Jim was quite sure the man must have spent every available cent he earned on entertaining and the finer things of life. Then again, maybe it was the international influence, the broader scope he was supposed to have for his job.

Recently, Jim and Marian had been invited to a number of McBride-sponsored events, and even though they were only business colleagues, Larry knew that Jim was a valuable addition to any evening. The Fairmonts were not old money, nor did they have a great deal of wealth, but they lived very comfortably with a sense of style that came from existing in a world Larry McBride didn't really understand. They lived in a two-hundred-year-old-house—that had been Marian's parents—in Fordstown, New Jersey. It sat in an area of similar homes on one-acre lots not far from the train station, which provided access to one of the primary commuter lines into lower Manhattan—Fordstown was an upscale town even 100 years ago. The New York theater district was a half hour to forty minutes away, depending on if you took the train or drove. The City was filled with museums and art galleries of every possible kind and the Public Library system was probably one of the best in the world. So opportunity was present. It was just a matter of taking advantage of it. And New York always proved to be one of those places where you were in control of your own destiny. Certainly, there were pressures from all sides, both good and bad, but the responsibility was still with the individual. Jim's parents were both in education, one at the University level and the other a local private high school. He grew up in an environment of books and argumentative discussion and was well prepared to mix with the Somerset County social scene. He and Marian hob-knobbed with the Pingry and Princeton crowd that traced their families back to the mid-1700s. He had considered teaching once, with thoughts of living the college professor's life but then decided, from a purely practical standpoint, somewhat prodded by financial considerations, to enter the world of commercial banking. In preparation, he did his mandatory time on Wall Street with Chase Manhattan Bank, learning the business until he had been actively recruited by First State. He now worked out of the Morristown Central Office, an easy drive from his home.

He spotted McBride again, this time, uncharacteristically on his hands and knees digging through a box of books under the table marked *BIOGRAPHY A-M*. Jim was two aisles away and could clearly see the intensity in Larry's face. It fascinated him so much that he just stopped what he was doing and stared. A man trying to look at the books on the table in front of him finally became tired of waiting for Jim to move and said: "Excuse me, can I get in here?" meaning the exact spot where Jim was standing.

Jim, startled, said, "Oh, I'm sorry. Certainly," and moved out of the man's way. Once set in motion, he kept moving toward the end of the row but continued to watch McBride on the floor. He seemed to be more interested in the boxes than the books in them. He kept looking at the identifying marks on their sides. Finally, McBride seemed to find the box he had been searching for, as he grabbed it with both hands and began to empty the books from it. By the time Jim was at the end of the row just behind McBride, he saw him pull some papers from the bottom of the box. He checked them over carefully and then stuffed them into the cover of one of the books he had previously removed from the box.

"Find anything interesting," Jim said in the friendliest tones he could muster.

Larry was startled by the comment and cleared his throat. "Oh, nothing special. One or two. A bit slow this year."

"Same here. Look, I'm really sorry about earlier at the door. I really didn't mean anything."

"Oh, I know," Larry said, now under control and flashing his best salesman's smile. "I shouldn't have snapped that way. You're an okay guy, Fairmont, it's just me. I have another appointment today at ten, and I really wanted to spend more time here. Anyway, I have to be on my way. Nothing seems to go right when you need it to. There just never seems to be enough time for anything."

"Not work I hope?"

"Actually it is. Some of these small exporters seem to work twenty-four hours a day and expect you to do the same."

"I guess it's a different breed. We old time domestic bankers just don't have a good handle on the international side. Hopefully, next week's international seminar will open our eyes a bit."

"That's why we're here. But I really do have to take off. I'll see you next week."

McBride tucked the book, into which he had placed the papers, under his arm and headed for the exit. Jim watched him as he made his way toward the nearest door, the one where they had come in. He was obviously in such a rush to leave that, when he reached Jean Slattery's desk and tried to pay for the book, she was clearly happy to remind him of the procedure and pointed to the back of the room, explaining that purchases had to be paid for at the exit in the back. McBride started in that direction but stopped at another table—the *TRAVEL* section. He looked to see if anyone was watching him, then placed the book he had obtained in the *BIOGRAPHY* section onto the *TRAVEL* section table, headed back to the entrance, now empty handed, and went out the door.

Finding all of this to be curious and certainly intriguing, Jim headed for the *TRAVEL* section table to see what it was that Larry had left behind. *American Caesar* by William Manchester was not a particularly valuable, although certainly noteworthy, biography of General Douglas MacArthur, even though it was a first edition. So it was puzzling that McBride had picked it up at all. Jim then began looking at it more closely, flipping through the pages and then the inside cover. *From the Library of L. A. McBride* jumped at him from the page. It was stamped in black ink in a most conspicuous place.

Why his own book? Jim mused.

It was not unusual to make a gift of some books to the sale. He had done it himself when he was cleaning up, getting rid of duplicates of those volumes he decided he didn't really want any longer. It was better than throwing them away, something it would be very difficult for either Jim or Larry to do. But why seek out a book you gave up only to search for it madly and then leave it behind? And what happened to the papers? Taking the book with him, Jim headed back to the *BIOGRAPHY* section and began to search for the box the book had come from. Like McBride, he ended up on his knees and wondered if anyone thought his conduct as strange as he had viewed Larry's to be. His search was not unlike McBride's, except that he had no idea of its object. He checked box after box until, upon opening one of the books, he came across the McBride library stamp. He then started emptying the books, as Larry had done, but found nothing unusual. Most of the books were biographies of one type or another and were a mix of hard cover and paperback. He assumed that McBride had been doing a cleanup of his biography section and this box was the result. With the box now empty and nothing to explain McBride's actions, Jim considered giving up when he saw a box, similar to the one he held, marked "Special Donation," a few feet down the aisle under an adjacent table. Jim began emptying the box and flipping through the books. He now understood why McBride had been upset about there not being that special donation section this year, as that would have made his search much easier. What Jim expected to find he had no idea but felt compelled to look—and suddenly there it was in the bottom of the box—another sheet of paper. Presumably, it had fallen into the box somehow when Larry did his weeding of books for the sale. Jim retrieved it. It appeared to be a sheet of some kind of letterhead stationery belonging to Alliance Automotive Export Corp. He stood up with the paper in his hand and left the box empty, with its former contents spewed on top of other boxes of books. He stared at the piece of paper, trying to determine what was different about it when he saw the words "Invoice No:" and a signature.

McBride wasted no time getting out of the building, taking the steps two at a time. On arriving, he had parked his car on Liberty Corner Road rather than in the school parking lot, so he would not be blocked, as so often happened on the first day of the book sale. He exited the door and headed to the left, crossing in front of the Liberty Corner Presbyterian Church, the way he had come. Halfway to his car he reached into his jacket pocket and retrieved the papers that had come from the box. He unfolded them and spread the sheets out slightly to count them and then stopped dead in his tracks. There were only four sheets. He was missing one.

"Damn!" he muttered aloud to himself and then began to analyze the situation.

Should he return to the book room and look for the missing sheet or go home first and make certain he didn't miscount? No, he was sure there were five sheets missing, he had to go back. It had to be in the second box. He didn't bother to look for it, as he didn't feel he needed to, once the papers were found in the first box. Turning to head back to the school, he took two steps and stopped. What about Fairmont? What would he say to him? How would he explain his return after having left in such a hurry?

Maybe he could sneak in and out without being seen, since he knew where to look, and the second box of books must be near-by. He knew it had not been emptied as he had carefully looked on all the tables and none of the books he had donated were on display. He would try it. But not by the front entrance. He stuffed the papers back into the inside pocket of his jacket and re-entered the school by the door designated as the exit from the sale area.

As he went past the payment table, the woman behind it, who had a simple cashbox in front of her along with three ball point pens for check writing, was about to speak but Larry spoke first.

"Sorry, just forgot something. Be right out," he said and whizzed right by her.

He stopped at the doorway to the book room to get his bearings and see where Jim Fairmont might be. McBride saw him standing in the middle of the *BIOGRAPHY* section looking at a sheet of paper. Mc Bride knew exactly what it was, but he wondered if Fairmont did.

CHAPTER 2

The Invoice

Jim concluded his tale with "I can't imagine what he was doing."

"It must have something to do with the paper you found. Are you sure it was blank?"

"Oh, it was definitely blank. I thought it was a sheet of stationery, at first, but it turned out to be an invoice form of some kind. Alliance Automotive, I think. Oh, and it was signed. Yes, that was a bit curious."

"Are you going to give it to him?"

"How can I? He would think I was snooping on him or worse—spying." Jim reached up into the cupboard where they kept the coffee.

"Weren't you?"

"Well, not in the strict sense." He retrieved the package of de-caffeinated coffee beans and placed them on the counter. The coffee brewer was already on the burner.

"No, I suppose not. You just hid behind some books and watched his every move. Then, after he left, you ran over to see what he left behind and then crawled around on the floor of a public building searching for what he may have missed. But you weren't spying." Marian, as usual, had reduced the event to its basic components. It was something she did very well: analyze and get to the heart of things. Jim always accused her of being extremely logical in the most un-logical of ways possible. He always found it absolutely amazing because she was rarely wrong. Instinct, intuition—whatever it was—it worked.

Marian continued sorting the mail on the kitchen counter into her usual three groupings: bills, mail to look at and, the largest pile, mail to throw away. "So, what are you going to do?"

Her light brown hair, which was cut just about shoulder length, framed her face as she worked. She looked younger than her fifty-two years, and that was, of course, by design, although, aside from the hair tint, her look was natural, almost plain, with little makeup. It was almost a uniform that many women who resided in well-to-do suburban areas seemed to wear in the 1990s, although that was changing rapidly. More than fifty percent of the women in Fordstown didn't have business careers of their own. Of course, thirty years ago that number would have been ninety percent. The reason for the massive growth of suburban areas was directly attributed to the two-income household, a good many of them DINKS—Double Income, No Kids.

"Nothing, I guess. He doesn't know I have it and it is blank. Maybe the other papers had writing on them, so this isn't important. Who knows?" He was now searching for the coffee grinder.

"It's in the cabinet under the microwave."

"Why is it there?"

"Because that's where it belongs."

"But I didn't put it there."

"Of course you didn't. When would it occur to you to put something back where it came from?"

"That's not a fair statement."

"I never said it was fair, only true."

It was a losing battle for him but one he greatly enjoyed. Frustrating, exasperating, but enjoyable.

"So how did you do at the book sale?" Marian continued. "You never did tell me if you found anything of real interest. I wish I could have come along. I could use some new reading material. I finally finished *Summer's Lease* and have nothing left."

"Can't help you there. Ended up with just the two books on the table, and Dos Passos and Masters are not among your favorites. Maybe we can stop by the bookstore later."

Saturday afternoons were reserved for general errands they would do together. Theoretically, Marian could handle all required chores during the week, since she was employed locally, being the proprietor of The Garden Walk, a store dedicated to odds and ends for the formal garden: sun dials, benches, plant hangers, and small specialized tools. However, she usually put in more hours a week than Jim, as she was also an elder in the Presbyterian Church—not a term she particularly fancied—served on one of its committees, and was on the board of trustees of two charitable groups as well as the Junior League.

"Good idea, I wanted to stop by the shop later this afternoon and see how Florence is making out." The "mail to throw away" category was unceremoniously deposited into the wastebasket under the sink. "Another tree down the drain. You know, sometimes I actually feel guilty throwing away all that paper. I guess when you're in the business of helping to make things grow you get to feel a little queasy when you see something nurtured for twenty years or so just tossed away."

"I suppose you could read the stuff."

"Not on your life! That would give credence to the idiots that sent it to us in the first place." Jim was about to make a reply about the questionable logic of Marian's two statements but decided better of it. "So you're not going to do anything about it."

"About what?"

"The paper, of course. Larry—remember—this morning?"

"Oh, yes. I didn't realize we were back on that."

"Never left."

"Just a minor detour." The coffee grinder came to life and Jim quietly counted six seconds to himself so the grounds would not be too fine.

"Which you missed."

Jim paused when he finished counting. "You did disguise it rather well. Shifting from a misplaced blank invoice form to junk mail to the unnecessary felling of trees."

"We never left the issue of paper. All neatly tied together."

"I see." He paused and then returned to the original subject. "No, I really don't see that I have any choice but to leave it alone. I suppose the only thing I could do would be to keep my ears open when I'm over at the international seminar next week. If there is some sort of crisis going on, I'll try to find out what it is. If it seems to relate to a missing invoice form, then I'm really not sure what I'll do."

The coffee grounds were transported to the coffee maker, which already had its filter in place, and Jim poured some hot water from the kettle over the grounds, just enough to wet them down.

"Why?"

"Think of it Marian, I find a blank invoice form in a box of books donated by the head of the bank's international department, which apparently belongs in the Newark office thirty miles east of here—where Larry works—at a book sale in Liberty Corner. There's no way I can make a connection to the bank without implicating McBride. Not to mention me snooping." Marian was about to speak, but he stopped her. "I know you can make it all seem perfectly logical and reasonable and I'm sure everyone would believe you, but there is no way *I* could make it believable." The initial supply of water had dripped through the grounds leaving them moist but unmoved. Jim added more water, this time filling about a third of the hopper containing the grounds. "No, I really think I'm just going to have to forget the whole thing. Not bring it up at all. Throw the invoice away and forget that I ever found it."

"Whatever you say."

Marian knew he wouldn't, though. After twenty-six years of marriage, she could read him pretty well, although, every now and then, he would surprise her, but, usually, he would stick with something until it came to some form of conclusion. After all, he had stuck with her even after that weekend fling she had. Admittedly it was more than twenty years ago—after she left Bankers Trust, and he was still with Chase.

She met Jim when she worked in the domestic credit department and was doing some line of credit revisions on three banks in Harrisburg, Pennsylvania. She called Chase to see what their lines of credit were to the banks. The credit analyst for the Mid-Atlantic region was on vacation, so they referred her directly to Jim, who was the junior account officer. They hit it off on the phone immediately. Lunch followed in a couple of days, then the theater, and they'd been together ever since.

There were some dramatic times. The stupid night with Ed Campbell almost ended everything, but, on the whole, they made a good team. They really liked one another. The thing with Campbell happened in their fifth year. It was stupid. She'd dated Ed before she met Jim. He worked as an international credit officer trainee at Bankers, but the draft caught him when he couldn't find a national guard reserve unit. She met Jim about six months after Ed left for the army and married him ten months later. By the time Ed came back, she was pregnant with Jeffrey and her Bankers Trust career no longer existed. That now-infamous Friday still troubled her. She knew right away it was a big mistake and immediately told Ed, who she never saw again and had no idea where he was or what ever happened to him. At the time, Jim had become an account officer with Chase and had just left for a two week trip to the West Coast—he needed to be at a Saturday dinner in San Francisco hosted by Bank of America—and Marian's mother-in-law took Jeffrey to the beach house in the Hamptons that she rented for the month of July. Marian should have gone along for the week with Jeffrey, but the plan was for her and Jim to have the week alone. Then came Jim's unexpected trip to California and Washington. She felt cheated. She knew it wasn't Jim's fault, but she blamed him anyway. So she stayed home, angry and disappointed.

On Monday, she and Mary Talbot decided to have lunch at Llewellyn Farms where Ed Campbell spotted her. He and someone else from Bankers were having lunch with some international people from Warner Lambert and were a few tables away. He came over. They had a brief chat, filled with fun remembrances of the good old days at Bankers. He wanted to talk more, so did she. They agreed to meet at four p.m. at the restaurant in the Governor Morris Inn. They talked for hours in the lounge. Then dinner. Then a room upstairs. It was stupid. She never saw Ed again, although he called. She told Jim a few weeks later. She couldn't hold it in. She couldn't live a lie. It was eating away at her. Jim was stoic and quiet as usual. She wanted him to yell. She did. She cried. He went for a walk. When he came back, they talked for a long time. It was 1974 and times were changing: the war was over, the wage and price freeze lifted, the foreign investment controls removed, Nixon was gone. Time for a change.

Jim took the offer from First State. Ed Campbell was not spoken of again.

Now, Jim poured a mug of coffee. "Want a cup?"

"No, I'm fine."

"Oh, by the way, do you know a Jean Slattery? She was working the door at the book sale."

"Slattery. Jean Slattery? No, I don't think so. Why?"

"Larry got a little testy on the way in this morning and, of course, I tried to make some smart remarks and probably only made things worse. He was really intense this morning. I guess those invoice papers he misplaced must have been bothering him—now that I think of it. Anyway, she seemed a little taken back by it all." He took a sip of his coffee as Marian began sorting the middle pile of mail into *keep* and *throw away*. "I guess that's why he was so snippy at the door. The missing papers."

She gave him a questioning look. "I thought you were going to forget it."

"I am, I am."

"Good, have a couple of more sips and let's get going. I do want to check on Florence."

๛

McBride sat at his desk in the study of his townhouse and stared blankly across the room. The four blank Alliance Automotive invoices retrieved from the book sale lay on the leather desk blotter in front of him. What to do?

He wanted to make sure he didn't compound the problem by doing something rash or stupid—overthinking and over-reacting could be fatal. He had to take each step very carefully. Thinking back to the morning, he visualized Jim Fairmont standing among the book tables holding a piece of paper. Was it the missing invoice he was holding?

McBride shook his head, stood up, walked around the desk, and made his way to the bookcases opposite. The wall was twenty-six feet long and had specially constructed floor-to-ceiling bookcases built in to it. How could he be sure that Jim wasn't just holding a list of books he was trying to find? Should McBride really care? No, it had to be the invoice. Jim stood exactly where the second box of books should have been.

McBride scratched the top of his balding head, mussing what was left of his dark, once curly hair. He had to find out—but how? Turning, he began walking back to the large Chippendale desk in front of him. It was empty except for the handsome maroon, leather-bound blotter; the invoices; and the inkstand—Victorian, made of wood with crystal ink containers at each end of a pen tray. A metal bar forming a half circle like a rainbow, about three inches high in the center, formed a backdrop to the pen tray. There was a white card, four by six, propped up against the bar.

"The party!" he exclaimed out loud. *It'll be perfect*, he thought. He could engage Fairmont in cocktail party chatter, find out what he knew.

∾∾

"So what do you think of Florence?" Marian said as she drove through the center of Fordstown on the way back from The Garden Walk.

They had taken the Land Rover, as she had a wrought iron garden table she wanted to bring back to the shop. It was a small table, about a foot and a half in diameter, that she thought might look good in the back garden with some potted herbs on it. It didn't, so back to the shop, it went—one of the great advantages of owning your own business. She never thought she would be a garden person, but once Jeffrey started junior high school, she found herself with more and more time on her hands and decided to turn a section of the back lawn into a rose garden. She always liked roses.

It became an easy jump from roses to a formal garden. When she started looking for decorative pieces with which to populate it: small benches, concrete pieces such as rabbits, frogs and the like, sundials, wind chimes and other such items, she found them very difficult to find. The local garden centers really didn't have much. By the time Jeffrey entered high school, she had rented a small shop on Route 202 just north of town. Actually, it was a small, renovated house, as all of the shops in the area were, but it had a perfect front yard for displaying lawn furniture, arbors, and large planters.

"She seems all right," replied Jim. "It will be nice if it works out. Give you more free time on Saturdays. Is she going to work Labor Day?"

"She said she would. I gave her a key so she can open up. Told her I'd be in around noon. With Jeffrey not around to help out anymore, this may work out just fine." She stopped for the only traffic light in town.

"She seems pleasant enough. Has that friendly, chattering way about her that customers like. The small-town feel." The light turned green, and she eased through the intersection.

"Did you see that woman in the pink hat?"

"Oh, the one with the New York accent?"

"That's the one. The nervy one. I thought she handled her quite well."

"Oh, isn't that cute." Marian tried to imitate a New York accent. "'Harold come 'ere, ya gotta see this. Hay, lady, I was just lookin' at this, do ya mind.'"

"It's a good thing you had more than one."

"Even better, Florence managed to sell them both. I think the only reason the woman bought it was because pink hat made such a stink. Why is it so difficult for some people to be courteous or even pleasant?"

"It's the childhood imprint. Survival of the fittest. Be aggressive or be stepped on."

"That seems to be everywhere lately."

"True, look at the bank. The Larry McBride's of this world would have been relegated to the back office where customers couldn't see them. Do you realize that when I started at Chase, they purposely picked account officers that were tall—virtually everyone was around six feet? A few five tens and elevens here and there. The idea was to be an imposing figure. The physical image helped promote the mental one. And they trained you to have style. That was part of the reason for officer's dining rooms. And seasoning, my God, there was no way you would get near a customer until you had worked alongside an experienced officer for at least a year, maybe two—and that was after a two year training program."

Marian made a right onto High Top Road. Traffic was easier in the afternoon. Saturday mornings were madness. With the banks and the post office open only until noon, everyone was out doing errands around town from nine to twelve. Such was the suburbanite's lot: leave for work before dawn, return after dark, do all your town chores on Saturday morning and your house chores Saturday afternoon, relax on Sunday—and someplace in between throw in a round of golf or a little tennis. Jim continued: "It really is a shame. There doesn't seem to be any value placed on experience any more. We ran an ad last week for a commercial loan officer. Now, this is a VP slot mind you, and the requirement is for someone with a minimum of two years commercial loan experience. When I started the credit training program was longer than that, and if anyone made VP in less than ten years, they were considered to be on a fast track."

"Did you put the flag half up on the mailbox?" Marian pulled into the driveway.

"No."

"Take a look."

Jim rolled down his window while Marian backed into position so he could open the mailbox, which stood on a post made of half a wagon wheel. Marian had found it during one of her scavenger trips to nearby farms looking for antique metalwork that could be used for garden decoration. Jim mounted a standard mail box on it and sank it into the ground at the head of the driveway. Gave it a different look than the standard mailbox sitting on a post. Jim opened it and retrieved a white four-inch-by-six-inch envelope simply addressed to *Mr. and Mrs. J. P. Fairmont* and no return address.

Marian asked, "Who's it from?"

"No return address on it. Looks like a card or invitation of some sort."

"Opening might help."

"What a clever idea." A comment for which he received a playful punch in the left shoulder. Jim opened the envelope and withdrew a white invitation card with black lettering. "It's an invitation."

"From the Queen?"

"Not quite—McBride."

"You're kidding."

"No, he's having a Labor Day bash, or rather evening from the seven p.m. start, and we're invited. No RSVP required."

"Belatedly." Marian drove up the one-hundred-fifty-foot drive to the house. It was situated on a little rise and backed up to one of the local horse farms.

"I wonder," Jim mused. "You don't think this has anything to do with this morning?"

"You said he wanted to get together."

"Yes, but he was referring to next week."

"Maybe he just thought this would be a way of making up for being testy."

Jim nodded. "Could be."

She maneuvered past the front of the house and around to the back where the detached garage stood and stopped in the area between the house and the garage, a space that was designed to accommodate at least three vehicles.

"Do you think we should go?" he asked.

"Well, there are a couple of different ways to look at this." She parked, released her seatbelt, and stepped out of the car. "One would be to assume that McBride feels that we are socially deprived, which we are not, and have not been invited anywhere for Labor Day, which we haven't, and has taken pity on us. The second would be that he really doesn't want us to come but felt obliged to invite us since we live in the same town and both of you work for the same company." They made their way to the back door across the patio area. "And thirdly, it is possible he did feel he was a bit sharp, and this is his way of making nice, nice."

"What about number four?"

"Number four?"

"Yes, what if that invoice does have some significance, he was really not supposed to have blank copies in his possession, and he wants to find out if I saw them."

"But he doesn't know you have one."

"No, but he may think I saw the name on the papers he took from the box. I was standing right behind him, and it is possible." Jim unlocked the door.

"I think you're going overboard with this invoice thing. You don't even know if what you found was his, and, if it was, if it means anything."

"Why don't we go on Monday night and find out."

"How?"

"I'll just drop the name Alliance Automotive in casual conversation and watch his reaction."

"Are you sure you want to do this?" she said, going up the two steps into the kitchen.

"Why not?"

"Okay, Sherlock. Who knows? It might be fun. Beats sitting around smelling other people's barbecues."

Jim closed the door behind them.

CHAPTER 3

When Jim and Marian arrived at the party, they were greeted by a uniformed maid. McBride usually hired two people for the evening to serve but also to do double duty working the door on the way in and out. Clean-up would be done by a separate woman who would come in the following day and not by his regular housekeeper, who he didn't want to burden with after party duties. They exchanged pleasantries with the maid as they entered and were ushered directly into the living room. The festivities were well underway, and the faint tones of Chopin's *Nocturne in E Flat Major* could be heard in the background. Two large windows facing the street on the right, with a loveseat in between, dominated the room as one entered. At the far end of the room, an antique Victorian sofa separated two wing chairs. Tables that would normally be in front of the sofa had been removed so that guests could circulate. On the left wall was a large three piece, seven foot high display case with the shelves illuminated for dramatic effect and highlighted McBride's rarest and most valuable books. It also contained artifacts from various countries around the world that he had visited.

"Jim!" came the call of a female voice from the milling crowd.

He searched the somewhat familiar faces for its owner and, as he focused on a seemingly dismembered hand waving at him above a cluster of heads. Marian whispered in his ear, "I know who that is. You're on your own. I'm heading left. Catch up with me if you ever break free again."

"Coward," he whispered back, as she let go of his arm and slithered into the crowd.

The hand and the voice belonged to Martha Alexander Livingston Chamberlin, affectionately known as Mattie, and a constant fixture at McBride's parties—and many others. Twice divorced and once widowed, she was resigned to the life of a companion, which she truly enjoyed. In her mid-sixties, a fact she did not hide, she was slightly on the chubby side with a moderately tasteful amount of gray hair. Life was too short to waste on planning, so spontaneity became her hallmark. Those who did not know her often took her outwardness for boisterousness, but there was a difference. She truly loved life, and it just came through. She could be whatever you like: earthy, elegant, charming, but always a lady, never rude. She was McBride's favorite partner at the theater, ballet, and philharmonic. Safe, and visible—perfect for McBride. At this moment she was also loud. Jim had known her for as long as he could remember. Her family had lived in the area for more than 200 years and were direct descendants of William Alexander Lord Stirling of Revolutionary War fame.

As she emerged from the milling crowd, which parted for her as the Red Sea must have for Moses, she continued talking: "Jim, I had no idea you were coming." She grabbed his arm and extended a cheek, which he dutifully kissed. "Where's Marian?"

"Off being sociable."

"I wish I had known you were coming. Ended up taking a ride with the Bradys. Wonderful people, but so quiet. I would have called."

"Decided at the last minute."

They strolled arm in arm into the main room, weaving their way through the usual array of local people worth knowing, and found two empty seats on the sofa against the wall.

"Mattie, what's the reason for the gathering? I know there's always a theme, or perhaps I should call it an excuse, even though it's Labor Day."

"We're celebrating a painting."

"A what?"

"A painting. That one over there." Mattie indicated the representation of an old man looking softly down at them from the delicately lighted frame on the adjacent wall. "Larry has made a new discovery. He's quite sure the painter will be famous someday." She leaned forward and whispered in confidence, "The gallery said they had it on good authority that 'The Donald' acquired one of his paintings last month."

Jim sighed. "Oh, my God."

"Now, now, my dear, be kind."

"Yes," he said, laughing, "I shall be kind. Oh, my, yes, I shall be kind," and they both laughed.

Marian meanwhile made her way to McBride's display cases where she found Carl and Olivia Hansen admiring a carved wood bust of a gaucho.

"He does have some nice things doesn't he?"

"Marian," greeted Olivia, "How are you?" They brushed cheeks in the best of polite society rituals.

"Marian." Carl offered his hand. He was like that. Kisses on the cheek were reserved for family and extremely close friends. Carl was raised in an era when life was a bit more formal. He spent more than forty-five years in banking, with most of it on the domestic correspondent side, where the country club and formal dinner evenings had been mandatory. He had a Bushesque look to him: tall and slim with graying hair and sharp, angular features.

"So, how does retired life suit you?" Marian asked Olivia.

"I love it. Now if we could just get Carl something to do, it would be wonderful."

"Carl, don't tell me you wish you were still at work?"

"No, not really. It's just the habit that's difficult to break. Getting up every day at the same time and going to the same place for forty-five years sets quite a pattern."

"I thought you were going to spend all your free time on the golf course?"

"Sounded good at the time. When I was working, I looked forward to those two rounds of golf each weekend and an occasional one during the week with a customer, but the bloom came off the rose after about a month. Don't get me wrong, I still love the game of golf, but I've come to the realization that, when I was working, I used it as a diversion—a safety valve to take the pressure off. Now, the pressure is gone, and the game's purpose has changed."

One of the serving women came alongside the group with a tray.

"May I get anyone something to drink?"

Carl addressed Marian. "What'll you have?"

"Some white wine, please. What kind is it by the way?"

"A Mâcon Villages Chardonnay."

"Yes, that will do nicely, thank you."

"Olivia?" Carl encouraged.

"Oh, I'm still fine," she said raising slightly her half-filled gin and tonic glass.

Olivia had never been much of a drinker. The half-filed glass would last her the evening. Short in size—she was but five feet tall—but not in stature, she liked being in control. It made no difference if it was social or emotional, she needed to be aware of what was occurring and manage it as much as possible. She was subtle, but sooner or later conversations would be guided to topics in which she had an interest or people she did not wish to speak with would find themselves more comfortable out of her presence than in it.

"Nothing for me, thank you," Carl concluded, dismissing the server. Carl Hansen didn't drink. Although that was not always the case. Being on the customer contact side of banking he became caught in the three-martini lunch pattern back in the 1950s before vanity waters, and ice tea came into vogue. There were a number of tough years when it looked like he was on the verge of destroying his career, his marriage, and his family. Finally, his mentor at the bank took him aside and laid it all out for him. There were no Betty Ford centers to help, just reach down deep inside and pull yourself together. He did what he had to do. He changed his pattern: no more customer lunches for a while; no drinks before, during, and after dinner; he avoided entertaining; and refused invitations. After about three months, he eased back into the routine, but soft drinks were the replacement. At parties, there was the tonic water with the twist of lime.

"So tell me, Marian, where is Jim?"

"Mattie has him."

"Oh, my. Well, they do get along. If anyone can handle Mattie, it's Jim."

"Have you seen Larry?"

"He was here just a few minutes ago. I thought I heard a telephone ringing."

"I'm sure we'll see him later. Is it true you're finally going to move?"

Olivia replied with a barely audible sigh: "Well, the house is up for sale. I can't believe we've been in it for almost forty years. We'll keep Carl's parents' house in Silver Lake, New Hampshire of course." A passing couple stopped to greet Carl, who turned away from the conversation. "The timing of our trip to Marco Island this year will undoubtedly hinge on how the sale goes." She glanced at the couple and a slight frown crossed her face as she failed to recognize them.

"Somehow, I can't imagine Jim and me ever moving, but I suppose we will eventually. It just doesn't make sense to stay here. We have the summer place up in Maine but we'll probably head south like you and Carl. Although, I don't think we'll do Florida. I need a season change and Florida, at least the southern part, is too consistent, too much uniformity. No, I think the Carolinas would probably be more to our liking."

Olivia suddenly focused on Carl: "Well, Carl, aren't you going to introduce us?"

"Oh, of course. Olivia, this is Eduardo and Alicia Domingo. Olivia, my wife and this is Marian Fairmont. Marian's husband is a colleague of mine from the bank, or perhaps I should say former colleague, since I'm no longer there. The Domingo's are from Venezuela."

"How very interesting," said Olivia as she extended her hand in greeting. The ritual continued until all had exchanged pleasantries." How do you come to know my husband?"

"From the bank," replied Eduardo—who spoke with only the slightest hint of an accent. Carl was very helpful to us a few years ago. Our son was attending Drew University in Madison and had lost the check we gave him to pay his tuition and Carl came to the rescue."

"That's our Carl," interjected Marian," always the banker with a solution. So tell us Carl, what did you do?"

"It wasn't that complicated. Felipe—"

"That's our son," said Eduardo. Alicia was quiet but listening attentively. Her English was passable but she was somewhat reticent about speaking since she knew her accent was quite strong.

"—yes, Felipe came into the Morristown Central Office to report the lost check. It was drawn on the Newark Main Office and I happened to overhear Felipe's plea for help as I passed the customer service desk."

Eduardo elaborated: "Felipe was very upset, as it was the last day of registration for classes and the university would not permit him to register unless the first tuition payment was made. He still would have been able to participate in a late registration program, but was afraid that he would not be able to sign up for some of the classes he needed, as by then they might be full."

"And so…" said Olivia.

"Oh," said Carl. "I just asked what the problem was and, when I learned that his parents were in Caracas, I took him aside and put in a call to our host."

"Larry?" Marian said.

"He is the international group manager."

Then she turned to the Domingos. "And that's how you came to know Larry McBride and ended up here tonight. That's wonderful, but what did Larry do?"

"He checked the account and relationship files and then put a call through to Eduardo in Venezuela and explained the situation," Carl continued. "There was no time to replace the check, so I suggested to Larry we could have an official check issued, provided I had a valid request in hand. Larry instructed Eduardo to contact his bank, which was Banco del Sol in Miami, and have them send us a tested and verified message instructing us to issue the check to Drew University for Felipe. Everything took about two hours, and Felipe registered that afternoon."

"Was the original check ever found?"

"I don't believe so. We did put a stop payment on it."

"Knowing Felipe," said Eduardo, "I'm sure it was in his pocket, and he sent it to the laundry."

"I think we have all been through that one," said Marian, offering a look of sympathy to Alicia, who smiled and shook her head knowingly.

"When did all this happen?" inquired Olivia.

"That was two years ago. Felipe is now in his senior year. I met Carl for the first time at the end of that school year when I timed a business trip with bringing Felipe home for the summer. Our visit this year is timed with the start of school, and Larry kindly invited us to come to his party."

"Was it short notice?" said Marian.

"I beg your pardon."

"Oh, nothing. Just a thought. What sort of business are you in in Venezuela?"

"I own, what you would call auto dealerships—as well as some other interests."

McBride suddenly appeared out of the crowd and stood at Marian's elbow. "Everyone enjoying themselves?"

All heads turned in surprise.

"Larry," Olivia said, "we were all wondering where you were."

"Overseas phone call."

"On Labor Day?"

"Not where this phone call came from. Eduardo understands these things," he said, while extending his hand. "How are you? Alicia, good to see you again. How is Felipe?"

Alicia spoke for the first time: "He is fine. In school again."

"And Marian, glad you could come."

"Delighted for the invitation."

"Sorry for the short notice. Where's that book hound husband of yours?"

"Firmly in the clutches of Mattie, I'm afraid."

"Ah, Mattie. She is something else, isn't she?"

"We were just hearing about how you all met."

One of the serving women stepped into their midst with a tray of various hot hors d'oeuvres. She said nothing, but the aroma from the tray immediately stopped all conversation.

"My goodness, don't they look good," said Olivia. "I must admit, Larry, you do put us all to shame." She reached for a small pastry wafer followed by a flurry of other hands reaching for the tray and the cocktail napkins on its side.

McBride turned to Eduardo: "If you have a moment a bit later I'd like to have a little chat."

"Of course, how about now?"

"Fine. Why don't we go into my study?"

"Be back in a few minutes." He said to Alicia.

"Oh, we'll take good care of her," said Olivia.

She was good at this sort of thing, having done it so often. It had been her job. It was what the wives of senior bank officers were supposed to do. When she first married Carl, she was a nervous wreck, afraid that she would not pass the inspection of Judy VanDrost, the wife of Carl's boss. She knew that his career

was in her hands. If he was ever to become an officer, she would
have to measure up. She still remembered that first reception so
well. It was at the Somerset Hills Club, and she was in a complete state of panic for two weeks. She had visions of Judy
VanDrost being the evilest witch alive. When the day came, she
was almost sick. Her stomach had more butterflies than she ever
thought possible. But Mrs. VanDrost was nothing like she expected, she was motherly—almost grandmotherly. She immediately took Olivia under her wing and introduced her to everyone
she could. She talked quietly and smoothly. And when she
smiled, put her arm through Olivia's, and walked around the
room with her, an enormous weight was lifted, and she became
Olivia's model. She would do the same. She would be there for
the wives of others and never let them become uncomfortable.
She would control the atmosphere. And she did—for a while. But
the world changed, and the young wives of the 'seventies and
'eighties didn't need her help—at least, most of them didn't.
Many of them had jobs of their own. In fact, the reverse began to
occur: instead of her making them feel comfortable, many of
them did their best to make her feel uncomfortable. She had not
held a paying job since marrying Carl, and they were quick to put
her down for not having a "life of her own," as they would say.
She had difficulty understanding them. There was no reason to be
rude. They might consider themselves successful, but she had
made a difference. She gave her time to the United Way, to hear-
ing-impaired children, to the Red Cross, and the Visiting Nurse
Association. She was happy when Carl retired. They didn't fit in
anymore. Caring for others was out of vogue. Grab what you
could and run with it. Me. Me. Me, was the cheer of the 1980s
and the 1990s, and she could never be that way.

McBride closed the door behind Eduardo and motioned the
Venezuelan to the sofa at the left of the entrance. "Have a seat.
You favored Dewar's if I remember. Can I get you one?"

"Yes, thank you. Water, no ice."

Eduardo looked around McBride's study. The bookshelves
were very impressive. They covered three of the four walls from
floor to ceiling, and the rich, dark wood set off the books themselves. Eduardo, instead of sitting down began to move toward
the shelves to the left of the sofa. "This is a wonderful room. You
must spend a great deal of time here."

"I do. It's a good place to work."

Eduardo thought of his own home on the outskirts of Caracas. He lived in the mountains between the city and the airport. It was a large house with a full time staff of three and additional help as needed. It was a comfortable life, but lacking in many ways. As a prosperous businessman, there were few things he could not afford in Venezuela, but there were many things that were just not available at any price. While there were good universities there, you would be foolish not to send your sons to the United States or England. And medical care—if there was something serious to consider, then Miami, Dallas, or New York were the answer. Cuts and bruises were for Caracas, illness was a matter for elsewhere.

The exchange controls in Venezuela were dangerous. In order for Eduardo and those like him to survive, they must have access to hard currencies like the US dollar. No hospital in Miami took Venezuelan bolivars for surgery nor would a university for tuition. You could charge with an American Express card but you still had to pay AMEX in dollars. But now Venezuela said no! No more moving of hard currencies out of the country. Now you had to turn them into the central bank so that reserves could be increased. The excesses of the 1980s caught up with Venezuela. Although a petroleum-rich country, it continually got itself into one debt crisis after another, further exacerbated by high inflation and unemployment rates. Imports from hard currency countries were restricted, with a priority schedule being put into place. No longer did the marketplace set the volume of automotive imports, a need had to be verified. More than three million vehicles already roamed the extensive highway system, but they needed spare parts. For Eduardo, it meant he was importing very few cars, but many of the parts were still on the preferred import list. He tried to boost the export side of his business, but it was not easy. The state owned and controlled most of the heavy industry and had its fingers into the intermediate and consumer sectors as well, making the government one of his competitors for import licenses.

"I assume you have a good security system in the house. I am not a collector, but it would appear that many of your books have great value. Have you ever read any of the works of Romulo Gallegos of my country?"

"Yes to the first two parts of your question and no to the last." McBride handed him the drink he had prepared and motioned him back to the sofa. "I must admit that books are not as lively a commodity as jewels or precious metals. If there were to be a burglary, I'd be more concerned about some of the editions being damaged while some drug addict tried to get the television or VCR out of the house. As with most collectibles, you have to know exactly what you're looking for. With a painting, it's easy to find: you put it on a wall and turn a spotlight on it. A book can sometimes be a needle in a haystack. But yes, I have a security system attached to a private service, mostly for insurance purposes. This man Gallegos, what sort of things does he write?"

"In Caracas, as with most developing countries, security is something you also buy, but it is usually human rather than electronic and carries an automatic weapon. As far as Romulo Gallegos is concerned, he is one of our greatest writers. From him, you will learn much of what it is to be a Venezuelan. He writes of the soul of our land. In fact, he was so popular with the people of Venezuela he was elected president in 1947. Unfortunately, it is not always good to be too popular with what you would refer to as the man in the street, as that is where you usually end up. Gallegos was ousted in a coup the year after his election."

"Sounds like an interesting fellow," McBride said as Eduardo took his seat. McBride moved the chair near his desk around to a convenient angle. "Please sit for a minute. I'd be very interested to have something of his." They both sat. "Now, tell me how things are going. How is Felipe doing in school?"

"Very well, but he will be glad when it is over."

"Any plans?"

"We are looking at graduate school now: the University of Pennsylvania seems most likely."

"Will you be taking him back to Venezuela to work in the business?"

"Eventually, but I think he will spend some time with an American company or two. At least, that is what he has said he would like to do."

"Any interest in banking?"

"It's always a possibility."

"Well, you just let me know if I can be of help."

"Certainly, Larry, it is very kind of you to offer."

"How is business going?"

"We're holding our own. The exchange controls make life difficult for us, but I can't say they are completely wrong. When we have an unfavorable trade balance, we cannot offset it as America does with investment, tourism and, of course, college tuition fees," he said with a slight smile. "Venezuela may not be a truly poor country but we are far from being wealthy. We need to develop self-discipline in our buying habits but we also need to have a strong, visionary plan for the country—a long term one and stick with it. Unfortunately, we just seem to move from crisis to crisis. As soon as we seem to solve a problem we go right back to the policies that got us in trouble in the first place. Our problem is that we do not have faith in the government and they have no faith in the people. It is a never-ending cycle. In a few years, all will be back to normal."

"I guess the idea is just to survive these few years however long it happens to be."

"Yes, but we're okay."

"Good, I'm glad to hear it. I know a couple of your competitors are having some difficulties. You know we have quite a few exporters on our books that sell to Venezuela and they have seen their sales dropping significantly."

McBride's existence as head of international operations was a direct result of the growth in importing and exporting companies at the bank. The increasing size of the traditional international banks in the New York area such as Chase, Citibank, and Bank of New York had pushed the smaller importers and exporters off to the local New Jersey banks. While these banks had always served local import houses their interest was more domestic oriented: mainly personal, payroll, and general operating accounts. If they provided any form of international service, it was usually on a correspondent basis with one of the larger banks to whom they referred their customers, with the result being that, as the company grew, it began using the larger bank more and more and eventually cut out the local bank almost entirely. But now with statewide and interstate branching everything had changed. The local banks were being gobbled up one by one. Now New Jersey was dominated by Chase, First Union, Bank of New York and Fleet. Of the locals, First State was one of the few left. To survive they bought talent from the New York banks, which is how McBride ended up at First State. Even though the senior management did not fully understand foreign exchange and the risks associated with letters of credit and or export and import collections, they assumed they could hire someone who did. Someone who had experience with the New York banks and would like a chance to run their own show. Enter the Larry McBride's of banking.

Eduardo sipped at his drink: "We, of course, are under pressure like everyone else. But I have managed to put some reserves away before the exchange controls went into effect."

"I'm not surprised. You've always struck me as a good businessman. You know it's too bad the Venezuelan exchange control authorities didn't use more common sense. I remember some years back when the Far East was in a protectionist mode for many of their economies. A number of the countries put in tight monetary controls, but some of them, Taiwan being one, still permitted the maintaining of a foreign exchange account offshore into which five or ten percent of export proceeds could be kept for local operating and sales expense. It made a lot of sense. But being required to sell one-hundred percent of all hard currency earnings to the Central Bank…well, I'm not convinced they have their heads screwed on straight on this one."

"I tend to agree with you."

"Well, you know I would like your business, Eduardo, and if you ever feel that you need some help you know where to call. Remember, there are no restrictions on our maintaining US dollar accounts for a Venezuelan national. Venezuela may not be particularly happy about it but it's a fact of life and a few regulations aren't going to change it. Can I tell you something in confidence about a good customer of mine, Alliance Automotive Export Corp.?" Larry leaned forward in his chair.

Jim had finally broken away from Mattie and was hiding near the front door, nibbling away at some hors d'oeuvres left on a tray on the hall table.

"Are you sure those are safe?" said Marian sneaking up behind him.

"At this point I don't care. Do you know that Mattie knows the calorie, fat and sodium content of every snack food ever created? Every time I tried to reach for something, she would give me a chemical analysis of it. The reason you come to one of these things is to eat everything you're not supposed to." He reached for something red and white on a one-inch-square piece of brown bread.

"I thought we came to sneak up on Larry."

"Well, that too. Where is he?"

"Last time I saw him, he was heading for his study with Eduardo."

"Eduardo? Who's Eduardo?"

"One of the guests."

"That's a lot of help. Of course he's a guest."

"Not necessarily. With a name like Eduardo he could be a waiter."

"True, if there were waiters here."

"Point taken."

"So who is Eduardo? Does he have a last name?"

"I think it was Dominguez or something like that. Anyway he's from Venezuela and McBride did him a favor once. Carl and Olivia know them as well. In fact Carl introduced them."

"Them?"

"Eduardo and Larry."

"No, no, no, no. You said Carl and Olivia knew 'them.' How many Eduardos were there?"

"Oh, the 'them' is Mrs. Domin…something."

"What happened to her?"

"Olivia has her under her wing."

Marian, from where she was standing in the archway between the entrance hall and the living room, suddenly spotted someone she thought she recognized at the far end of the room. He was tall and distinguished looking in a dark suit but his back was now to her. She knew she should know him, but from where?

"Why don't we go find Olivia and Mrs. D. and then, when Larry brings this Eduardo fellow back, we can chat, and I can slip Alliance into the conversation someplace?"

"Okay, we should probably circulate anyway, just to see if anyone in town remembers us. Besides, it looks like there's no more food left in this part of the house."

The tray was empty.

Smiles appropriately in place, Jim and Marian began to circulate. They would have two rooms to cover plus the patio and deck off the back. It was amazing how similar parties of this kind were. There was a homogenization to them unlike city parties where more fashion trendy types actually wore clothes that one might see in *The New York Times* fashion supplement. The mix could be from evening gown to tee shirt or jeans to tux or a mix of both. Out in the country where real America lived—or claimed it did—Brooks Brothers and Talbots had everything under control. The suburban world had a certain crispness, cleanliness and uniformity to it, but then most county folk didn't think graffiti was an art form.

They shook hands, they smiled, they laughed, they looked concerned, they listened intently, they agreed, they disagreed, they told anecdotes, they greeted old friends, they met new people, they made it to the dining room where they could see across the room and out the sliding glass doors to the deck where Olivia Hansen and Alicia Domingo were standing with two other women and—that man again. Marian was sure she knew him.

CHAPTER 4

An International Seminar

Shouldn't you be on your way by now?" Marian asked as she came into the kitchen and found Jim nursing a cup of coffee and staring out the window to the patio.

"I've got time. It's only a quarter to eight."

"But I thought you got up early to go to Newark this morning?"

"Oh, shit! What the hell am I doing?"

"What time does it start?"

"Nine-fifteen."

"You should still be all right. I-Seventy-Eight is never as bad as I-Two-Eighty."

"I know, I just hate being late." He got up, folded the paper, and took a last sip of coffee.

Marian made her way back to the kitchen after saying goodbye to Jim at the door to the garage. Now, for a second cup of coffee and some quiet time to sit and look out the window into the back yard. Time to watch the birds at the feeder by the fence, swooping down from the cover of the magnolia tree, moving the seeds around with their beaks until they found the one they wanted, usually a sun flower seed if they could get it. Then they would dart back to a branch, get comfortable, and diligently peck away until the casing was breeched and the meat exposed to be quickly eaten. The routine was repeated over and over again by the house finches and the black capped chickadees. Watching them was hypnotic, like watching the flames in a fireplace. Time passed. Her mind went blank until she was awakened by a thought that crept in unexpectedly to bring her back.

"Ed Campbell!" she said out loud with a start. *Could it have been?* she thought. *That vaguely familiar face across the room last night.* That quick glimpse of someone not seen for so many years. No, she tried to convince herself. No, it didn't make sense. But why would she think of him? She hadn't given him a thought since—she couldn't remember when. Why now? It must have been something in the way the man moved. She tried to visualize the scene of the night before—the milling crowd, the noise, the chatter, the conversations with old and new acquaintances, Jim's fencing with McBride. She concentrated and tried to bring it all into focus.

ↄ∞ↄ

They stood on McBride's rear deck, making small talk with another of Jim's colleagues from the Morristown office and a couple that were frequent customers of The Garden Walk. The deck ran across two thirds of the back of the townhouse with access from the kitchen. Next to it were French doors from the dining room, which were open onto the screened deck. Marian stood facing into the dining room with her back to the view of the park. From her vantage point, she could see straight through the doors, across the dining room, through the archway that led into the room across the hall separating it from the living room and then through the second archway and right out the front window. The crowd milled about, and she looked up as McBride came onto the deck and stood with his back to the open French doors. She tried to focus on the scene, to zoom in with her memory.

She remembered McBride saying, "Well, how is everyone here tonight?"

"Enjoying ourselves immensely," said the Garden Walk customer. What was her name? Martha, Maggie, Mildred, something with an M. "It was so nice of you to invite us."

"Well, what are neighbors for? I'm glad you could come. And, Mark," said the one from the Morristown office who worked for Jim, "good to see you again. Jim, you've got a good one here. He spotted that Polywrap export collection business right away." McBride patted Mark on the shoulder as he paid him the compliment.

"Knowing the right questions to ask is the key to any sales effort, whether it's domestic or international," Jim responded. "All it takes is experience. It's not the sort of thing you can teach. You learn by doing, by being in enough situations. One and one may look like three and a dead end but knowing enough about a business, the right question can sometimes make it all add up."

At this point, Marian remembered McBride shifting a bit to his right and of her having a clear view into the living room. Jim was speaking again: "That's especially true in some special industry situations. Take automotive, for instance. The idea of floor plan financing for an auto dealer seems awfully simple, the inventory is so visible, but there are more traps and loopholes to get hurt by than almost anything else. Must be that way on the international side as well, Larry?" Marian's eye caught an image of a man move by the archway and over to the wall filled with books in the living room. It was the same one she saw earlier when she and Jim had started to circulate. She tried to zoom in on the man's face, but the movement was too fleeting. She couldn't see him clearly enough.

"Well, not entirely Jim, our focus is more on the appropriate financing tool rather than the industry. Mostly it's a function of risk: the bank versus the customer and the customer versus its customer. How much risk can each handle and what's the best vehicle to protect everyone."

McBride shifted back to his left again, blocking the view just as the man she had been following again appeared. This time he turned in Marian's direction. She tried to filter out the conversation but she couldn't because she was a part of it. She remembered how neatly McBride sidestepped the issue as she faced him and joined in. "I'm continually amazed at how much of my merchandise has a foreign origin. I mean, I buy directly from distributors and catalogues but don't always know where it was made until I open the boxes."

"That's very true. All those knick-knacks that you see in tourist type shops, 'Souvenirs of New York City,' and then look at the bottom and see it was made in China."

Jim tried again. "I suppose the only one that's pretty self-evident is when buying a replacement part for a foreign car?"

"Even there." McBride shifted again, but the man was gone. "You can't be sure anymore. After all, most Honda's seem to be made in the US now."

"No easy answers anymore I guess, Larry?"

"No. No easy answers."

"So, Larry, tell me about the painting." jumped in the neighbor.

☙❧

Marian re-wound the whole exchange again in her head and this time tried to focus specifically on the image in the living room. He seemed to be about the right height—around five feet, ten inches. The hair was dark but not black. There was something about the movement…

This is silly, she thought. *I've got to get to work.*

☙❧

Jim pulled into the parking garage across from the bank. The old headquarters building of the Essex National Bank of New Jersey now housed the International Department of First State, as well as its Trust Operations. Built in the 1930s and now a proud Newark landmark on Broad Street, it once stood as the home of the largest bank in Essex County and, for a brief time, the largest in the state—before the approval of state-wide branching and the acquisition wars began. The bank was actually at its peak when New Jersey split into three banking regions, enabling it to expand into Hudson County to the East and Morris to the West. Then the mergers began. First State began to take shape when it merged with the Bergen State Bank—then the largest bank in the region—a defensive as well as offensive move. New Jersey found itself being squeezed by both New York and Pennsylvania financial institutions whose states were moving faster on the deregulation front.

Major corporations were moving out of New York City to the New Jersey suburbs, but the local banks didn't have the size or the strength to accommodate their domestic and global needs. The New Jersey Legislature continued to limit the expansion of their own native financial institutions and thereby opened wide the gate for everyone else. That had now changed, but only after almost completely destroying the native banks. Jim had been through most of it—the mergers, the expansion and then the contraction in the late 1980s. Now not only the New York banks came west across the Hudson River, but banks from all over the country as well. They picked off the weak and vulnerable one by one. First State was trying to build itself into a super-regional, recognizing that it was of such a size, five billion in assets, that it was on the small side to effectively play in global markets and too big to call itself a community bank.

The international department had the look and feel of the way banks used to be. As you entered from the elevator hallway, you went through two wooden doors instead of the usual glass. Inside you were met by a receptionist, who would take your coat and hang it up for you, formally announce you to the person you had come to visit, and then escort you inside to the platform, which actually was one—a raised section of the floor where the officers had their desks. There were two private offices—the manager's, who also had a sitting room that was dutifully decorated with gifts and artifacts from around the world, and the assistant manager's, which was more modest.

Pictured on the walls were original paintings depicting scenes from various countries where the bank did business rather than cheap prints and posters chosen by a decorator for color effect. The oak paneled walls gave a warm and solid feeling to the space. The main problem with the entire picture that Jim walked in to was the decade—it was the 1990s, not the 1950s. Electrical cords and wires were in evidence everywhere. The desktop computer and mainframe terminal had not been envisioned when the room was last re-done after World-War II. The original lighting was much too dim for current day office work so that virtually every desk looked cluttered: there were personal computers everywhere, as well as video display units, diskette boxes, software user manuals, extra filing cabinets, printers and supplemental lighting—a massive array of electronic devices to replace the typewriter and personal interaction. Visiting one of the old offices always brought Jim back to reality, he saw how it was when he started in banking in the early 1960s and, while it seemed a more dignified, measured, and personal-customer-oriented time, it would not work today. The customer had changed, the way of doing business had changed, but most of the banks were still playing catch up.

It was exactly nine fifteen when Jim entered the reception area and introduced himself: "Good morning. I'm here for the International Business Development Seminar."

"Oh, yes," replied the mid-twentyish, Latin looking receptionist, typist, secretary, clerk. "That's being held in the large conference room. You're from the bank aren't you?"

"Yes, Jim Fairmont from Morristown."

"Oh, yes, Mr. Fairmont. Do you know where the room is? I'd be happy to show you."

"No that's all right, is that the one here on the left as you go in?"

"Yes, that's it."

"Good, thank you." And Jim breezed by her.

Entering the meeting room he took a long look at its rectangular shape designed to accommodate approximately twenty-four people positioned around an oak table specifically designed for the room but clearly showed its age. At the far end of the room a stand-up projection screen dominated the view with a projector positioned on the end of the table and facing it. Wires were stretched across the room to the only available outlet about twelve feet away. In front of each place at the table lay a folder with the bank's logo on it, a pencil, with the bank's name on it, and a one-sheet agenda for the meeting. At the entrance, which was actually at the back end of the room, a coffee service awaited the participants, which included a variety of breads and pastries. The room already contained twelve people evenly divided male and female, most of who were clustered about the coffee table.

"Hello, Jim," Adam Turner said in greeting. Turner, an assistant vice president, worked for Jim as a relationship officer out of the Union Office.

"Morning, Adam. Looks like I got here on time. Got a bit of a late start this morning."

"From the look of the agenda, we won't get going till nine-thirty. McBride built coffee time into the schedule. Plenty of time. How was traffic?"

"Pretty good. The toughest part is getting from I-Seventy-Eight to downtown." Jim made a move toward the center of the table where he selected a chair and placed his briefcase on it. "Let me get squared away here for a moment and then I'll join you for coffee. I need to talk to you about Rayburn anyway." Adam nodded and headed to the coffee urn. Jim opened his briefcase and retrieved two manila folders, one marked Rayburn and the other marked ATP, Inc. Four of Jim's people were to be at the seminar, and this was a good opportunity to cover some topics in a face-to-face manner, rather than over the phone. He was responsible for all major relationships based in the state and, while his group was headquartered in the Morristown Central Office, he kept people in regional centers within the heart of their geographic territories: Newark, Jersey City, Paterson, and Union, among others. They got together twice a month but were in constant contact by telephone and e-mail.

Making his way to the coffee, Jim greeted other First State people along the way. The mix was a cross section of people from Trust, Corporate, Retail, International, and some trainees. If nothing else, these seminars gave people who normally only knew one another by telephone a chance to meet face to face. There were a number of "Ah, we finally meet!" type comments and an occasional, "You sound tall on the phone." To which the response was: "I wish I sounded thin." There was some joking and some serious discussion going on and an occasional solitary soul sitting at his place with coffee, Danish, and newspaper.

"So tell me about Rayburn, are we really in jeopardy of losing the whole thing?"

Adam took a quick sip of his coffee: "It is possible. We got the business as a direct result of the Manny-Hanny Chemical merger—they were with Man Han, never liked Chemical—they were an easy mark. We had a small operating account and got the chance to bid on the cash management business. We grabbed the lock box and controlled disbursement stuff right off and then became a tier one bank in the revolver. Chemical, or should I say Chase now, is trying to buy the cash management business back on price and the AT at Rayburn says they're making some noise about rebates on the international side with their Hong Kong imports. Chase has apparently decided to put together a coordinated effort for a change. I hear they're actually game planning relationships."

"What sort of help do you think you need?"

"I think we can probably hold them off on the cash management side, but we're definitely vulnerable on the import side, which is why I need to talk with McBride. We shared it originally with Irving Trust, but since they lost their hostile take-over battle with Bank of New York, BONY's been sound asleep on the export import business. If Chase is going to break in, I'd rather see them take the BONY piece than ours. Chase is still trying to figure out who they are while their new parent, Chemical, is still trying to digest Manny Hanny, but they know the international corporate side better than anyone."

"They're more tuned into global reach than import export though."

"I think we'd better sit down."

The table had filled and Larry McBride and two other people, one male and one female, were standing up by the projection screen.

"Good morning, everyone. I'm Larry McBride, head of international, and I'd like to welcome you all to our International Trade Awareness Seminar. As they say in the airlines, 'If international trade is not your destination today, this is your last chance to get off. The doors will be locked in five minutes.'"

There were a few smiles and chuckles around the room.

"To get started, I'd like to get a sense of your objectives to make sure we're on the right track. So, if we can just go around the room and each of you would introduce yourselves—name, rank and serial number sort of thing—and then give us an idea of what you hope to get from today's seminar."

This was pretty standard stuff, but Jim was impressed to see that McBride actually took notes about what each person said. In fact, McBride made two columns on a piece of paper and split the responses fairly equally on each side. When Jim's turn came, he introduced himself as group vice president—corporate banking and simply said he wished to learn more about the bank's overall international capabilities. McBride specifically acknowledged him with a nod before moving on.

Adam Turner responded last. "Adam Turner, assistant vice president, corporate banking north, working out of the Union Office. My particular interest is really two-fold: I'm looking to get a better understanding of the international trade products and services the bank has but I also want to know more about how they operate, how to identify the type of product a customer might need so I could direct them to something we might have that they aren't making use of and that they, in fact, might not know exits."

McBride immediately responded: "Absolutely perfect. In fact, you just described the whole purpose of this series. Remember, we are not Citibank or Chase or even Bank of New York who can afford to have trained specialist in every field. We have a few basic disciplines that some of you represent, but on the whole you really have to know it all. And key to that is the ability to recognize a potential product need. That's really what this is all about. Now while you were introducing yourselves, I was making notes about your interests and divided them into two categories, which just happen to fall into the way we have structured our program today. One is the general understanding of the trade products and services themselves: letter of credit and its multiple varieties: documentary, clean, import, export, stand-by, etc.; collections: import, export; foreign exchange; foreign drafts and secondly, the financing opportunities they present, which many corporations do not totally understand.

"Now, to take you through all of this, let me introduce you to two people. First, we have Jane Moran, vice president of our international operations department, who will take you through the various products themselves and show you how import credits differ from export credits, even though every import is an export. Then after a short break a new member of our team, Ed Campbell, who recently joined us as vice president and assistant head of international, after spending fifteen years in the international division of the former Continental Illinois in Chicago, will take us through the financing side and into the more exotic nuances of assignable and transferrable credits, red clause credits, substitution of invoice options—"

Jim's head popped up from the pad on which he took notes.

"—and a variety of stand-by, bid bond and performance credits. In between, we will have a break, and, at the end, we'll do a little role-playing before lunch, which will be at one p.m. Any questions before we start?"

CHAPTER 5

Remembrances of Things Past

The Tuesday after Labor Day was always a slow customer day but heavy on bookkeeping and inventory. Marian spent the morning by herself in the store reviewing the sales receipts and entering them into her PC based inventory management system. One of the advantages of running a store out of a former home was its variety of rooms. The house began as a scaled down center hall colonial with a living room on one side and the dining room on the other, with a stairway up the middle to the second floor and the three bedrooms.

She had most of the wall separating the old dining room from the hall removed, and a counter sales center was set up across from the entryway and nestled against the stairway. Ten feet behind the counter she had a doorway created for access to the kitchen, now the office/storage room/coffee break area. There were three display rooms downstairs, and two of the three bedrooms upstairs were also used for merchandise, with the usual *MORE UPSTAIRS* sign over the stairway. On the wall behind the counter was an arrow guiding patrons to the rear of the store and directing them *TO THE GARDEN*—which was out the back door—where winding walkways displayed a variety of benches, trellises, lighting, hanging baskets and numerous other outdoor objects.

The newly fenced yard forced browsers to retrace their steps back through the shop so they would have to pass the front counter on their way out of the store. Out front were the more sturdy items such as concrete birdbaths, garden tool sheds, and displays less likely to disappear into a fraternity house exhibit or onto a teenager's bedroom wall.

Labor Day weekend had been a good one, which she

expected, since there had only been that one brief shower on Saturday morning and the temperature had just enough of a chill to it to remind everyone that fall was on the way. Two shoe boxes full of receipts loomed in front of her. The cash register took care of the money side of things but the inventory reconciling always proved to be the time consuming task. She could well understand why bar-code readers had become so popular so quickly. However, that level of sophistication was a bit out of her reach yet. Sitting at the old kitchen table in the office—with the door open so she could see the front door—her activity for the morning would involve going through the receipts one by one to see what needed to be replaced and what could be held off until next season. Florence had started on the plan for the Christmas garden displays but Marian still needed to figure out the sale items to be sold at a deep discount and thereby make room for the specialty seasonal materials that were already being ordered.

She switched the store sign to OPEN but didn't expect to hear the clang of the front door chimes until almost noon. The quiet without interruptions would allow her to focus. The only sound expected would be an occasional hum from the PC as the hard drive searched for something. The radio was purposely off. A contentment drifted over her as she worked away with the receipts and the sales tags. The warm coffee and the overcast day, with a gentle breeze that moved the trees and plants in the display garden ever so easily, just added to her comfort. As she worked, the effortless movement of the bird feeders swinging back and forth caught her eye. Looking up, she stared out the window. It had a mesmerizing effect, and her mind began to drift.

I wonder if it was Campbell, she thought. *It's been so long. Why has it suddenly all come back? God, I haven't thought about him or that time in years. I can still see his face, though. Llewellyn Farms. The place is still there. Not like it was then. And the Governor Morris. It used to be the only hotel in the area. That was before Parsippany decided to turn the whole town into an industrial park.*

She visualized the lounge at the Governor Morris where they met. It was dark, as all such places were then. No big screen TV for Monday Night Football. Just a quiet, comfortable place to talk, discuss business, and unwind after a long day. She remembered ordering a scotch and soda. Ed had a vodka and tonic. They were in the middle of the room. She asked about people they knew at Bankers Trust and then began trading stories.

The fictitious international credit reports brought back most of the memories. Banks from all around the world would send trade inquiries to the New York banks in the hope of drumming up new business, and they always included a credit report. All the credit trainees and junior credit analysts used to make bogus ones just for fun. Reliable international credit information was almost impossible to get in written form from a foreign correspondent bank. The only way to find out the real truth was to get it in person, and you would still have to read between the lines. All the written reports just listed the business they were in, their reported capital, and then invariably stated, "…the principals are of a good family and are of high moral and financial standing." The US bank would then put the usual disclaimer on the report indicating that "…the information provided has been obtained from sources deemed to be reliable and is given without responsibility on our part."

Over a second round of drinks, Marian told Ed about the fictitious report she had made up on a gold dealer in Dubai, who was trading in just about everything illegal you could find up and down the Persian Gulf. The fictional dealer wanted to expand his activities into the importation of well water pumps and supplies from the US and Europe. The phony report, after providing extensive references to the material the company wished to represent, then elaborated on the smuggling nature of the trader's mainstream business and the successful and extensive nature of their bribery capabilities with government officials and ended with the usual protestation of moral fiber and honesty and the credit disclaimer. It became a classic and distributed all around the domestic credit department, where everyone had a good laugh. The only problem, as it turned out, was that one of the domestic account support people got hold of it and, not realizing it was intended as a joke, sent the report to a water pump supplier in Paterson, New Jersey, who was looking for a contact in the Middle East.

Marian sat in the office staring out the window and visualized the whole conversation of more than twenty years ago, as though it took place only yesterday.

ⲉⲟⲉⲟ

"When I heard from trade support that the report had been sent out to the pump supplier in Paterson, I almost died. Gillie—do you remember Gillian Roche?"

Ed shook his head, no.

"Well, Gillie sat at the desk next to me and told me just to keep quiet. Since it was just a phony company and a phony address, nothing would ever come of it. But about two months later, someone in trade comes by with a file on Gulf Import Specialties, Ltd., which is the name I had made up for the smuggler. It turned out that the company in Paterson was interested and responded to my Dubai inquiry and—you won't believe this—it turned out that a company called Gulf Import Specialties actually did exist. They were legitimate distributors for GE, Westinghouse, Phillips, and a bunch of other prime names. They hadn't thought of water pumps before but thought it was a good idea and wanted to talk about an exclusive distributorship for the New Jersey company, who was so happy with the prospect that they opened an account with Bankers and gave them all their export business."

The laughter at the table turned some heads in the normally quiet room, which did not go unnoticed by them. Ed reached across the table, grabbed Marian's hand, and whispered, "Bankers certainly lost a valuable asset in you. Think of all the postage and telex expense they could have saved by just having you invent replies instead of sending off for them." Which resulted in more giggles, but this time subdued, as they knew they were being noticed.

Marian made no effort to remove her hand from Ed's. "I think we're disturbing the serious business set. Do you know we've been here for over an hour and a half? It's almost six o'clock."

"You're right," Ed said, glancing at his watch. "Look, do you have anything you have to do. How about some dinner? It's just across the hall."

"Well, I…no, eh…not really." She continued to hesitate, and then the alcohol spoke: "Oh, why not?"

It was that easy.

At dinner, the stories continued along with another scotch and soda and vodka tonic and then a bottle of wine. They were having fun, and now the heads were turning in the dining room as they did in the lounge. Ed started to tell stories and explained how, after returning from Vietnam, they put him into the international credit-training program and then assigned him to the global business development group, developing international business from US based corporations. He had his own tales to tell from the training program, especially the nine months he spent in letter-of-credit operations and the infamous *XYZ-files*, the training examples of letters of credit gone bad, through stupidity, carelessness or fraud.

Dinner ran well past two hours. She felt loose and relaxed, but there lingered an anger—an anger at being left in the lurch by Jim, who she envisioned as having his own dinner at a landmark hotel someplace in San Francisco. Great food, atmosphere, and service while she supposedly sat at home all alone with a TV dinner, a book, or maybe a crummy television show. If he could have fun with old friends and business associates, so could she. The justification came as easy as the next cocktail.

But then, somewhere along the way, the mood changed from fun and laughter to serious eye contact and then touching. The after-dinner drinks did them both in. It was back to laughing and giggling again and then the idea of a room. She couldn't recall who suggested it. They just decided to play prom night: she would hide in the shadows while he got a single room for the night and then they would sneak her in to it.

She sat at the PC, staring out the back window with a smile on her face, and suddenly the front door chime rang.

తుళ్ళ

The slide projector in Newark gave its familiar click-clack as Ed Campbell began his presentation on using letters of credit as a financing tool. It was something Ed enjoyed doing—giving seminars. He found he had a flair for it. The army helped him with that. People often forget how much classroom instruction there is in military training and as a second lieutenant at the artillery school at Fort Sill, Oklahoma, he learned very quickly how to put together lesson plans on everything from camouflage and concealment to health and hygiene. The army had formats and procedures for everything, and plenty of help and guidance was available, whether you wanted it or not. Standing before groups of men in a classroom setting became second nature. Stage fright never became an issue. Teaching a subject was an order, not a volunteer vocation. You learned quickly how to control your audience—how to keep their attention, how to get them involved, how to make them learn. He became good at it, and people told him so. Banking didn't change anything. When he left Bankers Trust to take the Continental Illinois job, one of the requirements was to be able to participate in bank sponsored international trade seminars for customers. It was amazing how little some import/export houses really understood about the role of the letter of credit and its bible: the *Uniform Customs and Practices for Commercial Documentary Credits*. Every time a new UCP revision was approved, the seminars would begin again.

"These are some of the topics we will cover this afternoon."

Jim and the others in the room focused on the screen which now displayed a blue background list of yellow bulleted topics: Transferrable Credits, Assignment of Proceeds, The Red Clause Credit, Advances, and Acceptances.

"As you will quickly see, this is a very small list of financing techniques, but the variations of this list are limited only by the creativity of the issuer of the credit. Always keep in mind that a letter of credit is nothing more than an agreement between two parties as to how the payment for merchandise will be accomplished. The bank is essentially an agent of the importer. The terms can be pretty much anything as long as they conform to the UCP rules."

He clicked to the next slide. *Transferring the Full Credit*. Ed began to move around the room. He quietly laid down the clicker next to Jane Moran and walked behind the chairs until he made his way to the other end of the table, talking the whole way. He learned a long time ago that there was nothing worse than reading your own slides. The presenter's job was to embellish on what is projected, to explain the statements or graphics beyond what the viewers can read for themselves. A good presenter also knew his slides and didn't need to wait for them to appear on the screen before talking about them.

The best approach was to lead into a slide, to have the slide actually reinforce the presenter's point. Ed had also learned that the quickest way to lose an audience was to stand behind a podium of any type. The object was to get them involved by becoming part of them not by hiding from them. Walking around, up and down aisles, behind tables, at the back of the room, the side, served to keep the audience involved and attentive. He also used their expertise—*Learn from them and they will learn from you.*

"So, our first topic will be transfers." He nodded his head and Jane Moran switched the slide and the words "Transfer of the Letter of Credit to a Third Party" jumped onto the screen. "This is probably one of the most common financing tools you will find," he continued, "but at times it can be tricky. In its most basic form, you will have a transfer of the full credit to another exporter. This is possible only if the credit clearly permits it and, if it does, it will state it clearly in its terms. The other party now becomes the exporter or shipper of record. This becomes important because now the invoices and all shipping documents will bear the name of the new shipper and all proceeds of the shipments will be paid directly to the transferee."

For the next half hour, Ed reviewed letter of credit feature after feature with question after question coming at him from all sides of the room. His focus honed in on the type of company that would make the most use of it as a financing tool and how to identify what bank services would fit into a marketing approach to new and existing customers. He reminded them that, for an export letter of credit, First State Bank's customer was the foreign bank that issued the credit and not the beneficiary of the credit, who probably wasn't even a customer of First State, but they could be a prospect, and a desirable one.

As the first break time neared, Ed had one more topic he wanted to cover. The slide changed again, and he continued his way around the room, stopping this time at the middle of the table on the right side. The slide said *Assignable Credit—With/Without.*'

"There is another form of the same credit that is of interest to us, where the original beneficiary may not end up as the actual shipper, and that relates to a credit that permits one set of invoices to be exchanged for another." Jim's head popped up. "In the case just mentioned we were dealing with a commodity, cotton, where the grade is more important than a manufacturer's label. What happens if we switch to something a little different, like a manufactured item? In this next example, instead of cotton, we have an order for electrical automotive switches, and our company/shipper doesn't want the buyer to know what is paid for them or even where they were obtained. Under the previous transaction, it made no difference since the cotton grower had no interest in selling to England directly. But for the switches, our friends at Materials, Inc. may not want to reveal their sources for a variety of reasons. So we use what is known as the substitution of invoice. Materials, Inc. makes up its own invoices on its own letterhead form as though it was making the shipment from its own stock. It lodges with the bank the newly completed invoices that comply with the terms of the export letter of credit and then requests the bank to issue a second letter of credit that will have a lesser dollar amount than the first or primary one. When documents are presented for payment under that second letter of credit—this is all called a back-to-back transaction—all of them also comply with the terms of the primary letter of credit except for the invoice. As the second letter of credit is paid, the invoices that are presented are swapped out for the ones lodged with the bank, and then the same documents can be used to pay the primary or first letter of credit and be sent off to the buyer. All parties are then paid, and the English company purchasing the goods will have no idea that Materials is not the actual supplier of the merchandise. The difference between the two credits goes into Materials' account."

Jim gave a quick look around the room to see if he could see McBride and, not able to find him, inquired: "Is that legal?"

"The switching of the invoices? Sure."

Jim pressed on. "So the company lodges blank invoice forms with the bank, and then the bank completes them and switches them over."

"Oh, no! You don't want to get involved in touching or adjusting the documents. The invoices should always be completed in full and lodged with the bank at the time of the application for the assignment of proceeds and the domestic letter of credit to the actual supplier. The invoice substitution must be simultaneous, or you run the risk of exposing the bank to being uncovered for the whole transaction. You don't want to be responsible for completing any of the documentation that will be needed. The bank is not in the business of creating documents, only validating them. There are a number of other elements involved here that can create extensive credit risk, but I figured we'd keep it fairly simple for the benefit of this seminar."

"So a company wouldn't lodge blank invoices with us. Or for that matter, any bank."

"No, that's just asking for trouble."

"Could you give me an idea of a specific reason?"

"Well, we're drifting a little on the topic, but the main reasons would be liability and audit. The problem with having blank signed invoices around would be that you would have to account for them. No sensible bank would want to take on the responsibility of re-typing the invoice from scratch and introduce the possibility of error while doing it. So that the bank would pay both supplier and the beneficiary and then run the risk of being turned down by the English company's bank, who picked up a typing error in the invoice. Not a good practice. Good question, but we have to move on, or we won't finish all of our topics. We can talk more about this off-line if you like."

"Okay," Jim acknowledged, "just the risk management side of me coming out."

"Good. Now—" Ed turned and looked at the screen as it changed. He was now back in control of the clicker. "—that last customer is one that will be moving substantial amounts of money through an account which will provide opportunities to generate a variety of fees. Next, we are going to take a similar transaction only this time we will focus on the importer and the way a letter of credit could be used to provide financing to the supplier/exporter when an assignment of proceeds or a transferrable credit would not be viable. This one is called a 'red clause' credit." Looking at his watch, "I tell you what, we're pretty close to break time, so let's pick that up in about fifteen minutes."

Jim was scribbling on his pad.

McBride…blank   signed   invoice…why?????   Alliance…who?????…Risk ????

∽∾∽

Marian looked up from her keyboard as one of the chime clocks announced three in the afternoon. She immediately grabbed the phone on the desk and dialed Jim's number in Morristown.

It was instinctive. They talked every day. Many times they dialed one another simultaneously.

"Mr. Fairmont's office."

"Hi, Paula. Is he in?"

"Oh, hello, Mrs. Fairmont, no he's in Newark all day."

"Of course, he is. I had to push him out the door this morning. Sorry about that. Just tell him I called."

"Are you at the store? Do you want him to call back? He's been calling in during breaks, although I think they should be finished by now."

"No, it's nothing important. He'll probably call later, anyway."

"Okay."

Marian hung up the phone, leaned back, and stretched. She didn't enjoy sitting for long periods of time, but inventory had to be done and, being a critical function, she didn't want to leave it to someone else. Work with people designing their gardens: planning the flowers, the accent pieces, the seating, and the lighting—that was the fun part. The books, the inventory, and the amount of time it took had not been anticipated when she envisioned the store. She knew business survival meant paying close attention to the books and accounting, but you had to have a balance between the fun part and the mundane. Small businesses that failed usually did it in the first few years for very basic reasons: great product, great marketing ideas, no sense of the cost of doing business, no financial discipline, no staying power.

Jim knew the pitfalls. He had been involved in a wide variety of bad loans and bankruptcies over the years, but he didn't preach, just watched cautiously from the side. He let her lead and only made suggestions when asked or when it looked like she was headed for trouble. There were some disagreements of course, but Jim would always back off. He knew this was her dream, and she had to make the final decisions, right or wrong. For Marian, she had to be careful to make sure that her decisions were not grounded in anti-Jim sentiment just to prove she could make the right decisions at the right time. The phone rang.

"Garden Walk."

"How's business?"

"Jim! I just called you in Morristown."

"I'm not there."

"So I found out. How's the seminar? Anything interesting being learned?"

"Actually, quite a few things. We were finished after lunch,
but I decided to have a little strategy session on a few problem
customers. The seminar is a good idea. McBride should be applauded."

"Well, that's a switch."

"That's because I'm in clear view.'

"What does that mean?"

"It means I'm sitting in McBride's territory out in the open,"
he said in a low voice.

"Okay, how about some yes-and-no questions?"

"Sounds good."

"You're supposed to say 'yes' or 'no.'"

"That was a 'yes.' Yes is an affirmative statement. They're interchangeable."

"Didn't I say that once? It sounds like my sort of logic. I
couldn't stand our both being on the same wavelength."

"You're a good teacher."

"And you're a good student."

"Try me."

"Okay. Did you learn anything about invoices today?"

"Quite a bit."

"That was another affirmative?"

"Yes."

"Good. Anything that makes you think something is going on
that shouldn't be?'

"Possible."

"Was that a 'yes' or a 'no'?"

"I'm not sure, but I do think the potential is there. There were
some comments made by McBride's number two that peaked my
interest. I've arranged a meeting in Morristown to review some
issues about the Rayburn relationship. Adam's coming up tomorrow afternoon, and I can raise my own issues at the same time."

"You mean there really is something going on?'

"I think so."

"Illegal?" she said with urgent surprise.

"That, I'm not sure of."

"Unethical?"

"That may be a little closer to the mark."

"Is it something to be concerned about?"

"It could be."

"How?"

"That was not the right question."

"Maybe we should hold this off until later."

"I think you're right. Besides, by tomorrow, after I've had a chance to speak with Campbell, I'll have a better idea of where I am."

"With who?"

"Who? What? Oh, Ed Campbell. He's McBride's new number two. Look, I have to be off. I need to stop at the office before I come home."

Silence.

"Marian?"

"Oh, still here. Yes, will you be on time?"

"I expect so. See you later."

Jim hung up the phone and looked around the room. He had been sitting at one of the empty desks in the middle of the international platform area. No one seemed to be paying any attention to him. He was the last one there from the seminar and had been using the desk and phone to respond to telephone messages. There had been a steady stream throughout the day. He hoped he wouldn't have to go to Morristown today and could just head home, but no such luck. He stood up, put his briefcase on the desk, opened it, placed the steno pad he'd been writing on inside, and headed for the door.

But Jim had been wrong. Someone was interested.

Larry McBride stood at the entrance to his office and watched Jim make his call. Then he quickly moved away when he saw it was finished. He immediately went to his phone and dialed a number.

"Yeah."

"I think we may have a problem," McBride said simply.

"Serious?"

"Not really sure yet."

"How do you know it's a problem?"

"I just know."

"Want me to do anything?"

"Not yet."

"Okay, but don't wait too long. Nip it in the bud."

"Not entirely sure what he knows."

"You sure he knows something?"

"That, I'm sure of, but I'm not sure he's put all the pieces to-gether yet."

"Has he started asking questions?"

"I think he's about to."

"Don't wait for him to start. Give him answers. Anticipate the questions. You play *Jeopardy*? He thinks he has an answer, supply him with a question that fits."

"Okay, I'll work on it."

"But don't let it drag on. We've got a good thing going here, and I don't want to lose it."

The connection ended.

CHAPTER 6

The Dilemma of Ed Campbell

Marian shut down the store promptly at five, stopped for groceries on the way home, and started dinner at six-thirty, expecting Jim to be home shortly. The chicken came off the fire part of the grill at seven-fifteen and now sat on the grill's upper deck in an effort to keep it warm.

The baked potatoes were merely moved to the back of the main cooking area and out of the way. The patio table was set. She fidgeted. Kept moving the chicken around. Turned the potatoes again and again. Sat down and then got up again.

She still hadn't figured out how she would remind Jim who Ed Campbell was. The name didn't seem to have made an impression on him. She would have to mention it. You didn't exactly forget the names of people who almost caused the breakup of your marriage, but then maybe you do, especially if you've never met them. No face to put with the name. But how to bring up the topic? You just didn't ask enthusiastically how old Ed is. It had to be sort of disinterested. Maybe she could try curious and inquiring, but it couldn't be obvious, as though she wanted to know—even though she did. But why? Maybe it was just natural curiosity.

The whole idea was dumb, but it had to be raised somehow. She hated the idea of just accidentally running into him with Jim someday, and Jim saying, "Oh, you're *that* Ed. Campbell."

No, that wouldn't work. Marian couldn't let things sit. They had to be dealt with—immediately. Procrastination was not her strong suit. If she didn't get it off her plate, it would fester until she became a nervous wreck. Of course, it did occur to her that it might be a different Ed Campbell. The name really wasn't that uncommon. But, no, she was sure.

Finally, Jim pulled into the driveway and made his way up the thirty yards toward the garage. Spotting him, she headed to the kitchen to get the corn. It was more than ready. She could lay out the dinner while he was changing.

Jim opened the bottle of Chablis and poured some into the glasses on the patio table. Everything was ready. It took him no more than five minutes to change into the chinos and a long-sleeved, checked shirt. In anticipation of the chill that would come later as they ate, he brought along a sweater for each of them.

"You were later than expected." Marian was carrying the corn and the butter dish to the table. They had exchanged hello's and welcome home kisses on his way from the garage, through the kitchen and then upstairs to change.

"Yeah, I know. I really hadn't planned on going back to the office. It's not like the old days when I was traveling and could cut out early after a business call. Now they find you, no matter where you are. The electronic umbilical cord. Why don't I retire, you sell the store, and we'll disappear to Grenada or St. Lucia?"

"You're not old enough."

"I feel old enough."

"I could say you look old enough, but that would be unkind—and also untrue."

"Thank you, I needed that."

The chicken tasted good, just the right amount of barbecue sauce, and the corn was the sweetest of the year. The recent chilly nights of September had turned it just right. They ate in almost complete silence except for a few menu comments. After a hard day of dealing with people, they both usually looked for a respite in the one safe haven they knew they had. Being outside made everything taste better. As Marian moved the coffee pot to the table and then sat back in her chair she decided it was time to dive in:

"So, how did our Mr. McBride do today?"

"How does that saying go? 'You've got to give the devil his due,' or something like that." Jim poured himself a cup of coffee as he spoke. "He set things up pretty well. This series of seminars is going to be valuable, and I intend to get everyone into them that I can. However, having said that, I still don't really know what to think of him personally."

"Haven't succumbed to his charms, have you?"

"Not a bit. There's just something about him that bothers me, and I can't put my finger on it. He seems like such a weasel sometimes, even if he does know what he's doing. If there's one thing I'm sure he does know, it's where he's going and how to get there. That sounds like a cliché, doesn't it?"

"You? A cliché? Never!"

"He just never lets up," Jim continued, having acknowledged her playful barb with a smile. "You know if I didn't feel so ambivalent about him I probably wouldn't have given this invoice thing a second thought. And this uneasiness about him is really bothering me. I can usually put up with most people. There really aren't a lot of people I would put into the dislike category."

"I must admit that's true. You're usually just the other way."

"Old McBride just brings out the worst in me, I guess."

"So what about this invoice? Is there really something to it or are we just dealing with some anti-McBride sentiment?"

Jim thought about the question and rubbed his chin. "No, I really think there's something going on. As I said before, it may not be illegal, but I'm sure it's unethical. There were a couple of things said today that make me think that, and one of them in particular related to invoices. I've got to ask some questions of this new guy who gave part of the seminar. He's the one who mentioned this invoice swapping thing."

"Invoice swapping? Is that legal?" Marian again questioned.

"Apparently, if it's all up front and above board. Everything documented and recorded. But if that was the case with McBride, he wouldn't have been so uptight about losing one, or for that matter, even having one. I'm more convinced than ever that there's something fishy going on."

"If this is supposed to be a legitimate practice, would there be something written up about how it works?"

"There would have to be."

"Okay, why don't you get some material on the topic and find out how you turn a legal transaction into an illegal or unethical one?"

"You know you have a really, truly devious mind."

"Was that a compliment?"

"Of course. Why do you think I married you?" Jim said with a smile.

"My devious mind?"

"The primary reason."

Marian hesitated. *You can't say anything. Not right now,* she thought. *The time and the conversation are wrong.* "Well, I would appreciate it if you could come up with another reason,"

"Okay, let's say that's *one* of the primary reasons."

"I guess when it comes to deviousness it takes one to know one."

The sun had already set as Marian began placing the dishes in the dishwasher. Jim did the rinsing and Marian did the stacking. It was a team effort, each one doing the task they did best.

"Jim, there's something I have to ask you,. This fellow Campbell, is he about five feet ten, dark hair?"

"Yes, he is—well, the hair is grayish-brown. Why do you ask?"

"Well, there was an Ed Campbell that I knew at Bankers."

"That's a long while ago."

"A million years," she said almost to herself.

"What was that?"

"I said 'A million years.'"

"Yeah, it does seem that way. I sometimes think the time I worked in New York was just a dream, somebody else. Another person, another time."

"Yes, I feel that way. But what I wanted to say was that this could be *the* Ed Campbell. You know, from twenty years ago. The West Coast trip. The bad time." Marian stopped stacking dishes. A slight shiver of tension ran through her.

Jim was silent. A long, dead-silent pause. "Do you really think so?"

"Jim, I don't know. The name just hit me. I have no idea why it comes to mind. It just did." A sadness came over her, as though a cloud suddenly drifted into the kitchen and hovered over her head.

Jim could feel her tension. "Well, it was a long time ago. I had forgotten. I'd never met him, so I wouldn't know. Maybe it's not him."

"You're right. I could be over reacting. It was a million years ago, as we said. Everything's changed. He didn't act as though he knew you today? Of course, he wouldn't—you two never met."

Jim put down the dish he was rinsing and reached out to her.

They hugged gently, softly, quietly.

"It was a million years ago," he said, realizing he felt suddenly uneasy, memories he really didn't want to recall coming to the fore. "A million years ago. A world and a time gone by. If it turns out that this Ed Campbell is *the* Ed Campbell, then, so be it. An acquaintance is back from another time. And that's how it will be. That's how it should be—and nothing more."

Marian increased the pressure of her hug and the cloud began to disappear; the tension eased but Jim knew he now had a whole new set of problems sitting out there to face.

"That's how it should be," she repeated softly and then thought, *But will it?*

"Okay. Settled," he said, releasing his grip on her. "Now, let's get these dishes done."

❧❧

Grace Fredericks finished up her dishes and placed a dishtowel on top of them in the drying rack next to the sink, a second dishtowel rested over her shoulder. Tommy had fallen asleep earlier when she cleared the table. The day-care center worked him hard today, and he just couldn't keep his eyes open. She smiled watching him sleep away curled up on the cushions in front of the television. She muted the sound on the TV so he wouldn't be disturbed while she did the dishes. Even the noisy neighbors in the apartment next door didn't disturb him. The attention needed by a four-year-old seemed never ending, but also served as the best time of the day after the long hours at First State. A good time but also an exhausting one. She loved Tommy dearly. His enthusiasm and love made her feel secure.

The telephone rang quietly. It was always kept on the low setting so Tommy would not be disturbed. Removing the dishtowel from her shoulder, she rushed around the serving counter of the one-and-a-half-room apartment and lunged for the phone just as it started its second ring. One and a half rooms was what the advertisement said—a stretch by anyone's imagination. A not so "great" room with a kitchen area.

She created some privacy for herself by dividing up the room with two four-foot-high book cases.

Tommy had one side while she claimed the other—where a

daybed and a television on a dresser chest made for her private space. "Hello," she said, almost breathlessly and in a half whisper.

"Ms. Fredericks?"

"Yes."

"Ms. Fredericks, this is Larry McBride from the bank."

"Oh, yes, Mr. McBride."

"I'm sorry to bother you at home but I wanted to speak with you in private. I hope I didn't catch you at a bad time?"

"No, it's all right. Is something the matter?" Her first instincts were that of fear—fear of being fired, fear that she had done something that would jeopardize her position, fear of losing Tommy. Black and a single mother trying to raise a four year old, she was vulnerable to everything.

"Certainly not. No. I wanted to touch base with you about possibly transferring to international. I heard you were looking for something more than just secretarial pool work, and I have an opening that may interest you. Forgive me for calling you at home but First State does not have a particularly enlightened internal transfer policy. As you may be aware, I'm not supposed to pursue anyone internally that has not already initiated a transfer request. You haven't have you?"

"Oh, no."

"Well, my secretary Gloria, Gloria Martinez, I believe you know one another."

"Yes, I know Gloria."

"Well, Gloria said that she thought you would be perfect for the opening we have and would jump at the chance to go beyond secretarial work."

"This wouldn't be a secretarial position?"

"No, it wouldn't. It's in our customer service area. I've done some checking on my own and, personally, I think it would be a win-win for us. You've had good reviews. You've got a good telephone manner and know and understand the bank. I think it would be a perfect fit."

"Well, I must admit I feel as though I'm going a bit brain dead where I am. Don't get me wrong, I like working for Mr. Fairmont's group, but typing letters and reports all day does get a little boring sometimes."

"Well, I can definitely guarantee you variety, challenge, a

significant pay increase, and a chance for advancement. Besides, I think it's in the bank's best interest to promote people internally. It's good for everyone."

"It sounds tempting."

"Why don't you give it some thought? Gloria's agreed to play go between, and I'll see that she sends you a job description. However, we can't talk again until you file the formal transfer request. I'll have Gloria send over that job description, and then you let her know what you think. If you're interested, I'll have her post the position opening, and we'll go from there."

"Okay, but what would I do then?"

"The way it has to work is that you have to put in for a transfer—officially—and it will have to be approved by Fairmont. Do you think there will be any trouble there?"

"I don't think so. Mr. Fairmont has always been fair. I think he would like me to move on to something better."

"Good, take a good look at what I'll send over and then let Gloria know what you think."

"Okay, I will."

"Excellent and I'm sorry to have bothered you this way but that's the way the system works."

"Oh, that's all right."

"Well, good then. And keep this to yourself for the time being. I'll tell Gloria to expect your call tomorrow."

"Yes."

"Excellent."

Grace gently placed the receiver into its stand, trying to make as little noise as possible. She then walked over to the bookcase and peered over at Tommy—he slept undisturbed in the area she had cordoned off for him.

As she walked back to the kitchen and the dish towel, she began to think about the phone conversation and the future. Yes, her future and Tommy's. She didn't think of the location of the international inquiry department and the travel implications. Instead of taking fifteen minutes to get to work, it would now be more than double that with both a train and bus ride, which would create day-care problems. But that was for tomorrow's reflections.

♋

McBride hung up the phone and smiled at his success. It was easy. Dangle a little honest extra money in front of someone who really needed it, and you had them. He knew he had Grace Fredericks. It would take some time for all the paper work to be signed off and, for the time being, he would have an information source near Fairmont that he could use in a number of ways. Perhaps even be able to feed Fairmont some information that would satisfy any questions he had and make him think he had a back door connection to international.

If only McBride hadn't panicked at the book sale. If he had provided a plausible explanation for the invoice at the time, none of this would have happened. They could have laughed it off. But the time for that had passed. He had to protect himself, as he felt Fairmont was becoming just a bit too suspicious.

CHAPTER 7

A Defensive Plan Develops

Grace Fredericks began Wednesday with a little extra bounce in her step. Up at six a.m., a bit earlier than usual, she had two and a half hours to get Tommy up, dressed, fed and ready for Tiny Footprints, and do the same for herself. She always ate breakfast at home with Tommy rather than just grabbing a Danish and coffee at the truck parked in front of First State on The Green, as many of her co-workers did. More importantly, she wanted to spend the time with Tommy at breakfast, and Peter D's truck food didn't fit into her budget. A good solid breakfast of juice, cereal, toast, and coffee would start her day, along with the usual conversation with Tommy about her daily plans. He would listen and ask questions, and then it would be her turn to ask questions about what he would do that day.

Being in an "up" mood, Grace chose a blouse of cheerful red, yellow, and pink flowers and hummed a tune as she got ready for work. By seven-thirty, they were both ready. Plenty of time to catch the seven forty-five New Jersey Transit bus to Footprints in Morris Plains. Grace and Tommy lived on Horace Place in a four-story brick building that housed twenty families, situated only one block from Speedwell Avenue where they would catch the bus. She could have taken Tommy to the day-care center run by a local church and within two blocks of Horace Place, but she preferred Footprints, where a number of people who worked at First State took their children. A good many companies were finally coming to grips with the needs of their employees when it came to child care and setting up day-care centers on site, but First State rejected the idea. The bank used the usual argument about insurance risk and shareholder liability, as everyone knew they would. With deregulation proceeding at full speed, the bank's plan focused on employee redundancy potential as a result of mergers, and benefit increases such as employee day care centers were not on the table. After all, there would be a lot of bankers out on the street looking for jobs in the next couple of years so offering added benefits to retain them made no sense. If not for the ride to Morris Plains, she could walk to The Green and the bank and be there in ten minutes. But, no, she would take the bus to Morris Plains, get Tommy settled into Tiny Footprints, and then hop on the bus back to Morristown and be at her desk by eight-thirty to start the day.

When Jim's secretary, Paula Enright, arrived, he already had his daily agenda well underway. He arrived just before eight a.m. and parked his car in the underground lot at Headquarters' Plaza, the office complex across the street.

His pattern rarely changed. Peter D's breakfast truck had his coffee and buttered roll waiting for him even though he just finished breakfast at home with Marian. Briefcase in his left hand and paper coffee sack in his right, he looked like everyone else as he made his way to the fourth floor and the Corporate Banking Department. His office looked south over The Green and had an impressive and soothing view of both the Episcopal and Presbyterian churches. He always took a moment to stand behind his desk and look out the window for just a few seconds before he turned on his PC and took off his jacket. This was quiet time, when the day could be sorted out in advance, when the voicemail messages could be written down, when the email messages could be reviewed and printed, and the To-Do list could be formulated. Work would be ready for Paula when she arrived.

"Morning Mr. Fairmont," Paula called as she plopped her purse on the center of her desk. Calling him "Mr. Fairmont" always seemed the right thing to do. She could never quite come to grips with calling him Jim. It just never occurred to her. Jim, on the other hand, never referred to himself as "Mr.," believing that doing so conveyed a sense of self-importance, and made a negative statement about a person—another sign of his growing dinosaur status in the corporate world of banking. It would be fine for others to convey the title of "Mr." but to anoint oneself? No, you just didn't do that.

He strongly believed companies requiring their customer service people to answer the phone, "This is Mr. Smith, how can I help you?" were trying to intimidate their own customers.

So Jim always answered, "Jim Fairmont." He would always identify himself the same way, "This is Jim Fairmont…" when calling others. When calling Paula to pick up his messages, he would use "This is Jim…" and would have no problem if she were to call him Jim but she had chosen not to do so.

The whole idea of greeting nuances was something that Jim continually tried to impress upon his calling officers: always refer to the client as Mr. or Ms. and wait for the customer to refer to themselves in the familiar before *you* do. It always seemed simple enough, but in today's world, formality didn't seem to exist in the public education system and certainly not at the college level. Unless you were at a military institution or you ran across a professor who had the courage to wear a shirt, tie, and suit to class and to stare you down over the top of a pair of cut-off reading glasses, should you dare not refer to him as "Professor" Smith, you were never even exposed to the concept of common courtesy. Unfortunately, there didn't seem to be enough of such people around anymore to give students a good taste of formality.

Manners were another topic altogether, where had they gone? Were they not taught anywhere, anymore? Jim had no problem in his early years at Chase—there were no options—you referred to your boss as "Mr." just as he referred to his. You knew your place and what was expected of you. He often wondered when everything started to change and finally began to look to the Viet Nam War where the art of misinformation and deception—as well as outright lying—by respected government officials and business leaders forever changed the playing field. So when Paula referred to him as "Mr. Fairmont," he did not see it as a possible barrier between them but as her dealing with a situation in the manner in which they both felt the most comfortable.

Paula settled into her normal routine. First was a change of shoes. The bottom right hand drawer of her desk had a remarkable variety of them—at least four pair in different colors. Off would come the flat comfortable walking shoes and on would go the black medium heels. In the bottom drawer of the file cabinet behind her would go her purse. Next would be to look at Jim's calendar that she kept on her desk. There were two notations: *eleven-thirty a.m., Adam Turner-re the Rayburn account and two p.m., Ed Campbell, Int'l—also Rayburn.* She picked up the bound, American Express appointment calendar book and walked into Jim's office. The book was green, and Jim had the companion pocket version out on the desk in front of him.

"I've got Adam at eleven thirty and Ed Campbell at two," Paula said. "Anything to add?"

"No, but see if you can finagle a table for two over at The Office for lunch. Adam and I are going to need some serious time together before Campbell gets here."

"Okay."

She immediately turned and headed back to her desk. She was the traffic cop again. Later she would be a "go-for." She understood why so many of the new secretaries that were coming up shied away from the job she had as a career. Times were changing. The millennium loomed only seven years away; the predictions of all jobs being in jeopardy because of the introduction of the personal computer was actually coming true. Secretarial positions were being consolidated, eliminated or completely revamped as Executive or Administrative Assistants. Everyone needed to justify their existence, do something meaningful, be part of the decision making process, and, above all, be a contributor to the bottom line. It was not that working for Jim Fairmont was bad. In fact, as bosses went, he was quite good. It was just that she and everyone else felt vulnerable and knew they had to have a visible role in order to survive—like all the bank tellers being turned into point-of-sale staff. It wasn't just a matter of personal achievement, as some people tried to put the spin to it, it was all about survival. The word secretary had developed a negative connotation.

ℰ✒ℰↃ

Larry McBride opened the door to his office and stepped into the doorway.

"Gloria, do you have a minute?"

Although it was still before nine in the morning, the International Department had been running at full speed for hours. McBride usually came in around seven. The bank didn't do a great deal of foreign exchange but did maintain small operating accounts in a number of European and Asian trading centers, especially those where their US clients had offices. The bank did not trade currencies for its own account but did a modest volume and usually offered better rates on small dollar amounts than could be obtained at the large money center banks. McBride made a point of staying aware of European foreign exchange trends and being in by seven a.m.—noon in London—gave him time to be aware of what had happened in the markets if he received a call from a customer early in the morning. Also, since a good deal of the export financing that the bank did was with Latin America and the Caribbean, much of which was on Atlantic Time rather than Eastern, he could be available for discussions with First State's correspondents at their opening of business.

Gloria Martinez looked up from her desk. "Sure Larry," she said and then got up to follow him back to his desk, grabbing a pencil and a pad along the way.

Gloria was dressed to impress in true Latin style. She stood five feet five with jet-black hair just slightly more than shoulder length. The dress was red and black and contoured to accentuate every angle of her Bally's Gym honed body. The makeup included liberal amounts of eye shadow crafted expertly to accent her dark almond shaped eyes. Gloria was a Latin knock out with all the front office appeal that Larry required to impress his guests from south of the border. She was the ice breaker at all his meetings.

The admiring glances from customers usually precipitated some extensive praise to Larry as she left the room. It became an almost common reaction for one of Larry's clients to bite on his knuckles and role his eyes in the air as she walked past him. Gloria had no illusion as to what Larry was doing and played her role to the hilt. She enjoyed the admiring glances and encouraged the occasional flirtatious chatter. Larry was well aware of her value and paid her well. He knew it was generally commented among many of the Latin bankers: "Have you seen McBride's secretary over at First State? Next time you're in New York go see him. Believe me, it's worth the trip."

For Larry, whatever edge he could get he would take. There were a lot of comments about the relationship between Gloria and Larry, but McBride kept everything strictly business. He made a firm practice of not getting involved with anyone in the office, having learned his lesson six years earlier when he was on a special trade financing trip at the request of Manufacturers Hanover's Europe Division. His overtures to a junior member of his group resulted in her filing a sexual harassment charge against him with her division manager.

The woman accused him of tying her performance on the trip to her cooperation with his advances and wasn't afraid to take the heat for her charges. He ended up being severely reprimanded by the Europe Group within three months of the trip. Seeing the bank's "aloha" room on the horizon, he made the move to Security Pacific International in New York, as soon as he received an offer from them. It was a touchy time. Sexual harassment was gaining visibility in the work place and not just hushed up or overlooked.

Thirty years ago it was unheard of for a bank to lay-off staff, much less fire an officer outright. It was understood that, if you and the bank must part company, you would be given a private office somewhere in the Personnel Division, before Human Resources became the politically correct terminology. From that vantage point, you would have access to a secretary, telephones, and all the resources necessary to secure another position without the taint of being let go by your current employer. There would be no severance pay, and you would remain on the payroll with full benefits until you could find a position with another bank. It was the civilized, gentlemanly approach that had its pluses and minuses: banking maintained a dignified, wholesome, competent public image—a secure, honorable place of employment—while passing off a good many incompetent, inefficient, bumbling managers on the public and other companies.

However, in a federally regulated, rate-controlled environment, bankers didn't need to be innovative or creative to have successful careers. They just needed knowledge and consistency. Then came the twenty-percent interest rates of the Carter and Reagan years, the savings and loan crisis, and the beginning of the de-regulation of the commercial banking system. The playing field became uneven, with banks being able to set the interest rates they would pay for deposits but the money center banks still felt they were being forced to compete with one arm tied behind their backs, as non-banks and foreign banks were free to maneuver in the marketplace without the specter of the state and federal authorities peeking over their shoulders in the same way. The end result was the increase in risk taking and "strange bedfellow" combinations in the name of increased earnings, as the free deposit base of banking disappeared. First State needed to compete, needed to protect its customer base from being eroded by European and Japanese banks, needed to get into areas it had not exploited previously, needed the high commissions and yields that could be obtained from an international trading portfolio, needed someone with the background of a Larry McBride, who learned his trade in the New York market, knew how to play the game and had learned his lessons well.

So as Gloria Martinez slipped into one of the two straight-backed chairs in front of his desk and crossed her legs so that her dress rose more than six inches above her knee, McBride simply averted his eyes and focused on his topic of concern. "I had a talk with Grace Fredericks last night, you know—pool secretary in Jim Fairmont's group but mainly assigned as a go-for for John Porter of Community Affairs over in Morristown. How do you think she'd do in customer service over here?"

"Probably fit pretty well. Is she looking for a transfer?"

"Possibly. How well do you know her?"

"A bit. We've talked over the phone from time to time and attended some corporate ed. classes together. She seems pretty sharp. Certainly has a good telephone manner. What brings her to mind?"

"Nothing special. She always seemed pretty competent when I've called over there. Would like to fill our vacant slot from inside rather than go out in the street to look for someone."

"That's true." Gloria, as the manager's secretary, knew everything that went on in the department. She served as personnel record keeper, had access to all staff information from performance reviews to salary, and worked closely with the employment department to file progress reports on any openings in the area.

"I think it might be a good idea if you gave her a sales pitch on us. I'm not supposed to be talking with her about a transfer and can't have Susan in customer service get involved until the papers are put through."

"So?"

"So let's see if I can arrange for you to go over to Morristown one day and maybe you two could work up some lunch—my expense—talk shop, tell her how wonderful we all are over here," he said with a smile.

"Oh, sure, a laugh a minute. This place is a zoo!"

"But an interesting zoo. You must admit it's never boring."

"I'll give it that. If she's looking for stimulation and a moving target, this is the place to be."

"And that's the best approach to take—innovation, change, action. Nobody wants to be just a secretary anymore."

"What am I, chopped liver?"

"You are not the traditional secretary. You practically run the place, and you know it."

"Yeah, I know, but when do I get the title? Executive Assistant to the Group Manager would be nice."

"Look, you're one of the few people left in the place that really is a secretary. You can actually take shorthand—in two languages. You're not like these kids today who take these secretarial jobs, most of them can't even spell."

"That's what spell checkers are for."

"Okay, you win, as usual. But if the Fredericks woman calls you, you give her a sales pitch. And I will talk to personnel about changing your designation."

"No problem."

"One other thing. Ed Campbell tells me he's going up to Morristown to meet with Turner and Fairmont about the Rayburn Corp. Have Susan pull the customer service file on them and see if you can get a copy of their account analysis. And make sure the latest charges and fees are on it then tell Ed I'd like to see him before he leaves. He's coming in first, isn't he?"

"He's here now. I saw him earlier."

"Good"

Recognizing the dismissal tone in McBride's voice, Gloria immediately got up. "Do you want to see him now?"

"Anytime is good. Just have him peek in."

"Okay." She headed back to her desk, where she immediately dialed Ed Campbell's number. His office was on the other side of the floor so, even though the international platform area was an open one, she couldn't tell if he was there or not. The phone rang three times, and then voicemail kicked in. "Ed, this is Gloria. Larry would like you to stop by for a few minutes before you head out for Morristown. Nothing special. Just some words of wisdom about Rayburn. Bye." Next was Susan's number

"Customer Service. Susan Ross."

"Susan? Gloria."

"Hi, Gloria, what's up?"

"The boss want's a quick look at the Rayburn file. Could you bring it over first thing?"

"Sure, anything else?"

"Oh, yeah, dig out a recent charging sheet."

"I think we just did an analysis. That name's been getting a lot of attention lately. There should be an up-to-date one in the file. I'll bring it right over."

"Thanks. Bye." Gloria put back the phone, thinking, *The joy of having competent staff around you.* Susan had at least fifteen years in international and knew everything about everything. *Larry keeps talking about people changing jobs all the time, but he doesn't mean we peons. It's all those young college types who keep job hopping to get ahead. The rest of us stay put. No one seems to keep statistics on us. Talk about secretaries, they got rid of all the secretaries and replaced them with voicemail, electronic calendars, and word processing programs, so now they pay some young kid five years out of college thirty or forty thousand dollars a year, and he spends more than half the time typing his own letters and reports and the other half making copies and distributing them. It takes two of them to do the job it took one good secretary to do when my mother worked for the bank. Ah, well, that was forty years ago. Times have changed. Now everyone wants to be the boss. No one wants to work for anyone else. Get your head together, Gloria, this is the nineties, it's the individual, not the group, that counts. Do what you have to do to get the job done, worry about your piece not the whole. That's for the guys that make the big bucks.*

McBride's PC sat on the credenza behind him. He tapped the space bar, and the password protection window popped into view. He entered the required eight alphanumeric characters and then watched the WordPerfect template he had been working on pop into view. It was a three column format with the first being a text description field of thirty-five characters, the second and third were decimal field columns. Approximately half the page was filled with product descriptions on the left, a unit price in the second column and then a total in the third. He reached into the drawer in the credenza just left of the keyboard and took out a dark brown, three section separated, hard press board file folder. The file tab read: *Alliance Automotive Export L/C# 011075*. He opened the file to the back section and removed a set of shipping documents that he had placed there the day before and then positioned the one marked *INVOICE* on top where he could copy from it. He began typing. The descriptive information in the thirty-five character column matched what he was copying from, but when he got to the number fields, he looked under the invoice to a separate piece of paper and typed in those numbers instead. When he was finished, he reached into his briefcase that was open on the floor next to his chair and removed a sheet of paper. He then positioned the sheet of paper into the manual feed slot on the paper tray of the LaserJet printer next to the PC and clicked the left mouse button on the Print icon. As soon as the paper dropped into the tray, he removed it and then replaced the invoice he copied from with the new invoice. The original he placed on his desk while he took the substitute and placed it into the proper order within the loose documents that were in the file and closed it. On the front of the file was a separate label with a printed notation.

REFER ALL INQUIRIES AND
CORRESPONDENCE TO:
L. A. MCBRIDE
INTERNATIONAL BANKING GROUP MANAGER

The original invoice he then placed into his briefcase.

A short while later, Ed Campbell made his way across the room to Gloria Martinez's desk, his five-foot-ten frame covered in true banker's ware—dark suit, white shirt, blue-gray tie. His thinning brown hair was cut a comfortable length with some gray beginning to show around the edges. He looked a bit younger than his fifty-five years.

"Is he in?"

Gloria looked up: "Just stepped down the hall. He'll be back in a moment."

"I'll just curl up here for a bit then." He made his way to the little anteroom by McBride's office. There was a small sofa, a coffee table with some business and international magazines on it and two straight-backed chairs at either end of the table. Ed took one of the chairs and put the folder he was carrying onto the table. "Gloria, how long have you been with First State?"

"Oh, let me see…must be…just ten years."

"Always international?"

"Pretty much. Why?"

"You're good you know."

"Yeah, I know. You sound like someone who needs a favor."

"No, no," Ed said with a smile. "No ulterior motives. Just a compliment."

"In that case, thank you."

"You have to realize I spent my time at the giants: Continental and Bankers. It's a long time since I've been exposed to the kind of atmosphere First State has."

"Not sure what you mean."

"Well, there's a sense of knowing what the total picture looks like. The place is still small enough so you get to see everything, not just one small piece of it. You have that kind of awareness. You have your finger on things. Actually, I find the place a little like the old Bankers Trust where I started. Used to work over at Fourteen Wall. Have you ever been over there?"

"No, I haven't."

"It was an interesting time the mid-sixties. The banks used to be headquartered on Wall Street, or Pine Street or Hanover Square. That was before they all moved up town to the Park Avenue area. I guess only Morgan and Bank of New York are left. You should have seen the banking floors. The one that always impressed me the most was Irving Trust Company's at One Wall Street, just across from where I worked. Magnificent art deco, three stories high. Red mosaic tile walls with gold borders. The tellers' cages rimmed the room and were gleaming brass. The tellers themselves all wore maroon jackets. It was impressive to walk in there."

"What happened to it?"

"Oh, the room is still there, but now it's an officer platform area. When Manufacturers merged with the Hanover Bank the headquarters of the two banks were consolidated at the Wall Street headquarters of Manufacturers. Irving Trust, which had its headquarters at the corner of Wall and Broadway, bought up the rest of the block along Broadway, Exchange Place and New Street, which was where the Hanover Bank was, tore down the buildings and built a massive addition to its One Wall Street address, instead of moving uptown like the rest were doing. That's where they moved the banking floor to—all modern and up to date."

"Sounds like a history lesson," said Larry as he came upon them.

"Actually it was pretty interesting," said Gloria. "We could probably use a little history around here. Make people feel they belong to something—improve morale."

McBride responded with ice in his voice. "The only morale booster that counts anymore is a pay check. Corporate graveyards are littered with companies with history. The present and the future are what counts. These are the only things you can control."

"Well, I still think it would help if people had an understanding of the traditions of the place where they work."

"Trust me on this one Gloria, the only people that count are the ones that buy the stock and they're not a bunch of wealthy dowagers who remember how nice a teller was to them in 1935 or that the bank saved the farm for Cousin George or that great Uncle Harold was the President in 1890. They're mutual funds, pension funds, and investment bankers, and they don't care what you were or how you got here. Their interest is the next quarterly earnings statement and whether you will be a survivor during the next industry shakeout."

"Well then, I think there's something very wrong with the process."

"It's just that the process is changing," added Ed. "We're in a transitional phase. One of the lessons being learned is that bigger is not necessarily better. Mergers used to occur for the purpose of eliminating competition but that was legislated out and now they're looking for greater operating efficiencies, but it doesn't always happen. Now we're into 'lean and mean.' We've had too many years of growth and good times since World War Two. The recession of the past couple of years was a wake-up call for a lot of people. There's a massive correction due, and the smart money knows it; they're trying to find the right survival tactic."

McBride ended the discussion: "Enough Business Philosophy One-O-One for today. Ed, come in for a minute."

"I still think traditions are important," said Gloria.

"So write a book for staff awareness—on weekends."

Gloria stuck her tongue out at McBride's back as he led Ed into his office.

"Grab a seat for a few minutes. I just wanted to go over the Rayburn stuff before you meet on it."

"Sure."

"I've been looking over the reports Adam Turner has been filing, and I don't see how we can match Chase on this unless we can put together that correspondent agreement with Hang Wing Bank that I've been working on. Chase has a branch in Hong Kong, and there's no way we can match the rebates they're offering without an agreement in place with a local bank. "

"Larry, I'm not convinced that rebates are the real issue here."

"But that's what we're being asked to match."

"That's what Turner is saying, but based on some of the things he's mentioned I think that's more a symptom. Rayburn has a much bigger problem."

McBride put down the pencil he was holding and leaned back in his chair. "In what way?"

"It's one of the reasons I need to talk with Turner and possibly visit with Rayburn myself. Turner is a domestic guy. Payroll accounts, controlled disbursement, check processing, domestic cash management with a revolving credit or two thrown in is what he knows and does best. Rayburn is one of the few major US consumer electronics firms left. The rebates on the letters of credit are a way for them to cut costs, but look at the position they're in: they are either minority partners or have joint venture investments in their manufacturing plants in Asia. They need to increase the capacity of the Asian plants, but that's a risky move if the market moves against them. If we can come up with a way to provide the financing and investment they need and yet control their risk we could have a real edge."

"Have any ideas?"

"A couple, but a lot depends on what Rayburn really wants."

"According to the latest charging statement, it looks like they are worth between one hundred thousand dollars and one hundred fifty thousand dollars in revenue to us. I wouldn't like to lose that."

"Neither would I."

"Okay, do what you can with Turner. Are you also seeing Fairmont?"

"Yeah, we're meeting in his office. Any problem there?"

McBride paused just slightly before answering, "I doubt it. Fairmont's an old timer. He still goes on the basis of what's good for the bank is good for him. My objective is to protect international revenue."

"I'm a bit of an old timer myself."

"So I heard, with all that stuff with Gloria."

"No problem is there?"

"Not as long as you focus on the part of the bank that pays your salary. As far as Gloria goes, she's good stuff, got her head screwed on straight. She plays mother hen around here. Does a good job, keeps the staff away from me—and you. You'll see. Let's you focus on revenue with a capital R and our bottom line. I give her and everyone else as much freedom as possible, as long as they stay focused on *my* agenda."

"I gathered that. Anything else?"

"No, just do what you have to to save Rayburn, that's why you're here."

CHAPTER 8

Mentoring the Next Generation

The Office restaurant sat just off The Green in the middle of the Morristown shopping district, which unlike the downtown areas of many smaller towns, still presented itself as a viable place to visit and shop. The big malls were still a good distance off in Summit and Bridgewater. The restaurant was true to its name in that its decor was that of a business office but with a 1940s and earlier theme. Old stock certificates peppered the walls, vintage typewriters were strategically placed, and advertisements from fifty and sixty years ago were framed and placed all around. It was a hangout for shoppers, as well as the local business crowd.

"I believe you're holding a table for Fairmont."

"Eh, I, oh, yes." The host—appropriately decked out in a broad-striped shirt with elastic armbands—stammered. He was about to say "We don't do reservations" but then saw the note pasted on the stand in front of him. "No problem, Mr. Fairmont. I have your table right over here in the corner."

"Thanks."

As they shifted into the booth, Adam Turner placed the tan file folder he was carrying onto the table.

"Can I get you something to drink?" inquired the host.

Jim responded first. "Just some iced tea.'

"Same here."

He made the notation on a pad. "Terry will be your server." He distributed the menus. "The daily specials are on the inside leaf. Enjoy your lunch."

"Thanks."

"Are you buying or am I?" said Adam.

"The bank will buy this one."

"A rare treat, indeed. My boss over at the Union Office makes us buy our own lunch."

"Smart fellow. Takes good instruction. I'll have to say something nice about him next time." Jim, Adam's boss, said all of this with a straight face. It fit into the relaxed give and take of his management style.

"I'm sure he'll appreciate that."

Adam spotted an old stock certificate that was pasted to the tabletop under the glass. "Kind of an interesting place. Don't think I've ever been here before."

"It's clever. The theme restaurant concept. Usually means the food isn't too good. Need to distract you with something else. You end up reading the old stock certificates and accounting ledgers—takes your mind off what you ate."

"That bad?"

"Not really. The place is the exception that proves the rule. They do lunch really well. I've never done dinner though."

"I'll keep it in mind."

"So tell me, do you have any good news for me before lunch?"

"One or two things."

"Good. Let's order first, and then you can butter me up while we wait for it."

Jim liked Adam. He was young, thirty two to be exact; Jim often joked at staff meetings about how young everyone was, claiming to have file folders in his desk that were older than most of them. Turner was a New Jersey native, as were most of the young bank officers. New York got the out of towners. Young MBA types didn't leave Peoria to come to New Jersey. Adam had a degree in history from Drew University and an MBA from Rutgers. He first worked in the treasury department of a Warner Lambert subsidiary, but when it was sold to a company in Ohio the local finance activity was consolidated, and he jumped to First State. That was five years ago. For the last eighteen months, he'd been working out of the Union Office and corporate banking.

Jim took a sip of his iced tea and pushed away the nearly empty plate of fish and chips he probably shouldn't have had for lunch and then picked up his napkin. "So now that the good news and lunch are out of the way, it's time for the bad news. Let's talk Rayburn."

Adam had already finished his Caesar salad with the sliced, grilled chicken and was working on his second iced tea. "Well, it may not be all bad. One thing I've learned is that Mike Rivers, the treasurer of Rayburn, is not a fan of Chemical. They were the lead in the revolving credit back in the early eighties when Rayburn was shutting down domestic manufacturing left and right and some of the New York banks wanted out. Given the numbers Rayburn was putting out, I wouldn't blame them, but Rivers, who was the domestic cash management guy at the time, took it personally. After Chemical and Manufacturers Hanover merged they made a bid to get back in, but Rayburn said they were happy with Chase."

"And now Chase is really Chemical?"

"Right. And Rivers is still in control and not suffering from Alzheimer's."

"He's that old is he?" Jim said peering over his glasses.

"Well, let's just say he has a more than adequately functioning memory."

Jim's smile became more pronounced. "Nicely done."

"Well, anyway, I think it leaves us an opening. Let's face it, there aren't too many banks left. The only one I can see being a problem is Bank of New York. They could probably get a foot in if they wanted it but haven't made a move. Citibank, I don't really see as a factor yet. No one ever seems to want to voluntarily do business with them, but they get it anyway because Citi is the only one with the geographic spread and product line to handle them globally."

"So there's hope?"

"There's hope if we can solve this international thing." The waiter drifted back and cleaned off the table.

"Do you think we'll lose our domestic piece?" Jim asked, serious again.

"Not all of it. We should be okay on the controlled disbursement and the local payroll, but I can't believe we won't get beat up on the Fed wire and ACH business. That's the sort of thing the really big guys do well, especially with all their automated PC based products. Frankly, I think we should be prepared to lose that, no matter what we do."

"The new money transfer windows won't help us?"

"Not really. Not against Chase or Bank of New York."

"So we're back to the international again?"

"Yup."

Jim sat back and thought quietly for a moment. "This letter of credit software from Bengal Products that McBride put in last year is okay?"

"No problem. Some big players are using it, so I'm told. No complaints. We look like everyone else."

"So we're back to pricing and the rebate thing."

"Looks like it."

"Tell me something, do you understand how this works? I'll be honest, the word 'rebate' has a nasty ring to it. Maybe I'm old fashioned but there's something about rebating fees to a customer that just doesn't sound right." Jim played with his spoon as he spoke.

"I'm told all the major banks do it for their high volume customers, but, no, I haven't the faintest idea how it works. That's what I'm hoping this guy Campbell will tell us."

"Speaking of Campbell, what do you know about him?"

"Not really that much. McBride seems high on him. I've talked with him a couple of times, and he seems all right. Long on international banking experience. Thought his presentation at the seminar last week was good. An old timer, like you." Adam said with a slight grin.

Jim peered over his glasses again, smiled, and shook his head.

Adam countered in a theatrical voice. "A deep understanding of the business acquired through years of experience dealing with a wide variety of multinational companies."

The check arrived.

"That's a little better. Why don't you pay that and we'll go? It's after one-thirty."

"Do I detect a penalty for insensitivity?"

"No, but I'll keep it in mind. You pay. I approve. You get reimbursed."

"Gotcha."

CHAPTER 9

Marian Exorcising Old Ghosts

Marian found herself in a reflective mood as she sat at her desk. Wednesday morning turned out to be surprisingly busy which she attributed to the good weather, although now clouds were rolling in and bringing a fine mist with them. It looked almost foggy out there now. Lunch, a bologna on rye and a Diet Coke, sat in front of her. One-half of the sandwich was gone, but most of the other part remained on the white deli paper in which it had been wrapped. Seeing the leftover food, she suddenly could hear her father's voice. *'Don't leave anything on that plate. I paid good money for that. You ordered it—you eat it.'* Funny how things popped into your mind from nowhere. It had been a long time since she had thought of her father. He had been dead now more than thirty years.

Patrick Kelly had always been somewhat of a mystery to Marian. This undoubtedly came from her being the youngest of four children. He was thirty-six when he married and fifty-two when Marian was born. Her three brothers had worn him out by the time she came along. Having been born in the last century, he was raised in an era of the autocratic parent and then found, when it became his turn, the world had changed. Believing that he should raise his children as his parents raised him and all the generations before him, with the father being the seat of authority in the family, he found it difficult to cope. The late 1950s and then the early 1960s were an emotional disaster for him. Television and rock and roll controlled his children. The high cost of education forced his wife to find first a part-time job and then a full time one. He became depressed. At the age of seventy, he had a daughter in high school, two sons in college and a third in the Army. After a lifetime of working for the City of New York as a court reporter, he saw his wife forced out of the home to provide the extra income needed for his children's education and the luxuries that were fast becoming necessities. Marian was twenty-two when he died and she could not remember ever having a meaningful conversation with him. During the last year of his life, she spent most of her time away at college in Washington DC, and, whenever she came home, she found him in the same place—the overstuffed chair in the living room watching television.

Marian touched the remains of her sandwich with her index finger and pushed it about on its wrapper, as she drifted back in time remembering how her mother catered to her father as though she were some kind of indentured servant rather than a wife with a life of her own.

The misting grew heavier and turned into a very light rain as she came back to the present. She kept daydreaming until spotting a squirrel scooting across the yard in the light rain, take a running leap onto the top of a wrought iron patio chair, and then again out into space, flying at the long wire that held the bird feeder elusively out of its usual range. It caught the wire, then smoothly slid down it onto the squirrel guard, and then, hooking a claw in the tiniest of spaces between the guard and food chamber, stretched itself out across its top. Then it let go of its grasp and, while falling, reached out, and caught the edge of the perching shelf, pulled itself up to the ledge, got comfortable, and began a much-deserved meal of sunflower seeds.

"And you, you crafty devil," said Marian out loud, "have it all figured out. You have your priorities all worked out and stay focused on them while we humans spend our time over analyzing everything. You're probably our successor on this silly planet."

Ah well, she thought, *here I sit thinking myself unique, the center of my universe, trying to make sense of the world, trying to understand it all, all this complexity and you my clever squirrel know it all: to survive the day, to be healthy enough to defend yourself, to hone your skills and rely on your cunning to keep your species going for another generation. Whatever it takes— find a way.* That was what her mother had done, and that was what Patrick Kelly had done. Their generation succeeded. Their offspring had achieved a level of affluence and success well beyond what they themselves ever had, something the current generation seemed unable to accomplish.

"Okay, enough daydreaming." The clock on her desk said two-fifteen. "I wonder where Florence is."

CHAPTER 10

Exploring a Rayburn Solution

Grace Frederick's desire to move to another position within the bank was not an unusual one. With companies making every effort to eliminate secretarial positions, anyone currently performing purely secretarial duties knew they were expendable. The eliminations, however, usually extended to middle management only. Senior management never seemed to lose their secretaries but did manage to disguise them. The "new" positions evolved with the designations executive assistant, assistant to the president, or administrative assistant. However, the new job description looked an awful lot like the one for a secretary that existed twenty years ago, except for the "word processing" skills requirement.

One-on-one secretarial assignments below the senior executive level were rare, so it was no surprise to Jim when he learned that Grace would not be replaced, and his secretary, Paula, would also take care of the needs of John Porter, the director of community affairs, who had the office next to Jim. John did not have a staff, and some of Paula's new duties were to watch his phone and calendar and take care of occasional visitors. John's primary responsibility involved representing the bank at the various civic and charitable functions in which the bank was expected to participate. Someone had to attend all those fund raising dinners the bank was invited to by the United Way and Catholic Charities, the Friends of the Chamber Orchestra, and the Big Brothers and Sisters and so on.

And, of course, there were the organizations that decided to name the chairman or president as "Man of the Year," "Father of the Year," "Banker of the Year," and someone had to coordinate buying up tables at the awards dinner at $1,000 or $5,000 each and then fill them with employees and guests who would applaud enthusiastically at the appropriate time. That was the task of John Arnold Porter.

The bank's travel department took care of booking hotels and rental cars, while Grace would just gather up the information and pass it on to Porter, who kept a large calendar book on his desk with everything in it. Someone had to screen all of the requests and make the appointments required. It was also John's responsibility to chair the bank's committee on gift giving and the matching gift program. John was perfect for the position as he actually attended the ballet, opera, symphony—as well as other artsy functions—and was a member of three or four art museums on his own, well before being obliged to attend such functions on behalf of the bank. In a previous era his family connections—his mother was a descendant of Thomas Hayward of Declaration of Independence fame—knowledge of art, music and literature, as well as his political finesse, would have made him senior management material.

However, in today's free market banking environment, the attributes of Attila the Hun were far more valuable in the executive suite than those of a John Arnold Porter, although they were still needed from a defensive image standpoint, similar to women and persons of color on boards of directors.

"So, Grace, all excited about becoming an international expert?" Jim said, cheerily greeting his departing staff member, seeing she seemed somewhat nervous.

"Oh, Mr. Fairmont, I'm so sorry."

"Sorry?"

"About leaving like this. I was sure I wouldn't have to leave until a replacement was found. I feel so guilty."

"Don't be silly. This will be great for you and you'll do extremely well," he said, while positioning himself on the edge of the desk and peering into the box she was packing.

"I'll keep in touch."

"Grace, you're not going to Siberia. It's only Newark—but then again—" he teased, trying to cheer her up, and received a smile in return. "You realize you'll be dealing with a lot of the same customers that you did here. Of course, it will be somewhat different, since it will be international. But then, we seem to have a lot more contact with international these days. Besides, we in-

tend to use you as a resource. You're one of us and we don't intend to let you forget it."

The thought also occurred to Jim that perhaps she could be of
help with the McBride invoice matter. Here was an opportunity
to find out a few things before going to internal audit and making
a fool of himself.

"Oh, I won't. If there's anything you ever need that I can help
with, please let me know."

At this point Ed Campbell came in for the scheduled meeting
about the Rayburn account. "I think I'm a few minutes early."

"No problem," responded Jim, as they shook hands. "Just trying to make sure Grace here knows where her friends are."

"I'd heard you made a smart career move," Ed said to Grace.
"Congratulations, you'll love international and never be bored.
Not that domestic banking is ever truly boring, it's just…shall we
say?…predictable."

"She's already sold, no need to sell her anymore," said Jim,
heading for his office.

"Good Luck," was Ed's parting comment, as he headed after
Jim.

Jim felt a bit uneasy about this meeting because of the Marian
connection. He wasn't sure how he should handle it. He could
always be flippant: "Nice to finally meet the guy who had an affair with my wife." But that wasn't his way. Then there was the
clear the air approach: "By the way, I know all about you and
Marian, but let's be friends anyway." No, that wouldn't work
either. No, the best way would be no way. Let it stand. What he
would love to happen would be for Ed to raise it so Jim could go
into a forgiving mode: "Well, it was a long time ago. Times were
different." And let the issue die. But that was not to be. Besides, a
business meeting was not appropriate for a personal discussion of
this type. *Keep to business. Keep personalities out of it.*

"Say, Ed, we've got about ten minutes or so before Adam gets
here, can I talk you into some coffee?"

"Sure."

"Just put your case over there," Jim said, pointing to a chair at
the side of the room, "and we'll make a quick run to the cafeteria."

"Fine."

"Paula, we're off to the cafeteria," Jim said on the way out.

"If Adam comes while we're gone, have him stay put. I'll bring him back some coffee. Would you like anything?"

"No, I'm fine thanks."

Then Jim turned to Grace, who stood next to Paula as they continued to review community affairs activities. "What time are you leaving today?"

"Oh, I'll be here all day. I'll be getting Paula up to speed on how to handle Mr. Porter's calendar and showing her where the files are kept and how to arrange the material. We're going to be tied up with Mr. Porter in a few minutes so we had planned it for this afternoon."

"Oh, good. Be back in a few minutes."

Jim and Ed went out the door of the office and headed for the elevator.

"Do I get the feeling that international is getting the better of the deal with Grace?" Ed asked.

"Absolutely."

"What brought on the transfer?"

"Just opportunity knocking. Grace is a single mother with a little one in daycare. The secretarial grade levels just don't go anywhere, and we both know there's no real future for them anymore."

"How'd she find out about the opening?"

"Well, it seems she's friendly with your boss's secretary. I guess they all know one another. Secretaries are such a rare breed, they tend to flock together like endangered species. When the spot opened up, McBride called her directly and offered her the job. I'm not supposed to know that."

"He didn't clear it with you first?" Ed said with a note of surprise.

Jim gave him a raised eyebrow as they reached the elevator and he pressed the "down" button. The cafeteria was on the basement level. "Let's just say that there was no requirement to."

"Oh," Ed said with a shrug.

"I understand your feelings. The old way would have been to clear it with me first as a courtesy, and I would have applauded the opportunity. I would never hold back her or anyone else."

The elevator came and was empty. Jim held the door for Ed.

"However, having said that, we both know that times have changed. Inter-divisional predatory raiding practices are frowned upon, but opportunity advancement by referral is not. Also, there seems to be a tendency toward over protectionism of good people these days."

"That's an interesting way of putting it. I had a department head working for me at Continental one time who actually gave some of his more valuable staff people bad reviews, just so that no one would take them away from him."

"Really?"

"It was an interesting situation. He had two documentary examiners on the import letter of credit side that were absolutely terrific. They could spot anything and process documents in half the time of anyone else. He was scared to death to lose them, so he gave them mediocre reviews but made sure they always received raises."

"But didn't the employees react to the bad reviews?" Jim asked. The elevator hit "B" level and the doors opened. He stepped out first this time.

"They didn't know."

"They weren't reviewed?"

"He kept two sets of reviews. That's how we found out. The review he showed the employee was a good one, which the employee was happy with and signed off on. Then he made up a second one that was less flattering that he sent to HR with a forged signature."

"That's outrageous!"

"One of the problems of the modern workplace."

"You folks didn't have a management incentive plan by any chance, did you?"

"Ah, you caught that, did you? Yes, but it was somewhat informal. The division managers were given a pool of funds they could distribute at will to managers of departments who had excellent performance and productivity records."

"So how was he found out?"

"Someone made an inquiry about one of the staff with regard to a supervisor position that was available over in GFT."

"GFT?"

"Sorry. Government Financed Transactions. We operations types live by initials. Anyway, the GFT department manager knew the guy was good and figured this would be a great opportunity for him. So he pulled his HR file and couldn't believe the reviews that were in it. Figuring there must be some sort of personality conflict involved, he informally approached the import docs—sorry, import documents—manager, who, instead of being delighted at the prospect of getting rid of a mediocre performer, said point blank that he was too valuable to let go."

"So how did they catch him?"

"The guy in GFT just didn't buy it and went to the division manager. They talked to the docs examiner, who had heard of the opening, and mentioned that he was surprised he hadn't been called before because of his outstanding ratings."

They were at the coffee line.

"Why don't you get yours first? I'll get Adam's." Jim watched as the three Styrofoam cups were filled. "You know, this idea of substituting employee evaluations reminded me of that trade finance seminar you folks ran the other day where you were substituting invoices. Also, the other night the topic of letter of credit fraud came up, and it seemed, on the surface anyway, to be pretty easy to get away with something."

"What was the letter of credit fraud about? I've got it," Ed noted as they made their way to the cashier. "You've got your hands full, anyway."

"Thanks. I'll catch you next time. Don't remember the product but it had to do with changing documents without authorization." Jim tried to see if he could get Ed to talk informally about invoices without revealing his suspicions about McBride.

"It's not as easy to do as you might think. When it comes to documents, they're checked by a lot of different people from the exporter to the freight forwarder, to the bank to the importer."

"But it is possible?"

"Yeah, sure, but it takes a lot of planning and effort, especially on the banking side where credit extension is involved. It's one thing to just adjust a number or two that a freight forwarder or customs house broker might miss but when payment time comes, banks tend to look at *all* of the documents in a very, very critical way. That's why the letter of credit is being used in the first case." He handed the cashier a five-dollar bill and waited for the change. "Take all three out of that."

"So it's not that common or easy?"

"No. Good document examination and procedures work hand in hand with good lending practices. But, in the end, the operations people have to be the hard liners. They have a fixed set of parameters they have to follow, and if everything conforms, the money goes. Of course, it's easy for me to say that as we're not the ones on the hook for the liability, the loan officer is. They tend to see the customer accommodation element. They're sensitive to the risk of losing a customer to a competitor if you don't grant the credit they want or approve a bad set of documents, especially in today's environment where bank staffs are now being compensated, in part, based on income produced. But you should know all about these things. International operations job is just to process the transaction accurately and efficiently in accordance with how it is structured. We can advise of the risk—if asked—but don't have veto power. That's up to you loan guys."

"And we don't want you telling us how to handle a transaction." Jim decided to dive in. "Tell me about this invoice substitution technique. There seems to be something inherently risky about that."

They approached the elevator, and Ed hit the button this time.

"Oh, there is, especially with back to back L/Cs, where your customer is buying merchandise domestically for shipment abroad under another L/C. Your customer receives a letter of credit from a foreign buyer, for say, one-hundred-thousand dollars. He then comes to you and says he wants to issue a domestic L/C in favor of the actual manufacturer of the merchandise he has sold to the foreign buyer, but he doesn't have the cash to lay out up front. The exporter is usually an agent or distributor of some type. So he wants to use the export L/C as the collateral for asking the bank to issue a domestic L/C for a lesser amount, say, seventy-five-thousand dollars, directly to the manufacturer or supplier. The trick here is that the foreign buyer doesn't know who the ultimate supplier is and doesn't know the original unit price of the merchandise, so his L/C calls for the invoice of the exporter, your customer. In order to make the transaction work risk free to the bank, the set of documents that are presented under the domestic or subsidiary credit must be able to be used to pay not just the domestic credit but the export one as well. The problem is that the domestic one will have an invoice from the manufacturer for a lower unit price than that would be required under the export credit. Now, the one thing you don't want to do is to lay out seventy-five-thousand dollars and then go begging to your customer for an invoice for one-hundred-thousand dollars that you can present under the export L/C and get your money back. So what you do is have the customer make up the invoice required by the export credit in advance of issuing the domestic credit, and then when the documents for the domestic L/C come in you pay both L/Cs at the same time, using one set of documents and substituting the seventy-five-thousand-dollar invoice from the manufacturer for the one-hundred-thousand-dollar one provided by your customer."

They got onto the elevator.

"What happens to the twenty-five-thousand dollars?"

"That's the agent's profit and goes into his account."

"And this is pretty common?"

"I wouldn't necessarily say common, but it is a standard financing technique that's been around for a long time. You also wouldn't do this for someone just walking in off the street waving a six or seven figure export letter of credit in your face. *Know thy customer, know thy customer, know thy customer.* You've probably heard of that?"

"Part of my bible as well, although in today's sales environment, the stress doesn't seem as strong."

"Well, believe me, it's still there on the international side."

"Are the invoices always complete? I mean, would there ever be a reason why the bank would be holding blank invoice forms?"

"Not a good idea. You don't want a bank employee filling out a document that, if incorrect, would result in a bank liability. If the customer fills it out and it's wrong it's their loss not ours. We don't want to be an active party to the transaction."

"So the bank wouldn't keep blank company invoices around?"

"No reason to."

"But all this substitution stuff is okay? It's all legal?"

"Sure, everything is the same between the two invoices except for the name on the invoice and the unit price."

"So there's no way someone inside the bank could manipulate an invoice and pocket something for themselves?"

"Well, I didn't say that."

The elevator stopped at Jim's floor, and he got out first with the two coffees while Ed held the door for him.

"The truth is that a skilled L/C guy could always find some wrinkle, but that's where good knowledgeable management comes in."

"You mean that the current philosophy of a good manager can manage anything doesn't apply?"

"Big mistake when it comes to letters of credit, just as it does to foreign exchange. If the manager really doesn't know what he's looking at, there's a good possibility of someone cleaning out the cash drawer sooner or later."

They came to the office door.

"But what about the manager, who checks on him or her?"

"I think one of the things you'll find is that, with any bank that does a substantial amount of international trade and finance business, it will have someone at the senior executive level that earned his spurs, at one time or another, on the international side of the bank. If senior management doesn't understand international trade finance, then the bank shouldn't be involved in it, no matter how profitable."

Adam greeted them as they came in the door, "Ah, there they are. And I see you didn't forget me. It's not everyone who can get their boss to buy them coffee and deliver it personally as well."

"Don't push your luck," was Jim's reply. "Adam, you know Ed Campbell, don't you?"

"Sure."

They shook hands.

"Jim was just giving me the tour of the underground. First time I've been here. Now over in international, we provide coffee free to our people," Ed said with a nod toward Grace. "We do everything to keep them happy and contented."

"No more solicitation please, or I'll have to start downgrading some HR evaluations," Jim said.

"Given you some ideas, have I?"

Adam looked puzzled. "Am I missing something?"

"Nothing more than usual," was Jim's quick remark. "I'll tell you all about it later. Let's go in and see if we can find a way to salvage the Rayburn business. I have a feeling that Mr. Campbell may have an answer for us."

"It's called a 'Red Clause' letter of credit."

"Why am I not surprised?" Jim said, raising an eyebrow and shaking his head.

The meeting lasted just over a half an hour. Jim and Adam were introduced to another specialized approach to financing a company's international trade that they never would have conceived of on their own. Jim was getting more and more of an appreciation of the letter of credit as a vehicle for accomplishing tasks that could never have been achieved otherwise. He also developed an appreciation for the knowledge and style of Ed Campbell and, surprisingly, found that he didn't dislike him. Jim had his defensive mechanism in place but had difficulty maintaining it when confronted with Ed's professionalism. He was good at what he did, and Jim had to give him credit for it, but how far should he go. This was the classic case that he always preached about: being able to divorce one's personal feelings from a business situation. Keep the two separate: you shouldn't have to like someone in order to work with them. Easy to say, of course, but not always easy to do.

As the meeting wound down and Ed outlined an approach where Rayburn would be able to provide working capital to its affiliated suppliers without increasing its investment in them. Jim wondered if he might be able to bring Ed into his confidence concerning McBride. It would be risky, especially if Ed took Jim's suspicions back to McBride. Jim decided he would need more proof. But proof of what? He still had no idea if McBride was acting illegally or just unethically. He had to find out, and he realized that that would mean getting a look at the Alliance files in international. But how to do that without raising all sorts of suspicions?

CHAPTER 11

Manipulating an Invoice

Marian sat at her desk at The Garden Walk thumbing through the new Blue Bird China Corp. catalogue that came in the mail the previous week. Blue Bird was the source for most of the inexpensive odds and ends carried in the shop. They were all made in the Far East and sold amazingly well. But she also carried a higher end line of decorative vases, sundials, and garden wall hangings. People would come in and browse around looking at benches and arbors priced from four to six hundred dollars and fancy garden tools at twenty to fifty dollars each and then settle on a silly looking molded frog or rabbit for $7.50 or a ceramic family of snails at $1.50 each. Before all of Jim's suspicions regarding McBride and the invoice, it never occurred to her to consider what went into the acquisition and distribution of these odds and ends that surrounded her.

She sat there pondering the size of the overall business and the number of shops that would be ordering and carrying things like ceramic frogs made in China—not to mention how many Blue Bird China's there were in the US and then multiplying that on a global scale. She suddenly envisioned millions and millions of ceramic frogs stacked up in a warehouse in Shanghai or Hong Kong, with shipments designated for dozens of countries around the world. That $7.50 frog, which she bought for $4.00 was probably purchased by Blue Bird for under $1.00 and manufactured in China for pennies. It was fairly obvious how the K-Marts and Wal-Marts of the world could undercut her prices, since they bought direct and not through someone like a Blue Bird.

She suddenly had a thought, picked up the phone, and called Jim.

"Jim Fairmont."

"Ah, answering your own phone now, I see."

"Yes, well, new policy until I get the three-ring-divert feature added to my phone. Paula's huddling with Grace and going over some files."

"What's three-ring-divert?"

"Voicemail. If Paula or I don't answer my phone by the end of the third ring, it automatically switches to my voicemail box. Another one of those modern marvels designed to increase productivity by eliminating the need for secretaries or anyone else to answer phones."

"So why don't you have it yet since today is Grace's last day?"

"Capacity, my dear, capacity."

"Capacity for what?"

"System capacity. The bank keeps shifting more and more people onto the system as they suddenly realize that it's an expense saver but the original system that was budgeted for by telcops was not designed to handle the kind of volume being pushed at it by the mergers. But enough of my mundane daily trials. What prompts this pleasant interruption in my day?"

"I have an idea for you, regarding McBride. I was just going through *The Blue Bird* and—"

"Blue bird?"

"The catalogue I use for knick-knack purchases and realized that if I knew the names of the original manufacturers, I could buy direct and save a fortune."

"Buy direct from whom?"

"The manufacturers. All the stuff is made in China, and Blue Bird is a middle man. So I eliminate him, and I'm home free. Which I wouldn't do, of course, since they would have no interest in shipping me five snails, and I don't speak Chinese, but the concept is the same."

"Concept?"

"Eliminate the middle man."

"But you said you wouldn't do it. Or are you? And what does that have to do with McBride?"

"No, not for me but someone else, someone larger."

"Can you go back to the beginning?"

"It's very simple."

"Easy for you, difficult for me."

"Okay, Señor Wences, what I figured is that money could be made by selling the names of original manufacturers to the major customers of middle men so they could do direct purchases. McBride would know who the original suppliers are, since he sees the original invoices with the company's name and address. The foreign company pays McBride a fee or cut. What do you think?"

"I don't think so. It sounds too simple. Besides, once he provided the name, the deal is done. Doesn't sound that lucrative."

"Still think it's a possibility."

"I think we're reaching. Besides, what would all this have to do with a blank invoice? Why would he need a blank invoice?" At that point, Jim looked up to see Paula standing in the doorway to his office. "Gotta go. Talk to you later."

Marian was absolutely convinced that she was on to something and, even if Jim thought she was barking up the wrong tree, she decided she was going to follow her instincts anyway. But what were they telling her? And who could she talk to? She sat at her desk, staring off into space. *Okay*, she thought, *maybe it's not selling supplier names, but he is doing something with those invoices, manipulating them somehow. So let's get back to basics. What are the elements of an invoice?* With this, she reached into the side drawer of her desk, pulled out a file from a supplier, and retrieved a recent invoice. She then continued her silent analysis: *The only things that are really important are the merchandise description, the unit price, and the number of units.* She started doodling on the piece of paper. *If I were to switch one invoice for another, what would be changed to my advantage? The unit price, that seems obvious, but how does that help me?*

"I've got to talk to somebody," she suddenly said out loud and started cycling through options.

The name Ed Campbell popped out. *According to Jim*, she thought, *he's probably the most logical person to probe and yet— maybe not.* So far she and Jim had been ignoring the issue of Ed Campbell, and it had just been sitting there under the surface. From her side, it was even easier to ignore, as she didn't have to deal with Campbell, didn't see him every now and then.

Maybe they ought to just address it head on, clear the air. Good grief, it was how many years ago…twenty maybe. This was ridiculous. She knew it had to be addressed. Why doesn't she just pick up the phone and call Ed Campbell and ask him some straight questions about invoices? And then she thought, *sure, we could do it over drinks at the Governor Morris Inn. I don't think so.*

Besides, Ed was part of the bank and that would be for Jim to do. She would have to develop her own international expert. *Maybe Manny could help,* she thought. Manny was Manny Rosenberg of Blue Bird China. He was their chief sales rep, actually the director of sales, but handled The Garden Walk account and Marian's needs since he lived in town. He had been a friend— actually, more of an acquaintance, since it was one of those things where you see someone in the neighborhood and just politely pass the time of day without really getting to know them. Once she opened the shop, he had come in to browse around, and they recognized one another.

Why not Manny? Marian picked up the phone and dialed the number.

"Blue Bird China."

"Manny Rosenberg, please."

"Just one moment."

Marian thought of the brief conversation with Jim as she waited. *Of course, there was no three ring divert here, of course not. Blue Bird had a sales culture. They knew that to secure a sale you had to cater to the customer and to do that you needed to develop a personal relationship.* Jim had always told her that the most important step in the sales process was the first one, that first person you run into, the receptionist, the bank guard, the teller.

Many a deal was lost because of a bad experience a customer had on the banking floor lobby, but then an awful lot of relationships were maintained because of it. That was why big banks didn't do community banking well. Community banks succeed because of their lobby culture. Big banks tended to play defense, not offense. Their response to the first-person-you-meet syndrome was to eliminate it: eliminate the receptionist, the bank guard, the teller, and focus on the "user friendly" ATM machines.

Expense control and cost containment had become a primary focus, having resulted in promoting an employee culture that promoted self-preservation over doing what was good for the bank and didn't even consider the once primary directive of fiduciary responsibility toward the customer.

"Manny Rosenberg."

"Manny, this is Marian Fairmont."

"Hi, Marian. How's my favorite customer in North Central New Jersey?"

"Just fine."

"What can I do for you today?"

"Well, I've got a kind of strange request. Do you have a few minutes to talk?"

"Sure."

"I figure you guys know as much about letters of credit as anyone. The other night at dinner, we got into a discussion of letters of credit and how they can be used for fraud, and it seems a lot tougher than we first thought."

"You do come up with weird ones, Marian. Have you been approached by someone?"

"Why, no. What do you mean?"

"It's not unusual for someone to try and go around us and deal direct with the customer with the idea of selling you on the great savings you'll get."

"Oh, no, it's nothing like that. Besides, I can't believe I could place a direct order for frogs and rabbits that would be of interest to anyone but you."

"You'd be surprised."

"No, this was just a curiosity. International trade fraud was a topic of conversation the other night. I was curious about your take on it."

"Marian, we're not in the business of cheating anyone. Blue Bird is a reputable company, and we stand by everything we sell."

"Manny, relax. We're old friends. This is an old-friend call. You guys have been real helpful to me over the years, and I would never use anyone else. No. This is about ways in which a letter of credit could be used for fraud. We're all trying to come up with additional ideas for our next gathering, more case-history or story-type things, and I figured if anyone would know their way around the street you would. Okay?"

"Do I least get to come to dinner?

"A deal."

"All right. I kinda get the picture. Well, let me think just a bit." There was a pause on the line.

"I'm sorry if this is the wrong time or anything. I can always call back."

"No, it's okay. I was just thinking. You know, your question could be interesting, in that in there are some things that would be considered fraud or illegal in one country but not in another."

"Oh?"

"Yeah, in fact, we recently dropped a supplier in Argentina that wanted an over-price arrangement. That's where the order calls for ten boxes of fifty each, and they ship ten boxes of forty but get paid for fifty."

"But isn't that rather easy to figure out if the boxes are checked."

"Well, yeah, but let me give you a simple explanation of how it might really work. Let's say a buyer abroad wants to purchase five thousand of our large ceramic rabbits at ten US dollars each. We say okay, but the buyer asks for a favor. He wants us to agree to a unit price of fifteen US dollars and not ten. That way he can get approval from his local foreign exchange control for a payment of seventy-five-thousand dollars, instead of fifty-thousand dollars, for which he puts up the local currency equivalent with his country's central bank. When the letter of credit is paid in New York, we would get the seventy-five-thousand dollars. However, as part of the deal, the buyer want's the extra twenty-five-thousand dollars put into a US dollar account they have someplace in the United States."

"And this is all legal?"

"Well, I didn't say that. It's definitely illegal for the buyer but only in his own country, not in the United States. You see, what we're dealing with is foreign exchange controls in say, Argentina. The government wants control of the dollars leaving the country, so payments for imports have to be pre-approved and run through the foreign exchange office and the central bank. The importer is not permitted to possess US dollars—or any other foreign currency—and can only do business in the equivalent value in local currency, which probably has a double-digit inflation rate attached to it. This way, the buyer can protect his liquid assets by secretly shipping them abroad. The seller also has to be very careful as to how he records that twenty-five-thousand dollars, which is a whole other can of worms."

"But isn't the buyer taking a big risk? I mean, couldn't the seller just keep the extra twenty-five-thousand dollars for himself?"

"That's the trick. The buyer has to really trust his supplier. Not only can he lose the twenty-five-thousand dollars, but if his supplier reports him, he's probably looking at jail time in Buenos Aires or someplace. Of course, he does have some leverage, such as claiming to the central bank that it was all the supplier's idea, claims extortion, and notifies the US Treasury Department. Also, if the central bank finds out, they can always blacklist the supplier. In many cases, the buyer will offer a 'sweetener' in the form of a personal 'cut' of the twenty-five-thousand dollars."

"So what happens?"

"The buyer—as most smart international traders do—will have an account someplace in the US or another stable-currency country. The most common places are New York, Miami, Los Angeles, San Francisco, London, and, for obvious reasons, a few select Caribbean locations."

"And this is okay?"

"For the US, it is, as long as the twenty-five-thousand dollars is reported and shows up on seller's taxes in some way—consulting fees, finder's fees, personal service charges, whatever. It's pretty common for financially struggling countries to have all sorts of restrictions on citizens having foreign bank accounts. And it's not just Argentina. Once their economy gets on track, the controls are reduced or eliminated but then another country like Venezuela might impose controls or maybe Taiwan or Indonesia or someplace else around the world."

"But they open accounts in the US anyway."

"Sure."

"And it's not illegal in the US?"

"The US banks don't care. In fact, it's great business for them. Besides, foreign governments can't tell US banks what to do. I remember twenty or so years ago when Central America was in turmoil, people would show up at Miami banks with suitcases and trunks full of US dollars, and it wasn't drug money. It was the life savings of some local business guy. Hey, if I was in the same situation, I'd do it too."

"And there's nothing illegal going on?"

"No, not really. Just helping out a good customer. Just has a different twist to it, that's all."

"But you said you don't do it. Why? Look, Manny, tell me if I'm crossing the line here. I don't mean to put you on the spot or anything. This is just something that came up the other night, and it just peaked my interest."

"No, no problem, Marian. Look, when you agree to do this sort of thing, it becomes embarrassing sometimes. The people feel obligated to provide some form of compensation for helping them out of a tight spot. They start sending extra Christmas presents, they wine and dine you when they're in town, offer you free use of the condo and boat they bought in Hilton Head with the money you saved them. Sometimes, it can get out of hand. So the boss just decided he didn't want the hassle. Let's just keep everything business to business."

"Sounds like good advice to me."

"Well, I can't disagree. To be honest, some of these Latin American types tend to go overboard with this amigo stuff—the hug and brother routine. They practically adopt you into their family."

"Well, Manny, I appreciate your candor, as always. It looks as though I'm poking around the garden in the wrong place."

"Hey, weeds do grow."

"Now there's a line to remember."

"Seriously, Marian, no problem. We've been friends and neighbors for a long time."

"Well, thanks, Manny."

As Marian hung up the phone, she began to wonder if she had learned anything or not. Certainly, it was a new wrinkle on doing favors for customers but was it really so far off? Someone was coming in from out of town and was looking for theater tickets, so you got them, and you didn't let the customer pay. Next time you were in town, some football or baseball tickets could be yours in return. Business entertainment, business luncheons—they were a part of how things got done. Marian knew all of this and was now seriously wondering if they were truly letting the somewhat offensive personality of Larry McBride completely color their thinking about his professional activities and motivations.

CHAPTER 12

A Crisis with Rayburn Corp

The following week took a turn for the worse when, on Tuesday, Jim received a call from Adam just before noon. "We have a problem with Rayburn. Stewart Carney called and was really upset about some documents we rejected under one of their letters of credit."

"Don't documents get rejected all the time?"

"Sure, but that wasn't the real issue. Apparently, the documentary examiner offered to repair the documents for a fee."

"What do you mean 'repair'?"

"I'm not entirely sure, but it seems the export manager at Rayburn thought the discrepancy we were objecting to wasn't valid and accused the clerk of trying to hold them up. The export manager then called McBride, who defended the docs clerk and called the Rayburn guy a liar."

"He didn't!"

"It's all a bit confusing but, according to Stewart, he did."

"What the devil's gotten into McBride?"

"Well, anyway, Stewart was brought into it by his guy, who stood behind his complaint that he shouldn't have to pay a fee for having the documents corrected. Stewart then called McBride and said the conversation started off pleasantly enough, one head of international talking to another. I guess, like two old bulls in a pasture feeling one another out, it was all pleasant at first, and then McBride went nuts and started calling Stewart a liar again. Also something about a personal attack on McBride's integrity."

"Shit! You've got to be kidding? Where are we now?"

"Nowhere. I haven't called McBride yet, but Stewart Carney is looking for an apology and wants our clerk reprimanded. And he also wants his documents approved."

"Who do you think's in the right here? What do you know about Carney? Is he pretty straight?"

"As far as I know. I've never met him. Although Mike Rivers has told me privately that he's a real stickler, especially on performance and accuracy issues."

"Think we may have two hard noses bumping into one another?"

"Don't know, but this is certainly something we don't need right now."

"Okay, I'll call McBride and find out what our side of the story is."

Jim signed off with Adam and, after checking the number, immediately called McBride.

"L. A. McBride's office," came a very familiar sounding voice.

"Grace?"

"Yes. Mr. Fairmont?"

"What are you doing answering McBride's phone? I thought you were in customer service?"

"Oh, I am. Gloria went home sick, and there wasn't time to get a temp, so she asked if I could cover for her, since I'm still in training, and it was easy for me."

"How do you like it so far?"

"It's real interesting. At the moment, they're teaching me where everything is. I was surprised at how un-automated the place is. There must be thousands of files. The good part is they're all organized the same. That's what I'm learning now—where to find everything so I can respond to inquiries."

"Well, telephone work certainly suits you."

"That's what so interesting, but almost a quarter of the inquiries are SWIFT and telex. They'll have me doing those first."

"You certainly sound like you're enjoying it."

"Oh, I am. It's really different."

"Well, is he there?"

"No. He went out about twenty minutes ago. Said he had an appointment with a customer but would be back after lunch. He didn't say exactly what time after lunch."

"Did he say where he was going?"

"No, just out."

"Did he look or act upset?"

"He seemed in an awful hurry."

Jim hesitated, cleared his throat. "Look, I really need to talk to someone over there about Rayburn."

"I guess there's a real problem brewing. I've heard the name a couple of times this morning."

"Really?"

"Mr. McBride had one of the clerks in his office earlier and really gave him a going over. I couldn't hear exactly what it was about, as the door was closed, but it was loud."

"Interesting. I really would like to find out what's going on."

"Could Mr. Campbell help?"

"Was he involved?"

"I saw him speaking with the same clerk after Mr. McBride got finished with him. He's in his office. Would you like me to switch you into him?"

"Yeah, why don't you do that? And, Grace, thanks for the info."

"No problem. Hold on."

Ed Campbell again, Jim thought. *He seems to be everyplace lately*. Jim and Marian would have to talk. He didn't like this feeling of hesitation that came over him whenever he and Ed came in contact. Jim had to find some way to put the incident with Marian behind him. After all, it was so long ago, and they're all different people now.

The problem was that it happened so many years ago, it seemed as though it happened to someone else. The realization was that it didn't. Although Jim was fifty-eight years old, he didn't see himself that way. The person in the mirror in the morning was not the twenty- or thirty-year-old-he expected to see. The face was recognizable, but was it really him? Was he really as old as the mirror said he was? He had to be. Just look at all those books in his library. He'd read every one, and that didn't happen overnight. And there was his son Jeffrey, fully grown and looking older than *Jim* felt.

Truthfully, though, Jim hoped he would always be surprised by the face in the mirror because, if he wasn't, that would mean he was catching up to it and, when you caught up, there was no place else to go. Although his feelings about Ed and Marian could be considered unreasonable after so many years, they were very understandable.

Maybe coming to grips with it would be the best approach. He would have to work on it.

"Ed Campbell," came a voice on the line.

"Ed, this is Jim Fairmont."

"Oh, hi, Jim. Would I be right to say this call relates to the flap over Rayburn?"

"That's an easy one for you to figure out. Adam gave me a bit of a rundown, and I tried McBride, but he's out of the bank. Thought you might be able to help out with some background before I call over there and try to smooth a few feathers. Just what did happen?"

"I talked to José Peña who was handling the documents, and we've obviously got a huge misunderstanding on our hands. Rayburn, as you know, is primarily an importer, but they also do some exporting to Latin America from the West Coast, as well as some stuff to the Caribbean from the Gulf. This was a shipment to Peru, and one of the documentary requirements was for original signed commercial invoices in triplicate. What we received was unsigned so Peña called the customer. The export manager at Rayburn just told Peña to go ahead and sign them himself. José said he couldn't do that, but he could messenger them back to Rayburn's freight forwarder and asked for a fax with authorization instructions and agreement to all costs to get the documents repaired. José said the Rayburn guy just blew up and started yelling over the phone, made some comment about his ethnic background and how First State sure has a selective policy on invoice repair."

"What in the world did he mean by that?"

"Not entirely sure, but banks charge for everything now, and José was just asking for the out-of-pocket costs for the messenger back and forth and any other incidental expenses. José also said the guy at Rayburn referred to something about K E N Automotive, although José said he couldn't figure it out."

"Adam said that McBride got involved."

"He happened to overhear the telephone conversation and jumped on the phone. José said he was yelling at the Rayburn guy and the name K E N Automotive jumped out again. From what we could tell, McBride and the export manager have dealt with one another before. McBride ended the conversation by slamming the phone down and marching off to his office with José in tow."

"Have you spoken with McBride?"

"No, I didn't get a chance but did speak with José."

"What do you think is the best way to handle this?"

"The document repair issue is a simple one. We send the documents back to the freight forwarder that presented them. They make the adjustments and give the documents back to the messenger, who brings them back to us. José made a note in the file relating to the telephone call—as he's supposed to do—including date, time, comments, and who he spoke with, which, by the way, is a name we have to get, since things blew up before José had a chance to find out the name of the Rayburn guy he was speaking with. As far as the fee is concerned, we'll just waive it. As far as easing tensions, the best approach is for you to call your main contact at Rayburn's treasury and explain what action we are taking, apologize for any misunderstanding, tell them that all international types are a little crazy anyway, and we hope everything is okay. Then let him calm down his people, and we'll calm down ours."

"Okay, sounds good. But what about McBride? What got him so upset with the guy at Rayburn?"

"I'll talk to Larry."

"Okay." Jim hesitated. "Look, Ed, I really appreciate this. I'm really mystified at what would have set McBride off? I mean, I've known him now for about four years and, while we haven't had too much contact, I've never heard of him yelling at a customer—an employee, maybe—but he always seems pretty smooth with customers."

"My experience has been the same. Although since coming here, I've seen…well, let's just say he seems to be under a lot of pressure."

"All right, let's leave it at that for now, but I'd like to know something about this K E N Automotive Company or whatever it's called."

"I'll do some checking. For now, let's see if we can put this fire out."

"Agreed."

Ed hung up the phone, immediately left his office, and headed for the letter of credit files area on the other side of the floor.

First State, like so many banks today, was more a conglomeration of many banks rather than one cohesive institution. A series of mergers and acquisitions over the past ten years had put them into the ten-billion-asset size but, while that gave them some muscle on paper, they were a long way from being the equal of some of their peers. One of the reasons Ed came to First State was McBride's pitch to him about how they needed solid international operations experience.

Over the past few years, some of the acquired banks had some international exposure, which, when added to what First State already had, left them with a significant book of business. McBride had been running it all himself but wanted to be able to concentrate on the foreign correspondent side and offered Ed the opportunity to run the operations. Seeing the handwriting on the wall with the Continental merger, it seemed like a good idea, and so far, it had been. He liked the feel of working with a smaller operation and his relationship with McBride was working out pretty well, although he had to admit that Larry was a little different on a day-to-day basis than he was when one met him at banking conferences and social gatherings. But, Ed rationalized, that was to be expected. McBride did seem to go through some rather quick personality changes, almost like a mime sometimes changing from sad to serious and then to immediately flashing a bright smile and easy laugh. But again, he had a salesman's way about him and if that was the only side you saw, he was extremely engaging.

It was mid-lunch hour when he came into the file room, which contained a series of file tubs laid out in the middle of the floor. Each contained three rows of files at waist height so you could easily reach over and take one. They were all suspended in hanging folders and moved easily. The files were in numerical, not alphabetical, order and were segregated with a marker every 100 numbers.

There were separate sections for open and closed files and another major division between import and export. The file folders were also color coded, so you knew immediately which type you had. The numbering system was also different between import and export transactions.

Special transaction files, such as Eximbank, had their own numbering sequence, as did performance and bid bond letters of credit. New credits were at the front and old ones at the back. As with most domestic oriented banks like First State, there were far more import letters of credit than export. At a large international bank, the volumes would be reversed, as with an import letter of credit, the US company was the bank's customer and, with an export credit, the foreign bank was the bank's customer. This was always an important distinction for exporters to understand, as the US bank examining the exporter's documents was doing so in an effort to protect the interest of the foreign bank, not the US company, even if they had an account relationship.

Ed headed immediately for one of the computer terminals in the customer service area, which was just to the side of the file area. It was positioned so they could have easy access to the files to answer any inquiries that came in. He logged in with his own access code.

"Hi, Mr. Campbell," said one of the customer service clerks. "Anything I can do for you?"

"No, I'm okay, thanks. Just need to check on a couple of files."

An input template appeared before him, and he checked *EX-PORT* for credit type and then typed *RAYBURN* in the "beneficiary" field and hit *ENTER*. Almost instantaneously a list of fifteen letters of credit appeared on the screen. He wrote down the numbers on a piece of paper that was on the desk he was using. He then hit the *RESET* key to bring back the template screen. He checked *EXPORT* again and, this time, he listed *K E N AUTO-MOTIVE* as the beneficiary and hit *ENTER*. With a flash of the screen, nine letter of credit numbers appeared in front of him but, unlike the Rayburn numbers, six of them had asterisks next to them, which immediately told Ed that all the credits were associated with another one and were probably "back to backs." He wrote down the numbers and then headed for the file tubs. The first number on the export side for Rayburn was a credit issued by National Commercial Bank, Kingston, Jamaica. He quickly thumbed through it seeing that partial shipments were permitted and two had been made and paid without incident.

He put the file back, looked for the related one, and found the file missing. In its place was a "file out" card, indicating that José Peña had taken the file two days earlier. This was obviously the problem file that José was still processing. Ed methodically went through the other files one by one. They were all in the *CLOSED* section and had been completed and closed with all shipments having been made and a record of only one discrepancy recorded. According to the dox examiners notes in the file the matter was solved when the missing document was found in Rayburn's own file. Everything was corrected the following morning and the drawing was then paid without a problem. No indication anywhere that there was any previous invoice problem with any Rayburn shipments. So what was the export manager talking about?

Ed made some notes on the paper he was keeping a record on and put the last file back. Then, as long as he had the numbers, he decided to see what the K E N Automotive credits were all about. K E N was a name he wasn't familiar with, but that wouldn't have been unusual as he was still feeling his way around the customer base. The first file he looked for had an "out card" in its place. The file had been signed out by McBride more than two months ago. Ed made a note and went on to the next one. Again the file was missing, signed out by McBride just short of two months ago, clearly violating the forty-eight hour department rule. The third one was signed out by Gloria Martinez, McBride's secretary. He checked all the numbers that had asterisks.

They were all missing.

CHAPTER 13

McBride Expands His Network

The ring of McBride's phone yelled at him as he came into his office, and he knew, only too well, who would be the instigator of the noise. Alliance Automotive was becoming troublesome. He needed to find some way to get back in control. Two years ago, he approached them with the invoice substitution idea, and now he had four Venezuelan companies doing business with them. Domingo's company would make a good addition to his Venezuelan stable, if he could get him, but he didn't want to use Alliance as the exporter. Then again, Domingo was pretty sharp, maybe he already had something in place. He reached across the desk. "McBride."

"So how's everything?"

He recognized the voice immediately. "Just fine. No mention of anything. He has no idea of what he found and wouldn't know what to do with it if he did."

"You better be right. You know nobody around here knows anything about this. This was supposed to be a nice quiet business arrangement. Not to mention a pension nest egg—no risk."

"Relax, hang in for another six months. The exchange controls probably won't last another year, and then you can go sit on a beach someplace and forget about everything. Besides, you've made some really good business relationships,"

"McBride—"

"Trust me. Relax I've got some people coming in in a few minutes. There is nothing to be worried about."

"Okay."

McBride hung up the phone and then sank into his chair. *I've got to find a replacement for him,* he thought, *or maybe I don't. I wonder…*

If there were two things that Larry McBride did not lack, it was a sense of assurance and competency, especially when it came to international trade. McBride knew the trade finance business inside and out, and he *knew* himself to be the equal, or better, of anyone in the business. But when he was confronted with the social end of the finance world, when the Ivy League and near Ivy League types prattled on about music, art, theater, history, summer camps, college fraternities, school trips to Europe remembered and the like, his confidence would fail. It was why Mattie was important to him: she could carry the conversation when he couldn't. His remembrances were somewhat different from the other senior managers at First State. There were no summer camps only summer jobs, which he worked in addition to his weekend job making deliveries for Lombardo's market. There was the apartment building on Fourth Avenue and Fifty-Sixth Street in Brooklyn that had been home. Five rooms that held him, his parents, and two older brothers. But it was that summer job he had during his junior year in high school that made all the difference.

His father was a member of the local Knights of Columbus and knew everyone there. He enjoyed life, a good laugh, a good tune, a good beer. He spent the day alone, cooped up in the cab of a New York subway train but when the day ended he made up for it. He was a good provider and husband. As a father, he was just that, not a friend, not an older brother, not a buddy, not a coach, not a playmate. He set the rules, maintained order, and made sure you knew your place and your obligations. As a member of the family, and a male member at that, Larry was expected to contribute to its wellbeing. When he had his first job at age ten, fifty percent of the paper route money went to his mother to help pay for his upkeep, and it would continue as long as he lived under the same roof as everyone else.

He was sixteen in the summer of 1973 when his father told him to go down to see a Mr. Jerry O'Brien at the Atlantic Steamship Lines in Manhattan. O'Brien, a fellow Knights of Columbus member and an assistant manager in Atlantic's telecommunications department, had mentioned to Larry's father that there would be two summer positions available in Atlantic's mail room and if Larry would come in to see him, he'd make an introduction on his behalf to the personnel manager. The mailroom in the summer of 1973 would lead to the Bill of Lading Department in 1974 and after graduation from high school, to the position of assistant export declaration clerk. For the next five years, Larry McBride would live and breathe the movement of merchandise from one part of the world to the other. He knew every freight forwarder and customs house broker in the city, and he knew every ship Atlantic owned or chartered, inside and out. He knew how merchandise moved and how to move it. Above all, he knew what documentation was needed to make it all happen. He prepared documents that were handled by every major bank in the world. His horizons broadened.

He knew his knowledge of shipping and letters of credit far exceeded that of any of the bank officials with whom he now dealt. Larry knew he had value beyond what Atlantic had to offer and he was going to take advantage of the opportunities being presented to him. It took him a grueling, exhaustive, intense six and a half years to get his Business Administration degree from NYU at night. It was during those years that Mary Ellen left him. He had become consumed with succeeding—bettering himself. She, on the other hand, being the good Irish Catholic girl from Brooklyn, saw her duty as wife and mother. Children were not in his plans; they were anchors. The marriage was annulled—a wonderful word—his parents saw him as a disappointment. His surviving brother (the oldest was lost in Viet Nam) saw him as a jerk.

McBride, with his degree in hand, went on to become the head of the Import Letter of Credit Department at The Bank of the Pacific International in New York, an officer level position to which they could not promote him fast enough. He stayed three years and then left—after a hushed up sexual harassment accusation—to become head of international operations at Banc International New York. Four years ago, at age thirty-two, he became vice president and head of international operations at First State. He irritated people, and he knew it. It came with the territory. His six-figure salary and bonuses were more than justified by the amount of business he brought in. His contacts in the shipping industry, especially the forwarders and brokers, fed him every available piece of business they could. Larry was one of them, and he took care of his own. Now he lived in one of the best suburban areas in New Jersey, a place famous for the summer homes of the nineteenth century's rich and famous and more recently the residences of many of the twentieth century's new brand of robber barons.

He could attend the opera if he wished, Kennedy Center if he preferred, see a play in London if it interested him, entertain at the finest New York restaurants, but when confronted by a Carl Hansen, even a James Pace Fairmont, something inside of him would snap. He would suddenly be on edge, be on guard, as if waiting for a snub that would never happen because such people didn't need to snub. They treated everyone equally and courteously, whether they deserved it or not. It was worse sometimes to be ignored rather than abused.

Eduardo Domingo, a member of Latin aristocracy, was expected in a few minutes. McBride had no problem dealing with the Domingos of this world, probably because he knew they were interested in his expertise and respected it. In their eyes, he represented a knowledge base to be cultivated. A friendship developed on the basis of common business objectives was perfectly acceptable regardless of personal stature: one could be friendly and formal at the same time. The likelihood of a true personal relationship of any type developing was remote and understood by both parties, but that would not preclude strong business ties developing among people who, under normal circumstances, would have nothing to do with one another. Eduardo Domingo was wealthy, upper class, Venezuelan, with a pure Spanish heritage. His father sent him to the United States for his education—the University of Virginia—just as he now sent his son to Rutgers. He had taken the reins of Maquinaria y Caminos, SA, when his father decided to retire two years ago. Eduardo's younger brother Estefan managed the domestic sales and marketing.

McBride, always attuned to that going on around him, discerned movement outside of his office. Latins, notorious for their tardiness in their own countries, simply because it was the tradition, tended to be prompt and attentive when in the United States or, for that matter, any other country than their own. He headed for the door. Under no circumstance did he ever wish that a desk or other object would be between them. Symbols were important. McBride, for all of his young age, had his length of service and experience going for him. He had a ten-year head start on most of his contemporaries, who began their careers only after graduate school. From the early days of delivering ship's manifests and documents to merchant vessel captains, many of whom were European, he learned flair and courtesy. Things that might have gone over another person's head, he paid attention to and wanted to learn. He even substituted as a waiter from time to time on a vessel, whose captain decided to throw a going away, get acquainted, party for the select group of passengers that would be traveling to Stockholm or the Hague or Rio de Janeiro. He learned manners and protocol and patience. Above all, he learned desire.

"Eduardo, I thought that would be you," McBride said, the hand extended, smile sparkling, enthusiasm overflowing. The crisis of earlier in the day put behind him

"It's good to see you, Larry. I hope I'm not late?"

"No, definitely not."

Eduardo had embraced Larry's elbow with his left hand when they greeted. This was important: touching was critical. McBride counted on an "abrazo" by the end of the week, as the true show of Latin friendship. Without personal expressions of friendship, there would be no business done.

"Good," Eduardo responded. "Being on time is important."

"I agree. Many an opportunity has been lost due to bad timing."

"Not just bad timing."

CHAPTER 14

An Evening Out

Marian sat in front of her makeup mirror and worked the eyebrow pencil carefully and evenly through the center of her right eyebrow. "Do you think we'll end up like the Hansens?"

Jim was rummaging around the tie rack trying to pick out something that would fit the mood of the evening. "I'm not sure what you mean by 'end up' but if you mean would I like to have three homes, one here, one down at Marco Island and a third up in New Hampshire, I would be very hard pressed to say no to that."

"I suppose that's part of it. The other night at McBride's party, I was touched at how totally comfortable they are with one another. It was nice to see. I guess that's more of what I was getting at. They've been married almost forty-five years."

"We're pushing thirty." He finally chose a dark blue tie with muted white dots.

"I know, it's just that they seem to go together. I just can't imagine them with anyone else."

"I don't think I could either."

"He was always pretty good to work for, wasn't he?" The eyebrows were now perfect except for one small spot.

"I learned a great deal from Carl. I'll admit there were times he could be pretty difficult, especially when you came up against something he didn't understand, and he felt you didn't explain it fully. He was probably just the sort of banker that a lot of the old timers were. They were born and raised in an era of tight regulation and free balances. I look back on that time now and sometimes wonder why we all keep pushing for deregulation. It was so much easier. Banks couldn't fail, didn't have to pay interest on demand deposits, the interest rates paid were controlled by the Fed. You pretty much knew your cost of funds, and you lent it out at a nice comfortable but not excessive spread."

"And all you needed was a good looking toaster to convince a customer to switch banks."

"Well, maybe a little more than that." He now evaluated handkerchiefs. "There is one time I'm reminded of that stands out as the difference between what goes on today and thirty years ago. First of all, there were no credit cards and no FICO scores."

"You have no idea of how that blows away most of the kids today."

"Well, this was kind of like that. There was this young couple that came into the Bloomfield Central Office that Carl managed at the time, and they were looking to buy a new car. Carl made all the final lending decisions, and there was no such thing as a five-year loan.

New cars had three-year warrantees and banks made three-year loans. He sat there and went over every nickel in their budget and explained how they would have to trim down their spending in order to make the necessary payments. In fact, he tried to talk them out of the loan, telling them straight out that he thought it would be too much of a strain on their finances. But they wanted that car, and he spent more than an hour with them, making recommendations on how they should adjust their insurance and where they might be able to save a few extra dollars. He went over their plans for a family and the house they wanted to buy someday. He actually tried to talk them out of the loan, not because they couldn't afford it, but he thought a used car would be a better short-term strategy for them."

"Today we have the sixty-minute loan that's approved by a computer, and you never even get to see a loan officer, if there is such a thing anymore." Marian now evaluated lipstick colors.

"I think the politically correct term is 'Financial Service Representative.'"

"Oh, right."

"But to get back to your question about Carl and Olivia, yeah, it is something to look forward to. Carl is sixty-eight now. He stuck in there right to the end. To tell the truth, I'd love to bail out at sixty-two if we can. Hopefully, there won't be another merger before then. We haven't put the last one to bed yet."

"That's only three and a half years off."

"I think we should start thinking seriously about it though."

"We certainly won't be able to do it like Carl and Olivia."

"Not quite. They had a bit of a head start. Carl could have left at any time with the family money he had. Wouldn't be surprised if he never had to work at all. I can't believe they're going to sell the house on the Bernardsville Mountain. That was his parents' house. Their daughter doesn't want it. She's lived down in the Raleigh-Durham area for the last ten years and has no desire to come back to the cold and snow of New Jersey."

"I can certainly understand that. By the way, we do have someone to plow the driveway don't we?"

"All taken care of."

"Good." Jim, with tie in hand, moved in front of the full-length mirror that stood in the corner of the dressing area. "Are you looking forward to tonight?"

"All of Olivia's parties are worth the effort. And I certainly hope it will be less stressful than last week at McBride's"

"I wonder if he'll be there tonight."

"Oh, you don't really think so, do you?" she said, stopping what she was doing and turning toward him.

"They don't exactly run in the same circles, but it is possible. Out of courtesy, Olivia might have offered an invitation." Jim paused. "However, I don't think so. They might invite him to something else but not this kind of dinner."

"Maybe he's out of town. You said he always seems to be traveling."

"Not after what happened earlier today with Rayburn. What a mess. I can't believe how he acted. If it wasn't for Campbell, the bank would be in big trouble."

"Based on what you told me earlier I still can't believe how McBride acted. By the way, how is the great mystery coming?"

"You mean the invoice thing?"

"You have another mystery I'm not aware of?"

He gave her a look over his glasses. "If nothing else I'm learning more than I ever thought I would about the international side of things. I have a definite feeling that there's something fishy going on, but whether it's just McBride's slickness or something downright illegal, I can't say. Whatever it is, I'm sure it's risky."

"Why does he always have to push the envelope? He seems always on edge. Insecure or something?"

"Could be. I'm sure some psychiatrist would have an answer right off and probably tie it back to his childhood. I guess we might as well all give up after the age of five, our futures are set, our destiny established."

"You don't seriously believe that?"

"Not for a minute. I believe that every day we run into at least a dozen forks in the road that could change our lives and put us on different paths. Admittedly many of the paths will bring us back to where we were before. Every now and then though, you run into a fork that looks innocent enough but takes you off on a path that changes the direction of everything you do for the rest of your life. And there are lots of those."

"You won't get an argument from me about that. So what's next with McBride?"

"Difficult to say. By the way, I think Campbell is Campbell."

A short moment of silence. "You met him?"

"Earlier in the day, when Adam and I were trying to map out something on the Rayburn business. Seems to know his stuff."

"What does he think of McBride?"

"Non-committal, at this point. Which is how it should be." There was another pause. "Is there anything special about tonight or is it just the Hansen's usual mid-September dinner party before they head for Marco and set up for winter?" Other thoughts came into both their heads but nothing was said.

"Nothing that I know of." The black dress and white pearls were now in place.

"Anyone new going to be there?"

"Olivia always manages to find someone new to invite. You know, sometimes I think that Carl's retirement has been tougher on her than Carl."

"Really?"

"Well, she's always been such an active part of everything he did at the bank. The last few years, she went along on almost all of his trips, even though that sort of thing isn't usually done now days."

"No, it's not, but I'll tell you those were some of the most successful trips the bank has seen. This deregulation thing is changing everything. The east and west coast banks will eventually dominate. This trip was the last gasp of true domestic correspondent banking. There were dinners set up just about everywhere at some of the best restaurants and clubs in the country. Olivia gave a personal touch to the account relationships that tended to hold things together even when we were out bid on a piece of business. She was as much an employee of the bank as he was. I'm sure there will be some old business relationships at dinner tonight, as usual. Well, how do I look?" Jim stood in the middle of the dressing room, did a pirouette, and then took a position with his arms stretched out.

"Quite dashing for an old geezer."

"Oh, thanks."

"No, you look very nice. But then you always do when you dress up. Now, if I could only get you to wear a suit and tie when you're on the golf course instead—"

"That's sacred territory. One wears clothes for comfort."

"Or to scare the ball off the tee."

"Cheap shot."

"Agreed."

❧❧❧

The Hansen residence in Bernardsville was relatively unassuming from the street, being set back from the road by almost a full acre—the trees screened it very effectively. The best views of the property were in the deep of winter when all of the leaves were off the trees, and you could see all the way back to the house. Riding around the Bernardsville Mountain was a common pastime for many of the residents of the area. It, like Harding Township, a few miles to the northeast, managed to survive a good deal of the suburban sprawl that affected much of eastern and southwestern New Jersey. The Garden State still held up its image once you made it west to Somerset and Hunterdon Counties. But it was a struggle.

Local communities quite often made the mistake of believing that they can control industrial growth and reap the benefits of having the company pay taxes to support the town, but not have the company's employees use town services, except possibly for some road access. They didn't figure on the government stepping in and telling the town that it had a legal obligation to provide affordable housing for the workers in those companies, especially the low-income ones who had difficulty commuting, due to the lack of mass transportation. Towns like Basking Ridge and Pluckemin were once sleepy horse farm communities with a smattering of executive commuter type who would daily ride the Gladstone Line to Wall Street. Then came AT&T. What a great idea! A beautifully landscaped executive headquarters perfectly designed so that it was virtually unseen, tucked away at the edge of the Great Swamp. And then their old Long Lines Division also tucked away in Bedminster that if you didn't know where to look you would never find it.

They were good neighbors and held up their end of the bargain. But the government did not, and once the door was open, there was no way to stop the flood of companies fleeing New York City, Newark, and Elizabeth during the 1960s and '70s. Pluckmein, with no more than a few thousand residents and a four corners shopping area, suddenly found developers and others buying up the whole mountainside and planting hundreds and hundreds of condominiums, townhouses, duplexes and affordable single family homes up and down the hills and pastures.

The Burnt Mills polo matches were not the most exciting thing to do on a Saturday any more, now the challenge was to make it through the congested streets of the town and along Route 202 to the shopping center. Only Harding Township and the Bernardsville Mountain had the sense to say no to industrial growth. There would be no industry permitted, not the slightest hint of it. Pandora's Box would not be opened here. After all, the vice presidents and treasurers and presidents and chairmen of all those companies that moved into the region were smart enough to keep them out of their backyards.

The Hansen house stood at the end of a gravel roadway that served the original farm buildings dating from the early 1800s. The current house, which Carl's grandfather acquired in 1895, had been rebuilt after a fire destroyed a good portion of it in 1870. It had been renovated and up-graded a number of times since. First, they added gas, then electric and then a general modernization in the 1950s, when Carl and Olivia took it over, Carl's parents, having had enough of northern winters, moved permanently to Naples, Florida, but would always have the Bernardsville house to come back to in the summer should they wish. It was a white house with black shutters, as it had always been—as most of the houses in the area seemed to be—except for the newer, gaudy ones built by entertainers and sports figures, complete with their high walls and electronic gates and permanent guards. The King of Morocco's estate over in Far Hills didn't seem to have as much security, but then perhaps the king didn't have quite as many friends or enemies as the Tysons, the Houstons, and the like.

The greeting at the door was a personal one with Olivia doing the honors for all of the guests. A maid stood ready to take the coats and paraphernalia, but Olivia's smile and greeting were the first things you saw. There was the mandatory kiss on the cheek for old friends and a warm handshake for new ones, which would become a kiss on the way out. The guests were ushered into a large sitting room, where very few were actually sitting, and the twelve dinner guests would become re-acquainted or introduced by Olivia or Carl. A small bar and attending waiter were subtly tucked away in a corner to handle the drink requirements, while the front door maid did double duty, also circulating an ever-changing array of hot and cold hors d'oeuvres.

There are very distinct differences between cocktail parties, such as the one hosted by Larry McBride on Labor Day, and dinner parties, as done by the Hansen's—with the most immediate observation being in both the volume of noise and volume of people. Cocktail parties are mostly of the thirty-to-fifty-guest variety, with the inevitable mingling requirement and subsequent development of islands of conversation participated in by like-minded guests and friends. The dinner party, with eight to sixteen guests, quite often would have one topic of conversation that dominated for periods of time and would delve deeper into topics and issues. Side conversations also had a more significant depth and were frequently more focused in a one-on-one or one-on-two environment.

The sit-down dinner of the Hansen was an increasingly rare event in the 1990s, with the Super Bowl party becoming the dominant entertainment style, where everything was informal and politically correctly non-threatening. Conversations are sports team and personality related. The focal point was to be entertained, not to provide or be the entertainment, as would be the case at a sit-down dinner, where the participants developed the themes rather than commented on what a broadcaster, the effective discussion leader, presented. With the advent of television, it was inevitable that a "me" generation be developed, as children and consumers were and are catered to and continue to be the focus of multimedia presentations for four, five and six hours a day. The individual at which such an onslaught was focused saw himself as the center of attention, which, of course, he was.

As Jim and Marian entered the sitting room more than half the dinner participants were in active conversation. Some faces were immediately familiar, such as Ian and Doris Ryan. Ian, like Carl, was a retired banker, having come up through the ranks of Barclay's Overseas Division before joining the old Manufacturers Hanover Trust Company, where he had spent most of his career in the international credit administration area. They also spotted Michael and Cathy Ranieri, who were the principals of Ranieri and Ranieri, a local CPA firm. A third couple, or at least that was how they appeared, were unknown to them. The gentleman, elderly, was seated in a comfortable wing-backed chair and was speaking with Cathy Ranieri, who had taken the straight-backed chair to his right.

On his left, separated by a table containing a lamp with a magnificent glazed pottery base, was the unidentified woman. She was seated on a sofa and conversing with Doris Ryan who sat next to her in a perched position, it being unclear as to whether she was about to get up or had just sat down. The woman, with seemingly uncolored but well-coifed, gray hair, looked middle aged, but, as she conversed with Doris, kept a protective, or possibly possessive, hand stretched across the arm of the wing chair, where it covered the bony left hand of the elderly gentleman seated there.

"Let me introduce or, possibly, re-introduce you to some of our other guests," said Olivia while guiding them into the room. "Everyone! This is Marian and Jim Fairmont." Heads turned attentively. "Marian, Jim, this is Michael and Cathy Ranieri, Ian and Doris Ryan."

"Yes, I believe we have met," Jim said, while offering his hand to Ian and then subsequently to the other gentleman. Marian followed suit.

"Do you remember Cathy," said Michael Ranieri, placing his hand on his wife's shoulder.

"Of course," said Marian.

More hand shaking.

"And I know you know Doris Ryan," Olivia indicated the well-dressed occupant on the sofa across the coffee table from them. The response was some waving of hands, rather than maneuvering around the four-foot-by-four-foot table filled with hors d'oeuvres and a floral display.

"And this is Martin Washington," Olivia continued, indicating the elderly gentleman in the wing-backed chair, "and Gloria Westview."

"Very nice to meet you," said Jim, making his way in front of Cathy Ranieri to catch onto the now free, bony hand. "Gloria," he said, reaching then toward the hand that had just uncovered Washington's.

Marian was waving at them both from behind Jim and offering her own greetings and then did maneuver around the other side of the table to shake the hand of Doris Ryan.

"Hi, Doris," Marian said and then glanced over her shoulder at Olivia. "We're old friends," she said as she made her way to the vacant seat on the sofa.

"Yes, I remember now," said Olivia. "Something to do with schools, wasn't it?"

"Schools and children, the ultimate connection."

"Oh, I wish I had children," said the soft, wispy voice of the gray-headed Gloria. "It must be so rewarding." She extended her limp hand. "I'm Gloria. My husband and I so wanted to have children but it just wasn't in God's plan."

"Is your husband here?"

"Oh, no. William died eight years ago."

"I'm sorry."

"Oh, that's all right. It was a long time ago. Although, sometime, it does seem like only yesterday. I can still see him lying there so helpless." A small sigh escaped, as her eyes looked to the ceiling. Doris Ryan surreptitiously stepped on Marian's toe.

"Gloria was just telling me what a savior Martin Washington has been for her," Doris said to Marian while turning to face her and positioning her back to Gloria. At the same time, she managed to roll her eyes in a "Do you believe this?" movement. "Martin lost his wife a few years ago, and he has been taking care of Gloria of late."

Marian gave a look to the frail old man sitting in the wing chair.

Jim joined the ongoing conversation among the two men and Cathy Ranieri.

"Live by the sword, die by the sword. It's only fair. Newt deserved the criticism," said Martin Ranieri. "But it's all contrived. They really didn't have anything on him. It's not as though he really did anything wrong. I mean, he didn't steal or anything. What he did was not illegal. If he can't be convicted by a jury of his peers, it was just a partisan witch hunt."

"I don't disagree. I just feel Newt had no room to cry foul. He was the ultimate partisan. He knew better than anyone how the game is played. The problem was he never really believed they could beat the Democrats and was unprepared for the switch to defense from offence."

"Defense *is* an unfamiliar position for him," interjected Jim. "He certainly was effective as the beleaguered voice of the minority."

"Maybe that was his true calling," continued Ranieri. "The position of Speaker of the House was just above his capabilities."

"The Peter Principle?"

"Why not?"

"But what about Clinton?" continued the accountant "Now there's a crook but a real smart one. It just amazes me how he can deflect one attack after the other. Poor Newt was being beat up over *ethics* charges, and 'Slick Willie' just keeps rolling along. There's something wrong here that I just can't figure out."

"Not necessarily," it was Ian this time. "What I find very interesting about this country is its ability to have its leaders truly reflect the psyche of its people. Bill Clinton is a superb representative of the image of America. He is young and vibrant. He loves fast food. He expresses his commitment to all environmental causes but doesn't really trust environmentalists, he empathizes with the beleaguered middle class, while paying lip service to the poor and, indeed, encouraging the powerful in corporate America to expand their base. He is untruthful, he is expedient, he is unfaithful, he is contrite, he is truly sorry for all his transgressions, he is arrogant, he is powerful, and he is a small boy in a man's body. He is us—now—at this moment in time. He is America."

"God, what a frightening thought," said Jim. "Where's the bar?"

"So you've moved in with him?" said Marian engaging Gloria Westview in conversation.

"I wouldn't call it really moving in. Actually, I'm renting a room in the house. It's just so big, and Martin was so alone there with just the cleaning lady, who was coming in twice a week. We've become good friends. It was really difficult for him being all alone, no one to talk with or have dinner with. It's proved to be very healthy for both of us."

"Well, it certainly sounds like the old 'win, win' deal. I hope he doesn't charge too much."

"Oh, no. I don't actually pay rent." Doris was stepping on Marian's toe again. "I work part time and then take care of the cooking and keep things picked up for us and run errands and things."

"Where are you working?"

"At Epstein's. I'm in better dresses."

I bet you are, thought Marian, *probably also has a specialty in old men's pants*. "How nice, that would probably be the best time to run your errands and things as well."

"Doris added: "How are Martin's children taking it?"

"Oh, they understand."

I bet they do, thought Marian.

"Martin explained it all. It's really like a boarding house arrangement, only run by a widowed man instead of a widow woman."

"I hadn't thought of that, but I suppose there's something to it."

Olivia came into the room with two more guests, the Maloney's, and, this time, Carl was along. As the introductions ensued, Doris excused herself to Martin and headed for her husband, who was now engaged in conversation with Donald Maloney. In the midst of the twisting, turning, and jockeying, Jim found himself standing next to a vacated seat and decided to sit down.

"I'm Jim Fairmont," he said, introducing himself again. "Martin Washington, wasn't it?"

"Yes. You said Jim, didn't you? Never was very good with names. Don't know why I have difficulty remembering names of people I've just been introduced to but it's always been that way. Nothing to do with age. I think I've heard Carl speak of you. Are you a banker too?"

"Guilty as charged."

"Well, as a lawyer, I'd prefer to have you start off innocent." They both laughed a bit. "Well, as a former lawyer, anyway."

"It's been a long time since I've been innocent."

More chuckling.

"And I'm too old to be guilty."

Jim smiled in reply.

The female hand covering his closed and squeezed its charge. "Now what could you possibly be guilty of, Martin?" She was obviously keeping track of her own conversation as well as Martin's.

"Not much, at this point. Have you met Gloria?"

"Just during the introductions on the way in." Jim reached across Martin and took hold of her hand as it released the one on the chair. "Nice to meet you. Jim Fairmont. I belong to the stunningly attractive woman on the chair at the end of the sofa."

Marian responded by blowing him a kiss. "Thank you, dear." Then she turned to Gloria beside her. "I'll find out later why I'm being flattered."

"Oh, you men are all the same," said Gloria in her best wispy voice, as the hand returned to its former position and gave Martin a pat.

"It's all part of our master plan to achieve dominance through servitude."

"I thought that's the way women did it," said Martin.

"They started it all but, in coming to grips with liberation, we're finally learning the tricks of the trade."

"Well," said Gloria," I still feel that a man should be the head of the family. That's really his rightful position."

Doris whispered to Marian in return, "I can think of a couple of positions I'd like to see a few men in."

"Oh, Doris," Marian whispered while giving her a playful kick on the shin and a laugh.

Gloria remained serious and committed to her line of thought: "Martin could never be in a secondary position. It just isn't in his being."

"I'm just from a different era. When I first started work as a staff attorney for the old Lackawanna Railroad, there was no place for a woman. A few secretaries here and there but that was all."

"How long were you with the railroad?" Jim inquired.

"Right up until it was taken over by Conrail and then I went into private practice. Spent thirty-nine years with them. Of course, it finished out as the Erie Lackawanna and was the Delaware, Lackawanna, and Western before that. Started in 1928."

"All those mergers must have kept you pretty busy."

"Wasn't just the mergers. Railroading is right of way business not like the highways where the government owns the road. The railroad owned the tracks and charged other lines to use them. If the B and O wanted to have a train come to New York, it actually terminated either at our terminal in Hoboken or the Jersey Central's in Jersey City. Lots of legal agreements to work out. Lots of swapping going on back and forth. Oh, I know a lot about what went on. There actually wasn't supposed to be a merger between the DL and W and the Erie. It surprised a lot of people. What is it you do again?"

"Banking."

"Well, you might know then."

"Know?"

"About the difference between a parallel and an end to end merger."

"Hmmm."

"The DL and W was really looking for an end-to-end deal, and there was real surprise when the Erie deal was announced."

"Of course. In market out of market."

"That's it. What would be comparable would be some of the bank mergers that are going on now. An in-market deal would be Chase and Chemical getting together, and out-of-market would be First Union and First Fidelity. One lets you consolidate operations within a market while the other lets you expand into a new market."

"Of course. DL and W and Erie was a parallel deal as much of their operations ran side by side. Erie ran to Chicago through the southern border of New York State while DL and W stayed in Pennsylvania. Managed to shut down a good deal of Pennsylvania and just feed into the Erie route."

"I remember taking the *Phoebe Snow* one time. That was quite a train."

The conversation, the banter, the renewing of friendships, the telling of stories, the tales of children gone wrong continued. Drinks flowed at a moderate pace, and the h'ors d'oeurvres were consumed among a variety of comments about them, the decor, the hosts, and a myriad of other platitudes—some meaningful and some not.

At eight o'clock, it was time for dinner. The dining room seemed like something from an earlier era but then so were Carl and Olivia Hansen. Carl started his banking career with the National Newark and Essex Bank after graduating from Lehigh in 1952. Recruiting was done at the Somerset Hills Country Club by his father with the president of the bank who also belonged to the club. The country club connection has since evolved into the networking of today's industrial marketplace—moving from bloodlines to phone lines. Today's methods may be more democratic, but the previous method at least made a stab at putting a premium on character; understanding someone's bloodlines and the genes they carried and the assumption that the success of the father will rub off on the son. A focus on pedigree, a protected environment, and the long view was to be replaced by the over achiever, the survivor, trying to make it to the next fiscal quarter with improved earnings.

Having twelve for dinner would usually involve a buffet where guests could serve themselves at the dining room table and then find a place to sit, in either the living room or the dining room. Dinner at the Hansen's was the way dinner was meant to be presented. Seventy-five years earlier, only the owners and senior managers of industrial companies could afford formal entertaining. It was the Second World War that developed the middle manager and the ability to accumulate wealth, or at least savings. But they were GI Bill people who raised their children in houses with dining rooms intended to accommodate family gatherings at holidays.

The Hansen's table was magnificently appointed for twelve to sit comfortably and Olivia would have it no other way. To have guests carry food from the dining room to any other room in the house was not going to occur at a dinner she hosted.

If you were invited to dinner, it was presented to you in the dining room. Guests were not expected to roam around the house, looking for a place to sit and balance their meal in some precarious position, as though they were birds having taken seeds from a backyard feeder, looking for a safe branch on which to perch and eat.

No, Olivia, as usual, maintained control. She was the mistress of her home, and you took instruction from her as to where you would sit and what you would eat and drink. That was not to say that she was not gracious and polite when visiting others. While she would do her best to influence and encourage, she would always follow the lead of the host.

As a guest, if asked to perch on the edge of a chair with a plate of food on one's lap, a fist full of utensils in one hand, and a drink in the other, she could manage with the best of them, although anyone who had been to one of Olivia's dinners was quite often uncomfortable at asking her to wander around the house looking for a place to sit and eat and, usually, found themselves helping her locate in a comfortable place and paying great attention to her needs.

Olivia would protest the extra attention, as she was not uncomfortable. Royalty might make her uncomfortable, but certainly not someone from the Bernardsville Mountain or Fordstown. She was perfectly capable of handling herself at a formal dinner party for six or a super bowl party for thirty—that was how she was trained. It was a combination of experience, confidence, and courtesy.

CHAPTER 15

The Hansen Dinner

The dining room table was elegantly appointed with formal place cards announcing each guest's place at the table. The usual male/female spacing was adhered to with spouses sitting discreet distances from one another. Carl and Olivia were at the head and foot of the table, with Carl flanked by Gloria Westview and Donald Maloney and Olivia with Martin Washington and Mary Maloney. Marian found herself positioned in the second seat to Carl's left across from Michael Ranieri and Jim in the second seat on Olivia's left and across from Cathy Ranieri. Marian had Ian Ryan and Donald Maloney on each side of her while and Jim had Doris Ryan and Mary Maloney.

"Oh, Carl, this is just wonderful," said Gloria Westview, admiring the place setting. "I'm so happy to have been invited. You have such beautiful things."

"Why, thank you, Gloria," Carl said, "but Olivia, of course, deserves all the credit. I've never been very good at household things."

Marian pointed to the flowered centerpiece and waved her hand around the room. "Don't let him kid you, Gloria, Carl grows some of the most beautiful roses you will ever find."

"Well, roses are different," Carl said. "That's not what I would call a household thing."

"Oh, I just love roses," Gloria replied. "They smell so pretty. Martin was never a flower person, but I know he likes them, too.

Marion shook her head. "No, flower person doesn't come to mind when I look at Martin. Something go down the wrong way, Mary?"

Mary Maloney held her napkin to her mouth. "Just—a—little—water.

Looking down from her end of the table, Olivia seemed greatly concerned. "Are you all right, Mary?"

Jim turned to look at Mary to his left and reached behind her. "Here, let me give you a pat between the shoulder blades. It usually helps."

Mary continued to choke. "I'm—fine—thanks."

"It's amazing how easy it is to do that," Oliva mused.

"Well, yes," Donald Maloney replied. "Doris is somewhat prone to having things go down the wrong way from time to time."

Marian gestured at Mary's glass. "Just take another sip of water, and you'll be fine."

Gloria frowned, her face etched with worry. "I had that happen to me once in a restaurant. It was just terrible—and so embarrassing. Martin was so concerned. I thought I was going to have to leave the restaurant, didn't I, Martin? But there was this waiter that was so nice. He calmed me right down. I guess they see that sort of thing all the time. I think he was British. There's something calming about a British accent. Do you remember, Martin? That was in Hilton Head last year. Martin has a condo in Palmetto Dunes, and we go down there in the winter for a few months. Do you know Hilton Head?"

Carl nodded. "Oh, yes. We usually stop near there on the way south every year. Stay in a place called Beaufort. The Rhett House."

"That's a long drive from here, isn't it?" Marian asked.

Carl nodded his head, and the waiter began to make his way around the table filling wine glasses, starting with Olivia.

"About thirteen hours," Carl said. "But we take our time now. Don't have to rush. One of the advantages of retirement. We would always try to make the trip to Marco in three days before, which was a good ten to twelve hours of driving a day; now we can take our time. We try to keep it to six to eight hours now for a maximum. This year we've decided to go inland along I-Eight-One and stay away from Interstate Ninety-Five as much as possible."

"Before Doris and I moved to the US, I always wondered why you Americans always had such large automobiles," Ian remarked. "But it's the interstates, isn't it? Those long drives you took that we in England didn't. So how is retirement, Carl? We're just starting to settle in."

Carl leaned forward a bit in responding to Ian, who sat on the other side of Marian in the middle chair. "A lot better than I originally thought."

Michael Ranieri chuckled. "Well, your golf game has certainly improved. I don't think Carl ever broke ninety in his life. Now I'm losing money to him, left and right. Retirement suits him. I guess that's what happens when you get to practice all week long and then take advantage of your friends on the weekend. I may have to retire just to practice so I can get even."

More chuckles.

"Well, it certainly hasn't hurt you, Carl," Marian said.

"How long have you been out now?" Donald asked then shook his head. "I make it sound like you've been in prison, don't I?"

"Almost two years now," Carl replied. "Toward the end it seemed like one, a prison, that is."

Some chuckles all around now.

"Ian hasn't really settled in yet," Doris said.

Donald frowned. "Ian retired? Ian, I didn't know you retired."

Ian nodded. "Yes, just had enough. Working for three different managements in, what, six years. Just too much."

"I do that all the time," Donald agreed.

"Yes, but your moves are voluntary. I was with three banks in six years, and I'm still in the same office."

"Was," Doris corrected.

Ian blinked. "What? Oh, yes. *Was* in the same office. When you work for someone—or someplace—for more than ten years, it's difficult to break the habit. Getting up at five-thirty, rushing to catch the six-twenty, getting home at seven. And it's not like you're on an extended vacation. Now when you wake up at five-thirty, you realize you have no place to go. It's funny. You know when you're on vacation, but this sudden retirement thing—not easy to get used to."

Donald nodded. "You're not alone, Ian. I had my annual physical last week, and Dr. Schroder said that he's had an increasing number of patients showing up with stress related problems. Said it's increased dramatically. He's encouraged a number of people to take early retirement packages. Take them and run if they wanted to stay alive. Stress kills."

"I guess Carl is the smart one," Jim said. "He still gets up at the same time, has breakfast, and drives to the clubhouse instead of the bank. Puts in four to five hours of hard work on the course then has lunch with the same people he always did. But seriously, Don is right, and the problem is there's no relief in sight. The marketplace has completely changed. I don't believe this is a temporary phase—all the downsizing. It's an evolutionary thing. All those dire predictions of the 'fifties and 'sixties about computers imminently taking over is finally coming to pass. The workplace has finally caught up with technology, and there's no going back. In fact, there's still a lot more to come. The big difference is that it's usually senior management that is the last to catch on. They don't have the technical skills, so they keep hiring these young hotshots who come out of the best schools and have brilliant minds but have no people skills. They focus on numbers—people are numbers, headcount. They believe workers to be a commodity—interchangeable. They think the quality of the software is more important than its user. More changes will come with the next generation of managers, and, hopefully, a balance will begin to develop between productivity, the bottom line, and the worker. So far the gains achieved seem to have fattened the pockets of senior management and the Wall Street predators without any real benefits to everyone else. But I'm convinced that once all the dust settles some benefits will, finally, trickle down to everyone—God, I've learned to hate that phrase."

Ignoring the comments about his new golfing lifestyle, Carl shrugged. "I think you also have to understand the long view and not just forward but also backward. Banking deregulation was surely needed, but I think Mr. Reagan and then this fellow Greenspan have managed to throw out the baby with the bathwater. Reform and updating were surely needed, but not the way it's developed. I think the whole industry was completely blindsided when the Fed refused to intervene against the hostile takeover that Bank of New York initiated. The rest of us were clearly told that going forward there would be only two types of banks: predator or prey. If you consider yourself a predator then start pouncing hard and fast; if not, you're prey. Then you'd better start looking for the best deal you can get."

"Welcome to corporate America," Donald said. "One thing I've learned over the years is that the small independent company is the home of innovation. That's where most things start. That's what makes acquisitions popular. Buy someone else's innovation. Believe me, I know. All these banks merging isn't going to solve anything unless they find a new way to produce income. Improving income by cutting and consolidating expenses works for the short term and even that's not guaranteed. It's the dropping of the other shoe you and we should all be worried about. Where will all this new income come from?"

"How many companies have you worked for now?" Doris asked.

"I don't think there's a company left in Philadelphia that Don hasn't worked for," Carl replied.

More genial laughter.

Donald grinned. "Well, with any luck, I'll be able to get out before all these new breed financial types take the whole economy down like they did in the late twenties. Retire like Carl and Ian here."

Finally trying to get his two cents in, Michael leaned forward. "Oh, I don't think that's possible anymore. These are necessary adjustments to get us to a true free market economy. They'll certainly be some bumps along the way but the marketplace always rights itself."

"Ah, the accountant speaks," Jim said with a chuckle. "I suppose one of those bumps is this foolishness the Mutual Savings Banks are into. Switching to a stock company and going public to line management's pockets."

Michael shook his head. "That's just a temporary aberration. It's perfectly legal and a good investment. I've recommended it to quite a few of our clients. You might want to think about it. Good retirement move."

"I don't think so," Donald said. "It doesn't give me a warm and fuzzy feeling. There's a lot of funny stuff going on now. I know a lot of money has been made and it's all legal, I think. Although this whole thing about people "flipping" shares, there's got to be something wrong with that."

Michael looked anxious and became animated. "No, no. Look, the Fed wants the Mutuals to raise capital, and that's what they're doing. Greenspan and the Fed think it's okay."

"Greenspan seems to think everything is okay," Ian said.

Michael raised a hand. "Look, I admit there are some, on the surface, shady things starting to show up but the rule is that Mutual Savings depositors are the current owners of the bank and a five-hundred-dollar depositor has the right to buy—at the offering price with no commissions—the same amount of stock as a ten-thousand-dollar-deposit customer. And, yes, a lot of people have been opening minimum deposit accounts to buy a big chunk of stock and then immediately closing the account. There have also been cases of people being approached by third parties with money to add to their account so they would get a larger allocation of stock that they would pass on to the outsider. So yeah, there's a lot of stuff going on but that only because it's being seen as a really good deal. The average gain on shares in the first month after issuance is running between thirty and fifty percent."

Donald arched an eyebrow. "And if interest rates go up, like the Fed has already said they're going to do, to make sure inflation doesn't get out of hand, those stocks will tank."

Michael sighed, exasperated. "I just don't see it. There are more than twelve hundred mutual banks and savings and loans still out there, and the conversions are just going to keep rolling on."

Taking back control of the conversation, Carl cleared his throat. "Speaking of rolling on, couldn't resist the segué, didn't Mary say something about your changing jobs again?"

Donald laughed. "Heaven forbid, no. What's happening is the company is moving from North Philadelphia to King of Prussia, but we're keeping treasury operations in downtown Philadelphia."

Jim nodded. "That's right, Don, you're in cash management. There's no need to be in an office building with five hundred other people. Most of what you do is over the phone or by a networked PC."

"Smart move," Ian said. "One of the biggest time wasters ever invented was the so called weekly staff or committee meeting. In the last couple of years before I left Chemical, or rather Chase now, it seemed that was all we did: attend meetings. They were regularly scheduled meetings too: the weekly up-date, the transition planning committee, the operations and technology meeting, the liability review committee. They were all over the place. You could never get any real work done in the office—there were too many interruptions. So you came to the office earlier to have some quiet time to think. Your 'in-box' was usually cleaned out on the train ride home."

Doris frowned. "But surely it can't continue that way? Something has to give."

With the wine fully in place, the salads began to arrive.

"Not really," Ian said. "We just see it more clearly. All of us. We remember when, as they say, remember when we didn't have to make our own photocopies."

"When there weren't any photocopies," Jim added.

The mood of the whole table lightened up.

"Does anyone remember what cc followed by a colon on a letter actually means?" Martin asked

Jim shrugged. "Sure. Carbon copy."

"Carbons, of course," Doris agreed. "Do you remember carbons?"

"I remember carbon sets," Martin said.

"Carbon sets!" Doris exclaimed. "Oh, my goodness. They were the most wonderful invention. No more trying to line up the carbon paper or having it slip in the typewriter."

"Did they come out before or after Post-it notes?" Marian wondered. "Remember they were fastened at the top with that line of glue, or something, just the way Post-it notes are."

"That was the beginning of the era of super waste," Martin said. "From that point on people stopped using carbon paper. Use it once throw it away,"

"Excuse me just one minute," Oliva said as a server stopped to whisper in her ear, and she got up to leave the room.

"And it was the same with the copier," Martin said, "make ten copies when only five were needed. With carbons, you could get only six decent copies. Information-only copies were circulated around the office. The truth is that if you had to keep more than five people directly involved in everything you did, someone wasn't managing very well."

"The end result being in-box gridlock," Ian said with a chuckle. "Email and word processing are the same. They are praised as work savers and productivity tools, and I will admit they are—when used correctly but when are they used correctly? E-mail saves paper, except that everyone seems to print them out. A whole sheet of paper for four lines of text."

Having calmed down, Michael was happy to be on another subject. "Well, I think the 'using them correctly' comment is the key term. There's no effort to properly train people to have them use modern technology tools correctly. People today are given a desk, a PC, and a telephone and told to work but not given any real guidance on how to work effectively. An assumption is being made that the tool creates productivity, where the truth is that the individual using the tool creates the productivity and unless they understand how to use it effectively productivity gains never reach their full potential."

Olivia returned to the table. "Sorry about that, just wanted to make sure everything was okay."

"This artichoke stuffed with crab is just wonderful," Cathy said.

Olivia smiled. "Oh, thank you."

"I don't know how you do all of this yourself," Mary said.

Olivia chuckled. "Well, I do have some help. And I have my secrets."

"I know," Mary said, "but Anita, Ralph, and Michael are just serving and cleaning. If I had to cook for twelve, I don't know where I'd start."

Donald patted her arm. "You do it at Thanksgiving and Christmas."

"That's family. They don't count."

"Maybe not," Marian said, "but they're probably more critical."

Cathy nodded. "You're right there."

"I suppose that's true," Mary said.

"Where did you ever find Anita?" Cathy asked. "I think she's wonderful."

"She is," Olivia agreed. "Through one of the gardeners at church. He has the most wonderful touch with flowering plants. The azaleas, dogwoods, flowering fruit trees—they've never been so brilliant. I always passed the time of day with him when I see him, and one day I made the comment, 'Now if you could just find me a cleaning woman who could do for the inside of my house what you do for the church grounds.' And that's all it took. He said, 'You need a good cleaning lady, Miss Hansen? I get you a good cleaning lady.' And the next week he comes to the house with Anita. It was the funniest thing. He came to check out the house and make sure it wasn't too much for her."

"That would have made me a little uncomfortable," Ian admitted. "He could have been casing the place."

"To be honest, I did think of that—but, no, he was just concerned for her. Anita's English wasn't that good. She was only here from Columbia a month, and he wanted to make sure everything was all right for her. He negotiated her pay and working hours and tested her on being able to drive here. She lives in Dover."

"That was nice," Mary said.

"He was truly concerned."

"Was he a relative?" Ian asked.

Olivia shook her head. "I don't believe so, just her protector."

Don frowned. "*Just* her protector?"

"Yes, Don, *just* her protector. I'm quite sure. In fact, he did the same when I had referred her to a church friend, a member of my circle: Mimi Harvey. Mimi had lost her cleaning woman, and I recommended Anita, and, sure enough, Anita and Guillermo showed up together. He also found the woman who does Marian's."

"And he showed up the first day," Marian said.

Donald chuckled. "I wonder if he gets a cut of the action—a finder's fee—a sort of cleaning lady pimp or something."

Mary glared at him. "Oh, Donald!"

Donald shrugged. "Well, it's possible."

"Maybe not so farfetched," Ian said. "We forget just how the rest of the world works sometimes, especially with regard to male-female relationships. We've been sensitized to treating women equally, although some would not agree that we have achieved a particularly large degree of success."

"Not agree?" Donald asked. "Oh. Never!"

"Well, the truth is there's been a major shift in male-female relationships in this country in the past generation that does not exist in many parts of the world, especially Latin cultures," Ian continued. "Guillermo's helpfulness is really protective in nature. I'm sure he was raised to believe women are the weaker sex and it is the man's responsibility to protect them, especially those that are alone in a strange culture. He has probably taken it upon himself to watch over her, make sure she's not taken advantage of, have a decent place to live and work."

Donald snorted. "I rest my case—a cleaning woman pimp!"

"Don?" Mary asked in an admonishing tone.

"Sounds like simple ethical behavior to me," Jim said.

"Good point," Ian said. "There's a sense of ethics there. I'm sure he feels that it is something that is required of him to do because it is right and correct to do it."

Jim nodded. "Like the lost art of doing a good job for its own sake and not out of fear of being fired or penalized but because of self-pride and the feeling of giving a good days work for a day's pay."

"Now that's a lost art," Martin said. "But I suppose I'm old enough to remember what might be considered a quieter, gentler time between the sexes. When a man took his hat off to a lady and certainly wouldn't wear one in a restaurant—and would certainly not use profanity in mixed company."

The salad plates were cleared.

"Martin," Ian said, "I don't think the current generation understands what is considered profanity and what is not."

"But that's nothing new," Doris said. "Men have always been crude and coarse."

Marian grinned. "You tell 'em, Doris."

"Well, it's true," Doris said. "They may have tipped their hats and held the door but would still be ready to chase you down the street at the first opportunity."

"Yes and no," Ian countered. "The courtesy was a check on coarse behavior."

"There is something to that," Martin agreed. "In my day a man would never tell an off color story in front of a woman and certainly not use foul language."

"We're getting into fine-line territory now," Michael pointed out. "With all the changes being made, if you exclude the female office staff from hearing the story, you're discriminating against them, but if you let them in, it becomes sexual harassment."

"I don't think so," Jim said. "You may be overdoing it there a bit."

Marian frowned. "Did it ever occur to you that there is no place for off color stories in the office to begin with?"

The main course was brought in.

"Oh, Olivia, that looks wonderful," Mary exclaimed. "What is it?

"Filet of beef boursin."

"To be honest, although I do miss the office, I'm glad I won't be around when the rest of you are gone," Carl said. "I don't think I could handle being left with the new group. There's something about their brashness that I've never been comfortable with. I'm especially put off by the language, the cursing and swearing, the f-ing this and that. When I hear it, the hairs go up on the back of my neck, but it doesn't faze them at all."

"But it's everywhere, Carl," Doris said. "And it's not just the men."

"Oh, I know it. The movies, television. How did we ever get to this point?"

"I'm afraid I'll have to put it off to the schools," Doris said. "I mean, bad language has always been with us, but you never used it at home; I think all of us have had our mouth washed out with soap. It was just accepted. At school, there were standards for dress, for manners, for conduct. If you used bad language you were sent to the principal's office; now that's reserved for shooting someone."

Ian leaned forward. "This fellow Bratton ought to be brought back from Boston. He seems to have the right idea: focus on the basics; start enforcing the minor infractions, and you will avoid the big ones. There's been too much selective enforcement of the rules. My favorite has been the fifty-five mile an hour speed limit. Interstate seventy-eight out here is the perfect example. I have yet to see anyone drive fifty-five miles an hour. And everyone on that road knows they're breaking the law—but they do it— watching for the police car the whole time, radar detector on the alert. Actually, they should move it to sixty or sixty-five. Maybe even seventy. That's one of the first places children learn the new morality: acceptable behavior is what you can get away with— and it builds from there."

"I can remember the first time I went to Jeffrey's first grade classroom," Marian said. "It looked like kindergarten: chairs were all over the place, the children were walking all around the room. I was in shock. I had no idea things had changed so quickly. I expected the neat, orderly, rows of desks with everyone oriented toward the teacher. Form, structure, and discipline—it was all gone."

"That's happened everywhere," Michael said. "I'm in and out of lots of small and medium sized local companies doing audits, and they wonder why there are mistakes and errors. So much of it can be put down to organization, structure, and workflow. If you were to look at pictures of offices in the forties, fifties, and sixties, you will see neat, orderly lines of desks, file cabinets, and tables. The supervisor sat up front just the way the teacher did and the manager was in the corner office. Now we have workstations and cubicles that are a disaster. People are spread out all over the office, and the supervisor is indistinguishable from those being supervised. There is so much clutter in the workspace that, after accounting for the keyboard, the monitor, the printer, the computer, the in-box and the out-box, the action file rack, the light—because the fluorescent ceiling lights in cubicles are never in the right place and give more shadow than light—and personal pictures and effects, you are left with a two-foot-by-two-foot square to actively work—if you're lucky. The idea is to cram as many people into as small a space as possible to keep the costs down."

"I can't disagree with you," Michael," Ian said. "There is an enormous effort toward cost and expense control that has opened the door on risk. There is so much information available, and it moves so quickly, that it is extremely easy for items to fall through the crack."

"You're right there Ian, what the public doesn't fully realize is that there is now an acceptable level of error."

"Acceptable level of error—that sounds ominous," Doris said.

"Oh, yes," Cathy agreed. "We're back to cost management again. If an account doesn't balance or there is a reconcilement error you have to evaluate at what point it becomes more economical to write it off than to find it and correct it."

"Signature verification in banking is a perfect example," Jim pointed out. "The cost of verifying the signature on every check that's written would be outrageous and would be impossible to pass on to customers. At one time, an understanding existed between the bank and its customer 'You give me your money to hold, and I'll protect it for you.' Now it is your responsibility to protect yourself: check your statement and verify that all the

withdrawals are legitimate. Besides, ninety-nine-point-nine percent of all items processed are correctly signed. Forgeries are an
extremely minute number, given the level of checks processed."

"But that's volume, not amount," Doris said. "It would seem
that all you would need would be one check for a million or so to
make an impact."

"I didn't say that all signature verification has been eliminated, it just varies from bank to bank. Sometimes there are cutoffs,
say ten thousand dollars, where any checks over that amount are
verified. Also, there can be random checking where one check in,
say, every five thousand, is verified regardless of amount.

"But that's the visible part," Michael said. "There is an enormous amount of activity within every organization that slips
through the cracks."

"Haven't computers helped?" Marian asked.

Michael nodded. "Oh, yes. But only in areas that lend themselves to being computerized."

"It seems to me that everything is that way now," Marian said.

"Not really. In fact the most at risk areas are those that involve any form of manual processing. That's the most difficult
area for an auditor to monitor. That's where strict controls, work
flow rules, and procedures are critical and the office environment
works against you."

"We always found international credit operations to be very
different because it's almost all manual," Ian interjected. "Letters
of credit and documentary collections require, not just manual
processing, but also the close examination of documents by
clerks and sometimes managers. If you're not careful, you can
lose a great deal, and that goes for the bank as well as the customer. I remember when I was in the Seville office there was a
letter of credit from the US for three-million dollars for airplanes
and parts, the small ones they use in agriculture. The US exporter
shipped and submitted documents over a six month period for the
full three-million dollars, which was paid. However, the importer,
who was our customer, complained that they never received anything but spare parts—no aircraft—and wanted their money
back."

"That sounds reasonable," Doris said.

"Ah, but all the shipments and drawings under the letter of
credit were legal. The terms of the credit did not specifically

specify what percentage of the drawings were to be for parts and what percentage were to be for aircraft."

Marion blinked. "And they got away with it?"

"They did. Apparently, they never had the aircraft."

"But your customer, what did he do?" Marian wanted to know.

"Oh, they sued us and the St. Louis bank and the exporter and lost. In fact, the exporter offered to procure the aircraft for them for a second letter of credit—actually, since they had made a handsome profit on the spare parts, they could now afford to buy the planes."

Laughter and amazement all around.

Marion shook her head. "That seems crusty."

"That's an easy one," Ian said. "In reality, there was no deception on anyone's part, just sloppy record keeping on both sides, especially the Spanish importers, who should have spotted the problem early on. But the exporter, they said, didn't realize that they had sent too many parts in the first couple of shipments and blamed it on their export traffic department who, when they realized they had made a mistake, didn't tell anyone."

"Oh, right," Marian said.

"What about the banks, were they caught in the middle?" Jim asked.

"Certainly, but they were on good legal ground. The bank's responsibility was only to verify that what was specified in the credit was evidenced by the shipping documents and that those documents properly conformed to those listed in the letter of credit."

"And they did?" Jim asked.

Ian nodded. "And they did."

Marian frowned. "But shouldn't the bank have notified the company that only parts were shipped?"

Ian shrugged. "That's the importer's obligation. Remember, these were partial shipments made over a six month period. Each shipment was handled by a different clerk who only looks at his specific shipping documents in relation to the overall credit."

"So there was no real fraud?" Marian asked.

"None that could be proven," Ian said. "Just stupidity and poor management. Now if you want fraud. That's an easy one."

"How easy?" Jim asked.

"Jim, do you remember an account of mine called Quality Materials Inc.?" Carl asked.

"Quality Materials Inc.? That rings a bell, but I'm not sure."

"I remember them," Ian said. "I was in Canada then."

"Well, the banks were the ones that got burned that time," Carl told them. "I think they caught a couple of them but they played it very well. I don't remember all the details but it just shows how you can get caught in the middle."

"That was the one where they fudged the inspection certificate," Ian said.

Carl nodded. "That's right, go ahead, Ian."

"All the documents were properly prepared by the exporter: invoices, packing lists, consular invoices, quality inspection certificate, draft—everything set up just right. All the documents met the requirements of Carl's bank, and they paid out about five-million dollars. They then shipped the documents to the bank in Istanbul by mail and, as soon as the Istanbul bank finished verifying the documents, they charged the importer's account, but there was only five-hundred-thousand dollars available, and the importer wasn't answering its telephone. After a couple of days, the bank became suspicious and called the police. The ship took almost four weeks to arrive, but when they broke open the crates, instead of high-grade textile products, there was nothing but rags."

Carl sighed. "Now that was a court battle."

"But didn't anyone check the crates before they were shipped?" Doris asked.

"Oh, there was an inspection certificate submitted with the documents," Ian replied.

"Well then, it certainly seems that's who you go after," Michael said.

"The inspection company didn't exist," Carl explained. "Well, that's not really true. It did exist, but it was a shell inspection certification company set up by the exporters so they could generate a legitimate inspection certificate. No real independent inspection took place."

"Obviously pretty slick," Michael said. "Why in the world did the Turkish bank give them the credit?"

Carl shrugged. "Good question. Poor credit management I would think."

"Something like that," Ian agreed. "But this was a pretty well-orchestrated swindle. They were considered to be a reputable company with an acceptable track record when they asked for the five-million-dollar credit."

"Still, five million dollars…" Jim mused.

"You have to understand that the bank thought they were protecting themselves by having the original shipping documents consigned directly to them and not the importers," Ian pointed out. "That way if the importers couldn't pay, the bank could sell the merchandise and get the money back."

Marian frowned. "Run that one by me again."

"The idea is that actual ownership of the merchandise on board the ship belongs to the people who possess the negotiable shipping documents—the bills of lading generated by the shipping company. To protect themselves, the bank required that the shipment be consigned directly to the bank. That way, the importers couldn't get access to the shipment without the original bills of lading. If the importers couldn't pay, the bank still had five million dollars in high quality textile products they could sell and get their money back."

"I see," Donald said. "The key here was the timing—the wait for the actual arrival of the merchandise, which was probably three or four weeks, right?"

Carl cleared his throat. "Actually, the key was the mail time more than the arrival of the actual merchandise. When those documents were approved by our bank, we followed standard procedures and debited the Istanbul bank's account, credited Quality Textiles' account, and sent all the documents out by airmail. We also notified the bank by telex that their account was debited. Actually, we loaned the Istanbul bank most of the five million dollars to make the payment."

"How do you remember all of this?" Doris asked.

"Oh, I even remember this," Olivia said. "Believe me, when you get interviewed by the FBI, you remember it. Carl was a wreck, as much as Carl could ever be a wreck."

Doris smiled. "Yes, Carl has always seemed so unflappable."

"It's true," Carl said. "There's something about being interviewed by law enforcement people that can be very unsettling. Of course, that's their intention. They make you feel like a suspect, and I guess you are. So yes, this is etched very well into my memory."

"So how long did it take the documents to arrive in Turkey?" Jim asked.

Carl pursed his lips. "About four days, I believe."

"So they had about a four day head start," Donald said.

"Actually, more," Ian reported. "They probably should have had less if everything was done properly."

"Ah, so there was a problem in the bank—an inside accomplice?" Michael asked.

Cathy grinned. "The auditor's mind at work again."

"Statistics show that most fraud has an internal component," Michael said. "That's where the real risk is, not someone at the front desk with a gun. Did you know that, according to the FBI, more embezzlement occurs at churches and charities than anyplace else?"

"So was there someone on the inside?" Cathy asked.

Ian shrugged. "All the bank people were under suspicion for quite some time, but nothing was ever proven."

"How do you remember all of this, Ian?"

"Like Carl, when you're interviewed by law enforcement people you tend to remember details."

"How were you involved?" Marian asked.

"That five million dollars was transferred to our bank in Toronto and then transferred elsewhere."

"Is this sort of thing common?" Jim asked.

"Well, I wouldn't actually say common," Ian said, "but I assure you that most managers of bank letter of credit operations have a good deal of court experience."

"I've been attending a seminar on international trade finance of late, and this whole area seems awfully complicated," Jim confessed.

"And tricky," Ian agreed. "You see the whole purpose of a letter of credit is the act of substituting the credit of one party, a bank, for another, the importer."

"So two people who don't know one another feel comfortable with one another," Doris said.

Ian nodded. "Exactly."

"And this goes on all the time?" Marian asked.

"Well, not all the time but the potential is always there. Jim, your fellow McBride should have plenty of tales to tell," Ian said.

"Why is that?"

"When he was with Banc International in New York, he headed up the Fraud Committee of the CIB—the Committee on International Banking."

Jim stared at Ian. "Really?"

"He worked with just about every bank in North America on international trade disputes."

Mary pushed her plate away. "Well, this may all be very interesting, but I would like to say to Olivia and Carl that this has been a lovely meal, and I think they are just wonderful to have us."

"Yes, of course," Donald said. "This has been excellent."

Carl nodded his head to the waiter, who immediately began to clear the table of the dinner dishes.

"Oh, yes, Olivia," Doris agreed. "I think you've outdone yourself this time."

"Hear, hear!" Ian added.

Donald raised his glass. "A toast to Carl and Olivia."

Marian raised hers too. "Yes, definitely."

"I must admit I don't know how you do it," Mary admitted.

"Those asparagus things were wonderful," Cathy said. "What were they?"

"Asparagus Biendles with a lemon butter sauce," Olivia answered.

"And those potatoes," Donald asked. "What do you call them?"

"Gratin Dauphinois"

"They were delicious," Gloria agreed. "You must have worked so hard on all of this. I could never do something like this. Carl, you must be so proud of Olivia."

"Oh, yes. She's been quite a trooper these past forty years."

"Forty years!" Gloria blinked in surprise. "Oh, isn't that wonderful?"

Everyone applauded.

"If you have some time," Jim said in an aside to Ian, "I'd like to pick your brain a bit one day about this international stuff."

"Sure, Jim, anytime. One thing I do have now is time. Just give me a ring."

"I'll call you next week."

Olivia nodded to the server, and he began serving desert. "Well, thank you all so very much," she said. "I'm so glad you've all enjoyed everything. We did so much want to get together with everyone before we headed south."

"When are you leaving?" Martin asked.

"In two weeks."

"And you're going down to the Naples area?" Ian asked.

"Just south of there. We have a place on Marco Island."

"Oh, yes," Ian said. "We're looking around, ourselves, at the moment, mostly North and South Carolina."

Olivia frowned. "Not Florida?"

"It's such a long drive."

The door to the kitchen opened, and Anita began to serve coffee.

"Oh, my," Mary said, upon receiving her dessert.

"Now that is really something," Donald agreed.

"It's a French apple tart," Olivia said.

"It looks positively indecent," Ian said.

Jim and Doris looked at Marian.

"Don't look at me. I wouldn't touch that line for anything."

Everyone laughed.

CHAPTER 16

Debriefing the Dinner Party

The chit-chat continued through dessert and coffee with Mary being thoroughly shocked to learn that the Ryans had lived in six countries around the world—two of which were in Africa—while Ian was with Barclays. Mary, of course, had never left Philadelphia. The idea of moving from her mother's house, which she lived in since a child and to which her parents added a wing for Donald and her when they were married thirty-five years ago—was unthinkable. Donald's frequent job changes were usually related to Mary's refusal to move and, since Mary had more than enough money to ease the pain of living in place, Donald could afford to do as *she* pleased, although the last two moves had been more difficult, due to one being a downsizing and the other a merger. He was let go both times, without the moving option being offered. Of course, he wouldn't have gone, even if asked, but it was always nice to know you were valued. However, he found his age and salary had become a major factor. There were lots of young cash management professionals around, all with their MBAs and CCMs, neither of which he had. What he did have was knowledge and experience, something he perceived to be of little value in corporate America any longer.

Coffee and after dinner drinks were served in the living room with everyone seeming to occupy the same positions they were in prior to dinner, as though some sort of territorial imperative existed. Gloria resumed her position next to Martin, and the hand patting continued. However, Marian decided to break the pattern. She moved from the sofa, where she and Doris had been with Gloria and found herself in conversation with Michael and Cathy Ranieri.

"Who does your books for you?" Michael inquired.

"A CPA friend in Bernardsville, Joseph Solomon."

"Oh, I know Joe. Good fellow."

"We've used him for personal taxes for years so it was a natural move for him to do The Walk."

"Well, if you ever become unhappy, Ranieri and Ranieri would be happy to help out."

"We're probably a little small for you folks."

"Not really."

"How many people do you have now?"

"Including Cathy, we're up to fifteen."

"We just moved into a new office on Maple Street in Morristown," Cathy said.

"Well, that's certainly a good address. They probably ought to change the name to accountants, lawyers, and doctors drive. Those old mansions and Victorian houses are certainly being put to good use."

Cathy nodded. "Business has been good. The economic growth of both Morris and Somerset counties has been a real plus. A lot of the smaller firms have been expanding and we've also gotten a fair amount of business from the large multinationals in the area."

"I thought they only used one of the big eight firms—I think there are still eight—with all of these consolidations it's tough to keep up; I wouldn't be surprised if we're now down to the significant four, or something like that."

Michael leaned forward. "There's still plenty of competition out there though, and more than enough work to go around. We've been brought in by them on a number of special projects. We couldn't handle a full company audit by ourselves, of course. On the other hand, we're brought in to supplement a large company's internal auditors. It's all part of the outsourcing syndrome. Companies are not willing to fully staff an area that has peaks and valleys. Actually, it's good business practice: cuts expenses and increases productivity. Even Jim's place had started doing it."

"First State?"

"On the international side."

"Really?"

Michael nodded. "That's what was so interesting over dinner—the letter of credit stuff. One of our junior people left us a few months ago to go with a Summit firm that is beefing up because they're doing some of the First State audit on a subcontract basis."

"Does he have special international experience?"

"Well, some. He did some work on a freight forwarder account for us once, but I don't think it's really necessary, most of what's involved is number crunching: checks and balances and the like. It's really pretty straight forward."

Marian's mind was clicking away—there were just too many loose ends that seemed to be working in McBride's favor. But she knew that she and Jim still had no idea what it was that McBride was doing and if, in fact, it was illegal. And why did she care anyway? Everyone was taught to stay within their own sphere of responsibility—worry about your job and not someone else's—that was the modern way. But it wasn't the way she and Jim were trained. They were taught to consider the good of the bank first and make it the primary focus, rather than what was good for them personally. Now the reverse was in place, and the change was brought on by both sides: the bank with cost cutting to maintain short-term profits and steady earnings growth, while sacrificing the loyal employee when necessary, and the employee keeping his or her options open for self-preservation. "The more I learn about the international side of things, the more I would say it's anything but straight forward. It seems a specialized area that requires specialized knowledge."

"To some extent that's true, but it's not entirely the way it works these days, Marian, just the opposite is not uncommon. In theory, if you send someone in with little or no experience they'll tend to ask the dumb question; they'll look at an operation with a fresh perspective and see things skipped over by a more practiced eye, someone who tends to see what should be there rather than what is."

"Sorry, Michael," said Jim, "but I'll never buy off on that one. I've too many years of reviewing financial statements put together by accountants. If you don't know what you're looking at you'll miss the problem. As far as I'm concerned, the more experience and specific knowledge you can bring to the table the better. Your junior accountant may be able to properly age receivables and payables, but without experience, he'll probably miss the fact that some of those receivables are overstated or don't exist."

"Ah, but that's why there are senior experienced people looking over their shoulder and, more importantly, why there is an internal audit function as well as an external one."

"Well, I suppose that's true, most fraud is uncovered by internal auditors." Why hadn't he thought of this before? This could be the answer, do some nosing around the internal auditors, and see if his suspicions really meant anything. It would be easy enough for him to do. A casual off-the-record conversation with Robert Bradley of audit. Drop a few hints and/or suspicions and see if they run with it. "I guess we just have to hope the internal audit function never goes away or ends up being out-sourced completely, like so many other functions."

"Just because something is out-sourced doesn't mean it's bad or inefficient."

"I realize that. Most banks would never get off the ground today if they couldn't outsource."

∽∾∽∾

Dinner parties and cocktail parties never formally ended. Unlike a reception, which occurred within a fixed time frame, the dinner party just faded away. There was no formal end time announced as it relies on the lemming syndrome, where some guest, usually a close friend of the host, makes the first move to leave, which triggers the others to follow. Each, in turn, would then make their declarations of having had a wonderful evening. and within a half hour, everyone would have left except for the straggling couple, who were either extremely good friends of the host—or thought they were—and decided to have another drink and a private chat. There were also the guests who decided to have a personal debriefing chat or had a topic they needed to speak with the host about and had not had the opportunity to do so during the party. In truth, neither guest was usually welcome. The affair was over, the host was tired, and regardless of how much help they have had, just want to get the place cleaned up so they could rest.

Offers of help to clean up by straggling guests, while seemingly polite and courteous, were often an intrusion on privacy, unless the offer came from a close family member. While the "Great Room" concept of combining a kitchen with a living or family room area was a welcome venue for family, it could sometimes be most invasive with guests. The kitchen was where one got away from guests. It was where hosts were able to plan and converse in private, where the host provided instruction to serving help, and where they got the opportunity to talk about guests. It was the last place a host wished to be pursued by a chatty guest with a glass of wine.

So when Gloria detached herself from Martin and made her way to the kitchen to see if she could help Olivia with any clean-up chores, Marian knew it was time to leave. Olivia, of course, would be most gracious in declining Gloria's offer, no matter how irritating it might be—after all, Gloria was invited because of Martin. Marian, as she had done a hundred times before, sought out Jim in the room and sent him her usual telepathic signal.

Being married for twenty-six years, it was uncanny how they could communicate. It was not just a matter of finishing one another's sentences from time to time, but of actually coming up with the same ideas at the same time, of instantly knowing what the other was thinking. So it was not surprising when Jim turned and made eye contact with her. It was confirmation, for Jim knew exactly why she was looking at him.

☙☙

At home an hour later, Jim and Marian did their usual analysis of the evening. Although they had some discussion in the car on the way home and before bed, it was primarily about people and conversations. Gloria Westview and Martin Washington were an obvious topic:

"When I'm gone are you going to get yourself a younger woman?" was Marian's initial out of the blue comment. Jim gave her his usual "where did that come from" look but then realized the source.

"Do you think Gloria has a sister? That hand patting stuff, I could really go for that."

"What do you think he sees in her?"

"Companionship, someone to talk to, and probably someone

who will talk about something other than health and sickness and operations and medication."

The conversation was a walking one, with Marian moving through the house closing blinds and turning down the thermostat, while Jim made his way to the bedroom and started removing his clothes.

"You really think that's it?"

"I wouldn't be surprised. It's probably what keeps him going."

"How old do you think he is?"

"Got to be at least eighty-five, the way he talked about railroading in the 'thirties."

"But what does she see in him?" Marian said, entering the bedroom, the house now having been put to bed.

"That's a little more difficult to say. It's easier to relate to Martin's motivation than Gloria's. He seems to have gotten the best of the deal."

"You think she's after his money?"

"They're not married." Jim thought for a moment. "So she really doesn't have any legal standing. You're a woman—"

"Glad you noticed."

"—why would you want to hook up with an eighty-plus-year-old man—someone almost forty years older?"

"I wouldn't. I'm looking for a twenty-five-year-old."

Jim threw one of his socks at her and they both laughed.

"Seriously, you think it might be a father fixation," he asked.

"I have no idea. I can't relate to her at all"

"How about Mary Maloney?"

"Now, there's someone I really can't relate to," Marian said. "Do you realize that Mary and Olivia were at school together and have remained friends all this time. I mean, I like Olivia, she's a classy lady, and I've met Mary before, and I just don't see them as compatible. Mary is such a dunce—and so provincial."

"Maybe so, but it does seem they get along."

The analysis of the gathering would continue until the final light went out.

At breakfast the following morning, Jim again brought up the conversation of the previous evening. "Did you hear what Ian said about McBride being a fraud expert? I wonder if we really are on to something." He put his *Wall Street Journal* aside for a moment.

Marian was looking through the "want ads" of the *Star Ledger* to see what people might be selling in the way of garden equipment—benches and the like. It was one of the ways she supplemented her inventory at The Garden Walk, adding old and antique ones to the new pieces she carried. Admittedly, it was sometimes difficult to tell the old from the new as so many things were made to look old. But Marian wasn't into antiques, she just wanted to carry items that looked good, were useful and would sell. She replied: "Personally, I think the audit route is the best idea. After all, that's what they're there for."

"You're right, as usual. Internal audit may be the answer. This whole affair has turned out rather interesting, though. I mean, I knew the international side of banking, especially the trade area, was a different world. I just didn't realize how different."

"I suppose it's just one of those things we take for granted." Marian now put her paper aside and took a sip of morning coffee. "More than half of the inventory at The Walk has a foreign origin. I buy from catalogues put out by US companies and never see all that goes on in the background. I mean, someone actually travels to China or the Philippines or Indonesia and orders the stuff, has it shipped to the US, and then around the country. They go through all the trouble that we never see: the foreign exchange risk, the quality control, the international shipping. Can you imagine spending…what was it?…five million dollars for 'quality' rags?"

"I guess that's what's so fascinating about all of this and why it's so easy to dream up schemes for McBride to be involved in."

"I suppose there's always the possibility that everything McBride is doing is on the up and up."

"I suppose so, but my instincts are telling me something else."

CHAPTER 17

Appeasing Charlie Field

The cab headed up West Broadway with the usual bobbing and weaving maneuvers that were appropriate for New York driving and boxing, which have a lot in common. It was one of those ugly yellow whales that dominated the New York Taxi fleet. New York cabs had to be the most uncomfortable in the world, except for other US cities that used automobiles that were designed for the driver's comfort and paid little attention to back seat passengers, who were supposed to be no more than five foot five, had no need of leg room, and wore Teflon clothing so they could slide across a seat that only an airline executive could love.

However, McBride wasn't paying much attention to what was going on around him, as the cab made its way through TriBeCa in lower Manhattan. McBride had considered driving in from Newark, but it remained just that: a thought. Driving at midday was too much of a hassle, so he took the PATH subway from Newark to the World Trade Center. It was only four stops and a twenty-minute ride and then a five-minute cab ride to the Tribeca Grill, where he was to meet Charlie Field of Alliance Automotive for lunch.

The meeting with Field was set up last week, prior to the Rayburn blowup, but he added it to the discussion agenda for their usual monthly Monday meeting in an effort to placate the often excitable Charlie Field, as the Rayburn matter had the potential to be a loose cannon that needed controlling. Alliance had one of the largest stakes in McBride's win-win-win-win "revenue enhancement" arrangement and was the first company Larry recruited. These monthly meetings were usually good natured and involved more good food and drink than serious talk, but that had changed somewhat with the missing invoice that Jim Fairmont found.

Larry shuffled through some papers in his briefcase as the cab hit the cobblestones of the TriBeCa side streets. Reading was impossible. He looked out of the window as they passed some of the remnants of New York of 150 years ago. The artsy crowd was taking over, as well as the new Wall Streeters: the twenty-somethings who worked the Street and now lived in the converted loft buildings. There were still remnants of the old Washington Street produce markets that had not been replaced by office buildings, schools, and apartments. Although somewhat ignored by the current tourist industry, the area remained an architectural wonder, even though its most prominent feature is the Salomon Smith Barney headquarters building on Greenwich Street near the Grill.

The cab made a right turn and came down the one way street to the restaurant where it double parked to let Larry out. He put a ten in the plastic sliding cup of the window designed to protect the driver from his passengers—or perhaps the other way around—and slid uncomfortably across the seat to the door, something there is no elegant way to do in a New York cab. Oh, for the old Checker cabs.

Arriving a few minutes early for his one thirty reservation would not be a problem, as he knew Field was visiting some shipping companies around 17 Battery Place. Finding a cab there usually involved walking to the Downtown Athletic Club, where the yellow monsters tended to congregate. Alliance had their offices in Journal Square in Jersey City and Field had scheduled a visit to a freight forwarder in Exchange Place on his way back to the office, so they planned to take the PATH back to New Jersey together.

Their relationship was a friendly one, but Larry had no misconceptions about Field: he didn't like mistakes, and he took no prisoners. He was a native New Yorker like Larry, but he was from Astoria, Queens, which was a little different from Larry's Bensonhurst beginnings. They understood the same language but Field—a NYU night school grad like Larry—who had also worked for shipping companies and freight forwarders all through high school, college and beyond—took a different career path in branching out on his own. He started Alliance twenty years ago and had done extremely well. Now fifty-two, gray, and balding he was in his super-prime, on top with a four-thousand-square-foot house on an acre in Livingston, New Jersey, a content wife and two girls about to head for college. He had scratched for it all, and he wasn't going to let anything impede the realization of his plans.

The twelve-forty-five p.m. reservation group finished up, so tables were becoming empty as Larry approached the hostess keeping guard over the reservation book. She had the usual New York air of command and control—no small town friendliness here, no greeting like you were a long lost friend. You were here to eat. She was here to make sure you had a reservation—make sure you belonged. She didn't say hello and didn't offer a "Good afternoon" when you came up to her little stand with the book on it.

"McBride. See if you can get us a table in the back where we can do some work."

"No problem." She nodded while placing a check mark next to his name. "It'll be a few minutes."

"That's fine. I'm the first. I'll be at the bar."

She nodded again and made a note next to his name. No unnecessary words, no chit chat, just do the job right.

Larry took control of a bar stool, ordered a glass of Chardonnay, and sat for a few minutes watching the theater: the world of a New York trendy lunch spot. There were a few tourists here who stood out, but this was a serious lunch place for the Wall Street crowd. Appropriate business attire, both the men and the women. Wall Street was now a state of mind, not a place. The banks were pretty much gone from the physical place of Wall Street itself as the financial district had expanded well to the North along the Hudson River. The Smith Barney tower across the street could keep the restaurant full without a problem all by itself, but within a reasonable walk stood the overpowering presence of the World Trade Center and its associated financial companies kneeling below it. City Hall, another short walk away also added to the steady stream of regular patrons. Shirts and ties still held their own in the world of dress-down Fridays, which had expanded to everyday for some firms. But dress-down didn't extend to sales representatives—if you worked for AT&T or J P Morgan you didn't go visiting and entertaining customers wearing a golf shirt. Same was true if you were selling paper or furnishings to the Street. And, certainly, if you were a banker visiting with a customer, you wore a suit or appropriate female business attire—as there were more women banking reps now than men. So the room was filled with whites and blues and browns with an occasional splash of red in a tie or scarf. Hair was neatly trimmed, and there were no male earrings or tattoos visible anywhere in the room. That was not to say they were not there but people with visible tattoos and earrings didn't make it past HR at any organization that was hiring for customer contact work. You wanted the customer to focus on the product being sold not the salesperson, as a rule.

Charlie found McBride at the bar. "Been waiting long?"

"Just a few minutes. Traffic was good. I probably could have walked up." McBride said, turning and taking the outstretched hand.

"It's a long walk."

"Yeah, but I could use the exercise."

"So could we all," Charlie said while patting his slightly protruding mid-section. "The wife is always after me to join a health club. I tried it once, but I swear the place was full of fags. Struttin' around the locker room in their altogether showin' off their wares. Makes me uncomfortable. The only naked bodies I like are the ones that waitress over there is covering up."

The bartender came over.

"You got Bud light on tap?" Charlie asked.

"Yes, sir."

"Good. Hit me with one." Charlie turned to McBride. "Won't be able to go back with you later. Have to see some people at Two Broadway. We got a table?"

"She said it would be a few minutes. I asked for a spot in the back."

"Good, we got some talkin' to do. You got yourself a lady friend yet?"

"I'm working on it."

"You stayin' away from company property? Don't want to make the same mistake twice. I don't know about things today. First thing I learned workin' was you don't stick your pen in the company inkwell. But I guess you young guys don't understand that sort of thing—no inkwells anymore, before your time. Gotta come up with a new saying that says the same thing. Suppose it's tougher today, though. Women all around the place. Used to just have them as secretaries and you wouldn't have to be bumping into them all the time during the day. Jesus, will you look at that one over there?" Charlie indicated a group of four young business types just getting up from lunch: three men and a woman. "Look at the legs on that. Shit, they go up to her armpits and the skirt barely covers her ass. Can you imagine working next to that all day?"

"I'm sure it's not easy."

"Not easy? Shit, man that would be darn near impossible." The beer was delivered. "If she worked for me I'd fire her ass in a minute. Hell, I wouldn't have hired her to begin with."

"Can't do that these days, Charlie. Got to deal with qualifications only."

"Yeah, I know, but it sure doesn't make it easy." Charlie took a sip of his beer.

"Charlie, how the devil do you survive in today's business world?"

"Survival is my business," Charlie said, dead serious, and stared directly and hard into McBride's face.

"Mr. McBride," said the hostess, coming over to the bar. "I have your table now."

"Okay," McBride said, and they both picked up their drinks and briefcases and followed her across the room to a table for four, which was set for two, in a back corner.

The one-thirty time frame had been chosen as there would be no rush to get them out to make way for another seating. The trick for a luncheon spot in Lower Manhattan was to make sure you get three sittings out of every table. If you were waiting for a table, any smart restaurant always gave you a menu to study at the bar, and all the specials were posted in multiple locations with the hope your mind was made up by the time you sat down. The system worked for patrons as well as wait staff, who were both trying to maximize their time. It was the tourist who drove everyone nuts. They come in for a New York dining experience while everyone else wants lunch. They had time to kill while the waiter would just like to get them out of the way, as they were disturbing the pattern.

The table was near a rear wall, and Charlie took the seat that looked out into the room while McBride sat facing him and the wall. He ordered another beer and the shrimp and pasta special, while McBride stuck to his same wine and ordered the filet of sole with the fancy sauce. Bread and butter were delivered by a bus boy while the orders were being taken. The waiter moved away and then it began.

"So what's goin' on at the bank, Larry? Everything under control?"

"We're doing okay."

"What about this guy who thought he knew something? Fair something or other. He's not a problem anymore? You seemed pretty worried for a while."

"Turned out to be nothing. I guess I over reacted when he found that blank invoice, but he was never able to figure out what it was for."

"You sure now? He never asked you about it? Never came over and said 'Hey, Larry, old buddy, did you drop this?'"

"Look, he's a domestic guy, wouldn't know what to do with an international trade transaction if he fell over it. No, that's a dead issue. Besides, I've got one of his people working for me now, and I've pumped her a bit already about what he might know." McBride, of course, had not pressured Grace about anything yet, but he planned to when the situation dictated it.

"And?"

"Nothing. No, she never heard of Alliance and has never been asked to check on anything. I'll have her run inquiries back to Fairmont's office, now and again, just to make sure nothing's going on."

"That was pretty careless of you, Larry."

"Hey, shit happens, Charlie."

"Yeah, I know. Don't get testy. You and those books of yours. Why don't you collect something easier, like painting or rugs?"

"I like books! What can I tell you?"

"Okay, okay. But just watch it. This is a pretty good deal we've got going, and I don't want to see it messed up. If you have the slightest hint there might be something going on, you let me know, and we'll find a way to deal with it. No point in being too greedy. The guys on the other side will understand. They don't want to lose this pipeline. How many companies you got lined up now?"

"There are four," McBride lied. "You, K E N Automotive, Export Marketing Association, and Traders Caribbean." Actually, there were four automotive-related but others in other replacement parts and equipment fields.

"And overseas?"

"We're up to twenty now." McBride again understated the number. "And I've got a good lead on another one in Venezuela."

"Who?"

"Maquinaria y Caminós, SA."

"Domingo's outfit?"

"Yeah, you know them?"

"Larry, when it comes to auto parts importers in Latin America, I know everyone. Watch Domingo. He's quality stuff and well connected and may be interested in more than capital flight. I'd be careful with this one. Personally, I'd love to do legitimate business with him, but he's pretty tight with the big guys. Next time you're gonna meet with him let me know, I'd like to make a pitch for some business, forget the capital flight stuff, I just want a shot at regular trade."

The salads arrived, and they quietly ate for a minute or two.

Then McBride broached the topic he came to talk about. "There's something that came up last week that you should know about."

"What's zat?"

"There's a guy by the name of Sam Kramer over at Rayburn Corp—"

"The electronics outfit? Don't tell me they're gettin' into this?"

"No, no. This guy's their export manager. He's new, but he worked for K E N Automotive before going to Rayburn. He knows the routine. K E N is a small outfit. You know Kenny was working out of the basement of his house until a couple of years ago. His wife still runs the books from there. In an outfit that size, there's no way for someone *not* to know what's going on."

"What're you tryin' to tell me, Larry?'

"We had a problem with some documents. Unsigned invoices. Kramer wanted us to repair them. Our guy refused without authorization and slapped them with a fee. Which is standard practice."

"Tell me about it. All you banks got fees for everything now.

I'm surprised I don't have to pop quarters in the men's room when I visit you."

"Yeah, well, anyway, Kramer was trying to cover his ass and didn't want to show he blew a set of dox, and he jumped all over my examiner. Words were exchanged."

The main course arrived, and the salads were moved to the side. "The plates are a little hot," said the food deliverer who was handling them with a towel. He was not the person who took their order, more efficiencies to keep things moving.

"Okay, thanks," Charlie said. "Go on, Larry."

"As I said, words were exchanged, and he mentioned to José, that was the dox examiner, that he never had a problem with invoice repair when he was with K E N Automotive. That we changed invoices all the time, as well as other documents, without even asking, and there was never a fee. Just made sure everything was done right and paid, no matter what."

"How would he know what you did or didn't do?"

"I'm not sure. All I can figure is that K E N is a small shop, just Kenny, a secretary, and an assistant. Kenny may have mentioned something, or the guy just figured it out on his own."

"I'm gettin a bad feeling here, Larry. Is there anything else I should know?'

McBride hesitated. "There could be. The reason I know all of this is I heard part of the conversation between Kramer and José, so I jumped on the phone before it went too far. Kramer really pissed me off, so I blasted him. Told him he was incompetent. He then said he knew all about the deal with K E N and the special customers."

"Terrific, I really need this!" Charlie put down his fork, pushed his plate back, folded his arms, and leaned back in his chair.

"Charlie, I can't prove it, but I'm convinced he really doesn't know the deal. He may have suspected something, but I can't see how he could really know what was going on."

"Unless Kenny told him."

"But he wouldn't do that. That would be stupid. He knows that only the five of us are to know how this works."

"Maybe so, but I wanna know for sure. The feds would really like to know about that something extra we've been putting away on the side. And you'll be in deep shit trouble with all those accounts."

"Yeah, I know. I'm just wondering if we should completely shut down."

"Wadda ya mean shut down? I can't shut down. Some of these guys are my biggest accounts now. Hey, I'm not just makin' money on the side like you are. Ninety percent of what I'm doing with these guys is legit. I'm they're prime US supplier for some product lines now. Wadda they supposed to do, start placing orders with other guys? No, that's not gonna fly. We gotta have a meetin'. The five of us, and we gotta make sure this Kramer guy is just blowin' smoke." Charlie leaned forward and started eating again. "You sure there's no problem at the bank?"

"Positive. I've got all the open files locked up in my office at home. There isn't even anything at the bank to find."

"And you're sure there's no problem with those accounts?"

"The accounts are all legit. The US has no restrictions on foreign individuals having accounts in US banks. The foreign governments may not like it, but that's their problem."

"Larry." Charlie waved his fork at him. "I sure hope so. You got me into this deal, and I got a lot at stake now. I run a straight business…well, pretty straight anyway. I don't wanna get caught with my pants down, and I definitely don't want the tax guys after me. I've had run ins with them before, and it's no fun. That's why I got me a real accountant this time, and I pay him serious money."

"He doesn't know about this, does he?"

"No, he doesn't. That's what's beginning to worry me. He doesn't know about the account in Panama either." Charlie paused and then leaned forward. "You're absolutely sure there's no drug money in any of this?"

"Positive. This is strictly a capital flight deal to get around exchange controls. All these guys are legitimate businessmen. You know them; you've seen their operations. When the exchange controls go away, then the deal goes away."

"Yeah, okay. But I'm still worried."

CHAPTER 18

Curious Behavior

As part of his regular routine in trying to learn as much about First State as he could, Ed often joined the international operations crew over lunch in the cafeteria at their designated table—actually a number of separate square ones pushed together to make a large rectangle that expanded and contracted, depending on the number of people sitting at it. Here the letter of credit issuing clerks, document examiners, customer inquiry staff, secretaries, and their supervisors and managers could meet in an informal atmosphere. They would relax in conversations about televisions programs they watched the night before, favorite baseball or football teams, commuting problems, raising children and just about any other topic that someone had a comment about, including customers and office work problems. Serious personal conversations were reserved for smaller, private groups but if you wanted to know the full story about what happened with a customer, such as the full, unfiltered problem with the Rayburn documents that were rejected and caused such a problem for everyone, this is where you would find it.

Today he sat among some of the supervisors of the international department, including Jane Moran and the heads of the customer inquiry and refinance units, and raised the question, during the regular lunchtime banter, about files being signed out for long periods. Jane commented that everyone was very good about it while Laura of customer inquiry said no file was ever out for more than a week without verifying its location. She couldn't remember the last time a file went missing, and she would know as file accuracy and maintenance was one of her responsibilities. Jane and Laura each had about thirty years with the bank and its predecessors, all of them in international related activities—when they joined the bank, international was only a three person operation and an offshoot of the main office branch. They were mainly involved in feeding international business on a third party basis to their two New York correspondents. Jane acted as the operational liaison between First State's customers—actually they were The State Bank of Essex County then—and the two New York banks, who didn't wish to deal direct with Jane's customers, as the New York banks were looking to State Bank of Essex County to assume any credit risk.

Jane's job evolved as the business evolved and the Port of Newark began to replace New York as the premier shipping point in the region. Her banking education was on the job and the courses given by the American Institute of Banking. Since she lived in Jersey City, she usually attended the classes that were held at the Woolworth Building in lower Manhattan. The classes were taught by bankers about banking, and there was no better education for bank operations people anywhere. If anyone would know how things worked at First State, she would. As head of operations, her duties included being the official signer for the department, she also endorsed bills of lading on behalf of the bank, signed checks and drafts, approved documents and initialed adjustments.

When two signatures were required, one of them was always hers, with the other being either McBride or Campbell, and they always made sure she signed first because then they knew it was right.

After lunch, as he looked at the papers in front of him, he knew it was Jane's expertise he needed before deciding whether it would be a good idea to approach McBride. He picked up the phone and called.

"Jane Moran."

"Jane. Ed. You have a few minutes?"

"Sure, be right in."

While waiting, Ed got up from his desk and looked out his window down onto Broad Street, Newark's main business street. He felt nervous and fidgeted with the pencil in his hand. He had seen the pattern before: a manager controlling the files of an account. Accepting McBride's offer to come to First State seemed like a good idea at the time and an opportunity to move into McBride's seat if he decided to jump somewhere else. He assumed McBride had bigger plans for himself, most likely running a major European bank's operations in New York. But this thing with adjusting invoices for customers bothered him, and now the missing files triggered all sorts of bad feelings. He hoped there would be a logical explanation.

"Can I come in?" Jane said at his door.

She was the picture of the operations manager. The long sleeves of her blouse were rolled up to the elbow, she had a pencil in her hair, which was short and uncombed or rather decombed from running her fingers through it as she analyzed a problem set of documents. She knew her job inside out backward and forward. Nothing fazed her.

"Please," he said as he motioned her to one of the two chairs in front of his desk and then sat down himself.

"You're looking serious this afternoon."

"It's just one of those days. Let's hope you can put some things to rest for me about the file system."

—

McBride came back to his office at three fifteen still mulling over his conversation with Field. Although everything seemed okay, he had a gut reaction that something was wrong. The process couldn't be stopped the way Field thought it could. If it had to do with laundering money it would be easy: just stop the transfers. But the way the deal was structured he had at least fifteen letters of credit open with over $5,000,000 in merchandise involved. If he tried to stop the process the buyers would just find new suppliers and his "ultimate win, win, win, win" scenario with a win for the foreign buyer who was moving his assets into dollars, a win for the exporter who was increasing his sales plus getting an "inconvenience fee," a win for the bank that was reaping all the extra income in the form of letter of credit commissions, foreign bank accounts and refinancing fees, and, of course, himself with his finders/agent fee, would become the "ultimate lose, lose, lose, lose" disaster. The phone ringing interrupted his thinking.

"Larry McBride.'

"Hey, Larry." It was Charlie Field. "You know, I got to thinkin on the way back to the office about this loose cannon

Kramer, so I gave Kenny Mitchell a call—this guy's a coke head!"

"A what?"

"A druggie. Kenny fired his ass a month ago for screwing up documents."

"Shit."

"In spades."

"Now what do we do?"

"I got some ideas. Just hang loose."

"All right." And the line went dead.

McBride sat holding the phone for a few minutes and staring across his office at a painting on the wall but not really seeing it.

"Is everything okay, Mr. McBride?" said Grace, looking into the office and seeing him holding the dead line.

He started. "Oh, yeah. Just thinking." He hung up the phone. "It's okay."

"Do you want your messages now?"

"Ah, why don't you hold them for a couple of minutes? I've got a couple of calls to make, and could you close that door?"

∞

The next morning found Jim sitting at his desk, looking over the monthly sales reports. How he hated that term. He didn't think he would ever get used to the idea of banks being in the sales business. It just didn't seem right. He still believed that the primary purpose of a bank was to serve as the fiduciary agent for its customers.

Maybe he belonged with Carl Hansen: an antique, a relic of the past. Certainly, the financial services industry was not going to back away from its hard-fought gains to pursue financial income in all its various forms. But his heart wasn't in the chase for profit as the Holy Grail. Oh, he could do it and do it very well, but he still believed that a banker's job was to help his customers to be successful.

He still took great pride in making sound loans to smaller companies and then watching the companies succeed. To take an interest in them, work with them, guide them. That, of course, was the essence of community banking and that was what the banking giants couldn't do. He knew how they worked; how they cut staff, especially the senior people, senior in years that is, and replaced them with twenty and thirty somethings who were given little training but large "sales" and "incentive" quotas. "Get them to sign up for the product. Don't worry as to whether it will be really useful to them or not. That's for them to figure out." There was nothing more irritating to owners of a company that they have been running for thirty years than to have a twenty something with no corporate experience come in from a bank and tell them how to run their business. But that was now the bible according to John, John Paressi, the executive vice president, he now reported to, late of Citibank, who came to make his mark on poor First State and drag it into the modern banking world of fee-based services.

An article in *The New York Times* announcing the Citibank branch of the future proved to be an eye opener. They were cutting the teller positions at their "branch of the future" on Park Avenue and Fifty-Third Street from nineteen to eight and increasing the automated teller machines from eight to twenty. All the staff was now referred to as "sales people," and the branch itself was being referred to as a store. *Banking as we head into the millennium. What will the twenty-first century bring?* Yes, he knew all of this. He did what he had to do, and he did it well, but sitting there looking at his new monthly sales sheets in preparation for the quarterly report he would soon file, he longed for a way of life that was long gone. The ring of the phone interrupted his thought patterns.

"Jim, Ed Campbell. I've been doing a fair amount of research into our problem and I think we need to get together."

"You want Adam along?'

"No, let's just keep it simple. There are some things I'd like to discuss that I don't think I want to have other bank people involved with yet."

"How about lunch off-site someplace?"

Jim hesitated a moment, "Look, Marian and I were going to meet for lunch at Pierre's on Two-O-Two South. She knows everything and more about the problem, why don't you join us?"

"Well, actually, that might work out just right."

"Good. You know where it is?'

"If it's on Two-O-Two South of Morristown it can't be hard to find."

"It's not. It's just on the right hand side as you get around New Vernon. About noon?"

"I'll be there."

As Jim hung up the phone, Paula stuck her head in the door. "Mr. Fairmont, Mr. Paressi just called and would like you to call him when you're free.'

"Thanks." Jim immediately picked up the phone and dialed the number.

"Marie, this is Jim Fairmont, John just called me."

"Let me check and see if he's free." The line went dead as he was placed on hold. About thirty seconds passed and then Paressi came on the line.

"Jim, how're you this morning?"

"Just fine, John. Working hard on the numbers for the quarter."

"Terrific! Look, Jim, we've got the 'good news' meeting tomorrow, and I thought it would be a good idea to throw some applause at international and pat ourselves on the back at the same time. International has been pumping in some good numbers lately and has the boss's attention. You and your people went to that seminar McBride ran a week or so ago, didn't you?"

"Yes, we did, and I must admit it was extremely good. Very helpful and informative."

"Great. Look, what I need is a paragraph or so praising McBride and showing how we on the domestic side are stepping up our efforts to take advantage of the expertise he's put together."

"Sure, no problem. Have it to you by the end of the day."

"Terrific. Thanks, Jim." And he hung up.

Just what I need, thought Jim, although he should have expected it. McBride had been showing good numbers so it was only logical that everyone would jump on the band wagon and the "Good News" meeting was the place to do it. Jim attended the meeting in Paressi's place on a regular basis when Paressi was away and was always amazed at it. It was officially the "New Business Meeting" where each of the senior line managers reported new "wins"—how he hated that word—to the chairman and president. All the news was good: new accounts opened, new relationships established, new lines of credit approved, new loans booked. Hence, the good news meeting. Needless to say there was not a "bad news meeting" that was done in private on a one on one basis. In any event, Jim would have no problem putting together a paragraph on the benefits of the seminar. *Give the devil his due*, he thought.

He knew his business, and the hiring of Ed Campbell was also a good move. Ed proved to be as knowledgeable as McBride but also had a seasoning that went well with customers. Yes, Jim could give McBride a good report, even if his gut told him there was something wrong someplace. He just wished he could figure it out.

He reached for the phone again. As he dialed, he thought, *I better let Marian know we've got company for lunch and, if this turns out to be "the" Ed Campbell, we may need to chat a bit first.*

Marian had just opened up and was in the process of moving to the outside some of the display items she usually brought in overnight.

The phone rang just as she put a straw doll, Wizard of Oz type, on a chair just outside the entry door. She made it to the receiver on the third ring.

"Garden Walk."

"Do garden's walk?" Jim teased.

"No, but wisecracking husbands are sometimes asked to."

"Whoops, are we having a bad day?"

"Oh, not really. It's just that Florence called and said she was going to be late again."

"We're still on for lunch, aren't we?"

"Oh, yeah. She'll be in about a quarter to twelve. She was supposed to come in at ten-thirty. Some emergency at home. I really shouldn't be upset. I knew when I hired her this would happen. She really just wanted the job to get out of the house. It's not as though this was a big career move or anything. Actually, I would have loved to have had a job like hers ten years ago. But anyway, what's up?"

"Some McBride issues. Ed Campbell called to say he found out something about the Rayburn blow-up I told you about yesterday. He was kind of cryptic. Said he wanted to meet off-site, as though he didn't trust the phone." Jim hesitated. "I invited him to lunch with us. I hope that's okay?"

"Yeah, sure. It's okay." Marian's smile disappeared as her mind raced.

"It just seemed the logical thing to do at the time. Are you sure you're okay with this?"

"No, really, Jim, there's no problem. Has he mentioned anything?"

"No and neither have I, although I can't believe he hasn't figured out the connection. He's a bright guy. You're sure this is okay?" Jim began having doubts and wondered if he had made a critical error. But—too late to go back now.

"I'm okay, if you are."

"I'm okay. Let's just let it all play out. We're all adults with a lot of water under the bridge. Maybe we can put some of the pieces together about this Alliance thing and finally put everything aside."

"I should be there right around noon. Ed is coming from Newark."

When Marian hung up the phone, she continued to stand behind the counter. *Well, it was going to happen sooner or later,* she thought. *Might as well be today as any other.* Her stomach churned. It would be a long, tense wait until lunch.

Grace Fredericks sat at her desk in the customer service area examining a file folder. It was a sample that was used to explain where one would find key items in an export letter of credit file. It was hard covered and had multiple dividers with metal prong, page holders built into the insides of the covers and dividers. She was taking notes on where different papers would be filed when a voice interrupted her.

"Grace, do you have a minute?" It was McBride standing a few desks away.

"Mr. McBride, sure."

"Come on over to the office." He immediately turned and headed back to the other side of the building. Grace closed the file and then wrote a brief note which she placed in the middle of the desk. It said simply, *Susan. In McBride's office. Be back shortly.* Her supervisor was due back in a minute to take her over to the refinance unit to introduce her around and to give her an overview of its operation, and she didn't want her to think she had just wandered off. By the time she got to McBride's office, he was already seated comfortably behind his desk.

"Come in, Grace. Sit for a minute," he said, motioning her to one of the chairs in front of him. "You know I hate to do this but could you fill in for Gloria again this morning. I asked her to run an errand for me before lunch. She should be back around one. I'll square it with Susan. Sorry to be interrupting your training schedule."

"Oh, that's all right. I can bring some of the reading material over and do it at Gloria's desk."

"Yeah, that'll be fine. So tell me, how do you like things so far?" McBride said, leaning back in his chair and taking as relaxed a position as possible in the hope of making her feel comfortable.

"It's been very interesting. It's totally different from anything I've done before. I mean, I've answered inquiries for Mr. Fairmont but they were not really technical like these are. They were usually very general. Sometimes there would be a wire transfer question or someone looking for a Fed reference number or an account balance but certainly not the depth of detail that I've heard people in the unit handle." She became more comfortable as she spoke. "Some of it seems very complex."

"I'm sure you'll have no trouble catching on. You've got the right personality for it. Gloria was right about you. Besides, I'm sure you're quite familiar with a lot of the names since many of them are the same ones you would be dealing with out of Fairmont's office. You know, people like Warner Lambert, Lucent, Alliance Automotive, Thomas and Betts, Toys R Us—we deal with them all here as well, just a different part of the same companies."

"I guess that's true. I've talked to them all already." She hesitated. "Except for that Alliance Company. I don't think I know them."

"Well, no matter." McBride smiled to himself: *Okay, Field, I've covered myself. Fairmont isn't sniffing around.* "They'll be a lot of names that are unfamiliar in addition to the familiar ones." He stood up, and she followed his lead. "I think you'll make a great customer service rep, and it's really good to have you with us. Would you close the door on the way out? I've got some phone calls to make. Feel free to bring anything you need over from customer service."

"Sure, Mr. McBride, and thanks." Grace dutifully shut the

door behind her on the way out and spotted one of the telecom-munications clerks waiting at Gloria's desk with some papers.

"Something for Mr. McBride?"

"Yeah, I'm supposed to hand these to Gloria.'

"I'll take them. Gloria's out this morning, and I'm sitting in for her."

"You sure?"

"Yes. I'll see that he gets them."

"Okay, he's kinda funny about SWIFT messages."

"Don't worry." Grace took the papers as she went behind Gloria's desk.

"You got to sign for them." He handed her a long sheet which she took and initialed the two items with McBride's name next to them.

"Okay?"

"Yeah." He turned and left.

Grace took the two messages and realized from her limited training that they were letter of credit pre-advices. Advance notifications of letters of credit that had been issued and would be arriving by mail. One was from Venezuela and the other from Columbia. As she put them down, she spotted the name Alliance Automotive on the one from Venezuela but didn't recognize the Columbia one.

CHAPTER 19

The Luncheon at Pierre's

As he anticipated, Jim was the first one to arrive at Pierre's.

"Mr. Fairmont, how're you today?" The bartender greeted Jim by name, not because he was a regular with a favorite bar stool, but he used the restaurant place as a primary location for business luncheons for customers in the Morristown to Somerville route I-287 corridor.

There was a highway exit nearby, the food was good, and there were four dining rooms having no more than five or six tables. The restaurant was a converted and expanded private residence and the small rooms kept the noise level down, so you could actually hold a conversation at normal speaking levels without feeling everyone else in the room was a part of the meeting. "Waiting for lunch?"

"Yes, the rest of them will be here in a few minutes."

"Can I get you something while you're waiting?"

"Just some iced tea would be fine."

"Coming up."

Jim looked at his watch. It was eleven-fifty-five. He was glad he came down US-202 instead of heading over to I-287. He heard there was a bad accident south of Morristown last night that damaged the overpass at New Vernon. He figured the lane reduction would slow down Ed coming down from Newark, but Marian would have no trouble coming up from Bernardsville and it would give them a chance to talk before Ed arrived. They both knew this meeting was eventually going to happen and Jim was glad it would have a business related background where other topics rather than just "good old times" would be the main subject of conversation.

Marian came in just after his iced tea had been delivered. She headed for the hostess but then spotted Jim at the bar. "It's all right, I see him." She walked over to the bar and tapped him on the shoulder as she approached from the rear. "You all alone, big boy?"

Jim started, turned, and, seeing it was Marian, said, "Sorry, my wife's due any minute."

The couple at the bar next to Jim gave them both a strange look.

"Hi, hon," Marian said as they gave one another a hello kiss. "Been waiting long?"

"No, just got here. Had to make my way around that accident from last night. They're still working on it."

"I heard about that. Don't think it was a local or I would have heard more about it by now."

"The time of only locals being on the roads around here is long gone since they opened I-Two-Eighty-Seven."

"Yeah, I guess so. What are you drinking? I see it's brown. What a surprise?"

"Iced tea."

Marian waved at the bar tender. "Bring me one of these, please."

"Yes, ma'am."

"So," said Jim. "Florence showed up?"

"She was there just after eleven-thirty. She's been having trouble with her daughter at school. I really feel sorry for these women that are trying to work and raise families at the same time. How in the world they do it I don't know."

"Having understanding employers is one way. Most of the women I've seen trying to juggle job and family by themselves are usually terrific employees. They can't afford to lose their job so they tend to be more conscientious than most and less likely to jump from job to job like their male counterparts. So as a reward for doing a job well, you cut them a little slack."

"You may cut them a little slack, but I don't think many other people do."

"How about moving to the table, I hate sitting at bars."

"Fine."

The table was ready, and the hostess took them into the "yellow room" and put them at a table for four, which was the only corner table in the room. The other three corners had doors associated with them, one of which was to the kitchen. They sat next to one another with their backs to the walls.

"I hope you don't mind about my inviting Ed?" began Jim. "He sounded really anxious to talk and made a point of not wanting to do it on bank premises."

"It's okay. This meeting was going to have to come up some day and today is as good as any. Besides, I'm really interested to find out what he found out and why it's so hush-hush. Do you know if he ever spoke with McBride like he said he was going to do? You said last night that he was going to get to McBride after he returned from lunch."

"I have no idea, but if he found something suspicious I can understand why he wouldn't approach McBride with it, unless, of course, it didn't involve McBride." The waitress came over to the table.

"Hi, I'm Judy. I'll be your server today. Would you like a few more minutes before ordering?"

"We're waiting for another party. If you could just top off the iced teas, for now, that would be fine," said Jim.

"Sure, no hurry. Let me get some for you," she said and moved on.

Marian waited until Judy was out of earshot. "Do we really care if her name is Judy? Is she planning to join us for lunch and that's why we need to know her name?"

"The usual pet peeve?"

"Well, it is infuriating. Especially here. Save that for the Appleby's crowd. This is supposed to be a quality place. My first rule is if there's a cloth on the table the server shouldn't have a label."

"That's catchy. Ought to make it into a sign and you can sell it at The Walk."

Marian picked up one of the little packages of NutraSweet that were in a bowl on the table and threw it at him. Jim, laughing, held up his hands in self-defense.

"Ah, food fight," said a voice approaching. It was Ed Campbell.

"Hey, Ed," Jim said, starting to get up.

"Stay there. Marian, good to see you again." He held out his hand to her, and she took it.

"Hello, Ed," was her response, looking at him carefully, seeing a younger face hidden in the older one.

Jim motioned him to a chair.

Ed took the seat next to him. "You guys always act like this in a restaurant?"

"Only when provoked," she said with a smile while Jim rolled his eyes and then changed the subject.

"I see you found the place without a problem."

"It was pretty easy now that Route Twenty-Four is open. Only problem I had was near here. Apparently, there was some sort of bad accident last night; they still have one of the lanes shut down." Ed paused and gave a hard look at Jim and Marian. He had been mulling over the meeting on the drive from Newark. How would he handle it? Calm and collected. Not say anything? Wait till one of them brought it up? He knew that would be wrong, but he needed to get it out of the way. *Why wait? It's hanging out there anyway. Get it over with.* "You know—there's—something I have to say before we get into anything else. A lot of years ago, I made a really terrible mistake. And, believe me, it was my fault. I orchestrated the events. To be honest," he said, looking directly at Marian, "I felt sorry for myself. I'd lost you when I was in Viet-Nam—"

Marian looked like she was about to interrupt. He held up his hand. "Just let me finish first. I had no reason to expect anything. There was no commitment between us. We were just a couple of co-workers who had fun together, and I know all of that. But I got caught in the draft and, although other avenues were open to me, I made the decision to just accept it. I was single, no attachments so I figured I'd just let the married guys and those with kids do the national guard bit. I had no idea how difficult it would be, and none of us anticipated that we would end up being the targets of the protesters…well, not all of them. Actually, I was on their side. Anyway, it depressed me as I'm sure it did a lot of other people, and when I saw you that afternoon, it all just welled up inside of me, and I consciously decided to take advantage of the situation. I could have stopped when I found out you were married, but I was feeling so sorry for myself and angry I decided to take it out on you. I am so sorry. So terribly sorry."

A long pause and then Ed continued. "Jim, I really don't know what to say to you other than I'm sorry. I hope this won't damage our professional relationship." He dropped his eyes down, looked at the napkin in front of him, and then, nervously, reached for his glass of water.

Jim shifted uncomfortably. "This happened a long time ago, and Marian and I've have had lots of conversations about it since, although not recently. To be honest, it's been a long time since I've given it any thought at all. I thank you for your candor, and I'd like to suggest that we let the incident die right here. From a professional standpoint, I too hope we will do just fine, but if either of us honestly feels that our judgement is being impaired, then it should be put on the table."

Ed looked directly at Jim and then Marian. "My wife, Susan, and I have had some long telephone conversations about this when I realized who you both were and, to be perfectly frank, we agreed that I would resign and move back to Chicago until I could find something else if the past proved to be an insurmountable problem."

"I don't think that's necessary. Frankly, I didn't know you were married."

"Yeah, twenty years coming up in December. Twin girls. Just starting senior year in high school. It's why we made the decision about my coming here on my own. We wanted the girls to finish, not interrupt their lives. It's too important for them at this age. Besides, with the banking world what it is today, I could be on the street again—if First State merges or is taken over—only we'd all be away from our support groups in a strange town in New Jersey."

Marian made as though she wanted to make a comment but then Judy, the waitress, reappeared and joined the conversation, "Oh, heard you talking and I just remembered, there's a story about the accident in the local paper this morning. I'll bring it over." She turned to Ed. "Can I bring you something to drink?"

He nodded, pointing to what Jim and Marian were drinking. "Just bring me another Banker's Special."

She looked at him with a blank stare.

When he saw her confusion, he added, "Sorry, that's an iced tea."

"Oh," she said. "I've never heard of that. Be back in a minute."

Marian sighed but couldn't let it go. "Good help is so hard to find," she said sarcastically.

Ed and Jim both smiled and then Jim said, "Hey, if you'd like to throw something at her, this time, it's okay with me," and they all chuckled together.

The ice is broken, thought Marian, *maybe it won't be so bad after all.* She could understand why Jim had come to like Ed. There was an instant ease about him, a confidence, a maturity, which Jim always referred to as seasoning.

Suddenly, the room at the Governor Morris Inn popped into her head, and she started.

"Are you okay?" said Jim.

"Yes, oh, I was just thinking of that accident last night and how many times I'd passed that same spot. Gives me shivers."

"I must admit driving around here is no picnic," Ed agreed.

The waitress was back with the iced tea. "One Banker's Special." She smiled. "Are you ready to order?"

"Do you need some time to look at the menu, Ed," Jim said. "We've got it virtually memorized."

"Why don't you guys order while I peek just a moment?" he said while picking up the folder on the table in front of him.

The ordering of lunch was uneventful but a challenge for Judy, nonetheless. She managed to forget to tell them the specials, which no one was really interested in anyway, but eventually managed to say what they were, from an index card she had in her pocket, even after she had taken all the orders.

When she finally left, Marian couldn't resist. "So much for a tight labor market. If Pierre's is hiring 'Judys,' what can we expect from the Velvet Turtle?"

Jim and Ed smiled and then Jim decided to restart the conversation. "Ed, before we get into Rayburn and McBride, there are some things I think you should know." Marian stiffened in her chair. "First of all Marian knows all about the Rayburn flap and the problems we've been having but I also want you to know up front that I've had my problems with McBride. We're not exactly the best of friends. We do tolerate one another professionally but I don't think there's any love lost. It may be just a domestic versus international thing. I've known Larry since he joined the bank about four years ago and I'll admit he's done a great job in building our international business and making it quite profitable. To be honest though, I just don't like his style, and we've clashed from time to time. For the most part, I try to stay out of his way."

"Believe me, I understand and, frankly, he's made some comments your way."

"I'm not surprised. My problem is that I just don't trust him. I'm trying to be honest here, so you know where I'm coming from. I've always had the feeling that the good of the bank will always come second to his own personal objectives. I guess I'm somewhat old fashioned in my views."

Ed smiled. "I think Mr. McBride would probably agree with you on that."

"And you?"

"Well, having been through a few bank mergers that didn't go exactly my way, I've come away a bit from the bank first view, although I believe strongly in loyalty to whoever is paying my salary and I have an obligation to give an honest day's work for a day's pay. Now that may also be a bit of an old fashion notion."

"I guess before we go too much further, the obvious question would be 'Do you feel it is McBride who is paying your salary or First State?'"

"Oh, no question, First State," Ed replied. "I've seen too many situations where people make the mistake of tying themselves to their supervisors and then are left high and dry when their protector leaves. Prove your value to the institution first, don't neglect who you report to but don't lose sight of the bigger picture and responsibility."

"Okay, I'll buy that but before we get into Rayburn, let me tell you about something that happened at a charity book sale over Labor Day weekend that has been driving both Marian and me nuts, well…me at least."

Jim began his story about McBride's unusual and somewhat frantic behavior of rummaging through the book boxes at the AAUW book sale, the stuffing of the papers into his pocket, dumping the books he was apparently going to buy, and racing for the exit. He told of finding the Alliance Automotive Export Corp. invoice form and Jim and Marian's attempt to find out what it all meant. Marian chimed in and related her conversation with Manny Rosenberg of Blue Bird China.

"Ed, maybe we're nuts. You know, I've often wondered if I would have had a second thought about any of this if it was anyone but McBride; it's just that it was all so suspicious. Maybe I just should have just sent the form to him and dropped the whole thing?"

"Probably a good thing you didn't because then he would always suspect the reason you returned it. One of the things I've learned very quickly about Larry McBride is that he takes nothing at face value. He lives and breathes ulterior motives."

Suddenly, there was Judy with lunch. In distributing the food, she mixed up the orders and, after she turned to leave, Jim and Marian swapped plates. They were just ready to take their first bites when she was back again. "Is everything okay, guys?"

"Just fine," said Jim.

"Good. Let me know if you need anything. Enjoy," she said, turned, and cheerfully headed off to the kitchen.

Marian, of course, had to make a comment. "Well, I guess we have to give her points for attentiveness."

"Hey," said Ed. "This is a real nice place."

"Oh, it is," said Marian. "The foods always good, and I really like the small rooms and the house atmosphere. It's just this labor shortage problem that surfaces from time to time."

"I think you'll find that everywhere but let me tell you why I wanted this meeting." They all shifted in their chairs. "After we finished talking about that document examination flap yesterday, I decided to see if there were, in fact, some invoice problems with Rayburn shipments. I'm not sure where the Alliance invoice fits in, but I checked all the Rayburn files I could and found absolutely nothing. There's no indication that there have been any invoice document problems with any Rayburn shipments. Then, as long as I was there, I decided to check on this K E N Automotive name, but I wasn't able to, as all the files had been checked out and, curiously enough, they were all out to McBride or his secretary. In itself, this can be explained if there was some form of analysis or study of the company going on, which is fairly common. You pull all the files and verify the way the credits have been issued. This is especially true if back-to-back credits have been issued, which seemed to be the case with most K E N credits. You both understand back-to-backs?"

"I have a sense of them from Jim, and I've done some research on my own."

"She probably understands them better than I do right now," said Jim.

"Good," Ed continued. "You'll remember then that the key feature of the credits is that one set of documents should be able to pay both credits, with the only variable at times being the invoice, which can be substituted, so the original supplier's pricing is concealed. So I figured this is where the invoice comment came from the guy at Rayburn."

"So everything can be explained away legitimately?" Jim said.

"Technically, yes, provided that an actual review is underway."

"Are you saying that maybe there isn't?"

"Let me continue a bit. After I found all the K E N Automotive files were missing, I decided to check with Jane Moran. She's sort of the mother of international."

"Yes, I've known Jane for a long time," Jim said.

"Mother of international?" Marian inquired. "Are we getting a little sexist here?" She was feeling comfortable. This Ed she didn't know. The image she had of him didn't exist anymore. She felt confident she could deal with this. She only hoped Jim could as well.

"Not really," Jim responded. "Believe me, if Jane was male instead of female and had the same history and personality, she'd be the father of international. Or he'd be the father of international. Or one of them." He shook his head. "Oh, go on, Ed."

"First, I asked about the file out policy, and she confirmed that all files should be pulled for action only—such as payments, drawings, refinancing, amendments, etc. I then mentioned the K E N Automotive files and her response was: 'Oh, they're one of Larry's pets.'"

"One of Larry's pets?" Marian said.

"Yes, apparently, he has a number of them. According to Jane, Larry likes to keep his hand in when it comes to verifying documents and actually does the document work himself on a number of names. She said this keeps him up to date on what's going on and keeps his skills sharp. I asked her how many names were involved, and she said she wasn't sure, but she knew of at least three or four. He apparently has notations on all of his pet files to refer all inquiries and drawings to him personally. Also, the customers know he sometimes does the documentation himself, and when they are delivered to the window by messenger, they contain specific instructions to be delivered to L. A. McBride."

"But there's nothing really wrong with what he's doing? I mean, he's not really in violation of any bank rules?"

"Again, technically, no. Except that I've seen this before. We had a branch manager in our Taiwan Office who would keep pet files in his desk and would do all the negotiations on export refinancing himself. It turned out he was approving loans for non-existent transactions and taking a cut on the side. The files were always locked in a cabinet in his office, and all that anyone saw was the note indicating that the loan advance was supported by a shipment of 'certain' merchandise, which, of course, didn't exist. It all eventually came apart when one of the companies couldn't pay, so he kept rolling over the note as though they were new shipments and liquidated the old loans with the proceeds of the new ones. It got real messy in the end."

"Do you think we've got something like that going on here?" Jim inquired.

"I don't think so, but something screwy is definitely going on. What really bothers me is a couple of things you said earlier: you mentioned Alliance Automotive Export, which is one of the pet names, and the invoice form, which you found in a box of books that came from his home."

"Why would that be critical?" Marian asked.

"It may mean that he's storing bank material at home and removing the letter of credit files and documents from bank premises, which would be a clear violation of bank policy, not to mention not good business practice."

"I wonder if I could ask a fairly basic question," Marian said. "Why come to Jim? Why not go directly to McBride and ask him for an explanation?"

"That's a fair question." Ed sat back in his chair. "As I think I mentioned, I've seen this pattern before when I was in Taiwan. In that instance, the manager of the office was confronted by the local head of credit, who actually reported to him. Accusations were tossed about, and the credit department manager was accused of disloyalty and incompetence and fired by the manager. The manager also filed a lengthy report back to his superiors in the US explaining his actions. He, of course, was on strong ground because he was responsible for running an extremely profitable operation. The people in the States he reported to had taken credit for the good performance, and executive management was dolling out incentive bonuses to them. The credit manager, being fired for cause, was stranded in Taiwan and had to pay his own way back to the US He eventually filed a complete report, which got back to the internal auditors, but by the time a full investigation was done, which was three months later, the office manager had resigned and had taken a position with another foreign bank, this time in Korea and the loans that were made in Taiwan all started to go bad. The bank took some very significant losses."

Marian nodded. "And you think the same thing could happen here?"

He leaned forward again and whispered, "I don't know. In fact, I don't know for sure that there is something illegal going on. What I do know is that it's poor business practice and brings back some very vivid, bad memories."

"Taiwan?"

"It was a blood bath. The new manager started firing people left and right. The whole credit department was replaced, as well as the staff of the refinance unit."

"And head office didn't complain?"

"Head office concern is profit and head count. Who the heads were was not important. They were local hires and the manager could do what he liked as long as it didn't impact office earnings and performance."

"How did you escape?"

"I was an expat on a contract. To get rid of me would require head office approval because of the expense of shipping me back home. I was a junior account and credit guy at the time brought in from the US to concentrate on American affiliates, similar to what Rayburn has over there now. I don't think Susan really ever got over it. The stress and tension were unbelievable. She reminded me what she and the girls went through living under the tension in Taipei and used it as an argument when I took the First State job. And it wasn't just during the manager's blood bath but for a good six months after when the internal auditors were in tearing the whole place apart. Then came the new manager, who went looking for people who were loyal to the old guy, or even worse, had developed bad habits because of him. No, this is not something to bring to McBride and certainly not by me."

Marian pushed back her chair slightly and folded her arms. "So you both just sit back and ignore it?"

"No, we can't."

"I agree," said Jim. "But where do we go from here? Internal audit?"

"I don't think so. Not yet. We need to be able to not only justify an investigation but also *prove* that it's justified." Ed suddenly paused. "You know, I'm not sure it's fair for me to bring you into this. I mean, the only reason I'm confiding in you is that I know your reputation and feel that you're not automatically on McBride's side, no matter how much money he brings into the bank. My problem is that I'm new to the bank and don't really know anyone in international. I trust Jane Moran but she's an operational technician and besides it appears all the managers seem to have taken a McBride loyalty oath, although I'm sure if it came to the bank versus McBride, Jane would be in the bank's column. As I said, I'm new and could use some guidance around the politics of this place, but you don't have to really get involved."

Marian leaned forward again. "What did you have in mind?"

"I agree," Jim added. "But we *are* involved, so what do you think needs to be done?"

Ed took a deep breath and a long pause. "What we need is evidence of wrongdoing. It doesn't need to be elaborate, but it does have to be clear and incontestable. If we don't come up with something that is a clear violation of bank policy, a dismissible offense, then we have to drop it. If we bring anything less to internal audit, we'll be on the street instead of McBride."

"I could always use some help around The Walk."

"Thank you, Marian, but I think our main objective should be to make sure that doesn't happen."

"I'll support that," Jim said

"We do have a problem," Ed continued. "And that invoice you found could very well be the key. What we need to do is get our hands on some of those files McBride has been hoarding. My initial instinct would be that he has some of them locked up in his office someplace and that would be the first place to look. The only problem I see is that you said you found the Alliance invoice in a box of books that came from his home and that pretty much convinces me that he's been taking the files home and working on them there. That's both good news and bad in that taking the files off bank premises is definitely a clear violation of bank policy, as I said. But if we combine that with some clear evidence of unethical behavior, we have a good chance of nailing him. However, the bad news is that getting access to the files is going to be nearly impossible."

"Is there anyway of checking into what the files represent without actually having them?" Marian asked. She then paused and realized she had the answer to her own question and, looking at Ed and Jim, she knew they had it as well. They all looked at one another and then said in unison, "Follow the money."

And there were smiles all around the table.

"Aren't we having fun?" It was the waitress, back again. "I found that newspaper from this morning. About the accident you talked about. I'll just leave it on the chair here." She placed it on the empty chair between Marian and Ed. "Can I get anything for anyone?"

"No, I don't think so," Jim responded. "We're okay, thanks. And thanks for the paper." She turned and left. Marian immediately picked up the paper and began skimming the accident story on the front page while Jim and Ed took the opportunity to work on their lunch.

"Looks like the guy just lost control of the car," she said. "He must have been going awfully fast for some reason. Never heard of him, though. He must be from out of area. Samuel Kramer,"

Ed stopped eating. "What was that name again?"

"Samuel Kramer. Do you know him?"

"That's the name of the Rayburn guy. Sam Kramer."

"Which Rayburn guy?" Jim asked.

"The export manager. The one that blew up at José and had the run in with McBride over the phone."

CHAPTER 20

Evidence Building

T he plan to determine what McBride could be up to involved obtaining some closed files that listed K E N Automotive or Alliance Automotive Export Corp. as the beneficiaries. Next, would be for Ed to find companion files where the two companies were listed as the account parties, showing the connection to the domestic letter of credit part of the back-to-back transaction. After Ed reviewed the transactions themselves, he would pass the payment dates to Marian so she could forward them to Jim, using The Walk's e-mail account. Jim would then track the payments with the wire transfer department located in First State's operations center in Secaucus, New Jersey. Both Ed and Jim would then use their personal e-mail addresses to send any and all information found to The Garden Walk's address and thereby keep all the messages outside of the bank's system. Hopefully they would be able to find enough incriminating data to determine just what McBride was doing. The plan seemed reasonable and straight forward but would it reveal anything?

Arriving at his office forty-five minutes earlier than usual the next morning, Ed set up a folder for holding whatever information he found and labeled it Pierre and Company and then signed into the documentary credits system from his terminal. Switching the search indicator to *CLOSED* from its default *OPEN* setting he typed in *K E N AUTOMOTIVE* under the heading of *BENEFICIARY* and the screen displayed thirty letter of credit numbers in credit number order, which he immediately wrote down on a piece of paper and placed in the file. He could have printed out the list but the system printer was outside his office in a central place on the floor with access by everyone. Next, he changed the *BENEFICIARY* heading to *ACCOUNT*

PARTY, and five credit numbers came up with domestic letter-of-credit number sequencing. These would be the suspected back-to-back credits. High-level search data was kept in the on-line system for only twelve months from the closed date. At the beginning of the thirteenth month, the system automatically generated a hard copy report of the information being deleted, which was bound and placed in date order in the archive room. Ed wrote down all five numbers. He then moved to his PC that sat next to the system terminal and quickly formatted an e-mail to Marian from his personal AOL account and typed in the closed dates to be passed onto Jim. Leaving his office with the Pierre and Company file in hand, he headed to the back of the room and the door that went to the Letter of Credit Department Inquiry Section, where all the credit files were kept. Ed decided to go after one of the old K E N Automotive back-to-back letters of credits as a starting point.

⋐⋑⋐⋑

In Morristown, Jim's approach to researching information took a more roundabout route. He came in at his usual time but waited about an hour before signing into his personal AOL email account using the PC in his office. The message from Marian, with the subject of Pierre & Company, stood out.

> *Hi, Jim,*
> *Finally got hold of those disputed reference numbers we have for Pierre. Really have to clean up around here. You won't believe where I found them, but better yet we can discuss that later. Anyway, the dates involved are Feb 12, April 6, May 22, June 6, and July 6. Also have the invoice numbers: 786, 810, 905, 985, and 987. We can go over all of this later this evening at the store. Flo isn't in this afternoon, so I'm stuck late today anyway.*
> *How about dinner? We'll bring it in so we can go over everything.*
> *Love, M*

The message contained the numbers received earlier in the morning from Ed. She disguised the domestic letter of credit numbers from his message and inserted them as a part of her dai-

ly comments on her morning at the store but removed the year—
as they were all from 1992—and spelled out the month, so they
appeared current and didn't use bank or international code sequencing, giving the impression they related to shipments she
received at The Walk rather than merely forwarding Ed's original
message. She also copied Ed's personal email address as a bcc so
he wouldn't be shown on the original. Most people didn't pay
much attention to husband and wife messages, but they all felt it
would be best to not take any chances.

Taking his Pierre & Company folder, Jim took the numbering
from Marian's email and expanded them in the way Ed had instructed.

L/C Number Date:
10-00786 19920406
10-00810 19920406
10-00905 19920522
10-00985 19920606
10-00987 19920706

The plan he developed involved signing into the money transfer inquiry system from Paula's desk, when she stepped away on
an errand he concocted for her—Ed didn't have access to the system in Newark—and search for the letter of credit reference
numbers, which would be entered in the related reference number
field of wire transfers from K E N Automotive around the closing
date Ed provided. Although he wished he could get Paula involved, as she knew how to manipulate the system better than he
did, he didn't want her to know what he was doing.

Once Paula's terminal was free, Jim signed into the money
transfer inquiry system and formatted an inquiry based on one of
the K E N Automotive credit numbers. He pressed *ENTER*, and
almost immediately the screen flashed *INVALID ENTRY*. He
tried again with another number and received the same result. He
tried changing some of the other data, but *INVALID ENTRY* was
all he could receive. After fifteen minutes of trying, he finally
threw in the towel.

"Why is it whenever I really need the system, something's
wrong with it?"

Computer frustration was boiling to the top. It looked as

though he would have to involve Paula after all.

"Hi, Mr. Fairmont."

Jim looked up and saw the smiling face of Grace Fredericks. "Grace, what are you doing here today? I thought they kept you locked up in the Newark Office?"

"Still in training, so Mr. Porter worked out an arrangement with my supervisor that I could come over and help out on special projects until you find a replacement for me here. The bank is hosting the annual Boys and Girls Club fund raising luncheon this year, so here I am. Will be here a couple of days. Kinda nice to be back, actually."

"International a bit different for you?"

"It's really interesting, but the pace is something else. International inquiry is one crisis after another. The section has the nickname of Aspirin Alley. Didn't mean to bother you. Just wanted to say hello," she said, noticing his obvious level of frustration as he sat at Paula's terminal.

"Not a problem. Maybe we can chat a little bit later; catch up on what's going on." Jim stopped and held up his hand slightly. "Wait a minute. You're now with international inquiry. Do you have time to answer a question for me?" He wondered if this could be his answer.

"Sure."

"Is there something different about doing an international funds transfer inquiry as opposed to a domestic one? I've been trying to get into the system and keep getting *INVALID ENTRY* back."

"Actually there is. I just found out this last week in my training. The bank's funds transfer system was created a long time ago and is based on the old bank wire system. I was told that it's due to be updated, but the project is on hold because of all the mergers happening. In the meantime, Mr. McBride bought a new letter of credit software package that does all of its formatting, according to the SWIFT system. I haven't learned much about it yet, just the terms, but I do know there is a translation fix that lets the two systems 'talk' to one another. Ms. Moran is the one who worked on it. I actually did my first inquiry in training the other day and if you're in the L/C inquiry system and you need to see the details of funds sent or received domestically you just type ALT FTS and format your inquiry according to that system. Ms.

Moran created 'quick guides' for both systems. The opposite works for going the other way by typing in ALT L/CS and you get an inquiry screen for the new letter of credit system. Ms. Moran said everything will eventually be converted to the format used in the SWIFT system but, for now, we're stuck with this clunky way of doing things. Does that answer your question?"

"I'll say it does. Does Paula know about this?"

"I'm sure she does. Probably has a memo update about it somewhere. When I was here, we never did our own international inquiries—if we ever had one, which was rare—just passed them on to Newark and they would get the information for us."

"Makes sense. Thanks, Grace. Didn't mean to hold you up. No rush on the inquiry. Just curious. Will work on it later or have Paula do it when she gets back. By the way, are copies of the inquiry guides in this office somewhere?"

"Actually, I think Paula has copies under her desk blotter next to her PC." She pointed to the blotter just off to the side of where Jim sat. She thought about getting them for him but realized that would be encroaching on Paula's space.

"Grace, you're a life saver. Paula won't be back for a while yet, and I needed to check on a transfer." He peeked under the blotter and slid the guides out.

"If you or Paula need some help with them, just let me know. I'll be here all day. I have to go now, Mr. Fairmont. Mr. Porter's probably looking for me."

"I'll tell Paula you were looking for her, and we'll all catch up a little later."

"Thanks, Mr. Fairmont."

As Grace left Jim looked at the clock and realized he had a meeting coming up and couldn't spend any more time on doing inquiries, so he wrote the numbers down from Marian's email, put some questions down next to them indicating the information he would need, grabbed a meeting folder from the corner of the desk, and left.

Twenty minutes later, Paula and Grace were chatting outside Jim's office, and Grace related the earlier conversation about the international inquiries.

"I didn't know he had an international inquiry he needed done. Why don't we do it for him from my terminal and you can show me how to do it? I usually just call Lorraine in Newark and let her do it." Paula got up and headed for Jim's office with Grace following.

"So does everyone else. I see it all the time when I'm actually working in customer service instead of doubling as Mr. McBride's secretary."

"Really? I didn't know you were doing that too. Have you been doing it a lot?"

"Oh, not really and I don't mind. It's just that I was surprised that he asked me to fill in instead of one of the other secretaries like Mr. Campbell's or someone else."

"Find out anything interesting?" Paula asked while looking over Jim's desk.

"Well, it is different. I mean, an awful lot of unusual things come through his office. Naturally, there's a lot of international communications both telephone and telex and also SWIFT. It sure is a busy place."

"I didn't mean to pry or anything. I suppose there's some logic to asking an experienced secretary to fill in. This looks like it." Paula picked up the note Jim left for himself earlier.

"Oh, I agree. It's just that I'm so new. I had to spend a lot of time asking other people what to do."

"Okay, this is definitely the information for the inquiry," she said, looking at Jim's notes. "Look, why don't I just give the details to you and I'll look over your shoulder while you do the first one and then I'll pick up from there? It'll be great practice." Paula handed to list to Grace.

"K E N Automotive. I know that name. I saw some messages about it when I was sitting in for Gloria. Funny, Mr. McBride said I would see a lot of familiar names."

"He did?"

"Yeah, it was just in conversation the other day. He mentioned Warner Lambert and Thomas and Betts and a bunch of others that corporate deals with on a regular basis, and there was one name I hadn't heard of, Alliance Auto something."

"I suppose he's right. It's one bank, after all, just different sides. It's only the really specialized names that would remain a mystery to each side."

"Mystery is probably a good word. That name sure seems to be something special around here the way Mr. McBride controls everything about it. He makes a point of seeing everything that happens to it."

∽∾

While Paula sat at her desk in Morristown with Grace, investigating letter of credit payments relating to K E N Automotive, Ed searched for the original supporting documentation in the archive room of the Letter of Credit Department, looking through the *CLOSED* letter of credit section trying to find the old K E N Automotive and Alliance Automotive Export files. So far he had found only two Alliance and three K E N All the others still had *OUT* folder markers where the files should have been. The fact that so many files were out was not notable as the system was entirely manual and there was always a full tub of folders waiting to be refiled. Also, they were filed in the order of the date closed, the letter of credit number, and then the account party name, so the *OUT* folders were well disbursed throughout the file tubs. What he was able to find were the domestic letters of credit that were the companions to the export ones. He had six of them now. He had been moving them two at a time back to his office so he would not look strange carrying too many at once.

∽∾

Jim, in Morristown, walked over to John Porter's office to kill some time and be near the fax machine, which was on a table close to Grace's desk. He decided it was bad enough for Grace and Paula to have done the inquiries for him and to be involved to the extent they were, but he didn't want Grace reading the information being faxed to Marian at the store and innocently mentioning something to someone else. Porter and Grace were in the middle of assembling a seating arrangement for an upcoming dinner where the Chairman would speak about the bank's commitment to the Boys and Girls Clubs of New Jersey. The bank had taken two tables of ten with the Chairman hosting one and John Paressi hosting the other. There would be four bank people and six corporate guests at each table, and Porter was making sure the most significant and friendly customers would be surrounding the senior executives. One never put the chairman in a hostile environment—rule number one for keeping your job, and he definitely liked his job.

Jim's banter with Porter was innocuous enough, and he imparted some information about the personalities of his customers who would be attending the dinner as guests of the bank. Also, Adam Turner would be one of the sub-hosts. Jim declined, figuring this would be a good chance for Adam to get some informal exposure to senior management. As he stood in John's doorway, he heard the fax machine come to life. He figured it would be two or three minutes before it finished sending what he found, so he began winding down his conversation.

✍✍

Ed closed the door to his office, picked up one of the K E N Automotive files, and began pouring through it in an extremely methodical way. He took notes on a yellow ruled pad immediately. The plan was to trace all activity in a chronological manner—making as many notes as possible and, where possible, make copies of critical documents—then get the file back to where it belonged. He would then send all his notes and other material to Marian via e-mail and fax and destroy the originals.

Working quietly and intensely, he made notes on the pad where he had set up three columns: *DATE: ACTION: COMMENT:* The same format would be used in the email. The documents themselves, he would fax to Marian either during lunch or when he could be certain of privacy with the machine, which, while keeping track of messages, only recorded the telephone number of the recipient, the status and the number of pages successfully sent.

✍✍

Marian's first e-mail of the day from Jim arrived just before lunch. She checked her mail every half hour and set up two folders one labeled *Jim* and the other *Ed*. She printed each mail message and placed it in the respective folder for them to review that evening by phone. Even though Ed lived at The Hills in Bedminster, only a fifteen or twenty minute drive away, they felt it was better to stick to communicating electronically. She could see that

Jim's message involved a debit to a bank in Argentina and a credit to the account of K E N Automotive Export Marketing Associates at First State. Then came a debit to K E N Export Marketing Associates and three credits: the first going to Bank One in favor of Specialty Automotive Supply, Inc. in Ohio, then a credit to Miguel Garcia at First State, and the third one to Hoboken Commercial Bank in favor of Export Import Consulting Group. While she was printing out the first message, a second one came in from Jim and the text followed the same pattern as the first only this time a company called Traders Caribbean at First State was in the mix.

Jim still had a few more emails to send to Marian but decided, since Paula had gone to lunch, to see if his access code was still valid for doing account inquiries with regard to viewing a customer's statement—access was suspended if it wasn't used for more than thirty days and he usually had Paula do most inquiries. Luckily, he found he could get into the system. Armed with the K E N Automotive account number and relationship information from the bank's customer information system, he was able to see where it showed that, although the account was listed as being opened at First State's branch in Newfoundland, New Jersey, LA, McBride was shown as the principal contact. Jim entered in the data required and, sure enough, there was the K E N statement for the current month. He pressed the "print" key and then went to the previous month and did the same.

ဢ

Ed was looking over his notepad where he had listed out the transactions and suddenly realized there seemed to be some gaps in the dates. He was looking at notes that did not relate to one of the back-to-back transactions, but what appeared to be a straight export to Venezuela by Alliance Automotive Export. There was a discrepancy in the documents—the merchandise description on the invoices did not match, precisely, what was written in the letter of credit merchandise description field—and the documents and payment were held while First Bank notified the Venezuelan bank and requested approval to pay, despite the discrepancy. It took four days for the "discrepancy waiver" to arrive and for Alliance Automotive to be paid the amount requested by the draft

$155,850. However, what caught Ed's eye was the writing on the front of the letter of credit folder. Where the stamp usually went for a notification of the transaction being a linked to another letter of credit—making it a back-to-back credit—the box had been filled in and then crossed out. If it was originally a back-to-back, then there should have been a hold placed on the domestic supplier's letter of credit. He wondered what really happened. He quickly turned to the terminal that sat on the credenza behind him and formatted an internal payment inquiry for the date the documents were rejected and spotted a $120,850 transaction.

"Okay, now we're getting somewhere."

He quickly made some notes, shut down the inquiry screen, brought up email, and formatted a message to Jim via Marian.

CHAPTER 21

The Problem of Kramer's Death

Marian got up from her chair and stretched. Her back felt a little stiff from being hunched over her desk for almost an hour. She had about five messages from Jim and two from Ed so far. This was certainly not what she had expected when Jim first brought home that silly invoice form from the book sale. It seemed kind of like a joke then. It never really occurred to her that a simple piece of paper would lead to being involved in anything, certainly not sneaking around trying to drum up evidence about McBride. She thought it would be a simple case of making a few comments to internal audit and they would take care of everything, but what Ed said at Pierre's made a lot of sense. She supposed that if it had been a problem with one of the clerical staff, then audit would have taken over and they could have just forgotten about it, but to make an accusation against a senior department head, well, that was something else again.

And what about Ed? She was still in a state of shock about him. His coming out of the blue like he did. She hadn't thought about the Governor Morris Inn for so many years, and suddenly, now she couldn't get it out of her head. It was strange though, the Ed she met at Pierre's was not the same Ed. Oh, he was Ed Campbell all right, but he was older, more subdued, more serious; he was not the same person she had the affair with. That person was young, slim, and quick to laugh and make a joke. That person was like the person she still believed herself to be, not the person she saw in the mirror each day. That person was older and different but yet the same. The mirror reflected her physical appearance and not her mental attitude. The mirror didn't see her soul, her feelings, her beliefs. It didn't see the little girl with the cut knee she received after falling off her bicycle onto some broken glass. In fact, lots of times the face in the mirror was a stranger, a much older person that she didn't recognize. She felt like the mirror with Ed. The face looking at her was different, was older, with no history. She knew the younger Ed, the carefree, joking, athletic Ed, not this serious, middle-aged international banker—married, father of two—who faced her over lunch the day before. He was different. A different person, not the person she knew before, but then she wasn't the same, either. That person sneaking across the lobby of the Governor Morris Inn was someone she knew, just as that little girl with the cut knee was someone she knew, but she was no longer either of them. She knew exactly who she was and it wasn't the person staring back at her from the mirror, she was the sum of her being, her thoughts, her memories, her beliefs, her emotions, her experiences. The face in the mirror was also a part of her, and it dictated many of her actions, but it did not control her. She thought of a time before the "looking glass" became such a seemingly all-consuming force in our society, a time when mysticism and spiritualism were dominant. A time when others saw you, and you saw others, but you only experienced yourself.

"Hello?"

A voice interrupted her meandering and daydreaming. It was a woman's voice. Her first customer of the afternoon.

❧❧

Adam Turner peeked into Jim's office. "Afternoon."

"Oh, Adam. What are you doing sneaking around Morristown today?"

Adam stepped into the office. "Actually on my way down to Liberty Corner. Have an appointment with a new prospect at two-thirty. They just moved in from North Bergen. Had some time to kill so I thought I'd stop by. Heard the news about Rayburn?"

"No. What news?

"They apologized. Turned out that new export manager of theirs was a fraud. Had lied on his resume. Didn't really have a lot of international experience. Apparently worked for a small export house for less than a year, and that was it. You heard that he was killed in a car wreck, didn't you?"

"Yeah, it was just down the road."

"That's what triggered everything. Report said he was high on a 'controlled substance' but didn't identify it. The background checks the police did failed to match with what he told the people at Rayburn. He was actually fired from his last job for screwing up the documentation on some shipments. Anyway, the AT I usually deal with at Rayburn said they were pretty embarrassed and found some strange things in his desk. They didn't elaborate beyond that."

"Well, I'm glad that's out of the way. Sorry the guy got killed, but it sure was causing a mess. The strange things in his desk didn't have anything to do with us, did they?"

"He didn't say. Just that he had started contacting some of their customers and was trying to deal with them on a personal basis."

"How well do you know this AT contact of yours?"

"Pretty well."

"Think you might be able to get any more information from him?"

"Probably. Any specific reason?"

"I really would like to know what he was doing that was so suspicious—if it was—and see if he might have been using the bank's name at all. He apparently made some strange comments to our documentary checker. Would just like to close this out."

"Yeah, sure. I can check."

"Good. So who's the new prospect?"

⁊ℭ⁊

As Ed stood in front of the file tubs after returning two of the files he had taken for review, Gloria Martinez walked by on her way back to her desk. "Hi, Mr. Campbell."

Startled, he turned quickly to see who it was. "Oh, hi, Gloria."

"Didn't mean to sneak up on you like that."

"Oh, it's all right. I was just concentrating on something else, and I didn't see you coming. By the way, how's the training going with Grace from Morristown?"

"It's really been good. Learning a lot. She's bright and quick. Have her over in export doxs now to see how documents are actually being handled and the procedures the examiners have to follow and how charges are put through. It looks like she'll be there for a couple of days, although she had to go back to Morristown today to help with some project. But she should be a big help when she has to do investigations."

"Yeah, the more you understand about the process the easier it will be to track things down."

"Susan wants her to get a really good understanding of the area. Said they get an awful lot of inquiries about document handling and charges and fees lately."

"She's certainly right there. Documentary examination is the key to payment. Mistakes there can be very expensive." He walked Gloria back to her desk.

"That's what Susan always says. It's where most of the serious problems are."

"She's certainly right."

"Even the postage thing, it's really amazing."

"What postage thing?"

"Oh, where we add extra weight to each package of documents."

"Sure, I know what you mean now. The extra ounce or two is just to assure that negotiable documents don't get hung up somewhere for insufficient postage and cost the customer storage charges waiting for the original documents to arrive so the shipment can be cleared. It's always better to add that ounce just to be sure."

"But it's five ounces."

They stopped at her desk.

"No, it's always around one. Everyone uses one or two. Any more would be too much, be overkill."

"I'm sure it's five, Mr. Campbell. I could be wrong, though, but Susan would know for sure if it's a problem."

"Well, you're probably right. The last place I was at it was only one. I could be mistaken. Every place is different. I'll eventually get the hang of everything around here. Gotta get back to my office."

Five ounces, he thought as he left Gloria and walked across the room. *That can't be right. I've got to find out about this.*

He headed to the hallway and went directly to the elevators to make a quick visit to the mail room, which was located on basement level two.

⌘⌘⌘

McBride was pacing back and forth along the side of his desk. He'd attempted to reach Charlie Field three times this morning, ever since he heard about Kramer and the accident, but Field had not returned any of his calls. McBride picked up the phone and dialed Alliance's number again.

"Alliance Automotive."

"Charlie Field."

"One moment."

McBride waited impatiently.

"Mr. Field's office."

"This is McBride again. Is he in yet?"

"I'm sorry, Mr. McBride, but no, he's still not available. I'll make sure he gets your message."

"But is he in?"

"He's scheduled to be here for a meeting at three, and it's very possible he stopped somewhere in the building on his way up. He usually does, as you know."

Field was a firm believer in not trusting anyone, especially when his own money was involved. He drove his managers to complete distraction, as he was always second guessing them and forcing them to defend any decision they made. It was his position that it was his company, and he could go anyplace and do whatever he felt like. If someone didn't like it, to his way of thinking, it usually meant they were hiding something. Charlie was clearly visible to everyone who worked for him and everyone who worked for him knew him only too well.

"Okay, just tell him I need to talk with him."

"I certainly will, Mr. McBride."

Damn, this better have been an accident, thought McBride. He was definitely worried. Field could be a real hard-nose with a violent temper. He had seen him in action at Alliance once when he saw a truck being loaded wrong. The boxes were being stacked too high and not tight enough; he knew they would fly all around the back of the truck on the first sharp turn. He took off after the warehouse manager like nothing McBride had ever seen. He wouldn't have put it past Field to go after Kramer and confront him directly. *Maybe Kenny knows something. Kramer was his boy before he left for Rayburn.* He picked up the phone again.

❧❧❧

The afternoon proved to be a busy one at The Walk. Ever since that first customer, Marian spent the last two hours behind the counter or in the backyard helping customers decide on purchases. She didn't go near the office PC the whole time and hoped Florence would show up soon, so she could find out what was going on. The whole idea of their trying to develop evidence of fraud against McBride continued to bother her. In the beginning, it just seemed kind of playful, but now it had gone well beyond that. She hoped they came up with something today because she wanted to get rid of the whole business and turn it over to First State's audit staff and let them run with it. It was beginning to make her nervous.

Florence finally showed up at three, but it proved no help in giving her a break, as she ended up taking care of a large order from a customer interested in garden furniture while Florence worked the inside. The last customer who was browsing through the shop finally decided to leave, and Marian was actually happy to see her go without buying anything. She thought of putting up the *CLOSED* sign for a few minutes while she checked the PC but then decided against it. Florence left at a quarter to six, and Marion was so anxious to sign in to the PC that she made no less than three typing mistakes when entering her password. Finally, the mail for The Walk began to download. There were four messages from Jim and three from Ed. She began reading them to see if any needed to be re-sent when she heard the door chime, as the front door was opened.

It was Florence. "Marian, it's me again. I'm back in the office."

Marian called back, as she double clicked on another message to bring it up for printing.

"Forgot my packages," Florence said. "Thought you were going to close up?"

"That Mrs. Weber was back again for another look at the black metal arbor. She still can't make up her mind." Marian clicked on the next mail message. "I swear the thing will probably rust out before she makes a decision about it. She was in twice with me."

"Think she's looking for us to drop the price?"

"I doubt it. I think she really wants it but is afraid her husband will object."

The printer continued humming along, and she began to retrieve the pages.

"Heavy mail day?"

"Actually, eh, this is some material Jim sent over for me to look at." Honesty being the best policy when trying to cover up something, Marian decided to be straight forward—to a point. "It's bank stuff that will affect us both." She put one of Jim's messages into his folder and hid Ed's folder underneath.

"Changing the benefit programs again, hah. There seems to be a lot of that going on. Ed just got a bunch of new stuff on the medical plan he brought home."

"Ed? Oh, Ed, your Ed."

℘℘℘

The collection of material continued through the day, as schedules permitted. Before Jim had completed taking notes on the third month of K E N Automotive statements, his schedule got the better of him. There was the pricing committee meeting, the introduction to a new customer by one of his account officers, the credit review of two customers who's credit requests were to be presented to the senior loan committee for substantial line of credit increases and a never ending ringing telephone and e-mail interruptions. Ed's day was no better. Luckily he had started earlier in the morning, or he would never have gotten to the files at all. Ed ended up being tied up most of the day with two substantial letter of credit problems that Jane Moran brought him.

℘℘℘

When Florence left to pick up her daughter, who usually stayed for an after school club meeting or sports team practice, Marian was glad to see her leave as she was dying to get to the PC and print out the rest of the e-mails. The original plan was for her to close up promptly at five thirty and then stop at Kings Supermarket in Bernardsville to pick up one of their "dinner for two" specials.

She figured she could be home by six thirty if traffic wasn't too bad. Jim would be in between six thirty and seven and they would call Ed at eight.

With all the adrenalin pumping through her system all day, it was beginning to make her nervous. She had the same impression of Jim when she spoke to him after lunch. They figured it might be an embarrassment for McBride in some way and maybe a slap on the wrist might be in order. Jim could probably stay anonymous as the one who notified internal audit of the breech of policy but now Ed Campbell was talking serious, career threatening and possible criminal penalties.

And what about Campbell, she had mixed emotions about him. He wasn't the Ed Campbell she remembered and, actually, she was thankful for that. It was unnerving that he didn't seem to acknowledge her and their previous relationship directly, except for that one comment at Pierre's. But then she didn't really want him to bring it up. Every time she heard his name, she expected some reference to that night twenty years ago. It was disturbing. Upset that he didn't say anything and yet fearful that he would.

She assumed that the incident at the Governor Morris was more significant to her than it probably was to him. Should she have a separate conversation with him about it or not? She was convinced that all the psychologists in the world would encourage her to seek "closure" of the issue with him. To get it out into the open.

But that was the problem, aside from "closure" being a concept she didn't believe in, as she felt it was one of those new buzz words of the 1990s that probably did more harm than good. It only opened old wounds rather than healing them.

She looked at it as a prime example of the "me" generation philosophy, as it was designed to appease the feelings of the "me" person without any real consideration of the effect it might have on the person being "closed."

Having a frank conversation with Ed about something he may not want to talk about or worse may not have meant anything to him and a subject he would really rather forget—not to mention what Jim might think—didn't sound like a very good idea.

Let's just go with the flow, she thought, *let's just let the chips fall where they may. If the subject comes up, I'll deal with it but for now.* She remembered her father's advice. *Let sleeping dogs lie.*

✑✑✑

McBride was sitting on the sofa in his office, reviewing a report prepared by one of the college interns who worked in the international department during the summer, when Gloria came in.

"Oh, sorry. Didn't see you sitting there. Thought the office was empty."

"Just breaking up the routine a bit. Gets tiring sitting at the desk all the time. You know this is pretty good," he said, referring to the intern's report. "I think we can turn this into an article for one of those international trade magazines." The report was a study on mistakes customers made when completing applications for import letters of credit. "See if you can find the file on that PC she was using and put it on your machine. The file's name is in the footer." He handed the document to her. "I've made some editorial changes. Let's call it…" He thought for a moment. "Letter of Credit Applications—Doing it Right the First Time! That sounds pretty good."

"What was his name again?'

"It was the girl. The one from Drew. She was pretty sharp. Anyway, forget her, put my name on it. I did the editing."

"Oh, okay. Eh, here are the taxi vouchers you asked for."

"Good. I ran out, and I promised to take Mattie to the theater tonight."

"And Mr. Field's secretary called. She apologized for not getting back to you and said that Mr. Field would call you later."

"Terrific. I won't be around unless he calls before six. Anything else?"

"No, that's it. Do you need me for anything else?"

McBride looked at his watch. It was four-fifteen. "No, you can take off. I'm leaving myself in a few minutes. See you in the morning. Oh, and don't forget I have that eight o'clock breakfast meeting so I won't be in until nine-thirty."

"I have it on the calendar. See you tomorrow."

Field, thought McBride, *you son of a bitch. Everything has to be done on your schedule. Well, I won't be there to get your phone call. You sweat for a change.*

McBride had managed to reach Kenny Mitchell earlier in the day and talked to him about Kramer. Kenny confirmed that he had become totally unreliable with the cocaine use. He screwed up set after set of documents and then started blaming the banks, just as he had done at Rayburn. He said he didn't believe that Kramer really understood what was happening with the invoice and packing list adjustments, he just knew K E N Automotive was getting very special treatment from First State. After all, Kenny had joked, how many companies had the head of the international department checking their documents for them? Kenny was of the firm belief, although he had no proof, that Kramer's accident was just that.

He assumed he had a little too much dope and just lost control of the car. It wouldn't be unusual, and he was sure that's what the police report would say. McBride felt a lot better after that phone call but decided to leave the Field telephone calls in place, figuring maybe Field should do some worrying for a change.

McBride got up from the sofa, put the voucher pack on his desk, and left his office, heading for the men's room to clean up before meeting Mattie for dinner. On the way over, he spotted Ed Campbell with an arm full of files walking toward the other side of the building.

"Whatcha got there, Ed?"

CHAPTER 22

The Review

The phone rang promptly at eight o'clock, and Jim picked it up immediately. He and Marian moved the speaker phone into the dining room from the den where they could spread out the emails and investigation results and have the necessary room to write notes. They planned to evaluate what they had uncovered, determine where more information would be needed and set a target for involving internal audit, should it appear they had enough to take to Robert Bradley, who headed up the audit division.

"Hello."

"Hi, Jim, Ed."

"Right on time. Let me put you on speaker."

Ed was calling with his speaker already on and was seated in the bedroom that he had converted to an office.

"How's that?" Jim asked.

"Sounds good."

"Hi, Ed," Marian chimed in to let him know she was there as well.

"Hello, Marian. So, are we ready for this?"

"I guess so," Jim said. "I've got to admit this was a very stressful day. I'm not used to sneaking around the office the way I did. Oh, and before I forget, I had to involve Paula and Grace. Grace was in Morristown today filling in with Porter on a project of his. Didn't want to but I ran into a problem with access to the money transfer inquiry system, and she had the answers for me. Thought you had better know."

"How was she involved?"

"She showed Paula how to format an international inquiry, and they actually did the inquiries on K E N Automotive. It wasn't planned. They found my inquiry notes and thought they were doing me a favor, which they actually were, although I wish they hadn't. But it's done now."

Ed grimaced at the other end of the line.

"Grace had no idea why I was making the inquiries," Jim continued, "and I encouraged her not to mention it to anyone, since she's not supposed to be working for me anymore. Hopefully, she'll just forget all about it."

"Okay. I'll keep it in mind, though."

"One other thing—I had the impression from Grace that McBride was pumping her for information."

"Really?"

"I can't say for sure. It's just some of the things she mentioned. Apparently, he's been using her as a backup secretary and was making inquiries about mutual customers between corporate and international. I could be just getting paranoid. I'm sure if we hadn't started snooping around like we have, I wouldn't have thought anything about it. It could be nothing."

"Something else to keep it in mind, though. How could he be suspicious of anything?"

"You remember that party of McBride's, the one over Labor Day weekend?"

"Yeah."

"Well, Marian and I were playing amateur detective to see if that invoice we found meant anything, and we sort of tried to drop the name of Alliance Automotive Export to see if it registered with McBride—"

Marian cut in. "Actually, we never mentioned the name to McBride directly. We just tried to work it into the conversation, while he was present, in the hope that he might use the opportunity to acknowledge it and maybe volunteer something.'

"And?"

"He never blinked. Acted like it went right over his head."

"I don't think anything goes over Larry's head. Are you sure he heard you?"

"Reasonably sure. I mean, he was standing there in a group of six of us."

"But you made no indication that you knew the significance of the Alliance name?"

"We didn't know the significance," Jim said. "If there is significance."

"If it's anything like what's going on with K E N Automotive, there's significance."

"Then you found something?" Marian said.

"I take it you haven't had a chance to go through the emails?"

"Oh, I skimmed them a bit, but I was just lucky to get them printed out. We were pretty busy today, and Florence was hanging around a good part of the day. It certainly looks as though you both were pretty active."

"Ed, why don't we begin at your end since that seems to be where everything starts?" Jim suggested.

"Okay. To begin with, I was never able to get my hands on one of the current K E N Automotive files where a back to back was directly involved. Obviously, that's where there must be some incriminating activity. The mere fact that all those files are missing is more than enough to raise suspicions of something occurring that shouldn't be."

"But what are all these other files that are listed it in your e-mails?" Marian had opened the ED folder, and both she and Jim were looking at the material inside.

"Ah, that's something entirely different that I stumbled on. I decided to pull a couple of the K E N files that were direct exports by K E N that didn't involve the issuing of a subsidiary credit to a domestic supplier. They all seemed pretty straight forward until I ran across one where a discrepancy was found, and the documents had to be shipped off to the foreign bank on an approval basis—"

Jim cut it in again. "I'm afraid you're going to have to explain some of this to us poor non-international types."

"I know, let me expand a bit. When the shipping documents submitted for payment under the letter of credit do not match up directly against what the letter of credit calls for, such as the merchandise description states two hundred dozen jeans and the letter of credit calls for two hundred dozen men's jeans, you have a clear violation of the terms of the credit, and there's no way to fix it. The buyer ordered men's jeans, and there's no clear evidence that that's what was shipped as the invoice and packing list just say jeans. This can be a benefit to the buyer when he's pretty sure the shipment contains men's jeans. However, where he would normally have to come up with the money for the shipment when the documents were presented in New York—or at least his bank would have to, even though the merchandise might not reach the buyer's port city for a number of weeks—now he doesn't have to pay until he's completely assured that the merchandise shipped is exactly what he ordered. What happens is that the New York bank will send a message to the foreign bank notifying them of the discrepancy found in the documents and ask them for an 'Authority to Pay' the exporter—the discrepancy not-withstanding. The importer's bank will then notify the importer and only provide the authorization when they feel comfortable. That could be a day, a week or, possibly, not until they have an opportunity to see the actual merchandise. Okay for now?"

"I think so," said Marian. "I got a quick education in this stuff the other day from Manny over at Blue Bird. Keep going."

"Well, any importer would be crazy not to take advantage of the situation and milk it for all its worth. So, depending on the relationship between the exporter and the importer, he might immediately authorize payment to someone he has a long history with or, for a new relationship, they would hold off payment authorization until the merchandise arrives in his port and he has a chance to examine it and confirm that they are the men's jeans he ordered. At that point, he gives the instructions to his bank to notify the New York bank that's it's okay to pay the exporter."

"This seems to be all strictly by the rules, isn't it?" Jim asked.

"As far as it goes, but this is the interesting part, when that authorization to pay the exporter arrived at First State, in the case of the K E N Automotive file I was reviewing, the date didn't match the payment."

Jim sighed. "I'm missing something. I don't quite understand what you're saying."

"I double checked our payment records, and it seems that when the payment authorization was received, the money was withdrawn from the foreign bank's account, as it should have been, but was not paid to K E N Automotive but, instead, was put into a non-interest bearing, cash collateral account."

"Why? Was there any reason mentioned in the file?"

"None. And just in case it was an exception, I decided to check some other files, not K E N or Alliance related, that had

'Authority to Pay' discrepancies. Guess what? They followed the same pattern."

"Ed," Jim asked, "what in the world is going on? Are you sure it's McBride?"

"Seems that way. Two of the credits were broken back-to-backs, and K E N was the account party on the domestic supply credits. Someone authorized debits to a cash collateral account or an over-and-short account to cover the payment to the domestic supplier and then reimbursed the account once the export credit was paid. All the files folders had that 'Notify LAM' stamp on them."

"So he had to know about it?"

"I can't see how he wouldn't?"

"Who else would know?"

"The payments section and refinance, as that's who controls the cash collateral accounts. There has to be a policy written down someplace for them to follow. These are just clerks performing a rote function."

"So if I understand what you're saying, someone is covering up a broken back-to-back transaction by making sure all domestic parties are paid on time even though we're actually waiting for approval from the foreign bank?"

"Can I ask a question?" cut in Marian. "Would anyone at the bank really care in this day and age? I mean, nowadays, if this was reported to senior management wouldn't they just say that as long as our customer is happy and no one is complaining, don't rock the boat. Isn't that the way business is being done these days?" Everyone was silent for a moment. "Well, isn't it? I mean, if you took this to the chairman, what would he say? 'Well, I'll have a chat with McBride.' Big deal! You guys still end up with a black eye and McBride gets a wag of the finger and a pat on the back with what amounts to: 'We appreciate your eagerness to develop ways to increase the bottom line, but maybe this is stretching it a bit. Let's see the policy put back to more conventional terms.' Let's face it, if you can't prove that McBride is walking home with a suitcase full of the money, you don't have anything." Marian put her finger on the heart of the matter. There was more silence.

"I suppose, technically," Jim began, "you could say he did benefit directly since under the profit plan structure his bonus is tied into meeting the plan, with some extra kicked in if he exceeds it. So the more he can kick up his revenues the more he earns."

"Still reaching," said Marian. "You're blowing the whistle on this means you reduce the bank's earnings. You guys are going to need more than this."

Ed jumped in, "Oh, I agree. This is just an indication of questionable behavior that can be used in conjunction with whatever else we find. The more and more I look into the international operations of First State, the more I'm convinced there's more to be found. The question is how do we find it?"

"Well, I have something in that regard," Jim said looking at the folder in front of him. "When Paula and Grace checked around the closed dates of those K E N Automotive credits you gave me, I found there was a very distinct pattern. Each letter of credit was closed with three offsetting transactions—one to the ultimate US supplier of the merchandise, one to K E N's account with us, and one to an account at Hudson Commercial Bank. It was the same for all of them. Just for the heck of it, I called a good friend of mine, Ian Ryan, who recently retired from the old Chase Bank and asked if he could have one of his contacts at Hudson do a check on an account. Ian, who's doing some consulting for them now, got back to me just before I left the office. He said that within a day or so of each credit received from First State, three additional transactions took place. All three were sent to Caribbean American Bank International, New York for further credit to Export Trading Bank of Antigua with two going to an account called AKEX International and the other to Harbor, Limited. All transactions seemed to be legitimate trade transactions, as they referred to specific letters of credit and merchandise numbers, so no one at Hudson would have taken notice. Also, we're not talking millions of dollars here and none of the reference numbers matched against any of the First State numbers."

"What were the dollar amounts?" inquired Marian.

"Ian gave me one example. Of a forty-five-thousand-dollar payment we sent to Hudson, there were two five-thousand-dollar payments, one fifteen-thousand-dollar payment made to Antigua, and the balance of twenty thousand dollars stayed in the Hudson account."

Marian exhaled loudly. "Is any of this telling us anything?

You're pretty quiet, Ed. Have you any idea what's going on?"

There was a pause on the phone line and then Ed sighed. "Oh, I definitely think something going on that's trying to be concealed. I think that's obvious at this point. Otherwise, all those transactions and subsequent transactions could have been handled by First State. Instead, the money is moved all around the place and then split into three pieces, and we have no idea if they get split even further later on. What I can't tell from what we have so far is if anything is illegal. We have some questionable practices going on. And it would appear the bank is being put at risk when you split off a back-to-back transaction, but there's no indication the bank has taken a hit anywhere. Also, if the money going to Antigua all belongs to a foreign national trying to move assets out of his country, in reality, it doesn't really matter to us. Jim, you said that your friend Ian found the same pattern with all the transaction information you provided?"

"I didn't have much to give him, only three of them but yes, the pattern was the same."

"I've got a hunch about all of this, but we're going to have to get another name to track."

"You mean Alliance?"

"Might as well be Alliance. I think it would probably also be a good idea if we could find out what McBride's other pet names are."

"There's probably someone who knows," Marian said, "and that's his secretary. In fact, I'll bet Grace even knows at this point, after having sat in front of his office for a few days. I'm sure she knows the names but has no idea why they come across her desk."

"I'm not sure I want to involve Grace," Jim said.

"I thought she was already involved?"

"Yes, but that was a very innocent request and could be easily explained away."

"How do you get the information then?"

Ed's voice came over the speaker phone on the Fairmont dining room table. "I suppose I could do it. Make some inquiries at the document window, see if I can find out if there's a list of special names that have to be referred to McBride. There may not be though. Just thinking about it, anything that came over the counter that way would probably have McBride's name on it to begin with. The document window isn't exactly a thinking person's job, and turnover is high." Ed visualized the small room at the entrance to the letter of credit department. It was pretty much the same at all the banks: six or eight metal or plastic straight chairs against the walls with one wall having a windowed counter that looked more secure than a teller's cage in the lobby. There was usually room for two people to work at once with separate stations, with a slot at the bottom of the glass to pass documents through and a round hole in the window to facilitate the hearing of instructions but not designed to encourage communication, in view of the contorted position you had to take to speak through the hole. There was also a locked door as well that, when opened, gave access to the department. The room was usually filled with messengers and "runners" from local freight forwarders, custom house brokers, other banks and, occasionally, someone from a customer who showed up to either deliver documents directly or to pick up a check. The people manning the desk were there to receive packages and provide receipts. Since one of the key elements in a letter of credit was the "latest date for presentation," it was critical for the presenter to have a clearly marked receipt showing what documents were presented and for what letter of credit. The problem Ed realized, upon reflection, is that asking the counter clerks to keep track of individual letter of credit numbers or customer names would be a lost cause and he was absolutely certain that McBride would agree. "No, I don't think the document window is the right place. I think the only place you're going to find anything is right on McBride's desk."

"Or his secretary's desk," Marian added.

"Are we back to Grace again?" Jim said.

Ed sighed then cleared his throat. "We could be. The alternative could be involving McBride's secretary directly, which is certainly a bad idea. Grace, on the other hand, may already know a good deal of what we need. She's been there, what, two or three times already. I'm sure she's seen lots of things come across his desk. You could, innocently, take her to lunch as a thank you for helping today and for old time's sake. She wouldn't have to know you're fishing for information."

"Oh, she'd know. Grace's a quick study. Besides, if McBride has been pumping her for information and if she thinks I'm doing the same, she's going to start asking questions we would not like her to vocalize."

"It still might work."

"Let me think about it."

"There is another avenue to follow, and that's the SWIFT and telex daily folders."

"What are they?" Marian asked.

"A copy of every telecommunications message the international department receives is kept in a daily file. It would just mean searching for recent messages with McBride's name on them."

"Wouldn't it look suspicious or at least unusual," Marian asked, "if the assistant head of international is rummaging through the daily files instead of having one of the clerks do it on your behalf? I know it would catch my eye."

"You're not recommending we use Grace again are you?" Jim said."

"Not necessarily," Ed said, and then the room became quiet.

Marian broke the silence. "So where do we go from here?"

"I think we should continue to follow the money," Jim said. "I pulled some of the K E N Automotive statements. Let me also get some Alliance ones, and let's see what happens to *their* letter of credit proceeds. If by chance any of them go to Hudson, I'll have Ian's friend check those as well. Besides, there aren't that many banks left anymore that handle the kind of international activity we're looking at."

"Well, okay," said Ed. He could be heard taking a deep breath and then a pause. At this point, he no longer sat at his desk but could be heard walking around the room. "Marian, are you going to keep being the go-between and assembler?"

"Yup, I'm in for the long haul."

"Okay. I think I'll do a little noseying around about Larry's pets. I'll bet Jane Moran knows at least one of the other names. She was well aware of his pets. I just have to figure out how to do it without making her suspicious, or even make my inquiry memorable, to make sure she doesn't accidently tip off Larry. I'll think of something. Anything else we need to go over? I'm getting hungry."

"No. I think that's it," Jim said.

"Okay, good night folks. We'll just keep doing what we're

doing and try to get together again tomorrow. "

They all hung up. Then Marian said, "We didn't set a time to talk tomorrow."

"We'll work that out. This is tiring stuff. Not just tiring—draining. I don't think I could ever be a cop. The stress would really get to me."

"Well, an undercover cop anyway. Besides, this is probably more stressful. Jim, what do you think about bringing in Carl Hansen?"

"Carl! What would make you think of Carl?"

Marian began putting their notes and papers back into the folders.

Jim started to undo the telephone to move it back to the office. "Carl may have been through something like this in the past. After all, he's been in banking forever. I was also thinking that since he and Bill Harrigan are close friends, he might be able to throw a few hypothetical situations at him. Maybe find a way to get this off our backs."

"This is kinda on our backs, isn't it? I wonder. Harrigan has what?…five years to go before he retires. Any scandal would be on his watch, but it should be well behind him when he leaves."

"Is that important?"

"Bite you're tongue. Nobody gets to be CEO of a bank these days without being a good politician. In fact, no one gets to be chairman of anything these days without knowing how to play the game, unless it's your company. So, yeah, you've got to not only evaluate the storm but also make sure you'll survive it."

"So maybe Carl isn't the answer?"

"No, I think you may be right, as usual." Jim walked over to Marian, put his arm around her shoulders, and gave her a hug and a kiss on the hair on the side of her head.

"We've gotten in over our heads on this one, haven't we?" she said, looking up at him.

"We're getting close," Jim countered, giving her another squeeze. "We're getting close."

He thought about involving Carl. *Maybe that would be the way to go. Carl, the senior ex-banker. The voice of wisdom that might be listened to.*

❧

"Number two sure has been busy today," said Gloria as she brought some mail into McBride.

"He's supposed to be busy. Why?"

"It seems every time I see him anymore he's got an arm full of files."

"I saw him carrying some files the earlier. I didn't think anything about it. Said he was doing research. Take a walk over there and see what he's doing."

"You mean spy?" she said with a huff.

"No, not spy! For peat's sake, Gloria, go and find out if you can help him. Spy! Give me a break. What the devil made you bring that up?"

"Well, things have been a little suspicions around here lately."

"How?"

She now had Larry's full attention.

"The extra time off for one. I mean you told me to get lost for a few days. You said I was overworked and needed a rest. You gave me some comp time and then brought Grace over to help instead of Anne or Louise."

"Whoa, hold on. Look, I gave you some time off because of all the extra work you've been putting in. That's it. Nothing more. As far as Grace is concerned, it gave me an opportunity to know a new employee who may head up inquiry one day. I also wanted to check her secretary skills and see how resourceful she would be in a completely new environment. Besides, why should you care? You think I'm lining her up to replace you? Is that it? Sure that's it, isn't it? Gloria, don't be so damn insecure. You're the best damn secretary I've ever had in my life, and the only way you'll get replaced is if you get run over by a truck or something. Now get yourself over to Ed and see if you can help him. No, wait! I'll do it."

"No, it's okay, Larry."

"No, I'll do it," he said, getting up. "I need a walk anyway. You just get your little rear end back to your desk and stop worrying about things you don't need to worry about."

Ed was sitting at his desk with a domestic letter of credit file open. It related to one of the Alliance Automotive export letters of credit he couldn't get hold of because as it was checked out to McBride. He had a yellow ruled pad next to him with notes on it, and the computer screen behind him was open to his email.

"You're a busy bee," said Larry as he stood in the door way.

Ed looked up, surprised, and instinctively put his hand over the writing on the pad, a move that was not lost on McBride. "Larry. You startled me. Didn't realize you were there."

"You certainly were concentrating. What in the world are you up to? Look at all these files," McBride said observing the pile on the desk.

"Research," said Ed quickly. He had already anticipated that someone might eventually inquire about what he was doing and had his story already worked out. Also, as cover, all of the files were of names not related to Alliance or K E N, except for the one he had in front of him. He just didn't think it would be McBride making the inquiry.

"Research?" McBride entered the office. "Got some sort of project going on? Haven't discovered something I should be aware of, have you?"

"Planning a seminar for customers." Ed leaned back in his chair by pushing himself off with his hand and, in doing so, shifted one of the files so that it more than half covered his notes. "I've always found that the biggest complaint customers have with any bank's letter of credit department is with the handling of documents. The whole idea of discrepancies. Most of them can be avoided if the customer just knew what they were doing. Thought I'd build a seminar around it. 'Avoiding Common Discrepancies in Documents,' I was calling it. Thought I'd use some real examples from our own files to show where problems and delays could have been avoided. Leave out the names, of course, protect the innocent—"

"Or guilty," Larry cut in. 'Sounds like a good idea. Gloria spotted you wandering around with all these files. Said you looked over worked. You need some help?"

"No, I'm doing all right."

"Too bad you didn't start this in the summer. We could have sprung one of those bright and shiny interns loose for you. In fact, I understand one of them did some work on import applications. Why don't you let me give you Gloria off and on? She's got a copy of the report the girl did. I'm going to be in and out over the next week, and something like this would keep her out of trouble." Ed could see McBride's eyes drift from the pad on

his desk to the inquiry monitor on the credenza behind him. He
seemed to be trying to read the names that were listed.

CHAPTER 23

Following the Money

Jim sat at the kitchen table sipping his coffee while Marian cleared the dishes. Finally, he said, "I do think you're right."

"Oh, that's good. I always like to be right. Now if I only knew what I was right about I would really be thrilled."

"Carl."

"Carl? Are we reversing roles here? I'm the one who's supposed to jump from subject to subject and completely confuse you."

"I'm sorry," he said, laughing. "Your idea of last night when you suggested bringing Carl Hansen into the picture."

"Oh, sure. I still think it's a good idea."

"The whole idea of our doing all this behind the scenes running around on our own doesn't make sense. From what I can see we have enough information in those two folders of yours to warrant at least an informal investigation by internal audit. When Ed calls at nine tonight, I think we should suggest discussing the matter with Carl and see if he agrees. I don't think I've had a decent night's sleep since we started playing super cop. This is not some spy movie we're in. I'm a banker, not a cop. I make loans, cops catch crooks. It's time to get things back into perspective."

Marian came over and put her hand on his shoulder. "I'm with you. I haven't had any sleep the last few nights either, and I find myself jumping every time the door at The Walk opens. I don't know why. I just keep thinking someone's going to walk in on me and catch me with all this bank information." She pointed to the two, now bulging, files on the corner of the table. "And I think what bothers me most is having to be devious. It's just something I'm not comfortable with. For heaven's sake, we go to church every Sunday, and at Circle, I talk about honesty and truthfulness, and we study the bible. Then, when I go to work, I start making up stories that won't be the truth, but not be lies either. It's like I've been taking lessons from Bill Clinton. I guess that will be his legacy: he taught a whole country that its perfectly okay to mislead and use other people to achieve your ends just as long as you don't *specifically* lie, if there is such a thing anymore. But then nobody seems to be responsible for his own actions if they can help it, especially in the nineties. I can't imagine what the next century will bring."

"My goodness, who wound up your soap box this morning?"

"Oh, it's just stress, I guess, and frustration. I don't know."

Jim came over, put his arm around her, and gave her a hug and a kiss. "Hang in there, Sherlock, we'll find a way to unload this."

The hug was interrupted by the ring of the phone. "I'll get it," Jim said and made his way to the kitchen. "Hello."

"Jim, this is Ian."

"Hi, Ian. Hey, I really appreciated the help yesterday. I hope I didn't put you out?"

"No, not at all. Gave me a chance to call up some old friends. That's what I wanted to talk to you about. Those transfers?"

"Yeah." Jim waved Marian over to him and whispered, "It's Ian," then he said into the phone, "No one got into trouble did they?"

"No, but there was more to it initially. Remember I mentioned there were two transfers with an Antigua address."

"Yeah." Jim moved to the kitchen table where they could sit next to one another.

"It seems there was a third transfer as well, but not on the same date as the first two. It usually occurred a day or so later and was moved to another US bank and not always the same one. Sometimes New York, sometimes Miami. Those accounts were usually in the name of a foreign individual, and there's no clear indication where the funds went from there, if anywhere."

"Are we talking money-laundering?"

"Not sure. But what I did want to warn you about is that my inquiry has now raised some concern with my contact at Hudson. He's looking at it more closely, and I have a suspicion he may refer it upstairs for consideration with regard to filing a suspicions transaction report with the fed. Even though his bank isn't involved, he feels he has an obligation to let his management know and let them refer it to their compliance department for a final decision. The only reason he didn't do it right away was that the amounts were so small."

"Whoa." Jim took a deep breath and gave Marian a concerned look.

"If they do, they won't mention my inquiry in the report, but you can bet I'll be mentioned informally as triggering the incident, which means I would have to mention you. The bottom line is that if you haven't formalized your own investigation at First State yet, I would suggest you do so as soon as possible."

"Ian, I appreciate that, and I certainly will. You won't get into any trouble, will you?"

"Me? No. Remember, I already have my pension in my pocket. The question is you. Do whatever you have to do to formalize whatever your suspicions are, and do it soon."

"Absolutely. We had planned on doing that tonight anyway, and this just forces the issue."

"What in the world are you guys up to, anyway?"

Jim looked at Marian before answering and, when Marian nodded her head affirmatively, said, "We're pretty sure we have a case of unethical behavior on our hands within the international group, but we're not entirely sure if there's anything truly illegal going on."

"How in the world would a nice domestic banker like you get involved in a case of unethical international behavior?"

"It's a long story, Ian. Why don't we talk tomorrow?"

"Any time."

"Ian, I really appreciate your help on this,"

"No problem. You've really got my interest up now, though."

After Jim hung up the phone, he and Marian made some quick decisions. The first was to follow their original instincts and call Carl Hansen, which Jim did. He explained a very small amount over the phone, and then Carl suggested they bring everything they had over to him that evening so they could evaluate it. Carl suggested that they could make the call to Ed Campbell at nine from his study.

Carl had retired a little more than a year ago but maintained close contact with the bank. His successor was John Paressi, a choice that was a surprise to many, but one that followed an increasingly common trend in banking and other industries: bringing in someone from the outside. The theory is that the individual would bring new, fresh ideas with him or her.

Not everyone believed in the new blood theory though. Unlike the corporate sector, banking had evolved to the "commodity" stage where they all had the same products and services and tended to be carbon copies of one another. The real problem became the "no respect at home" syndrome. If a junior officer made a recommendation of implementing a new or innovative procedure it would be suspect and in need of outside validation by a consulting firm. If the same idea came from a person recently recruited away from a neighboring institution, it would immediately be considered innovative and worthy of strong consideration for immediate implementation. Such attitudes also went hand and hand with the honeymoon and free ride periods, which permitted a new manager to get away with changes that his or her predecessor would never have been allowed, under the theory that the new manager had to establish his own style and needed to be given the tools necessary to succeed. This was, of course, how Larry McBride managed to get his little policies and procedures into place without someone questioning his every move. It also helped that he reported directly to the CEO of the bank, who had no international expertise.

Carl lived through the entire transitional period in banking. He had a bachelor's degree in history from Lehigh and joined one of the bank's predecessor in 1948 directly from college. He had watched it all change as congress and the various state houses around the country kept jerking the banking industry back and forth, in one instance expanding their powers and another contracting them. The one thing he learned in his forty-five-year career was how to cement relationships, not just within the bank but also the industry. He survived where others had failed because he knew how the system worked and had been a mentor to many of those currently in power both at First State and elsewhere. It was why Jim and Marian felt comfortable going to him with what they had, or believed they had, on McBride.

Carl met them at the door and, after the usual pleasantries, ushered them into his study, which was very un-bankerly. It was not filled with banking related memorabilia but with his books and research on the revolutionary war, especially as it related to the State of New Jersey. His undergraduate training in history never left him, and he contributed numerous articles over the years to historical journals and local newspapers, especially during the bi-centennial. Jim and Marian settled themselves onto the sofa and Marian placed her folders on the coffee table. Carl, before sitting at one of the chairs that sat in front of his Chippendale desk inquired, "Can I get you something to drink?"

"No, nothing. Thanks, Carl," Jim said.

"Coffee? Anything?"

"No, we just finished dinner. Sorry to put you out like this," said Marian. "Where's Olivia?"

"She'll be back in a minute. She's been babysitting in Raleigh for most of the week and just ran out to the store. One of the duties of grandparents these days, not that it hasn't always been. It's just the distance. Children and grandchildren used to live in town, or at least nearby. Now they're all over the country. Instead of a walk down the street, it's a ride to the airport. I would have gone with her, but we had the member guest golf tournament at the club last weekend. So tell me what you've gotten yourself into?"

As Jim and Marian explained what had been going on, Carl listened attentively. He took no notes. Being of the old school, he had been trained that it was impolite to do so. That's what memory and junior assistants were for. Besides, Jim had everything already written down.

"Tell me something, Jim, what do you know about this fellow Campbell? What do you think his motivations are?"

"I—I really haven't given it much thought. He wasn't the one who started all this. I was. I brought him in when I was looking for guidance, trying to find out if there was something going on that was either unethical or illegal or both. Something that might hurt the bank."

"The bank first," Carl mused. "So unusual to hear that anymore. What I'm trying to determine here is motivation. You just explained yours to me: protecting your employer. I understand that as you do and your reaction is consistent with what I know of you. I feel I would have reacted the same. But why is Campbell willing to go out on a limb?"

"I'm not entirely sure, but I do get a sense from him of there being some sort of code of conduct among people involved in international trade. It's just the way he talks. There seems to be some sort of belief or trust that international trade people have and expect from their peers. An extension of 'your word is your bond.' It's difficult to say. International people seem to be a tight group. They know one another, and if someone were to renege on an agreement, everyone would know about it very quickly. I understand there are international credit associations where such things are reviewed and discussed. That's not to say they wouldn't take advantage of an opening or a mistake, but it would have to be within the rules, whatever they might be. I don't know what to tell you, Carl, I just have a sense of his disliking unethical behavior. He also mentioned that he had been in a previous situation that had some of the earmarks of this one and it went on for some time and became pretty nasty. To answer your question Carl, I really don't know. I just haven't known him long enough." Jim thought of saying that Marian knew him better but realized that would not be a smart thing to say on a number of levels. Also, it probably wasn't true.

She knew Ed twenty years ago and had no idea how he might have changed. Marian sat there and had the same thoughts go through her head. She was hoping Jim wouldn't say *'Marian knows him better than I do.'* She knew she didn't. She knew a young, freshly out of college Ed Campbell. One without a life and work experience that would later mold him over a twenty-year period.

She couldn't answer Carl's question either.

"My concern here is one of personal gain versus the good of the bank," Carl continued. "Although it may seem that the good of the bank first is a dead concept, it's not, especially in the board room. It may be tempered with personal liability issues, but it is still there. At the executive committee level, one doesn't want to be branded as someone who hurt the bank, as hurting the bank will do damage to one's own career and could end it. So in leveling any type of charge against a senior officer immediately creates visibility, which means exposure, which could mean publicity and bad publicity is something for which you will always be remembered. So my concern here is that you have a great deal more to lose than Campbell. He's relatively unknown within the bank—you are not. If his motivation is to set himself up as the logical successor to McBride, and I'm not saying he is, he would need to position himself as the savior, the one who would have the solution to the problem—the one who would save the bank and not harm it."

"I understand that Carl. My problem is that we seem to have uncovered some very suspicious behavior, at best. Certainly, there seems to be some questions about ethics and poor business practices, that much I can see, and there seems to be some things going on within the international environment that I don't understand, but Ed Campbell does, and, from what little I really know about that side of the bank, I've got to admit it doesn't seem right."

Carl leaned back in his chair, put his hands together in prayer fashion, and looked up at the ceiling. Jim knew the position. He had seen it often enough over the years. After a long pause, Carl frowned. "Jim, you realize this is an internal audit matter."

Jim indicated agreement, silently.

"The question is how you make it one without getting smeared," Carl said.

Marian leaned forward. "Carl, do you think there's enough information available in these folders for internal audit to take action?"

"It's their job. If they need more, they'll find it. That's what they do."

"But if they tell McBride that they suspect some irregularities in the way he's been handling some files, won't those files suddenly disappear?" Marian said.

"Possibly, but knowing Robert Bradley, he'll figure out a way to get to the bottom of everything before approaching McBride. However, on second thought, starting at the top may not be the best approach. I think you might want to start a level down."

"You have someone else in mind?"

"Actually I do. There is a fellow in auditing on the 'Retail' side of the bank at the moment that has quite a reputation and is highly regarded by Bradley."

"But will he know what to look for?" Jim asked. "I mean, this is pretty technical stuff and, and as I've found out, a world away from the domestic side."

"If he doesn't, then your man Campbell can tell him. Besides, don't forget that some of the accounts you're looking into are individual international ones, so it won't be completely unfamiliar territory. Also, I understand he has a background in the world of money transfers and has done audits of the bank's funds transfer department."

"Who is he?"

"A man by the name of Anthony Carenza."

"Tony? Tony *the bull* Carenza? Interesting. McBride versus Carenza."

Everyone was silent for a very long five seconds. Finally, Jim spoke. "Sorry. Tony hasn't been around a long time, but with the recent mergers, he's developed a...shall we say?...reputation for getting to the bottom of things. So, Carl, how do we get this into the hands of internal audit and off our backs?"

Marian looked at Jim and thought, *Thank you, God.*

Carl made note of the Tony Carenza comment with a slight smile and simply moved on. "I think there are two things that need to be done. First, I'll approach Bill Harrigan, informally, and let him know the basics of what is going on in a semi-hypothetical way. In other words, I'll tell him he's got a problem without telling him who it is and see what his reaction is. I have a pretty good idea of what will happen. Second, you have to get the rest of your material together into a coherent format. I think you know what *I* would look for."

"I've written enough of them over the years. I haven't forgotten."

"Good."

"What about the phone call to Ed Campbell?" Marian asked.

"Can we do that now?" Carl said.

"It's a little early, but I don't see why not, as long as he's there."

"Okay, I'd be interested to hear what can be added to what you already have."

The conference call with Ed Campbell took place at ten minutes to nine from Carl's den. When Jim told Ed where they were calling from, there was a long silence from Ed's side of the line. Finally, Carl spoke up and explained his background; about how he and Bill Harrigan, the CEO of the bank, had been close for more than thirty years, of how they had worked side by side developing the corporate relationships that were now the core business of the bank. He also explained that he had enormous confidence in Jim Fairmont and that the primary purpose of his becoming involved was to see that what they had uncovered was placed into the hands of people who were experienced with handling such matters. He carefully explained that they had done their jobs as officers of the bank and now it was time to turn their findings over to professional investigators who, if it was warranted, would notify the office of the US Attorney and then let the investigation go where it might. All of this was explained in a very soothing and professional manner, which was typical Carl Hansen.

He was the father figure, even though Jim and Ed, who in their fifties, were already father figures to others. But it was different. Father figures today seemed to be positioned more like older brothers rather than sage advice givers. Carl was the respected voice of reason and experience with access to power. Jim was on a first name basis with Bill Harrigan, who was only five years his senior, but his relationship was a workplace one only.

Carl also made a point of giving some background information on Robert Bradley, the head of auditing for the bank. He carefully portrayed Bradley as brimming with integrity and one who would pursue the investigation to its proper end regardless of where it would lead.

Listening to all of this, Ed's range of emotion went from end to end. At first, he firmly believed that his short career at First State was definitely over and the smartest thing he could do would be to revise his resume as soon as he got off the phone. But as Carl spoke in that reasonable, competent, voice of experience, Ed's fears began to ease and, as had occurred with Jim and Marian, he could feel a weight being removed from his shoulders.

Here is a way out, he thought. *Maybe it won't be like it was in Taiwan.*

When Carl finally finished, Ed spoke up. "I suppose you're right. Sooner or later, this was all going to be public, and it's better if it's auditing that appears as the lead. Besides, I think there's enough of a pattern to warrant a good hard look."

"You found more names?" Jim asked.

"I'll say. Remember I mentioned the telex folder? Well, I made a formal inquiry about it. As part of my supposed project to develop a seminar on commonly avoidable discrepancies in documents, I asked Susan in customer inquiry to run down some examples for me using the telex files. She said she would have some of her people spot check over the past six months and see how many messages were sent to banks requesting discrepancy approvals. I told her I wanted to help, and she had Grace bring me the entire month of August. Grace was one of the two people she put on the project. Thought it would be good training for her."

"Grace," Jim cut in, explaining to Carl, "is one of my former pool secretaries who now works in international customer service." Carl just nodded his head. "Sorry, go ahead, Ed."

"The bottom line is that in going through the August material, I came across fourteen letters of credit that were copied to McBride directly. What was particularly interesting was that they were all from Venezuela and there were seven different beneficiaries. Alliance Automotive had the most. Also, I did some checking with Jane Moran, and it turns out that four of the seven are well known *pets* of McBride. Oh, one other thing. I found a memo from McBride about the suspense accounts giving specific instruction to park the payments for three days. All out in the open claiming it was common industry practice, which it isn't, but that if a customer were to complain, just back value it."

"Hello," came a call from the hallway. It was Olivia as she came in the front door of the house.

"So what does that mean?" Jim said on the speaker phone as Carl got up from his chair and gave a wave to Jim to continue. Carl headed for the door of the den. The door began to open as he reached it.

"To me, it means that McBride doesn't see anything wrong in what he's doing."

The door opened and, as Olivia started to speak, Carl signaled her to speak quietly.

Jim gave a wave to Olivia and continued the conversation. "Is he doing something wrong?"

"He's ripping off the customers. He's using their money for himself."

"You mean for the bank."

"Yes, the bank."

"The point I'm getting at is that in this instance he doesn't seem to be getting anything personal from this."

"That's true. But what's disturbing is the openness of all of this. If nothing else, this is unethical and poor business practice."

"Don't mean to argue the point. I'm just trying to find a focus.

I think what we're looking at is a bad practice that could bring harm to the bank."

Olivia stood quietly listening to the exchange, waved to Marian across the room, and then made her way over to her as Carl closed the door behind her.

"There's no doubt in my mind about that," Ed continued. "What continues to strike me is the openness. It's as though everything is fair game. Do whatever you can get away with until someone cries foul."

"Ed, it sounds like a bad practice, as I said, but let's face it, banks, in pursuit of earnings, have adopted lots of bad practices of late."

Marian got up to greet Olivia. They brushed cheeks in a formal greeting and then Olivia whispered, "Come outside with me for a minute so we can talk without interrupting them."

It would never have occurred to Olivia that Marian was a part of the activity that was going on or even that she might be interested in it. Marian was Jim's wife just as she was Carl's wife and they were expendable from the details of a business discussion. They were the support troops—not front line.

"Bad practices?" Jim said. "I'll say. Can you believe our operations people just approved a proposal to re-sort checks by dollar amount, so the largest dollar amounts are posted first? Sounds innocent enough but the idea is to create more bad check fees: have three checks bounce for insufficient funds rather than one."

Carl turned, a surprised look on his face. "You're not serious?"

"Oh, yes, I am. Paressi announced it only last week."

"And everyone agreed?"

"Not everyone. The problem is that the revenue jump can be significant. The retail people are making some noise. The concept is to have more checks flagged for insufficient funds but to adopt a practice of paying more of them into overdraft. So while the customer is unhappy about the twenty-five dollar charge, they are also grateful that the checks were paid. It's probably going to be Bill Harrigan's call. It was Paressi's consultants that came up with the recommendation."

"But that's—"

"Unethical? Bad business practice? Just plain stupid?" Jim cut in. "It's all around us, Carl."

"If that's a real consideration," Ed interjected, "I can see where my discovery of the three-day hold on funds will get a real yawn. How do they justify taking advantage of customers that way?"

Marian had stopped at the door when she heard the discussion take the turn. She and Jim had already had this discussion at home when Jim first told her about the proposal. "Customers aren't supposed to overdraw their accounts in the first place," she said. "You bankers can rationalize anything these days. Back in a minute." She scooted through the door after Olivia.

"It does raise a point, though," Jim pointed out. "There is a mind-set that we will have to deal with, and that's the earnings issue. If what we have uncovered hurts bank earnings, we'll be the goats, no matter what the outcome."

"All the more reason," Carl added, "to get your findings into the hands of the professionals. Internal auditing is *supposed* to be the goat, as you say. Hey, they're supposed to be the policeman of the bank's rules and regulations, as well as the governments. Let them do their job. If the bank decides that what McBride is doing isn't in the best interest of the bank, then they will make a recommendation that a policy be established prohibiting such action, if such a rule doesn't already exist. Not only that, you have no idea if auditing isn't already aware of what you have discovered and is either investigating the matter themselves or has already done so. Look, I applaud your efforts and, knowing Bill Harrigan, I'm sure he will too, although I can't believe he'll go along with this check thing you mentioned. Your efforts to protect the bank are laudable, but that's not your area of expertise."

"Carl, you have me convinced," said Jim. "So what do we do?"

Olivia took Marian by the arm and guided her toward the kitchen. "They look like they could use a cup of coffee and something to nibble on. Come and give me a hand."

Marian was about to protest and say *Hey, wait a minute, I'm a part of what's going on too,* but she knew it would be useless. Olivia was into full operational support mode. Men's work—women's work. Her job was to clear the way for Carl, to keep the interferences down to a minimum, to prepare the way so he could make maximum use of his time. She was doing her job. Even though Carl was retired and no longer involved in the bank and the business entertaining had declined dramatically, she continued as she always did. Carl seemed to have adjusted to his retirement without much difficulty. He just transitioned his time to other things like the club—both the one in New Jersey and the one in Florida—became more active in the financial review activities of the United Way, played more golf, and joined the board of directors of two local companies whose presidents were members at Somerset Hills Country Club. It seemed almost as though Olivia was having more difficulty adjusting to Carl's retirement than Carl was. But then Olivia hadn't retired. While Carl was transitioning, Olivia's world was turned upside down. Carl was her first priority, but he was away from the house for eight hours a day, five days a week. She had her own social calendar to maintain, her own circle of friends and activities that took up more than just time. They were an integral part of her life. Whether it was the Visiting Nurse Association, the school for the hearing impaired, the Episcopal Church, the Women's Association, the book group, she had a full schedule to maintain. Carl's retirement disrupted everything.

"Marian, if you would get those cups down and just set them on that tray there that would be wonderful," she said as she set about assembling the material she would need to make the coffee: fresh, decaffeinated beans, the grinder, the filter, and a carafe of bottled water.

As Marian retrieved the cups and saucers and began assembling everything on the tray she thought, *What am I doing here? Olivia's doing her job, but I'm a part of what's going on in the other room. Why am I here? Here I am helping her do her job and neglecting my own!*

She had to get back into the den, but she couldn't just tell Olivia she had more important things to do than make coffee for the menfolk. Olivia didn't regard Marian as one of the new breed of corporate wives that had their own agenda and careers. Even though Marian had The Garden Walk and it was a serious business, Olivia viewed it simply as a diversion. She believed Marian to be of her same mold. Marian, on the other hand, knew she was a transitional figure, one who had a career equal to her husband's and voluntarily gave it up to assume another career, that of raising children, and then move to a third career, as owner and manager of her own business. Carl had one career. Olivia had one career. Marian had three.

"Olivia, I just realized that I have some material in that folder that I brought that Jim is going to need. Could you excuse me a couple of minutes? I'll be right back."

"Oh, go right ahead. I'll be a while before this is altogether, and then we can have a nice chat. I've got to tell you about South Carolina."

"Something new?"

"I'll tell you when you get back," Olivia said, giving her a shooing motion out of the kitchen.

Escape, thought Marian. It wasn't that she objected to the way Olivia did things, that was Olivia, and she was entitled to do as she pleased. It was that Olivia made an assumption about Marian—although she was more than fifteen years her junior—that they were of the same breed, that Marian was one of the support troops, as Olivia was. In a way, Marian was flattered by Olivia's inclusiveness of her, but at the same time, she was put off by it. Marian viewed herself as an independent being, not someone that was a mere subset of another, although Olivia would never view herself that way and, in truth, such a characterization would be unfair, as Olivia's impact on the community through the campaigns she chaired and the events she sponsored would probably have a more lasting impact on the world than Carl's forty years of lending money.

The park in the center of Fordstown that Olivia campaigned for so actively and to which she donated so much of her time and money, will probably be there 200 years from now. It will have served as an integral part of a good many lives and bring joy and pleasure to many more over the years, all of whom will see the plaque honoring Olivia and her committee. Carl's risky loan to a startup company that became immensely successful and was subsequently bought out by a larger corporation will be long forgotten, just as the bank's name will be—if it exists at all—and Carl will undoubtedly be remembered as Olivia's husband rather than the other way around. It is the things that improve man's soul that are remembered, not that which improves his pocketbook.

As Marian reentered the den, Jim and Carl acknowledged her quietly. Carl was speaking, "That information certainly adds to the suspicious nature category."

"Carl, have you been involved in anything like this before?" said Jim.

"Not specifically this. There have been instances of operational improprieties that mostly involved the retail side of the bank. And there was a junior officer one time who was accepting too many favors and gifts from corporate clients, but that was all handled internally within the department. And, naturally, a good many people over the years have been let go for varying degrees of incompetence. No, as I think of it, this is the first time I've come across anything of the nature you've described." Carl paused thoughtfully.

"Is there something else?"

"Well, I really hadn't given it much thought before. I mean, it actually seemed quite innocent at the time but, in light of what you have been saying perhaps—"

Ed's voice came alive, "Did it have anything to do with international?"

"Yes, it did. Strange. Do you remember Larry's Labor Day party?"

"Of course," Jim said.

"There was a delightful couple there, the Domingos, Eduardo and Alicia. Did you meet them?"

"No," said Jim

"I did," said Marian. "They were from South America…somewhere…I believe."

"Venezuela. Very nice people. Larry and I helped them out with a financial problem they were having with their son."

"The lost check," Marian said.

"Precisely. I really didn't think anything of it at the time, but Eduardo made some gentle inquiries of me during the evening regarding the bank's policy toward the solicitation of accounts from Venezuelan nationals. It meant nothing at the time but, in light of what you've been saying, I wonder."

"Do you remember, at all, the specifics of what he said?" Ed asked. "Under the current rules in Venezuelan, nationals aren't supposed to have US-dollar accounts abroad. Although, in all fairness to Larry, there's no law that says US banks can't accept them. The trick here is that most banks don't actively solicit the accounts, knowing it would give them a black eye with the Venezuelan authorities—if they ever found out."

"It was along the lines of 'Your bank has certainly become aggressive in pursuing dollar deposits.' In fact, he wanted to know if we had a specific program in effect that was aimed at Venezuela."

"Why wouldn't he ask that kind of question of McBride?" Marian inquired.

"Don't know," Carl said, shrugging his shoulders.

"I wonder," Ed said over the phone.

"Speak up," Jim said.

"I was just wondering if McBride might possibly have decided that capital flight was a good product opportunity for the international division."

Suddenly everyone was silent. Finally, Carl straightened. "Ed, I truly believe that the best thing you and Jim can do at this point would be to assemble everything you have into a concise report, and I'll drop it in the lap of Robert Bradley. I will be more than happy to raise the issue with Bill Harrigan. I'm beginning to think we should let Bradley decide who he wants to run with it and not have us approach a subordinate."

"Then you think we definitely have something?" Jim said.

"You certainly have a case of suspicious activity by a senior official of the bank, and the fact that that activity may have been picked up by external elements make it important that the bank not be blind-sided should anything become public."

At that moment, the door opened, and Olivia appeared with a tray of coffee cups, utensils, napkins and a cream and sugar service. Marian jumped up and went to the door to help her.

"The coffee's decaffeinated, fresh ground, and I also have some hot water for tea, should anyone wish some," Olivia said.

"Thank you, dear," said Carl as Olivia placed the tray on the coffee table. "This is very nice of you."

"Marian, there's a tray of biscuits on the table outside, could you please bring them in while I get the coffee."

"Oh, sure."

As Olivia and Marian left the room, Jim said, "Ed, sorry you're missing this."

"So am I. And they say you don't lose anything by telecommuting. Looks like I've lost out on coffee and biscuits."

The comment produced a few smiles and chuckles on both sides of the line and seemed to ease the tension that had been developing during the evening. As Marian came back into the room with the tray of biscuits, Jim said, "Okay, Carl, will you raise the issue with Bill Harrigan before going to Bradley?"

"I will. I'll give him a call tomorrow morning and set up an appointment. In the meantime, I think it's quite important that you put together as much information as you can into as concise a format as possible."

"The usual one page summary with supporting material?"

"Precisely."

Ed cleared his throat. "Carl, when do you think we might be asked to provide what we have to Bradley?"

"I doubt that I'll get to see Bill Harrigan this week but I would certainly be prepared for the middle of next week."

Silence. Then Marian moved closer to the phone. "Should data continue to be assembled? I mean, the door has been opened to Hudson, and there still seems to be some outstanding issues that could be cleaned up."

Carl shook his head. "I think the main thing is to put together your suspicions and conclusions in a coherent manner and let Robert Bradley take over whatever additional investigative work would be required. If it turns out the US Attorney's Office has to be brought in, let him make that decision."

"Okay," responded Jim as Olivia came in with the steaming carafe of coffee.

"Ah," said Carl, "this is wonderful, Olivia. I think this is just what we needed."

"Hey, am I missing something else?" Ed squawked over the telephone.

"Only the best coffee and biscuits in town," Marian said.

"This doesn't seem fair. How bout I go to the Hansens next time, and you two stay home?"

"You get to travel to Hong Kong and other exotic places, while we domestic types get to go to Trenton."

"I know some people who think Trenton is quite exotic."

Somehow Marian's retort was not unexpected. "I don't think I want to know those people."

Olivia's coffee and biscuits had its desired effect—relaxing everyone. It was an old trick or, better yet, custom. She had timed it just right, as usual. Forty-five minutes was usually the maximum for intense conversation, after that the strain would produce errors in judgement or conflict. Olivia had seen it often enough at meetings and dinner and cocktail parties that she had attended with Carl. She learned it from a mentor, but it was fast becoming a lost art. The wife of an up-and-coming executive had a career of her own to pursue and was rarely considered a partner or even an asset in the exercise of his duties. Perhaps that was why women had had such difficulty in breaking that glass ceiling to the executive suite. Men did not make very good support troops. So many senior executives had had the loyalty and undistracted support of their spouses as they worked their way up the corporate ladder, something that was not available today to either sex. Perhaps that was why there seemed to be less civility in the marketplace. That was not to say that uncivility didn't exist, as it most certainly did, it was just that now there seemed to be an awful lot more of it and it was out in the open.

"Ed," Carl began, since the ice had been broken, "I don't believe we've ever actually met and I was wondering what it was that got you mixed up with the Fairmonts?"

Marian almost choked on her coffee and gave Jim a worried look.

"I've known Jim here for quite a few years," Carl continued, ignoring her, "and can understand why Mr. McBride's actions would awake his curiosity and why he would be disturbed by it, but what brings you to the table? I hope you don't mind my being so straight forward?"

"No, not at all. It's a fair question." There was a pause. "Quite frankly, I have a problem with honesty, or rather, the lack of it. At least, that's probably what you would call it. I guess you might say that I've seen what dishonesty can do, whether it be personal, private, or corporate. It tends to be destructive, eventually if not immediately. I've seen corporate dishonesty up close and at times have been both a willing and unwilling participant in its destructive effects. I know only too well that no good can come of it and it really bothers me when I find it. It's almost like the squeak of chalk on a blackboard. Quite frankly I took the position at First State because of what I saw and was asked to do during the last merger consolidation in which I was involved. I couldn't handle management's deception of employees and the way they were being used. But anyway, when Jim began questioning some of the things he was seeing in international, I suddenly realized there was a pattern emerging. There were little things at first and not just related to what we had been looking into with regard to the Alliance and K E N Automotive problem but before that. I came here at the beginning of August, and I just kept getting this uncomfortable feeling about the atmosphere in the division. It's not just something specific you can put your finger on, but it's there—it seems to be in the air. I don't really know how else to explain it."

"I think you've done just fine," Carl said. "I know that feeling only too well. I'm sure Jim has experienced it too." Jim nodded. "Everyone seems content and doing their job on the surface, but there's a tension running through the place."

"That's pretty much it. Although I must admit, that's probably a pretty common atmosphere in today's workplace. But to get back to my original observations and comments, I really have become a nut on this honesty thing. Don't ever ask me a question if you really don't want to know the answer."

"What about McBride?" Carl continued, "Why did you take the job with him?"

"Quite frankly, I firmly believe there are two Larry McBride's. The one I've seen in private sometimes is a true Hyde to the Dr. Jekyll that shows up at a conference or trade show. I knew him as a joking, pleasant, quick to tell a story and laugh type of guy and he knew his international trade inside out. I think that came from his shipping background. Although he's young, there's a confidence that just pours out. Now, to be honest, I did think he was too good to be true. I didn't think that easygoingness could run a division, so I knew a lot of what I saw was a front. I just didn't realize how much. That blow up he had when the call came in from the Rayburn export manager proved to be very typical. Carl, I don't think we may have mentioned that event to you. Jim can fill you in on that separately, but that was what started me down this road, although, as I mentioned, I was pretty well primed to go that way already. In any event, I think First State has a serious problem on its hands, and we've just been scratching the surface."

"Well, you have me convinced. Let me see if I can convince Harrigan. Ed, I appreciate your candor. I think we should let you off now so you can get some dinner."

"Yeah, I can smell that coffee and biscuits from here. Jim, I assume we'll talk first thing tomorrow, and I'd like to know more about this Domingo person.'

"Okay. First thing, tomorrow. And I apologize for springing Carl here on you."

"It's okay. I think it's probably the right way to go. We'll talk tomorrow."

"Night, Ed." Jim disengaged the speaker and broke the connection. "So, what do you think?"

"As the man said, the bank has a problem, but I don't think it's entirely the one you think it is."

CHAPTER 24

Asset Flight

It was Friday morning, and McBride was not happy. Two days ago, at dinner with Mattie, he began to get a feeling that something was going on around him that he didn't like. Being with Mattie relaxed him, made him think clearer. She was totally un-business oriented and had no interest in money, since she had far more of it than she could reasonably spend. The conversation dealt with art, music, books, and politics—all subjects McBride had no time for all week. Mattie took him away from the world of international trade and banking profits. But it was just that diversion that got him wondering. He started taking individual events, trees if you will, and began putting them together, so they started to look like a forest.

As Mattie chatted about John O'Hara and *Sermons and Soda-Water*, McBride was thinking of the book sale and then his party, to which he never should have invited the Fairmonts. Too much happened because of the invitation—their meeting the Domingos, the dropping of the Alliance name, the international seminar and Fairmont's questions, the Rayburn file, and the move of a secretary from Fairmont's group to international. He saw that as a win for him, a chance to steal a great employee and learn more about Fairmont, but he hadn't considered that it could be a win for Fairmont as well.

And then there was Campbell. Fairmont and Campbell were doing a lot together, and Ed was suddenly rummaging through old letter of credit files, and a number of them seemed to be tied to K E N Automotive. All of this just kept whirring around in McBride's head. As Mattie had switched from books to art and talked about an artist named Hodler and one of her favorite museums in Geneva, he began to wonder if he had become completely paranoid or if he had actually stumbled on to something. Maybe it was time to back off. There was certainly enough of a nest egg at the bank in Antigua. His problem would be Field, and he knew it would be a big one. Kenny had convinced him that Kramer's accident was just that, but somehow McBride had a sinking feeling that Field was involved.

For Charlie Field, backing off would not be an option, as he already had his eye on another small company he wanted to buy, and the extra money coming in due to the Venezuela connection would help. His plan involved obtaining a mortgage on his warehouse and McBride already suggested he go to another New Jersey bank for it.

McBride, on the other hand, didn't want any of Field's domestic business at First State, business where someone like Fairmont might end up dissecting Alliance Automotive's financial statements. It was all becoming too involved. The number of transactions had grown to the point of taking too much of his time. He seemed to be spending most of his nights checking and adjusting documents. He already cancelled a couple of out of town trips and planned to send Campbell on that trip to Hong Kong to finalize the Wing Sun deal. The problem with auto replacement parts and Venezuela was that neither one of them was seasonal—no break. And sooner or later, he was going to have to get some of the files in his office back to their proper place. By the time he and Mattie settled into their seats at the theater, he knew he would definitely have to start backing off, if not shut down all together. The question was how to do it without turning Charlie Field into a raving lunatic.

∽∾

It was seven-forty-five on Friday evening when Marian and Jim arrived at The Store for dinner. There would be five of them with Ian and Doris Ryan joining them and Ed Campbell. Jim had decided that he wanted Ian's international experience as an alternate to Ed's—not that he was suspect of Ed's knowledge, he just liked having an alternate opinion on serious issues. Good loan approval practices were hard to break.

The Store was chosen as, with five of them, they could take over the large table and a good portion of one side of the enclosed front porch that was used as an extension of the main restaurant. There was no possibility of McBride showing up, as he hated the place—too touristy and gimmicky—with the period dry goods store theme: cracker barrels used as tables for hors-d'oeuvres, farm implements and old advertisements on the dark wood paneled walls and a totally uninspired menu with a focus on, of all things, American food. It reminded him too much of the national chain with a similar theme, even though the food and wine at The Store were very good and presented the atmosphere of a small, cozy, candle-lit country inn and tavern rather than a bustling, impersonal restaurant chain family eatery.

There was a ten-minute wait for the table, which Jim and Marian anticipated, and Ed showed up just as they were being seated. Ian and Doris showed up five minutes afterward. Jim made the introductions and then they all comfortably settled in.

"Now there's a bank that has a lot going for it," said Ed, as he indicated the Midlantic branch across the street. One thing about the porch at The Store was the panoramic view of South Finley Avenue. The porch area had been closed in, but the windows had been maintained so the feeling of being on the front porch of a house was retained. "The trouble is they've made themselves too attractive. Some regional with an interstate ninety-five strategy will probably grab them. Someone that wants to cover the East coast from Connecticut to Florida. You'd be amazed how many people have them for their bank just so they don't have to pay ATM fees."

"Banking has truly evolved into a commodity business," said Jim. "There's not too much to distinguish one from another, especially on the retail side. Corporate's another matter. After all what does the average person need from a bank: a place to put your money when you get paid, a checkbook to pay bills and the ability to get your cash out when you need it?"

"My, what would we do without the ATM?" Doris asked. "You know, I don't think I've been inside my local branch in almost a year. Between the ATM and the drive-up teller, I sometimes wonder why they have branches at all."

"Now," said Jim, "there's a question banks are wrestling with. Are the ATM and the PC really the future of banking? And if they are, why are all these new community banks opening up all over the place? It's a real problem. The big banks see Doris here as their ideal customer. The automatic deposit of salary, the cash withdrawal by ATM, the deposit by the drive-up window, and bill paying by check. The only thing more they would like would be for the deposit to be at the ATM and bill paying by the PC. Doris is pure and simple core earnings."

"Somehow I never thought of Doris as pure and simple," said Marian, which produced a burst of laughter. It also produced Nancy, the waitress, who did not introduce herself, thankfully, but the hostess who sat them had identified her when leading them to the table. Marian chuckled. "Sorry, Doris, I couldn't resist that one."

"This one? When did you ever resist any one?"

"Oh, you'd be surprised at how many I let go by."

"Can I get anyone something from the bar?" said Nancy, smiling.

"It probably looks as though we've been there already," Ian replied.

"Well, I haven't," said Doris. "I'll have a vodka and tonic."

"Make that two for me," Ian joined in.

"That's three vodka tonics?" repeated the waitress.

"Oh, no, one each."

"Oh." She made an adjustment on her pad and then looked at Marian.

"White wine for me. A Chardonnay?" The waitress nodded and went on to Jim.

"Cabernet for me."

Another nod and she then turned to Ed.

"You wouldn't happen to have a Guinness, by any chance, would you?"

"Sure."

"Good, then a Guinness it will be."

More notations. "I'll have these for you in a couple of minutes and be back to take your orders. The specials are on the inside of the menu and also on the blackboard back here." She pointed to the wall in the center of the room. "Let me know if you need anything." And with a swish of her gingham, period costume, she was off.

"Marian, you're terrible," Doris said.

"Have to call them the way I see them. Opportunities present themselves, and they have to be taken advantage of."

"I sometimes wonder how she survives at the shop," said Jim. "I'm sure the opportunities for verbal darts are endless, especially with all the tourists that have been showing up of late."

"The shop is something different. I would never abuse a customer. I reserve that for friends and family. The customer is sacred. That's not to say that a good many things don't come to mind and I do have to bite my tongue from time to time but then I have Jim to dump it on in the evening. He's a wonderful dart board."

"Yes, well, if you see some stains on my shirt during the meal it will be just the results of leakage from past missiles."

"You two are a wonder," said Doris. "Now, Ian here wouldn't know if you threw a dart at him. To him, it would just go right over his head, even though everyone else would see it sticking right in the middle of his forehead."

"That's not entirely true. Just because I might choose to ignore it doesn't mean I'm not aware of it. Just being courteous, that's all. Being polite is important. You get points for being polite."

"Polite, my foot! You're dense as a post."

"Ah, so that's the problem."

"Marian, you're impossible," said Jim giving her a tap on the shoulder.

"You leave yourself open I can't be responsible."

"Jim," Ian said. "Do you ever get even?"

"Even? Even? You've got to be kidding. I'm just working on survival. I gave up trying to get even twenty years ago. Now I just sit back and enjoy the fun because you folks are along and I can be left alone—somewhat."

"Now wait a minute. I'm not that bad. It's all intended in good fun. Besides, you must admit you all deserve it. Poor Ed over there must think we're all out of our minds."

"No, no. Just happy to be on the side lines."

"Don't worry," said Doris. "Your time will come. Our Marian here has the quickest tongue in town."

"Now there's a line I would definitely stay away from," said Ian. There was a pause and then a burst of laughter.

The Ryan's and Fairmont's had been friends for a good many years. Ian and Jim met almost fifteen years ago when Ian was with Bank of Montreal. They were attending a conference in Toronto sponsored by the Bank Administration Institute and sat on a panel together discussing the differences between United States and Canadian financial statement presentation and analysis. They kept in contact after the conference, and when Ian was considering the move to Chase, he stopped by to see Jim and subsequently had dinner with him and Marian. When they came house hunting in New Jersey, Marian took Doris under her wing, and they became good friends. The Ryans eventually bought a house in Chatham Township, right on the edge of New Vernon and a ten-minute drive to Fordstown. Ian took his retirement from Chase, at the age of sixty-two—with the takeover by Chemical on the horizon. The package available was too good to pass up.

"Not to change the subject," Jim said, "but have you two decided what you're going to do yet?" Then he made an aside to Ed. "These two have been thinking about buying some property in the south. Can you imagine giving up the Garden State for North Carolina?"

"Where do I sign up?"

"Oh, great! Another one."

"To answer your inquiry, Mr. Fairmont," replied Ian in his best British accent. "I am obliged to reply in the affirmative."

"You're kidding," said Marian.

"No," said Ian. "We've decided to go."

"Where about in North Carolina?" said Ed. "I have some relatives in the Raleigh area."

The drinks arrived and Nancy quietly and accurately distributed them. She did her best not to interrupt the conversation, which was a welcome change from most restaurant wait staff. In fact, after the drinks were delivered, Nancy stood quietly while they continued talking, not wanting to interrupt. Finally, Jim said, "Why don't we get the ordering done, so we don't hold things up too much."

Ed picked up the menu that was sitting in front of him. "I haven't even looked at this yet."

"If you'd like a few more minutes I could come back."

"No," Jim continued, "let him look and we'll order, I think the rest of us have the menu memorized by this time anyway, and we saw the list of specials on the way in. I'll coach Ed here, and you folks go ahead."

The ordering took a few minutes to complete.

"So tell me," Ian started, "where are you with this mess you've stirred up at First State and how do you think I can help you?"

"We're looking for some independent guidance from outside the bank," Jim said. "We're at a bit of a crossroads. You already know some of the background, but we've come to a decision point: do we drop it in the hands of someone else or drop it all together?"

"So you've definitely found evidence of wrongdoing?"

"That's a good part of the problem," Jim continued. "At this point, I've become convinced that we, meaning us, can't find a clear path of evidence. I mean we're not trained investigators. If we had planned on being police, we would have gone to John Jay College of Criminal Justice or something, instead of business school. To be honest, I don't think we know how to bring this to a head."

"Just what is it that you think you've found? I know from what you've asked me to find out, it certainly rings of money laundering, but the amounts aren't world shattering."

"Why don't I let Ed pick it up from here? I think he has a better perspective and speaks your language."

There was a slight pause as everyone turned to Ed and waited for him to speak, which he finally did. "Ian, what I think we have here is a case of asset flight." Ian perked up and was about to say something but Ed held up his hand and stopped him. "Now I know exactly what you're going to say. There is nothing illegal about accepting asset flight funds as long as the money itself is not illegal." Doris looked puzzled, and the look was not lost on Ed. "Asset flight may be illegal in the country where the money is coming from, but as long as the funds were legitimately earned, or even inherited, if someone wants to move them to a US bank, there are no restrictions in the US preventing us from receiving them. That being said, if there is a reason to believe, on our part, that the funds may be tainted, then we're supposed to notify the Fed."

"So you think there's some funny money involved here?" said Ian.

Ed took a deep breath. "So far we don't really know. Look, I think there may be something a little trickier here. I have a feeling from looking at some of the transactions that the bank may be involved in soliciting asset flight funds and may even have gotten into promoting it as a way of increasing revenue."

"Ah," Ian said.

"That's a twist," Jim said. "When did you come to that?'

"It's been kind of in the back of my head for some time when I started putting together some of the names that were involved."

"Excuse me just a moment," said Ian, "but if that's the case, why the need for moving money all around and splitting transactions? Why not just keep the money at First State or at least try to keep it there? That's where the real income will come from."

"That's one of the puzzling parts. You're right. From the US standpoint, there's nothing illegal about handling asset flight funds but the secretive maneuvering around the transactions, the hiding of files, the protection of the names, the splitting of transactions, multiple bank transfers and the movement of funds to known safe havens says there's something else going on here. There has to be."

"Where there's smoke there's fire?" said Marian.

"Exactly. The problem is we can't find what's smoking. We suspect something, and we can smell it but we can't tell what it is and may never be able to."

"Which is the main reason I thought you could help, Ian," said Jim. You've been down this road before." Ian looked puzzled. "Oh, not with the asset flight business but with the overall issue of unethical behavior that, if uncovered, becomes a major embarrassment for the bank. The Mexico problem?"

"Oh, yes I see what you mean. That was quite a while ago and a couple of banks back. Wasn't even a US bank, in fact."

"I know," Jim continued, "but I believe this situation could be similar where the embarrassment to the bank may be more serious than the criminal activity, if there is any. Look, we have stepped into something here which may be more of a liability for Ed and me than it could be for McBride. We could easily be tabbed as troublemakers or whistle blowers or whatever. That's why I thought of you and that Mexican problem. Just how was that handled?"

"For the benefit of those of you who are unfamiliar with what Jim is referring to, which I guess is really Marian and Ed, since Doris I'm sure remembers what I went through on this one." Doris nodded her head. "The Mexico thing, as Jim so delicately put it, had to do with an officer of the bank who went local. Now what I mean by that is that he began adopting the local business way of doing things as his own personal style. There is a way of doing business in the US, Canada and most of Europe that is somewhat different from the way things are done in what one might refer to as a second tier developing country. There is the issue of a much closer relationship between banks and corporations, of favor and courtesies extended within business relationships. One helps one's friends. The point is that this individual began adopting the ethical business standards of the country in which he was located. The problem was that, while generally accepted behavior in Mexico for a Mexican businessman, those standards were not compatible with the British bank by whom he was employed. That being said, however, he was very good at what he did. Was very well connected and respected locally and considered a valuable asset to the British bank. The problem that Jim is alluding to revolves around a desk officer in London inadvertently finding out that the local representative had participated in some local business ventures with some of the bank's clients, and that his participation was not on an equal footing. That is to say, he was offered an equity participation at a price below market level. There was also the free use of vacation villas, boats, and trips. Now, this was not tied directly to any specific loan or business venture he might have recommended, it was just the way things were done among business friends. Am I painting a clear enough picture?"

"Oh, it's quite clear," said Marian.

Ian then looked at Ed. "Oh, I'm quite familiar with the problem."

"To continue, our desk officer based in London began questioning the conduct of our representative and brought a number of his business associations to light. Management was not happy. They were placed in a position of chastising their very popular and highly productive—income-wise—local representative and eventually had to re-assign him. Our desk officer, while publicly applauded for, quote, protecting the bank, unquote, was put on the shelf."

"But why?" Marian inquired. "He didn't do anything wrong."

"Oh, I agree. But the reality of the situation was that no one seemed to feel comfortable having him work for them. I suppose there was the thought that he was some sort of avenging angel who would be watching over them as well."

"I still can't believe they could all be so insecure," said Doris. "To think his career was damaged just because he was the messenger. He didn't do anything wrong. And I suppose the other fellow made out just fine?"

"Actually, I did hear of him a few years ago. Remember, he was very good at what he did and was a success in that post to which he was relegated. He actually left the bank to take a senior position with a Mexican financial group, where I think he still is."

"And the desk officer?" inquired Ed.

"Have no idea. I would imagine he eventually left the bank as well. Perhaps he's done well. I have no idea."

"Okay, Ian," Jim said, "you know pretty much what we have picked up on McBride, how do we unload it without being tainted?"

"You've got a bit of a different situation. As far as I can tell, you have the potential of possible criminal activity, if it could be proven that he was assisting in a money laundering scheme and knew the money was tainted. The problem is you don't know."

"How do you feel about Carl's idea of notifying senior management?" said Ed.

"It's a good one. I assume he's not naming names, just making a so-called heads up advisory."

"That's correct," Jim said. "He will not mention either McBride or us. He will just put Harrigan on notice."

"I personally believe it's probably the best approach and if Carl hasn't mentioned it, somebody had better get to auditing."

"He has," said Jim.

"Good. Your best bet for not being tainted by this is that there is no criminal activity involved, although when I hear the word Antigua ... I don't know. You just have to hope that what is involved is a bad, or better yet, an ill-advised business practice. That way auditing can take the lead and you two can drift into the woodwork. One other thought, I assume you'll put something together in writing, make sure it's on blank stationery without your name on it. Also, deal only with the senior auditor or head of audit. I know I sound a little paranoid about this but you don't want to be involved or have your name attached to anything and that won't be a problem unless some illegal activity is suspected and the US Attorney's Office becomes involved. At that point there will be no way to stay out of it."

"Ed," began Jim, "it sure seems as though we have our work cut out for us this weekend."

"Anything you need I'll be happy to help with," said Marian. "I can leave Florence alone Saturday afternoon without a problem. You know there's one thing that has already bothered me about all of this and that's why would he do it? I mean, Larry is young, successful, has everything going for him, certainly is making enough money to support himself extremely well; why get mixed up in something that could ruin it all?"

CHAPTER 25

McBride Investigates

McBride felt nervous as he rode up in the elevator to the international department on the seventh floor. He intended to head for home but decided there were too many loose ends so he turned his BMW 740 around and headed back to Newark. He arrived just before nine o'clock and being Friday there were few people around. The elevator came to a stop. Sounds were enhanced in the quiet. The noise of the elevator door opening was something he never noticed before. The sound of his shoes echoing on the polished marble floor as he made his way to the oak double doors directly in front of him seemed extremely loud. Only half the lights were on in the outside hallway, which indicated that the cleaning crew had finished its work and moved on to somewhere else in the building. They would be around until late in the evening, as they usually were on a Friday, polishing floors and cleaning carpets—work that was not done during the week. He opened the door with his key and switched on the main reception area lights, which had also been shut down when the cleaning crew finished. A quiet eeriness permeated the silence. He often stayed late but rarely alone as the cleaning crew just worked around him and he usually left the lights on when leaving, as he knew the cleaners or a security guard would turn them off.

He made no attempt to go to his office but straight to Gloria's file cabinet, where she kept the key box. Larry had a hard and fast rule that everyone was to lock their desks and cabinets but a copy of the key was to be provided to their supervisor. Although the building was secure, and guards did patrol the floors on a regular basis, various pieces of equipment still managed to disappear. Even PC's and printers had been known to vanish so every item was cable locked or bolted down and every desk, cabinet and closet locked. Laptop computers were required to be removed from docking stations and locked into desk drawers or cabinets. No work was to be left out. It was all placed in fireproof overnight cabinets and locked. The file tubs had large covers that were put in place every evening. This was an area of the bank filled with negotiable documents that gave title to merchandise so that the shipping papers were always placed into fire proof drawers and kept secure.

McBride's object—the keys to Ed Campbell's desk and credenza. There would be only two keys since, although there were at least three locks on each desk—one for the center drawer, one each for the left and right side, and at least one and possibly two for the credenza, depending on its size—it was mandatory that the locks for each desk set be opened by the same key. The private office door would be closed but not locked so cleaning could be done. However, it was lockable and the door key was a substantial one, heavy and bulky, so it could be easily identified but the desk keys were smaller and not particularly durable. More than once a month the maintenance people were called to retrieve a key that had been broken in the lock of someone's desk. Non-official employees usually ended up carrying a minimum of two keys, one for the desk and the other for the rest room. The key for the latter was a particular necessity as more than one person had been attacked in the rest room. The constant flow of traffic coming on and off the floor with runners and messengers delivering documents, made the room a relatively undesirable place until the locked door policy came into effect. The restroom door locks on the seventh floor were keyed the same as the sixth and the eighth to keep unwelcome visitors from moving from floor to floor. More than once Larry had requested that an additional restroom be put inside the secure area of the department but the construction of the building, designed with the restrooms near the elevators on each floor for general access, made it impossible. It was a great irritant to Larry, as it was to the other managers, to have to carry at least four keys, since they had not only their desk keys but also the office and department doors, as well as the restroom key. Many had taken to leaving their office doors open and unlocked in an effort to cut down on the keys they carried. It was one of the events that triggered Larry's curiosity about what Ed

Campbell was researching, as he noticed his door locked at night when he knew it had been open before.

The spare key to the credenza that sat behind Gloria, where the key box was located, was always kept in the small glass bowl of paper clips she kept on her desk. The spare keys to the rest rooms were under her "in box." Everyone knew where the keys were, so if they left their keys at home or were out sick, access could still be obtained to their desk and work could go on. This whole issue of keys and access only developed during the 1980s with the advent of more portable office equipment and a more unruly looking group of delivery people, not to mention an office culture that was less than trustworthy. The security people had also changed. Once the province of former policemen, who had retired after twenty years on the force and then joined local banks as guards, where they would work until social security became available to them, they had been replaced by security cameras and outsourced to security firms, just as the cleaning staff had been outsourced and were no longer bank employees. The guards and cleaning staff constantly changed. You no longer saw the same face every day in the morning as you came to work and the same face in the evening if you stayed late enough for the cleaning crew to show up. The locking of desks and restrooms doors was as much a feeling of insecurity about the new security as it was anything else.

McBride immediately found the key among the paper clips. He opened the credenza, retrieved the key box, and quickly found the keys to Ed Campbell's office. Each set of keys hung on a small hook and were clearly marked on a round tag with a supervisor's name. On the reverse side of the tag was the start-up password for the individual PC. This was Gloria's doing. Quite a few staff people complained about giving up their passwords, claiming that to do so was a breach of company security. Gloria's argument was that the password was just another key and, by company policy, had to be included. Some felt it was an invasion of privacy and McBride told them point blank that if they wanted privacy, they should go home and, as long as they were using company property, then the company had a right to know what they were doing with it. Otherwise, they could provide their own PC and lease space from the company to work. Besides, there were no secrets on PC's any more as they were all networked and, via the network, data security regularly inventoried all PC's to make sure no illegal software was being used and only authorized individuals were using the internet. It was also the way in which the latest updates for anti-virus software were distributed to each PC in the company.

What had triggered McBride's suspicions were those files he had seen on Ed's desk earlier in the week. He recognized some of the names and Ed seemed startled when he first came into the office. Maybe it was nothing, but he had to be sure. He was becoming worried anyway. The whole operation had become too big. At first, it was a very simple arrangement. He had been approached by a Venezuelan importer, who he met on the plane to Caracas. They were sitting together in first class and struck up a conversation. McBride accepted an invitation to visit his office.

The topic of Venezuelan exchange controls was a natural one and was on the agenda of every meeting he attended. Venezuela was oil rich but its appetite for imported goods continually created foreign exchange problems. And whenever there was a downturn in oil demand, either real or artificial, Venezuela felt the pain very quickly. McBride's new acquaintance inquired about opening a US-dollar account with First State. He already had an account with a Miami bank but didn't want to keep all of his assets in one place. McBride agreed immediately. It was the beginning of a long relationship. It was also the germination of the idea of soliciting such accounts and to develop other business with the individuals as well.

McBride turned on the light in Ed's office and then closed the door behind him. The concise space had room for the desk and two chairs in front of it with a credenza behind, on which the PC, monitor, and printer were located and one bookcase to the side. The one window to the left as he entered overlooked an internal courtyard. As with most office set-ups, the senior person on the floor was the only person with a view. Those offices were usually set up in the same location on each floor. If you wanted to eliminate senior management, all you had to do was take out one corner of the entire building and leave everything else alone.

The desk was relatively neat but not cleaned off. There were a couple of thin file folders stacked on the right side, the telephone was on the left with the *IN* box in front of it. There were papers in both the *IN* and *OUT* boxes and some other papers stacked alongside the *OUT* box. He took a quick look at the papers on the desk and then dismissed them. McBride had no real idea of what he expected to find, but he figured the best place to look would be on Ed's PC. He switched it on and, while it initialized, he unlocked the credenza and desk. The larger drawer of the credenza was used as Ed's overnight drawer, and there he found some of the letter of credit files and a telex folder. The files were all related to either Alliance or K E N.

"Shit!" he said out loud.

The files were innocent ones, which concerned shipments to other than Venezuela, but if Campbell wasn't snooping, why weren't there other names? McBride opened the telex folder and found a sheet of paper, indicating letter of credit numbers where discrepancy SWIFT or telex messages were sent to banks. The folders were still referred to as telex folders even though few telexes were sent any more. Larry turned over the sheet and saw his initials written next to a series of other letter of credit numbers, this time in Ed's handwriting.

"What the fuck?" he mumbled.

The PC beeped behind him as the password window popped up. He entered the series of numbers and letters listed on the reverse of the key tag and then waited while initialization finished. Where to look? He immediately went to the WordPerfect program and, while he waited for it to start up, he took another look at the paper with his initials on it. The program came up and he immediately checked the list of most recently used files. All legitimate business stuff. He then went to Explorer and, while waiting for that email program to come up, he rummaged through some of the other drawers. The drawers yielded nothing of interest. He turned his attention back to the PC and checked the *SENT* folder but couldn't find anything of interest; the same was true of the *IN* folder. Larry then clicked on *READ MAIL* and, when the internet sign-on screen popped up requesting a password, he merely entered the password that was used as a sign on and the modem began dialing. He waited. Four messages eventually appeared in the un-read list. The last one was from thegardenwalk@ISSH.NET.

CHAPTER 26

Suspicions

When Gloria came in at eight o'clock she found McBride's door closed and a note saying that he didn't want to be disturbed for any reason. He had underlined the word *ANY*. She had no idea if he was alone or in an unscheduled meeting. Her calendar showed that his morning was clear until ten o'clock, when he was to attend a presentation on letter of credit technology improvements by a consulting firm that Ed Campbell had invited. So she did as told: no calls went through and he was unavailable to everyone.

Ed also arrived early, but his appearance at seven-thirty was due to an unusually good traffic day—I-78 seemed to be wide open with traffic cruising at seventy mph instead of the usual sixty. He put it down to a heavily overcast morning, so there was no rising sun to blind the eastbound traffic. He also managed to hit every traffic light in Newark just as it turned green. There wasn't even a line at the coffee wagon in front of the building. The day seemed to have started out well.

Entering the international department platform area, he knew someone had made it ahead of him since all the lights were on, although no one was in sight. Going into his office, he followed his standard routine: the coffee was placed in the middle of the desk, the briefcase and newspaper onto his chair, he removed his coat, turned on his desk light, and placed his coat on the hanger that rested on the hook on the back of the door. The next fifteen to twenty minutes would be spent reading his *Wall Street Journal* and sipping his coffee in quiet before the first crisis of the day hit. As he opened the paper to its full width, his eye caught the papers next to his *IN* box, the cover sheet was there but his "to do" list and "problem" list were missing. He kept track of problem letters of credit and follow up notes concerning them and reviewed it each morning making notations as to whom to follow up with for a status report. It was always kept on top, but this morning it wasn't there. He picked up the stack of papers and file folders and began leafing through them finding his list about a third of the way down. Someone had obviously moved it. His first thought was the cleaning crew. They had obviously been in over the weekend since his waste basket had been emptied and he had known them to inadvertently knock items off his desk in the past. He also knew they sometimes used the private offices to take breaks and finding unauthorized phone calls to the Caribbean and Latin America on the office monthly bill was not uncommon. In any event, it was entirely possible they could have been knocked off the desk by a duster and just hurriedly put back. It had happened before. But Ed had a funny feeling about it and decided to double check just to be sure. He checked the other items on the desk and found everything in order. The desk drawers seemed all right as well—nothing missing. He then swung around to the computer and turned it on while he unlocked the credenza and opened the drawers. He removed the files, folders, and papers from his overnight drawer and saw immediately that they had been moved. The K E N Automotive files were on top of the Alliance, just the reverse of the away he had put them away. The PC came to life and Ed immediately signed in and then went to his password log file. What he looked for was his own user name and access log. Since he was the assistant department manager he had also been designated as department security administrator and was responsible for viewing the unauthorized access reports and authorizing the issuance and re-issuance of passwords and codes to department staff. He immediately brought up Friday's data and stared at the final entry.

E CAMPBELL, FRIDAY 09/24/93, 2128, DATA FILE

Nine-twenty-eight p.m., someone was in his office looking at his network data file signed in as him. He immediately picked up the phone and dialed Jim's number.

At the same time that Ed was dialing Jim, McBride was calling Charlie Field. McBride had no intention of waiting any longer to let Field know that he was shutting down for a while. He made a list of the calls he would have to make and the messages he would have to send. He worked on it over the weekend and realized that the most difficult part would be the notification to the Venezuelan importers. At home, he had all the complete records of all out-standing, as well as completed, transactions and spent most of the time putting the information together to make sure he covered everything. He also reviewed every file he had in his possession and worked out a timetable for getting them back to the bank. He knew it was time to back off, and he had to tell Field what he was doing.

Charlie Field was sitting at his desk looking at the list of new orders that had been booked the week before when his private phone line began to ring.

"Field!" His response to a ringing phone always seemed like more of a challenge to the caller that his call had better be important rather than a simple answer and identification of who called.

"Charlie, glad I caught you. Larry McBride,"

"McBride, yeah. You got a problem?"

"What makes you think I have a problem?" *Field*, McBride thought, *always put everyone on the defensive; get an edge.*

"Because you wouldn't be calling me before eight on a Monday morning if there wasn't a problem."

"Okay, so there's a problem."

"What the fuck's the problem this time?" Field threw the pencil he was writing with down on the desk as he spoke.

"I think someone else may have figured out what we're doing."

"Who?"

"Ed Campbell."

"Your number two?"

"Yeah."

"Can't you control him?"

"That's not the point."

"The hell it isn't! Look, McBride, I told you this the other week. I can't back off. Venezuela is now my biggest account in the Caribbean region. These side commissions are getting to be more trouble than their worth, but the commercial business is damn good. I don't want that messed with. I'm not gonna lose it."

"Charlie, take it easy. Maybe we can find another way to keep it going."

"I don't see a problem with this one. Or maybe I do, and you're the problem and not this Campbell guy. Why the hell don't you just buy him off? Bring him into the fold? You don't tell him about the side deal. Just tell him it's a way to increase the bank's income. Tell him it's all legit."

"No, Charlie, not this guy. He knows his way around. That's why I hired him."

"He's got to have a price. Doesn't everybody? Maybe it's not money. Give him a bigger job. How 'bout another title. You bank guys are good at titles."

"No, Charlie."

"Maybe I should talk to him like I did that Kramer guy. Let him know what he's messin' up."

Suddenly McBride was taken aback. "You talked to Kramer?"

"Stupid crack-head. Yeah, we had a little talk. Let him know what he was messin' up. So he gets all excited, jumps in his car, and rams it into a bridge or something. Ah, druggies, they're all losers." Silence on the line. "You still there, McBride?'

"I'm here."

"I don't want this stopped."

"I don't have a choice, Charlie. Look, it's going to play itself out in six months, anyway. Venezuela got the IMF money it needs. It just goes away a little early. We'll find another country to work on." *But you won't be a part of it.*

"You're pissin' me off, McBride."

"Charlie, I can't help that. I've got to cover things here. Look, why don't you just short ship? You're doing it now, anyway."

"'Cause then my books are all out of whack. Right now I ship one hundred cases, my records show one hundred cases. If I ship fifty and my records show one hundred, my bookkeeping and inventory will go nuts. This is a sweet deal for both sides of the Carib. You sure you can't take care of this Campbell guy?"

"No, Charlie—"

"There's somebody else too isn't there? That other banker guy. The one you said didn't know anything. You really fucked up, McBride, didn't you? You're just too damn smart for your own good."

"Charlie—" McBride could hear the phone slam down on the receiver.

❧❧❧

Jim showed up at nine-fifteen instead of his usual eight-forty-five as he made a stop at Carl Hansen's to drop off the report they had worked on over the week-end. It proved to be an interesting document and followed the preferred format that Carl Hansen had long advocated: a one page executive summary, content page, analysis and detail sections, and exhibit section. The standard procedure was for the intended party to read the summary from which questions would arise. The content page would lead them to the answers contained in the detail pages. The usual joke was that the attention span of most senior executives couldn't extend beyond a one-page document. Nothing could be further from the truth.

The key element was time and getting to the heart of the matter. The summary presented conclusions and recommendations. If any of the conclusions were questioned by the reader, then they could be directed to the section in the document that provided the basis for the conclusion. If a conclusion was agreed to by the reader on the basis of the summary, then time need not be wasted by the reader in delving into detail unnecessarily. The most important part of the entire document was the credibility and track record of the author. For Carl, having Jim present the document gave it ten times more weight that if Ed had presented it on his own. Also, having Carl present it to Bill Harrigan gave it an even firmer boost—something that had better be taken seriously.

The construction of the report was orchestrated by Jim Fairmont. He did more of these than he cared to remember and they were not only loan participation proposals but also acquisition proposals and capital expenditure recommendations. Throughout his career, he had put together all of the different sections, depending on what had been assigned to him. This, however, was the first one he had put together outside of the bank and the first one that criticized the actions of a specific individual.

The executive summary was constructed by Jim based on the detail that Ed provided. That detail was contained in the emails that were sent to Marian at The Garden Walk address and were given back to him during dinner with the Ryans. Ed carefully outlined the unusual activity and practices that were occurring within the international department. Jim crafted the money transfer issues and their suspicious nature. As each element was crafted, it was faxed or emailed to the other party for review and comment. Marian also got her two cents in when she spotted something that seemed to be overkill or not relevant. Jim twisted and turned the text as best he could, as Ian had recommended, to give it a focus designed to protect the good name of the bank. He often called Ian to read some sections to him to make sure he was on track and solicit additional input. The whole object here was not to present a negative report citing deficiencies within a banking department, but to present a recommendation as to corrective action to be taken in a timely fashion that would put the bank on solid footing.

The idea was to avoid the possibility of embarrassing publicity and position the bank for the future. The name of Larry McBride was mentioned only once in the entire document. All other references referred to the "manager" or department policies. Again, the report had to maintain an impersonal tone. It was eight o'clock on Sunday night when everything was finished and agreed to. The only breaks taken during the entire weekend were when Jim met Marian for lunch on Saturday, she worked at The Walk from ten to five, and for the two of them to go to church on Sunday. After dinner on Saturday, Marian began her critique of some of the material and the first phone calls were placed to Ian. By the end of the day the meat of the document was together. On Sunday, Jim put together the summary and Ed did some additional editing of the second section to make it conform to the emphasis Jim placed on certain elements. The entire summary was read to Ian over the phone who also then had some style recommendations. It was a stress-filled weekend with no break. Even in Church, Jim found himself re-crafting sentences.

Even in the minister's sermon, dealing with John the Baptist, Jim found reference to what he was doing and, when the quote "...I am the voice of one crying in the wilderness..." was given, it surely struck home.

Sunday afternoon had proved to be the most stressful of the entire weekend with the assembling of the conclusions and recommendations. This was always the most critical part of any proposal. One learned very early that to be a successful manager a critical eye was not enough. The ability to detect deficiencies in a procedure or credit proposal was only half the job. The other half was proposing the solution and recommended course of action. To merely tell the world there was a problem was a useless effort. Senior management's job was to make decisions. To do that, they must be presented with options. Merely identifying the problem did not reap rewards but could classify one as a trouble maker. Ian had made it clear that, in the case of the Mexican desk officer, he had been tagged as a problem as much for the way he presented the information he discovered as for the information itself, which presented a problem, the solution for which someone was obliged to create. Jim did not want that to happen here.

All his career he was able to find solutions, find people who could deal with them. To discover that a company was in financial difficulty and would miss a loan payment was critical but finding a way to work with the company to solve its problems was essential. Contrary to the popular image of banking, the placing of a company into bankruptcy or foreclosing on a loan was the very last thing a banker wanted to happen. The object was to be re-paid and, usually, the only way that happened was by keeping the company afloat, as the company succeeded so did the bank. That's why experienced loan and credit officers made good chief executives. That's why Carl Hansen always stated that the best credit training for a loan officer was to participate in a bad loan.

Jim worked and re-worked the conclusion and recommendation section. This was the part where the input and expertise of Ed Campbell and Ian Ryan was so important. Questions were presented: If we are dealing with a formal policy of soliciting flight capital, what are the steps that need to be taken to correct the image of the bank in the minds of the target countries and what policies and procedures need to be implemented to prevent a re-occurrence? If money-laundering was part of the problem, what actions must be immediately taken with the regulatory and legal authorities, and what actions needed to be taken internally? If criminal activity was uncovered, what immediate steps must be taken to stop the activity?

If serious unethical behavior occurred, what new policies and procedures should be implemented and how can all employees be made aware of what constituted appropriate behavior on the part of the manager and the managed? In the final document, the answers needed not be specifically laid out in great detail but must be clear enough to suggest a direction. There must also be a positive feel to the document and not a negative one. And then all the recommendations must be summarized in one small paragraph for the executive summary. Here, writing and language skills become critical. It was one of the main reasons Carl Hansen always wanted his loan officers to have undergraduate degrees in liberal arts. He wanted them to have that grounding before doing graduate business work. Jim learned it well and followed the same policies in his own management and hiring approach.

In everything that was written and proposed, Marian was the final reviewer for she listened for the tone in the document. Each section she would provide comment, such as "too negative," "too technical," "too complex," "too wishy-washy," "not enough punch," "too simplistic." She had a fresher perspective, someone not involved in the daily routine of banking but coming from a banking background; of living in both worlds. Jim valued her A-plus-B-will-eventually-reach-F reasoning ability.

The document when finally put together was a total of fifteen typewritten pages, including summary and exhibits. Long enough to command attention but brief enough to reflect its preliminary nature as a document recommending a full investigation by internal auditing with the possible option of bringing in an external audit consulting group. The process was an exhausting one and they were glad to finally have it out of their hands,

The final version of the report was made into five copies—all nicely enclosed in the bank's presentation folders. Three were to be given to Carl and one each to be retained by Ed and Jim.

CHAPTER 27

The Pressure Builds

The day started badly for Larry McBride, and it didn't get any better as it wore on. Over and over, he told himself that he should not have become involved with Field and Alliance. Every place he now turned there seemed to be someone looking over his shoulder. This was supposed to be a nice quiet deal. This was supposed to be a nice "win-win" situation. The bank was happy with the extra profits that were coming in, so they wouldn't rock the boat. He made a few extra bucks on the side for his effort. Alliance and the other exporters were happy with the increased sales, and the Venezuelans and others were happy with all the money they were able to get out of their countries.

Best of all, it was all wrapped up in the cloak of straightforward commercial transactions. Who would ever suspect anything? Then there was Ed Campbell. He knew it was a risk hiring someone who actually understood the business as well as he did. He knew the risk, but it was one he wanted to take because the department continued to grow faster than he expected. Consolidation in the metropolitan New York area was pushing more and more local business his way, as medium and small companies with international needs bailed out of the banking giants when their existing banks were acquired, and the companies became very small fish in a new very large pond. Looking for the attention and importance they once had there was no place to go but to him and First State.

He needed Campbell's expertise, and it was paying off for him. Smart, articulate, and knowledgeable with more than twenty years of international experience behind him. The customers liked and trusted him. All that was to the good, but he knew there was a downside in that he was a purist. He knew the rules and followed them like a good international technician. McBride felt as though everything was closing in on him. And then that stupid invoice thing happened with Fairmont. *Who would have thought of Fairmont creating a problem? He needs a geography lesson to find Venezuela. And hooking up with Campbell? Who would have thought?*

Every place McBride turned, there was someone else waiting to point a finger at him to say '*Hey, kid, you're too smart for your own good. Little smart-ass kid. Thirty-three years old and thinks he's ready to take over the bank. You need some more season-ing—need a few more years on you.*'

"Seasoning, shit!" he said out loud as he threw his paper clip holder across the room at his sofa and then jumped up from his chair. "What the fuck do they know about seasoning? All of them. I've forgotten more about this business then they'll ever know. The ass-holes." He moved in front of his desk. "Gray hair. They think that makes them smart. Bull shit! A bunch of old farts!" He moved to the sofa. "Shit!" he yelled. There was a knock on the door, and Gloria started to come in. "Did I say come in?"

Gloria, taken aback by the hostility, stammered and then said, "Sorry, Larry. You've got a visitor."

"No way! There's nothing on my calendar."

"It's the manager of the Kennedy Boulevard Office in Hoboken. He says it's urgent."

"I don't have time to see him right now. Have him make an appointment."

"Okay." Gloria pulled her head back out of the door but could hear McBride mention something about "domestic shit-heads" as she closed it. "I'm sorry, sir, but he's got a conference call to Mexico that's already overdue. Can I set something up for you later today?"

"I was over here this morning for another meeting and was hoping I could speak with him. It's kind of important."

The speaker was in his mid-to-late-thirties and seemed to be of Hispanic origin, which would have made sense with the large Latin population that inhabited the West side of the Hudson River and was beginning to dominate Jersey City, Hoboken, North Bergen, and Fort Lee.

The bank had started to add more and more Latin staff to cater to the local population.

"I don't really think now is a good time," Gloria said. *Not if you want to keep your head on your shoulders,* she thought.

"I'll tell you what. Why don't I give you my name and number and you tell him I'll give him a call later in the day?" He took one of his cards out of its plastic carrying case. "Can I borrow your pen there?" he asked, indicating the one in the pen set holder.

"Sure, here," she said, handing it to him. "I'll see that he gets it as soon as he's free. His schedule has him pretty much in the building all day, and just after lunch may be the best time to call. Don't worry, I'll make sure he gets the message." She flashed her best smile at him as he finished writing on the back of the card and handed it to her.

He smiled back. "I'm somewhat new at the bank. Still finding my way around."

"I didn't think I recognized you. I try to keep track of the branch managers, since we do a lot of work for them. So now I'll add you to the list." That smile again.

"I'll do my best to make it easy for you." A smile in return.

Just then Grace came up to the desk to drop off a file. "Excuse me," she said as she made an effort to drop the file into Gloria's *IN* box.

"Sure," said the branch manager, moving out of the way.

"Grace, say hello to Rick Figueroa. He's the manager of the Kennedy Boulevard branch. This is Grace Fredericks. She's over in our customer service area. Someone you're probably going to get to know."

"Hi, Grace," he said, extending his hand. "You know I think we spoke on the phone last week. We needed help on a foreign draft."

"Oh, sure. I took the information down. Susan got back to you, didn't she?"

"Oh, yes, everything worked out fine. You guys were great."

"Sorry I couldn't help you myself. I've only been here a short while and still learning."

"I'm in a bit of a learning mode myself. Look, I don't want to hold you people up." He turned back to Gloria: "I'll call just after noon as you said."

"I'll give him the note. He's pretty good at following up and may call you first. Sorry I couldn't get you in to see him this morning."

"That's okay. I know how tough it can be to just walk in. Was in the building so just thought I'd give it a try." He looked at Grace. "Nice meeting you. It's always good to get to know the people, personally, who help you over the phone. I'll talk to you later, Gloria." He gave another smile and a little wave and started toward the door and the elevator.

"He's kinda cute," said Grace, as soon as he was out of earshot.

"Not bad at all. Maybe I'll spend some time over on Kennedy Boulevard."

"Maybe I'll go with you."

Just then the door opened, and a hassled-looking McBride appeared. His hair was mussed from running his hand through it. He had his overcoat over one arm. "I've got to go out for a while."

Gloria quickly looked at her calendar. "Did I miss something?"

"No, it's personal. Be back in a couple of hours."

"Any place I can reach you if something comes up?"

"Page me." Pause. "Or put little miss investigator on it," he said, referring to Grace. He then headed for the door, putting his coat on as he went.

The two women stood there and watched him go, obviously stunned. "Boy, is he in a mood," Gloria said.

"What did he mean by 'little miss investigator'? Am I in trouble or something?"

"Don't give it a thought. He tends to roll over people sometimes. You just happened to be in his line of sight."

"Gee, I hope I'm not in trouble."

"Believe me, it's okay. He gets snippy sometimes but never remembers it. If you mention it, he won't have any idea what you're talking about."

CHAPTER 28

Searching for Answers

As the afternoon sun began to warm Charlie's office, Charlie himself was warming up for another reason: the conversation he had earlier with Larry McBride really bothered him. Easy to irritate anyway, although much of it was for show—to keep an edge—this time he had a bad feeling. As he paced around the room, he just knew things were going bad. He stopped, reached across his desk, and hit the auto-dial button on his phone.

It dialed, and Gloria Martinez's voice came over the speaker. "Larry McBride's office."

"Is he there yet?" he boomed.

"No, Mr. Field, he has not come back yet."

"Well, where the hell is he?"

"As I told you a short while ago, Mr. Field, he went out earlier this morning and hasn't come back yet."

"And you're tellin' me you don't know where he is? I don't buy it. He's in his office, isn't he? Well, you tell him to pick up the damn phone."

"Mr. Field," she said, her voice beginning to rise, "he is *not* in his office. He left the building earlier and has not been back. If he calls in, I'll make certain that he knows you wish to speak with him." The more formal Gloria became, the more irritated you knew she was. "I have left two notes prominently displayed on his desk so he can't miss them, and I marked them urgent. I intend to put a third note next to the other two."

"Okay. Okay! I get the picture. You're doin' your job. But dammit, you tell him to call me. I mean it." He slammed down the receiver.

Charlie didn't like being in the position of having to rely on someone else to make something happen. It was his nature to be the locomotive and not the caboose. He went along with the Venezuela deal mainly because he saw the potential for increased sales. The side money he initially didn't care about—although he started to take notice when it got above the $50,000 mark. Field realized he'd made much more than he ever expected, especially from increasing his company's market share. McBride was the one who needed the side money.

Commercial bankers didn't make the kind of money investment bankers did. He figured McBride was barely making six figures and maybe picking up some stock options—if the bank was finally giving them—so the side money would have some meaning to him. But Field went along because McBride wanted everyone on equal footing, and he couldn't argue with the logic, although he had no idea how many other companies McBride had on the hook.

Field always felt uncomfortable, though. Sure, he walked on the edge and was tough on people, but he prided himself on never really screwing anyone, at least to his way of thinking. All of these things kept rushing through his mind as he walked to the window of his office and looked at the mid-afternoon sun.

"McBride, what are you up to, you little bastard?" he said out loud, then to himself, *This is a good deal. There are lots of other countries we can work with. Don't blow it.* He then began to think of life without McBride. *Why not?* he thought. *I don't really need the little prick. The side commissions don't really matter. I'll just cut him out. I don't need him to change invoices. I'll just short ship and adjust the books here. Besides, there's nothing wrong. I'm not keeping the overpayment. Just passing it on to the rightful owners. I'll be a public service. All I got to do is get out of the side money business. Fuck McBride!*

෧෨෧

The same sun was showing through Jim's office as the intercom buzzer on his phone caught his attention. "Yes, Paula."

"I have Mr. Hansen on line one for you."

"Thanks, I'll take it." Jim then switched buttons on his phone. "Hello, Carl."

"Jim, glad I was able to reach you. I just wanted you to know that I have an appointment with Bill Harrigan this afternoon in West Patterson at four-forty-five."

"The report's okay?"

"Yes, you did a good job as usual. There's certainly enough there for concern. I gave Bill a basic rundown on what was in it, and he immediately made time available. I'm going to leave here in a few minutes, and I'll make sure to call you tonight."

"Carl, I really appreciate this."

"Happy to do it. Besides, I've got a lot of years tied up in First State. I wouldn't like to see the place get a black eye."

"Thanks, Carl. I'll talk to you tonight."

Jim depressed the button to end the connection but didn't put down the handset. As soon as he heard the dial tone, he entered in the number for The Garden Walk. While someone else might have immediately called Ed Campbell, the second most concerned party in the matter, Jim's first instinct was to call Marian, the person who truly mattered to him.

"Garden Walk."

"Florence, this is Jim Fairmont. Is Marian there?"

"Hi, Jim. No, you just missed her. In fact, I can see her just pulling out of the parking lot. She'll be back in a few minutes, though. The bank just called to say that a couple of checks bounced, so she's going over to pick them up and call the people."

"The bank actually called?"

"Oh, they always do. Whenever a deposit comes back, they always call."

"Well, I guess that's the benefit of a small business banking with a local bank. You'd never catch us calling anymore. Wasn't too much was it?"

"Seventy-five."

"There goes the profit that was earned on something else. No wonder no one wants to accept checks these days. Would you tell Marian to give me a call when she gets back? I'm at the office."

"Sure, she won't be long."

"Thanks."

Jim put the phone down and reached for the bank telephone book which was in his top right hand drawer. His next call would be to Ed Campbell, but that wouldn't be successful either as Ed was, at that moment, in New Vernon, driving around and trying to decide whether to go into The Garden Walk or not. The past few days being around Marian again, after more than twenty years, had brought back memory after memory. She really hadn't changed. She was still the quick-witted, sharp-tongued Marian he worked with at Bankers. She was older and a little heavier but held her looks so much better than her contemporaries. He had been thinking over the past few days that maybe he had been foolish to let her get away. But then he wasn't there when she got away, he was in Viet Nam when she met Jim. It was all foolish thinking back this way, but he couldn't stop himself. He kept thinking of what his life would have been like if he had made other decisions.

What if he had made a greater effort to find a reserve unit instead of letting the draft get him, he would have been around when she met Jim, or maybe she wouldn't have met him at all? And what if he hadn't gone to OCS and stayed in the service an extra couple of years? And what about that night at the Governor Morris Inn? That was the real turning point. He knew she loved Jim and their night together was a terrible mistake for her and could have destroyed all she had. There was never any question in his mind about leaving. He sat at a traffic light and thought of that night. He could see everything as clear as if it was yesterday. The light was green. The car behind was honking at him. He made a left turn and headed down Route 202 for The Garden Walk.

It was all very disturbing and distracting.

As he drove, he switched to thinking of his wife Susan and the two girls and smiled. But then a picture of McBride edged Susan out. Did Ed make a mistake being uncompromising with McBride? Should he have just ignored what was going on around him and forgotten about doing what was right? And was it right? Maybe Marian and he could have been happy together? Maybe McBride should have been left alone?

Foolish thoughts.

We cannot be what we are not. And what we are is in our souls, as well as our genes. Often we're fooled by the mirror and believe what we see but the mirror doesn't see what's inside, it doesn't see what drives us to action and inaction, it doesn't see fear and courage, it doesn't see the little girl behind the woman and the sadness of the man behind the smile. What could have been was not and cannot be. What is past is memory, a phantom, a dream whose moment has come and gone and cannot be recaptured, as the people who played the parts are gone. They only existed for that moment in time and have moved on to evolve into others, shaped by each passing minute, hour, day and year. No, you can't go home again because home is gone, it's no longer there except in memory, a memory that is never a true reflection of the event—even for the participants.

໔๏໔

When Marian came back to the store, Florence was out in the back yard with a customer, looking at some bird baths. A note was stuck to the cash register, indicating that Jim had called so Marian immediately called his number.

"Mr. Fairmont's office."

"Paula, this is Marian Fairmont. Is he there?" The chimes on the entrance door sounded, and Marian turned to see Ed Campbell come in. She gave him a wave and signaled him to wait just a moment.

"Oh, I'm sorry, Mrs. Fairmont but you just missed him. He's off to a customer meeting in Parsippany."

"He called me earlier, so I was just returning his call."

Ed started to roam around the shop looking at the various knick-knacks.

Marian watched him as he moved about. "Any idea when he'll be back?"

Ed meandered into another room where Marian couldn't see him.

"Let me see." Paula flipped open Jim's calendar. "Oh, here it is. It looks like he should be back by three. Do you want me to have him call you?"

"Oh, just tell him I returned his call. Nothing important at this end."

"Okay, I'll tell him."

"Thanks." Marian put down the phone and then called to Ed, "Find anything interesting?"

"You've got some neat stuff here. Wish I had a garden," he said, while coming back into the room with the sales desk.

"What brings you to town?"

"On my way to Liberty Corner to see a customer. Had some time and thought I'd come see this Garden Walk place where I've been sending all these emails. See if it really existed."

"Want to make sure it's not a front for some secret contraband mail society?"

"Something like that. I'm impressed. You've got some really nice, first-class stuff here."

"Well, thank you. With complements like that, the least I can do is offer you a cup of coffee. I think Florence just made a fresh pot."

"Florence?"

"Florence Graham. She works for me part time. Actually, it's more like three quarter time lately. Come on back to the office." She came around the front of the desk and motioned for him to follow her to the back room. "Florence is out back with a customer. We have all the big expensive pieces out there. It's all fenced in, so they're less likely to walk away, if you know what I mean."

"I guess that's a problem in this part of the country. Although I guess it's become true in most major suburban areas."

"This used to be a relatively sleepy, small town. Have a seat." She motioned him to a teak wooden bench that sat next to her desk with the PC on it. "But once they opened up I-Two-Eighty-Seven through here, everything really changed. All the farms have been gobbled up and, of course, AT and T building its headquarters in Basking Ridge really opened Pandora's Box. There was no way to stop the flow after that. How do you like your coffee?"

"Just a little milk or cream." Before sitting down, Ed glanced out the window and spotted two women looking at some bird-baths. "That must be Florence."

"The taller one. The woman with her lives over in New Vernon and is putting in a formal English garden. Great customer."

Looking around the room, Ed commented, "This used to be a private house, wasn't it?"

"Built in 1910 or so. One of the newer ones. No real historical significance to it, which made it easier to convert for our use. It was pretty run down when Jim and I bought it." She handed him his coffee and put a cup down on the desk for herself and then sat in her office chair. "It was vacant for probably ten years before we took it over. Would have been a real chore to upgrade and modernize for living, but it's good and solid and works for the store." Marian paused for a moment. "Ed, what do you think is going to happen?"

He took a sip of his coffee while he composed his thoughts. It was a question he had been asking himself all weekend. "I'm not entirely sure. I really don't have a good feel for the culture of First State. Haven't been around long enough. To be perfectly honest, I've been trying to figure out how I got involved." Marian started to speak, but he raised his hand to stop her, "Now, don't get me wrong. I truly believe the correct thing is being done by filing the report and, as far as I'm concerned, there are enough weird things going on in international to warrant someone taking a good, hard look at the place. It's just that this was supposed to be a final career move for me. The reason I came to First State was because McBride is of the belief that he'll be moving up in the organization and told me the international department would be mine when he did, that there was no one there currently with the experience and knowledge necessary to take his place. What I'm probably doing is shooting myself in the foot. But having said that, I do believe what's being done needs to be done. I just wish it wasn't me."

"Ed, you don't know how many times Jim and I wished he never came across that invoice."

"Oh, I'm sure that's true. But if it wasn't Jim finding the invoice and questioning it…well, it would have been something else. I just can't believe McBride is dumb enough to do some of the things he's done. The mere idea that the head of the department has *pets* that are supposed to receive special attention is a starting place for disaster. Usually, the big companies get special treatment if they're big income producers, but the idea of the department head personally handling their transactions is just looking for trouble. And taking files and documents out of the office, I mean that's ridiculous. I guess the more I think about it, the more I realize that if it hadn't been Jim, it probably would have ended up being me."

He paused. "I always seem to be able to find fault with something." He looked at her, wondering whether he should continue but knew he had to. The only thing he knew for sure had to do with his suspecting someone of nosing around his office—he still had to evaluate that—besides, he didn't want to upset her and Jim any more than necessary. "I guess my getting mixed up in this just came a little sooner than I thought it would. Although, to be perfectly honest, if it hadn't been Jim who asked for my help, I might have considered stepping away, might have pleaded *new guy on the block*. The other night when Carl asked as to why I was involved, I realized that part of the answer was because of what happened twenty years ago." Marian tried to interrupt again. "No, let me finish. I've always felt guilty about that. Truthfully, it's been one of my saddest and most uncomfortable memories. When Jim came to me, looking for answers, I couldn't turn him away. I guess I felt I owed him the help. I assume he knows the whole story?" She nodded. "It's not that what I said to Carl was untrue, it's just that it wasn't everything. And don't get me wrong, I don't regret my participation in this. There's something definitely wrong going on. I don't know whether it's just unethical and unprofessional or it really is illegal, it's just that I think I saw my helping him as a way of compensating for the hurt I'm sure I caused."

"Ed." This time Marian wouldn't be stopped. "What happened twenty years ago wasn't your doing, it was mine." She told him about the vacation plans that were put on the shelf and how depressed she was over Jim having left her alone, about feeling cheated. "There was also something else working on me at the time, which I didn't realize until much later and that was a sense of jealousy. I was jealous of his success. I was the one stuck at home with Jeffrey. Oh, don't get me wrong, looking back now, I wouldn't give up those years for anything. I did the right thing in quitting Bankers when Jeffrey was born, but twenty years ago, it was eating at me; I just didn't realize it. I had as good a job as both you and Jim and was smarter than both of you to boot."

"You won't get an argument from me there. You still are."

"No, use it or lose it they say, and they're right. Experience is what makes one good at what one does. You can read all the books in the world on the perfect tennis serve but, if you're not out there day after day feeling the racket in your hand, positioning and re-positioning your feet, tossing the ball at different heights and tempos, you're never really going to be good at serving the ball. We all had the same book learning, but you both tempered it with firsthand knowledge and experience that I didn't have. I felt myself being left behind."

As Marian talked, Ed found himself watching her rather than listening to her. *Why did I come here?* he thought. *This is dumb. This is not what I need to happen. I've got to get out of here before I say something stupid.*

"My career wasn't just on hold," Marian continued, "it was destroyed. All of that was bubbling below the surface that night. I know that now. I was using you to get even, to somehow punish Jim for doing something that I would have done the same way but would never have the same opportunity. I was pretty mixed up and went and mixed you up along the way."

"You can't take all the blame. The Eve syndrome."

"The what?"

"Eve syndrome. Never heard that one?"

"No."

"I'm surprised. That's where, because of Eve, all mankind lost the Garden of Eden. Women have been taking the rap ever since." He made an effort to look at his watch. "Hey, I'm going to have to run."

"Oh, I get it," she said, ignoring his comment as she became interested in the topic. "The indoctrination of children as to how man was corrupted by woman. How if Eve never offered Adam the apple, we would still be living in bliss, while the truth of the matter was that Eden was lost not because of Eve's offer but because of Adam's acceptance. It was man's weakness of character that lost us Eden."

Ed stood up. "I was just realizing how much of that is still going on. Monica and Bill. Society put the rap on Monica while all Bill had to do was say no. He's the most protected man in the world and had a million ways to get out of it, but he didn't."

"I think that's what angered most women with any sense of real equality," she said while getting up herself. "Blame the offeror again not the acceptor. No real intestinal fortitude, as they say."

"That's why I can't let you take the blame." He was looking at her now in a way that startled Marian. "I could have walked away. I eventually did. I could have said no. The real decision was mine, not yours."

"Well, I appreciate your saying so, but it still haunts me some-times."

She looked away from him, and he made a move to leave the office, started walking slowly.

"I'm sorry if I've opened up some old wounds," he said. "I didn't mean to. It's just that it's been hanging over me, and this whole mess with McBride. I had to say something; to open things up; to get them out of the way and finally close it down. Especial-ly if we have a fight on our hands coming up."

Marian perked up. "Do you think we do?"

"Oh, yes. There's some major damage control ahead. And it's not going to be just from McBride."

CHAPTER 29

Looking for a Fall Guy

Dinner Monday evening was the now common "Meals for Two" from Kings Supermarket. With two people working and no children at home, someone finally figured out that a good portion of the American work force didn't have time to cook, and that included TV dinners and frozen entrees. The target market was originally young professionals in their late twenty's and early thirty's without families to worry about, but the market very quickly expanded to fifty something's, who were in the same boat at the other end of the age spectrum—now with two jobs and children in college. Marian was the one who picked it up tonight, as she closed up early. Both of them passed a supermarket on the way home, so there was always a phone call sometime in the afternoon to work out dinner logistics.

"Is Ed absolutely certain someone was snooping around his office?" Marian said, as she took the warmed up evening meal from the microwave. Tonight it was fresh made lasagna. She had transferred it to regular dinner plates. The meal came with a fresh salad, bread, and dessert.

Jim poured them both a glass of red wine. "As sure as he can be. Someone definitely signed into his computer with his password on Friday night."

"McBride?"

"I can't imagine who else."

"But McBride didn't say anything to him?"

"Not that I'm aware of. We traded phone messages. Ed left me one early in the morning, and I couldn't get back to him till late this afternoon, but he was already out of the office. Told him I would call him this evening after I've had a chance to speak with Carl. This all can't come to an end too quickly for me."

Marian was just about to tell Jim of Ed's visit to The Walk earlier in the afternoon when the phone rang, and she got up and answered.

"Oh, hi, Carl, yes he's right here. Hold on a minute."

Jim got up from the table and took the kitchen phone from Marian. It had the usual extra-long extension cord that permitted one to roam around the kitchen while holding a conversation. "Hello Carl, how're we doing?"

"I saw Bill this afternoon. He was certainly surprised. He's a good man, Jim, you'll get a fair hearing."

"I kind of thought that. How did he react?"

"Shocked. I had the impression that McBride was on a fast track, and a lot of people think favorably about him. Bill agreed that the best approach is having Robert Bradley put a full team in there and find out what's going on. He'll let the chips fall where they may."

"What happens next?"

"He'll call Bradley tonight so don't be surprised if you hear that someone showed up in McBride's office tomorrow morning."

"Is he looking for anything from me?"

"No. You step aside. Bradley now has the ball. The responsibility is now his, not yours." There was a pause. "Jim, I told Bill that this was not easy for you, and you did this reluctantly. Told him you had no choice once you received the information from Campbell."

"But that's not necessarily true."

The tone in Jim's voice changed, and Marian heard it. She watched him intently, as he suddenly began to pace as he talked.

"I'm the one who started all this. If I hadn't found that invoice form, none of this would have happened."

"I'm aware of that. But you must admit that you wouldn't really have really suspected anything without what he found and fed you."

"But it really wasn't like that."

"It's the best approach, believe me. Just let nature take its course."

As Jim hung up the phone, Marian became concerned, as she could see that he had heard something that disturbed him.

"What is it?"

"I have a sneaking suspicion that Ed is going to be set up to take a fall."

"How do you mean?"

"It was the way Carl said it. He apparently made Ed the heavy when speaking with Harrigan."

"But that's not what the report says."

"The report is fact, background. Now, we're talking impressions, gut reactions, and emotions. All the things that aren't in the report. Someone always has to be the heavy, and it looks like it's going to be Ed."

"But that's not fair."

"I know, but just as the first rule of making a complaint is to also provide a solution. There also has to be a heavy, just in case."

"Just in case what?"

"In case McBride talks his way out of everything."

"But there's no way—"

"There's always a way. Especially in the world of business and politics. It's a question of value. How valuable are you to the organization? You know the old joke that it's always the junior guy that goes to jail…well, in this case, if there's unfavorable publicity over this, Ed will be tagged as the cause."

"Even though it's all McBride's fault."

"Yup."

"Oh, this is ridiculous." Marian was up and moving around now, becoming more animated. "It's the bank's fault for giving McBride the freedom they did. They're the ones who are to blame. They liked the income he was producing, so they turned their back to it. They probably figured all along that there was something funny going on but didn't want to probe too hard because it might detract from the revenue stream. Why would Carl do such a thing?"

"You know Carl. He's protecting his own. He's always been that way. He's giving Harrigan a goat. If whatever we've put together falls apart, they've got someone to blame for all the disruption. Carl figures if McBride survives, he'd get rid of Ed anyway, so he was a logical choice."

"But it's *our* fault. No! That's not true either. The bank set the tone by giving him too much free rein and not really understanding the business."

"It's still people. The White House gets blamed for a lot of things, but the White House is an inanimate building, so is the bank. By saying it's the bank's fault, you take the blame away from individuals. Should Harrigan be blamed? The executive committee? The board of directors? What do we do, fire them all?"

Marian was finally calming down again. "What you're saying is there are no great men anymore. When someone blamed the House of Morgan for something, old J. Pierpont stood up and took the heat and clearly identified himself as The House of Morgan. Now, when a chairman or a president stands in front of a mirror, there are at least ten faces staring back, mostly made up of the board and legal advisors. *The buck stops here, but only if my legal counsel gets a chance to examine it first.*'"

"Exactly."

"This isn't a particularly nice world we live in, is it?"

"Not always, but it's not supposed to be Eden. We lost that, remember?"

"I'm not *that* old."

Jim smiled and then put an arm around her. "That's my girl."

"So what do we do?"

"Now, that's something we need to discuss."

CHAPTER 30

McBride Goes Missing

Tuesday morning brought the first hint of winter. It was cold and windy; one of those days that reminded you that fall could be a very short season. All those beautiful leaves that sparkled in the sun were now blowing through the air and curling up under bushes and burying flower beds. The trees would soon be naked, as the air had a touch of ice in it.

Jim watched from his office window and could see mini-tornados of leaves rushing across the park. Some people were struggling against the wind—one with a hand on a hat, another trying to keep a coat closed at the throat so the cold wind could not rush down and chill even more.

He watched one woman, who had come out of Epstein's department store with a shopping bag, try to get across the park and fail. She tried to cut across to the bank building but only got a third of the way and finally turned back. The wind was coming directly from the north and Epstein's was at the south end. The shopping bag had been only half full and each gust of wind filled it and dragged her back the few steps she had gained. Finally she turned and had all she could do to be kept from being blown right out of the park and into the street. She finally gave up, crossed the street and joined the other brave souls trying to make their way around the edge of The Green by moving from store front to store front.

There was a knock on his door, which was open.

"Morning, Jim, can I come in?" It was Robert Bradley.

"Sure, come on in." Jim was obviously surprised. He expected to hear from Bradley but hadn't expected him on his doorstep at ten-thirty in the morning.

"Mind if I shut this?" Bradley said, referring to the door.

"No, I think that would probably be a good idea." The door was closed. Jim picked up the telephone and pressed the intercom buzzer for Paula. When she answered, he simply said, "Hold everything for me for a bit will you." And then he hung up.

"A bit windy out there."

"Sure is. Was just watching a woman unsuccessfully negotiate the Green. That wind is really swirling. I remember days like this in lower Manhattan when you would move along close to the edge of a building, staying on the lee side as much as possible and then turn a corner and be blown back ten paces and not be able to move forward at all until the gust eased. The wind would blow so hard you could barely catch your breath."

"Oh, I remember that." Bradley was ex-Marine Midland Bank and had worked at the New York Headquarters building across from Chase Plaza. He removed his coat, having placed his briefcase next to the chair he staked out. "You should have seen the roads on the way down here. Debris flying everywhere among the leaves and branches. Large cardboard boxes are the worst. They just get lifted up from dumpsters or trash areas and come flying across I-Eighty. Traffic was just all over the place. Have to struggle just to stay in your own lane."

"Sorry you had to come out in all this. I've a pretty good idea why you're here."

"Your report."

"I thought so. Well, have a seat. Have you talked to McBride?"

"Not yet. Left a voice mail message for him at seven and spoke to his secretary about an hour ago. He hasn't come in yet. I've got a team ready to go in there this morning, and I wanted to notify him first. Harrigan has been trying to reach him as well. It's tough to give a manager notification of an audit if you can't find him. You wouldn't happen to know where he is? His secretary said he's supposed to be at his desk."

"Me? I'd have no idea. We don't have much contact."

"I didn't think you did, which raises the whole question of how you got involved. The report, obviously, doesn't say anything about that. Wanted to get your off-the-record impressions."

"It's a bit of a strange story." Jim then went on to explain how it all began and filled in, verbally, all the pieces that were purposely left out of the report. "We still can't say for sure what's going on because we were never able to get our hands on any of the critical files. I hope it turns out to be a case of an over-eager manager but those wire transfers…well, they certainly don't make it easy."

"Interesting. So Ed Campbell is really the one we need to talk with, although Tony would have gotten to him anyway."

"Tony?"

"Tony Carenza. He's leading the audit team on this one. He was to deliver the audit letter to McBride at nine this morning and is in the building in Newark right now. If McBride isn't back by ten, Tony goes after number two, which is Campbell, and delivers it to him. I hope they don't have to do that, though, but, under the circumstances, I'm not going to wait any longer. I assume Campbell will help out?"

"Definitely, you can talk to him directly, but I'm sure he'll give you everything he has." Jim was feeling a little uncomfortable at this point. He began to realize what Ian had meant about being interrogated by police. Bradley was not police but the next best thing. Jim had been through numerous audits before but this one had a different feel, this was one where there was something already identified as being wrong, not just a case of inadvertently failing to follow procedures or getting reports properly filed. He felt on the defensive and again beginning to question whether he had done the right thing or not. "In reality, I'm the one who brought Ed into this whole thing."

"And McBride doesn't know anything about any of this?"

"That I'm not too sure of." Jim told him about Ed's suspicions of someone looking through his office.

"So he could know? Interesting."

"Has anyone tried to reach him at home?"

"I've had a message left for him there as well. Jim," he said thoughtfully, "we've known one another for some time. This has the potential of being a real mess. Just how well do you know Ed Campbell? I keep coming back to him because he seems to be the primary point person, without him none of this would have come to light."

"I've gotten to know him pretty well, and I trust his judgement. I may not know much about international but he does and what he's said makes a lot of sense."

"Why wouldn't he have gone to McBride with it and confronted him?"

"That's something you'll have to take up with him. Besides,
remember I'm the one who started this, not him." Jim wondered
if Bradley had been given instructions of some sort to see how
much could be laid at Campbell's feet and was fishing around. If
he was, Jim had no intention of helping. He started it and he
wasn't going to let someone else take the heat.

"Tony will get to him. Do you know Tony?"

"I'm not sure I've met him, but I have heard of him."

"If you did, you'd probably remember. He's maybe five seven
or eight, two-hundred-plus pounds, looks like he's never missed a
meal in his life. He's my bull dog. I grabbed him from Citibank
about six months ago. If there's anything to find over in
McBride's shop, he'll find it. He's also one of the few people I
have who understands the international side. Interesting fellow,
Carenza. Came out of Queens, Astoria. Ex regular army. Still in
the National Guard. Well, look, I'm going to leave it here." Bradley got up from his chair. "I wanted to let you know, personally,
that the report you filed is being acted upon. Just wanted to fill in
some gaps and didn't want to do it over the phone. We'll take it
from here. Whatever we find will be reported directly to the
Chairman. I have no idea if you'll hear more from us about it. I'll
leave that up to Tony Carenza. No need for you to be involved
further unless Tony needs something and he thinks you can provide it." He extended his hand and Jim took it.

❧❧❧

At precisely ten o'clock, three men and one woman entered
the international department and headed for Larry McBride's
office. In the lead was Tony Carenza, who walked with a sense of
purpose, as he always did when making a surprise audit. In reality, all audits are supposed to be a surprise but were anticipated, as
they usually occurred ten to fourteen months apart. The last audit
of the international department had been performed nine months
earlier and the department received a satisfactory rating. Internal
audits of operating areas were primarily concerned with bank
policy and procedure and the validation of all internal accounts,
especially those dealing with the refinancing section, where all

the loans, advances and bankers acceptances were created. The approach was a broad brush one with a sampling done of various accounts and files.

This time it was a little different. Tony Carenza had in his briefcase a letter signed by Robert Bradley listing specific customer files and accounts to which the department was to provide access, as opposed to a more general letter that was more of an introduction of the audit team and scope of their review.

Normally, a list of data was required to be provided to auditing within a week's time to allow the audit team to prepare for their review. No time lapse was offered when there was any suspicion of irregular activity. He had his coat over his left arm and draped over his briefcase. His three team members also had their coats off, indicating that all of them had been in the building for some time. Actually, Tony had been the last to arrive, since he had come directly from West Patterson after his meeting with Bradley at seven-thirty in the morning.

Mark Lieberman, George Cleveland, and Mary O'Brian, the other members of the advance team, had been paged and told to go directly to Newark and wait for Carenza, rather than come into the head office. The three had met in the coffee shop near the Broad Street entrance to the building and then waited for Carenza. When he arrived, Carenza used the pay phone to call Bradley, got his final instructions, and headed upstairs. As he walked up to Gloria's desk, heads began to take notice of them. Lieberman had participated in the previous audit and had worked closely with a number of the international managers, especially Jane Moran. Jane also knew who Tony Carenza was and could tell that something unusual was going on.

By the time Tony introduced himself to Gloria, a buzz had started in the room.

"I'm sorry Mr. Carenza, he's not in."

"Do you know where he is or when he's expected back?"

"I'm sorry to say I don't. According to his schedule he's due here this morning. He may have stopped to see a customer on the way in and just didn't mention it. He does that from time to time." Gloria had a feeling something was up when she answered Larry's phone earlier and took a message from Robert Bradley. She knew who the auditors were the moment they walked through the door. Lieberman, of course, she knew and Carenza she identified from McBride's description of him "...short, fat, New York Italian guy, got to have a fifty-inch waist and be well over two hundred pounds. And that guy's supposed to be an officer in the National Guard? They must hide him in the back room some place so the troops don't see him."

The description was right. When he spoke, Gloria anticipated the New York accent but she could see in his eyes that she was dealing with street smarts that were three jumps ahead of her.

"What's his calendar say? When does he *have* to be here?"

Gloria looked down at her desk and opened McBride's Day-Timer. Something she really didn't have to do, as she knew his schedule by heart. However, she also knew the man in front of her would not accept her verbal assurances of McBride's office plans. Also, from her position, she could see Jane Moran heading for Ed Campbell's office and this would give her time to give Ed some notice as to the arrival of the unexpected visitors. She flipped through the page, stopped at the current date. "He has a meeting with George Mercer of computer operations at three this afternoon."

"Does he usually call for his messages?"

"Always."

"Have you heard from him this morning?"

"No, I haven't."

"Where can I find Edward Campbell?"

"He's on the other side of the room. The office in the corner."

"Would you please tell him I'm here?"

Carenza sensed something. A general feeling. He had no intention of waiting an extra hour.

"Yes." Gloria picked up the phone and dialed Ed's number. She offered none of her usual friendly chatty banter. One look at Tony Carenza's face told her that this was someone not to be fooled with.

Ed, of course, was aware that they would be coming. He just didn't know when. He also knew it would not be announced in advance to the department they were auditing, which was why audits of this type were usually called "surprise audits." He remembered when he first started in banking of seeing four men in top-coats and hats huddled in the cold in a doorway on New Street just around the corner from the Bankers Trust head office. They were the only people not going anywhere at two o'clock in the afternoon on a cold snowy day and looked somewhat suspicious just huddling and talking. But at five minutes past two they rushed across the street, flashed their ID to the guard and, while the senior member of the team sought out the branch manager, the others positioned themselves at the teller cages, as they were still called.

The tellers were then instructed to step back from their positions while the manager and head teller opened up a couple of new cages to take care of some of the leftover banking lunch hour crowd. The auditors then initiated their inspection of each of the formerly active teller stations. The object was surprise, although just as Ed was expecting an audit team to show up, the branch manager knew a surprise audit was coming, as he had requested it. There had been complaints of short changing customers but the daily positions of each of the tellers always proved out. Customer complaints of short changing were not unusual but the number had been increasing significantly. Usually when a customer cashed his payroll check at the bank, the amount included change, and it was easy for a teller to serve up fifty-five cents instead of eighty and hold back a quarter. If the customer were to complain on the spot, the teller would apologize and give them the quarter. If not, it would be pocketed.

Actually, in this case, it was buried in a souvenir cereal bowl of silver paper clips that the teller kept nearby. Each time the teller took a break, he would close out his position and take any personal work material to a designated work drawer, where they could store material. Since all tellers wore uniforms in the 1960s, they also had lockers where they changed their clothes and were required to leave their wallets and personal effects. What the auditors found was that the cereal bowl was filled with quarters on the bottom and covered with paper clips on top. They estimated that he was stealing ten to fifteen dollars per day from customers by simply short changing them. An extra fifty to seventy-five dollars a week was a tidy sum for a teller in 1960 and would more than double his take home pay. The auditors knew what they were looking for and it was just a matter of time before they found it.

Gloria knew there was something different going on today after receiving the phone calls from Robert Bradley, and now an audit team showing up the same morning, prepared to start work.

The usual procedure would be for the team leader to have a chat with the manager first and lay out the scope of the audit and enlist his support. With no notice like this, she immediately assumed there was something else going on and one of the managers was probably the target.

Jane Moran also knew something was up, since it was Larry McBride's usual practice with audits for her to be called in during the initial meeting with the audit team leaders. She was usually designated by McBride as the "point" person, to whom all audit requests, requirements, and preliminary reports were to be sent. It was therefore not unexpected when Ed asked her to remain in his office after she notified him of Carenza's unexpected appearance. She was there when Gloria brought Tony Carenza in and introductions were made all around.

"Normally, this letter would go to the department manager," Carenza said, as he passed it across the desk.

There had been no small talk, as that was not Tony Carenza's style. The schmoozing was left to Robert Bradley. Tony saw his job as finding the problem and demanding it be fixed within a specified time-frame. He had no interest in fixing blame or dealing in personalities either.

Ed nodded. "I'm aware of that. Unfortunately, Mr. McBride is unavailable but I'll relay to him whatever comments you have."

"I've left a copy of the letter with his secretary. We'll be here for the balance of the day and will need a place to set up shop."

"I'll see to that. Initially, you can use the conference room across the way near the entrance of the department. We usually use it for large meetings and seminars and its empty today. I'll have the schedule checked and see if you can have the room permanently. If not, I'll find you some other space where you won't be disturbed."

"Can it be locked?"

Ed looked at Jane Moran and she responded. "Yes, it can. Gloria, Mr. McBride's secretary has the key. I'll see that you're provided with one."

"Good. That letter outlines the scope of the audit. There are a number of files, records, and reports we will need, and if you could have someone start working on assembling them right away, I would appreciate it. What I would like to do for the balance of the morning is for someone to give us an overview and tour of the department to get us properly oriented. Also, if you can get me a current organization chart and personnel listing it would be helpful."

"No problem," Ed replied. "Jane here can give you the tour. She knows the place better than anyone, and I'm pretty sure Gloria can arrange for copies of the other material you may need. I'll have her put what she can into the conference room while you're touring with Jane." The latter was a vain attempt at easing the tension, which did not result in any change of expression from Carenza. Ed figured it went right over his head—but it didn't.

"Is there a designated smoking area on this floor?'

"No, I'm afraid the whole building went non-smoking at the beginning of the year. That's true, isn't it, Jane?"

"Yes. Afraid you'll have to go out in the cold on Broad Street."

"It's okay. I've done it before."

Jim wasn't sure whether there was a double meaning intended in the response about his being out in the cold or not. Carenza was clearly making him uncomfortable, something Ed didn't think would happen, since he knew the audit was coming, but this guy Carenza was giving him the creeps.

"Well, look," Carenza continued, "if you don't mind, I'd like to begin. The sooner we start the sooner we'll be out of your hair. I don't want to disrupt your normal routines or the department's business activity."

"No problem. Jane, I'll turn them over to you and—" Ed turned to address Carenza. "—if there's anything you need, please let me know, and we'll do everything we can to get it for you."

"I know you will. Thanks, but the only thing I'm missing right now is your boss." Tony extended his hand to Ed as he stood up.

Ed took it. *What do you mean by that?* He had no idea how much Carenza knew about Ed's involvement in the report, since no names were mentioned, or if he even knew of the report, which was unlikely. Although he may have been sent in on his own as they already suspected something. It was definitely unnerving. The handshake wasn't any better. It wasn't just a routine clasping of hands. Carenza's grip was strong, which Ed expected, but it was how Carenza held on to Ed's hand that second or so longer than he expected. As Carenza left the office, Ed made two quick telephone calls. The first was to Gloria for the organization chart for the department and key to the conference room and also to check and see if it would be available for at least two weeks. The second was to Jim Fairmont.

∾∾

"There's no sign of him anywhere?" Marian asked.

"He never came back to his office and hasn't called in." Jim reached for the grated Romano cheese. Tonight was pasta night, shells with some microwave heated sauce. Pasta was a staple at least two nights a week. "Ed said he checked with Gloria a couple of times during the day, and there was nothing."

"Has anybody searched his office?"

"What for?"

"To see what's there."

"You can't do that. I mean you have to have a reason."

"Can't the auditors?"

"That's not the way it works. What they do is develop a request list of files and reports and then submit it to the manager."

"Who's not there."

"No, the request goes to whomever the manager has designated as the 'point' person. With McBride out, Ed is the acting manager, and he designated Jane Moran."

"So she gets the request, spends all day looking for what everyone knows is missing, and is probably in McBride's office, while McBride gets an extra day to cover his tracks."

"The auditors are not the police. Their job is to collect information. If a file is out to someone, they are told the auditors need it, and they are instructed to provide it."

"Sounds too gentlemanly for me."

"No, in this case, the request will go to McBride's secretary, who will search McBride's office to retrieve the file. You just can't storm into someone's private office and go rummaging around."

"So what happens when McBride's secretary can't find the files and McBride is still among the missing?"

"Well, at that point, I guess, they'll have to bring the police into it. But I think they'll try just about everything else they can before that happens."

"Giving more time for McBride to cover his tracks."

"You know, he's not an axe murderer. This is white collar crime. Nobody's life is in danger."

"How would you like to go for a ride after dinner?"

"A ride?" Jim was not surprised that Marian had changed the subject, although he had a sneaking suspicion that there was a connection someplace. "Okay. Where do you want to go?"

"Just around. Leave the dishes, and we'll have coffee when we get back."

Jim drove and started out toward Far Hills, which was their usual route, but hadn't gone more than a few blocks when Marian suggested a turn. "Do you have someplace in mind as to where we're going?" he asked.

"McBride's."

"McBride's?"

"Just drive by."

"Marian, I don't think it's a good idea. Besides, it's dark. What can you possibly see?"

"Lights."

"Lights?"

"If he's home, the lights will be on."

"Marian, I don't think so."

"What can it hurt? No one will know. We just drive by, take a look, and head for home. We're only a couple of blocks away."

Jim was silent but kept driving toward McBride's. He knew this was not a good idea. All they'd have to do was run into McBride, but then he had to admit that he was curious too. After all, they did live in the same town. Driving by was easy to explain, should anyone ask, and who was going to ask?

Going past McBride's townhouse complex was one of the shortcuts you could take to get to the little shopping center down by the train station. Of course, weaving around the streets of the complex might be more of a challenge to explain than just driving through and since McBride lived toward the end of a street with no outlet and backed up on a park.

All of these thoughts kept weaving through Jim's head as he continued to drive toward the townhouses. Marian didn't say anything further as she could see where he was heading. In the darkness of between seven and eight o'clock at the end of September, she believed the car would be indistinguishable from any other.

Besides, she had already decided to do this during lunch, but became distracted with customers and never got around to it.

She was also still trying to find the right time to tell Jim about Ed's visit of the previous afternoon and hadn't figured out how to bring it up since being interrupted by Carl's phone call. She knew it was a mistake not to tell him right away, as the longer she waited to find the right opportunity, the more agitated she felt about it, which was a dumb feeling, since it was just an innocent visit from an old friend. Or was it? Of course, it was. Then why was she acting like there was more meaning to it?

Anyway, she was sure this was not the time to bring it up but was pretty sure it had better be a topic of conversation before the night was over. All Jim would have to do was hear it from Ed, since they talked all the time. But if he did, that would only prove that it was innocent. Not that anything happened. It was just a friendly drive by and a stop in to say hello between two old friends. That, of course, was stretching it. The one thing she really didn't want to happen was for Jim to hear of Ed's visit from Florence. Marian had introduced Ed to her just as he was leaving and told her he was one of Jim's colleagues at the bank, and Ed and Florence seemed to hit it off right away.

No, she was definitely going to have to tell him tonight—as long as nothing else got in the way.

"Well, we're here," Jim said. "Against my better judgement. So now what?"

"Drive around once, and then we'll head out."

"Sure you don't want to stop at his door and say 'Hi, Larry, just driving by. Understand the auditors are looking for some files you have. We'd be happy to take them back to the office for you.'"

"Well, I suppose we could."

"Marian!"

"Just kidding."

"I'll drive through the complex, and then we're out of here."

He turned into the entranceway. "We're not supposed to be involved anymore."

The speed limit was twenty-five miles per hour, so there was no way for Jim to just zip in and out again. Besides, almost every street ended in a cul-de-sac, which was designed to hold the speed down and eliminate through traffic.

Jim made a left and then a right and stopped at the head of McBride's street. "I'm just going to cruise down one side, turn around at the end, come back, and then we're out of here."

"I think there's a light on," said Marian, as she squinted at the darkness ahead of them. "I'm sure that's McBride's."

"Which one?"

"The fifth or sixth one up there on the left."

As they got closer, they saw that there were some people standing in front of McBride's townhouse, talking and pointing at the building. The lights were definitely on. In fact, *all* the lights were on, and the door was open.

As Jim eased the car past the entrance, more people were coming out into the street and milling about. Marian peeked around Jim to get a better look. It was definitely McBride's. Then they heard the siren of a police car. Jim looked into his rear view mirror while Marian turned completely around in her seat. They reached the end of the street, and Jim started to turn around just as the police car came in at the other end. The siren was turned off, but the lights kept flashing, the red, blue, and white colors lighting up the street as they bounced off the buildings and gave the once-calm street an eerie and surrealistic appearance.

The police car stopped in the middle of the street right in front of McBride's.

"What do we do now?" Marian said.

The lights were also bouncing off them and giving the inside of the car a red and blue tint.

"There's no way I can get by if he leaves that car the way it is."

"Pull over to the side there." Marian indicated a driveway and Jim eased the car along the curb and came to a stop.

"I think we should get out of the car. Our siting here may draw attention to us."

With the arrival of the police and the flashing lights, the neighborhood came alive. Having the police on the street was not a common occurrence, so virtually every building had either someone looking out the window or appearing in the doorway. It was a chilly evening so most people just stayed close to their homes, although one could clearly see some husbands being prodded to "…go find out what's going on," as they were handed a jacket.

Jim and Marian got out of the car and, as they started back toward McBride's, a man came up to them. "What's happening?"

"I have no idea," Jim answered.

Marian nearly jumped out of her skin when the man came out of the dark. She was now holding onto Jim's arm.

"Must be a robbery or something. I don't hear the fire signal," the man continued, now joined by another man and then a woman.

"That's right," the woman said. "There was no signal."

New Jersey relied almost exclusively on volunteer fire departments in all of the smaller city areas of the state and the call to volunteers was the air raid type signal that sounded from the firehouse. It usually sounded multiple times to signal a fire, and then within a few minutes, there would be cars and trucks with flashing blue lights rushing to the location identified by the fire dispatcher.

The police usually arrived first as they were tied in directly to the communications system. But no, there had been no fire siren. The group of five now continued heading toward McBride's.

As they reached the end of the building, they joined another group of five or six who had stopped to watch the action. A second police car now arrived, and the houses were bathed in the flashing strobe effect of the multi-colored police lights. The whole scene took on an eerie look.

"Hey, George, what's going on?" called a tall, thin man in a wind breaker and baseball cap to another man who was standing up near McBride's front door, which was wide open.

"Not sure. Some guy was makin' a big ruckus banging on McBride's door. Almost broke it down."

Every light in McBride's townhouse was on, and Jim could see one of the policemen walking from room to room.

"Lilly came out and told him to stop, and he yelled at her, started cursing a blue streak. She got scared and called the cops. I came out to give him a piece of—"

"Excuse me, sir," a policeman interrupted. "Need to get by. He then disappeared into McBride's townhouse, where a woman, presumably Lilly, was speaking with another policeman.

The tall man then said to another man of similar height next to him, "Good thing McBride's away."

"Is Larry away?" Marian immediately asked, without thinking.

"Yeah, Lilly said she saw him leave the night before last."

"Sunday night?"

"Yeah. On vacation somewhere, I think he told her. The airport limo picked him up."

"I guess it's a good thing he wasn't here."

"There was a lot of yelling," another woman chimed in. She had just come from across the street. "I looked out, and George and another man were yelling at one another. Good thing Lilly called the police right away. Some people try to handle things on their own but, these days, well, you never know who you're dealing with. It's best not to get involved."

"Yeah," said the tall man. "There are a lot of crazies out there."

"Do you think he knew McBride?" said the tall man's friend.

"Pete, it seems to me that if you're banging on someone's door like this guy was, you know who's door it is."

"Maybe he had the wrong place. I mean, why chase after a banker? McBride wasn't in the business of turning down mortgages or something. He was a high-finance guy. I'll bet it was a mistake or a nut case."

Jim nudged Marian. "I think we should try to get out of here."

Marian nodded. The crowd had grown while they were standing there and they had to weave through a number of people to get free.

"What's going on?" a woman asked them, arriving just as they started walking away.

"It looks like someone tried to break into that townhouse over there," Marian replied.

"Was anyone hurt?"

"Apparently not."

"That's Mr. McBride's place, isn't it?"

"Yes, I think so."

"Why would anyone want to do that? He's such a nice man. Do you know Larry?"

"Eh, yes."

Jim nudged Marian's arm in an effort for her to end the conversation and keep moving. He noticed that a car on the way in had managed to squeeze past the two police cars in the street and figured if someone could get in, they could get out.

"I guess it's just not safe anywhere these days. It's just terrible. And right here in our quiet little neighborhood. I don't think we've ever had a problem before. Where do you people live?"

Marian could feel Jim's grip tighten. "Oh, were just visiting some friends."

"Well, I hope you don't get the wrong impression. This is really a very nice neighborhood."

"I'm sure it is. We're going to try to make our way back," Marian said in an effort to break free.

"Oh, you're not on the street?"

Where is this third degree coming from? Marian thought. "No, our friends are over on the next street. We just saw all the commotion and came over to see what was going on." A pull from Jim this time. "We really have to be going."

It was then that she saw the man with the camera. He was taking pictures of the crowd that had gathered. Jim saw him as well and immediately turned his head away. If people still wore broad brimmed hats, he would have pulled it down over his face.

"Let's get out of here," he finally whispered as he pulled her away from the woman, who looked at them strangely as they rushed down the street toward the car.

"Were you planning to spend the evening chatting up the neighborhood?"

"I couldn't be rude. She was just being neighborly. If it was on our street, I'd probably be doing the same."

"Let's just try to get out of here before something else happens."

They finally made it to the car, got in, and then Jim started to ease down the street. There were a number of people milling around now, some were heading toward McBride's and other away.

No one was paying much attention to traffic, so Jim had to be especially careful and kept the car going at a crawl. He moved to the left side of the street in an effort to get by one of the police cars, the red and blue lights still flashing and bouncing off everything all around.

Suddenly, one of the policemen appeared in the street in front of them and then came over to Jim's side of the car.

"Hang on just a minute, and I'll move the cruiser so you can get by." He shined his flashlight into Jim's face as he spoke and made a point of getting a good look at Marian as well.

"Thanks, I'll just back up a bit then." Jim then said to Marian, as the policeman turned away, "This had got to be one of the dumbest things we've done in a long time. Everyone in the world is going to know we were here."

"Who's to know? Nobody's looking for us. Nobody's even looking for McBride, at least not yet. It's not as though he's a wanted criminal or something or, if he is, no one knows about it. So we took a little drive. We do live in this town, don't we? We can do that."

"Marian, no one in the world would believe that our cruising through the neighborhood was an innocent little drive. There's no outlet from this street. If someone were to recognize us, they would immediately assume we were snooping."

"What would they think we were snooping about? At this point, there aren't more than four or five people who know you put together a critical report about McBride, and not one of them lives in Fordstown. We just went for an evening ride, came in here to turn around, saw the flashing lights, and, just like everyone else, came over to investigate like a moth to a flame."

The police cruiser backed up and eased over to the side, and Jim began to move slowly forward. He was still on the left side of the street and, as he passed a sedan that was parked just across from McBride's, the occupant of the car looked carefully at Jim and then picked up a notebook.

CHAPTER 31

The Audit Begins

At the start of the audit, it was Robert Bradley who set the parameters, but Tony Carenza who set the tone. Meetings, schedules, conferences would now be at Tony's request and timetable. Demands would be made on both time and material. If his team needed a file, it would be provided, no matter who else might need it. One might borrow it back for a particularly good reason, but its temporary new home would be the audit room. If an auditor needed information and a personal meeting was required, you adjusted your schedule.

Under no circumstances was the auditor to be given the impression that anyone resisted cooperating. In fact, just the opposite was always true. Upon receiving an audit letter, the local manager would usually call all the supervisors together and remind them that they were to be helpful and cooperative. Whatever an auditor needed, they were to provide it. The staff knew they had to make themselves available for special meetings and interviews and to be patient with the audit staff, as they would be asking questions that, quite often, would seem somewhat dumb, as they, presumably, did not have the staff's knowledge base. So they would be obliged to look to them, the staff, for guidance and explanations, and the staff was to provide it—patiently, openly and accommodatingly.

The one thing the manager did not want to hear was that someone was being uncooperative, a word no one wanted to see in an audit report.

So when the call came through to Jim's secretary from Robert Bradley's office that a meeting was being set up for two o'clock on Wednesday afternoon in West Paterson, Jim immediately instructed Paula to clear his afternoon for it. If that meant cancelling other meetings and rescheduling them, then it would be done. If that meant finding a substitute to sit in with a customer or at an internal administrative meeting, a substitute would be found. It was an inconvenience and took up most of Paula's morning, shifting people and times, but she got it done.

And while all this maneuvering was going on in Morristown, similar activity was occurring in Newark, where another call had been received by Ed's secretary. Ed's schedule was a little easier to rearrange, as he didn't have the level of customer meetings that Jim did.

On Wednesday afternoon, when Jim arrived at the West Patterson office, he did so a few minutes early. He left Morristown at noon with the plan of stopping for lunch along the way. Above all he didn't want to be late, so he stopped at a diner on Route 46, just a few miles from the headquarters building. Ed's plan was the same, although they had not spoken that morning and neither was aware that the other would also be at the meeting or who else might be there, if anyone. Ed's luncheon choice was a diner where Routes 3 and 46 came together, slightly farther away from the place that Jim had chosen.

Jim was signing the log book at the security desk when Ed came through the revolving door of the lobby. They both made sure of being early for the meeting and planned on being ready when called to go upstairs. Although bank staff was not required to be announced, they were obliged to sign the log book, display their picture identification, and record their bank ID number in the log. Also, unlike customers, they were not required to be escorted through the building.

Since the failed attempt to blow up the World Trade Center two years ago, security was an imprecise art in these days of potential terrorist attacks. Corporations spent enormous amounts of money on security, most of it electronic in some fashion, and most of it circumvented by employees, as it was usually an impediment to efficient employee movement.

Many of the devices were either not activated or not monitored. The theory being, of course, that security could be tightened up at any time by management and the threat of detection was enough of a deterrent—the same argument used for the elimination of bank guards in favor of cameras, which cut expenses but did nothing to prevent robberies.

The real inconvenience and threat were to the employees who had to learn to live with it.

"Ah, so you *are* here," said Jim

"Yeah, I was just wondering if I was going to have any company." They shook hands, chatted about the traffic for a few moments, and then Ed moved in front of the security desk to sign the book. "To see Robert Bradley," he said to the security guard and then began writing in the log book.

Ed flashed his ID but then had to turn it over to read the number on the back, as he didn't have it memorized yet since the Newark office used automated turnstile equipment, which read the magnetic strip on the back of the card.

The same was true of the operations center although some additional security procedures were in place at such locations in order to preserve the integrity of critical data and systems.

Here at the headquarters building, where the general administrative, lending, trust and retail banking management were located, they tried to maintain security on a more personal level. Security guards were very much in evidence, even if they did wear custom blue blazers and were trained in courteous, friendly behavior.

The sign at the desk clearly announced that all briefcases were subject to search and quite frequently were. The routine was an expected one, something a visitor to senior management learned to put up with.

When Ed finished signing in, they both moved over to the sofa and lounge chairs that made up the large reception waiting area. The security desk officer would call Bradley's secretary, who would either come down to get them or just instruct security to send them up.

"I guess things have been a bit busy around your place," said Jim.

"Actually the audit team's keeping a pretty low profile. Carenza wasn't there this morning, but two additional people showed up. We've got them in the seminar room."

"Carenza's probably upstairs."

"I wouldn't be surprised."

"No word of McBride?"

"Gloria said he still hasn't called in. I wonder if we've stumbled on to something bigger than we thought."

"I think the problem may be that we still don't know what we've stumbled on to."

"Mr. Fairmont." The desk guard called to Jim, and they both moved in his direction. "You can both go up. Do you know where Mr. Bradley's office is?"

"Should be the fourth floor, south end of the building, unless they moved it."

"No, that's correct."

"You never know any more the way everything is constantly moving." They both picked up their briefcases and headed for the elevators.

"You know that Garden Walk place of Marian's is pretty nice. Only wish I had a garden; I'd send some business her way. I guess Marian told you I'd stopped in.?"

"Yeah. She does a nice business and really enjoys it. Although as with any small business it does get to be a twenty-four hour a day job. Were you looking for anything in particular?" which was a question that Jim was very interested in getting an answer to, as the elevator arrived and the UP light gave off a sub-dued chime as it lit up.

"Not really. I was on my way to Liberty Corner and couldn't resist stopping in. After all the e-mails I'd been sending there. By the way, do you have any hint as to what's going on upstairs? What's this fellow Bradley like?"

Jim would have really liked to pursue Ed's visit to Marian on Monday to find out why she didn't mention it for two days. He was starting to feel edgy about the relationship. He knew they liked one another twenty years ago so there was still a chance there might still be some compatible chemistry around—it made him uncomfortable—a little like finding out that one of the kids that you didn't want your son to hang around with when he was in high school just moved in next door. You wanted to have confidence that he could handle the situation and now recognized that the person was a bad influence, but you still felt uneasy because you knew there was a bond of friendship there once—the chemistry that found the problem child fun to be with. One might liken it to voters and Bill Clinton, who was clearly perceived as a fun guy to be with—bright, witty, intelligent—who knew how to have and to show you a good time But somewhere in the back of your mind you knew if you weren't careful there was a good chance he was going to get you into trouble if you kept hanging around with him, and you also knew that he'd be able to slough it off, but you wouldn't.

The elevator began to move after Ed pressed four and the doors closed. "Bradley's pretty level headed. Like any audit chief, he knows how to walk that fine line between protecting the bank while not imposing restrictions on its earnings. He's a pretty good politician. Auditors are a funny group in that they stick together. They don't really mix with the rest of the bank on a personal basis."

"That's kind of been my experience too. They're also pretty close to their counterparts around town."

"Yeah, I'm sure they talk all the time to keep up on potential scams that the other banks have uncovered."

"Now this guy Carenza seems to be cut from a different mold," Ed noted.

"As I said, I really don't know him other than he comes from Citibank."

"My initial impression is that he only knows how to play offense. Why I feel this way I don't know. I only met him once. And that was yesterday morning when he came in to set up the conference room and introduce the team members to us. He definitely made an impression. When I shook his hand, I had the feeling he was trying to tap into me. I don't know. I'm probably just being a bit paranoid. I'm starting to get some bad feelings about the whole thing."

"In what way?"

"I'm not sure."

"I probably shouldn't have gotten you involved."

The elevator arrived at the fourth floor, and they got out and began walking down the hallway.

Ed said, "No, I think you did the right thing. No matter what happens, there's definitely something screwy going on, the fact that McBride has suddenly gone AWOL has just convinced me even more."

"AWOL?" Jim, surprised, wanted to continue but they were at the secretary's desk outside Bradley's office.

Robert Bradley's status at First State was equal to that of a sector manager in that he reported directly to the chairman of the bank. The theory being that auditing should be as independent as possible and have direct access to the chief executive officer, whose primary objective is the growth and protection of the shareholder's investment. The chief executive, having achieved his ultimate career goal, would not be subject to the same performance pressures of those hoping to succeed him and would look at audit reports and recommendations with an unbiased eye.

So much for theory. The truth was that the chief auditor must be a master politician, as he continually walked on the edge of quicksand. His staff was charged with seeing that critical areas of the bank comply with the proper audit policies and procedures. However, strict policies and procedures may, a sector manager could argue, severely restrict operational performance— excessive control could be costly and thereby impact profits.

The auditor must know where to recommend tightening and where to force it. Quite often, timing was critical. Giving a manager eighteen months to correct or implement control versus three months could be the difference between meeting a profit target or missing it. If he tightened too much, the managers would complain. If he was too easy, he would be perceived as being lax and putting the bank in jeopardy.

The key to being successful was to implement rules that protect the bank from proven threats. The ideal proven threat is one that occurred at another bank and one that required some rules and procedures to be implemented to make certain it didn't happen in your own bank. Auditors were very good at keeping their own counsel. It was always difficult to argue with them as they were expected to always have the good of the bank as their main priority. If one argued successfully against them and the implementation of a new policy, then the manager's career could be on the line if something went wrong—unless he could get promoted and had moved on in the meantime—as it was the implementation timetable that was usually in question.

The auditor could always step back and say "That's a business decision for you to make. I can only outline the risks and let you know what others have done. If you feel confident that temporary checks and balances can handle the situation for now, that's fine, as long as there is a commitment for a permanent fix."

The auditor did his job, and it was up to the local manager to do his.

Robert Bradley's office was a carbon copy of other sector

managers with the usual desk, credenza, two chairs in front of the desk, the sofa for three, two end tables a bookcase and two additional chairs against the wall.

The only individuality one would have would be the family pictures and career mementos spread around the room. Even the art work on the walls came from inventory.

Bradley's secretary ushered them directly into the office where they found Tony Carenza already planted in one of the straight chairs, a good choice, since getting up and down from the sofa would have been a challenge for one of his bulk.

"Come on in," said Bradley, getting up from his chair behind the desk and moving around to the front to greet them. "Hello Jim," he said extending his hand.

"Hello, Robert."

"I'm Ed Campbell." Another hand shake.

"Good to meet you, Ed." Then Bradley turned to Jim. "I don't think you've met Tony Carenza."

"No, I haven't."

They all turned toward Carenza, who had also gotten out of his chair.

"But I have heard of you, and I'm sure I've seen you around." Jim extended his hand and was expecting some sort of retort from Tony such as "All good I hope." but there was none.

He didn't even speak, just extended his hand and there was the slightest perception of a smile but it wasn't really a smile, and there was that look in his eyes.

Jim knew he was being measured.

"Tony's hard to miss," said Bradley, giving reference to his obvious size and trying to lighten things up. Tony gave a bit of a smile in return. "He's given some stature to the department."

"Okay. Okay," said Tony, acknowledging the friendly barb.

"Tony and I have already met," said Ed, extending his hand but not looking forward to its clasp. Having gone through the experience once, he was not looking forward to it again.

Tony simply nodded his head in acknowledgment of Ed and then shook hands.

"Is that conference room working out all right?" Ed asked.

"Yeah, that's gonna be just fine."

"It looks like it's clear for the next two weeks so it's all yours. If you need it longer just let me know."

"Will do."

"You know, we can stay here or go into the conference room across the way?" Bradley asked.

The question was addressed to Jim as the senior of the two.

"Here will be just fine." Jim didn't confer with Ed on the answer. He preferred the more informal setting of Bradley's office to the starkness of the auditor's conference room.

"How about some coffee or soda?" Bradley inquired while moving back behind his desk.

"No, I'm fine," replied Jim

"Same here. Just finished lunch."

"Tony?"

The response from Carenza was a negative wave of the hand and a simultaneous shaking of his head, as though the two were attached by a string.

"Well, have a seat then."

Bradley turned to his secretary, who had continued to stand poised in the doorway while the introductions were completed. "No calls for a while."

She nodded and closed the door as she left?

Ed started to move to the sofa as Jim took the other available straight chair but then decided against it and moved to one of the straight chairs that was against the wall and moved it out near Jim's. Neither Ed nor Jim had any intention of being in a subservient position on the sofa with both Bradley and Carenza looking down at them. Bradley would have the advantage being behind his desk, the authority seat, but that was okay, it was his office and his meeting, but no way was Carenza to be given an advantage.

The move was not lost on Carenza who was smiling to himself.

"Sorry about the short notice. I appreciate your adjusting your schedules." said Bradley, taking his seat. "No trouble getting here was there?"

"No," said Jim. "This is probably the best time of day to get from Morristown to Patterson. Not like what you got stuck with yesterday."

"That was some storm. All that wind. Well, well." Bradley leaned back in his chair and put his hands together in a seemingly prayerful gesture that signaled the end of pleasantries.

"I wanted this meeting in order to fill in some of the gaps that were not in the report that was filed. The report got our attention and was very helpful, so now we need to put some meat on the bone in order to get a full understanding of what's been going on. I'd like to get this review wrapped up as soon as possible. To do that, Tony here needs all the head starts possible, so he doesn't end up covering ground that he doesn't need to. So let me give you an idea of where we are right now."

He moved forward, leaned his elbows on his desk and picked up a pencil and began massaging it. "First of all, McBride is still missing—"

"Still?" Jim interrupted. "I didn't know he was actually, officially classified as 'missing.' He hasn't contacted anyone in the bank at all?"

"No. We don't think so but let me get to that as we go along."

Ed noticed that Carenza was giving Jim one of his steely eyed looks that Ed had become familiar with.

"Since McBride isn't around," Bradley continued, "we don't have any input from him that might be helpful. So I'm going to ask that both of you give Tony here some extra help. Ed, you, of course, would be involved since the review is in your backyard but, Jim, I'd like you to stay involved as well."

"Anything you need. You know that, Robert."

"Same here," said Ed.

"Good. Tony and I both feel this may get a little messy before it's finished, and I don't think I need to tell you that whatever we discuss doesn't go any further."

Both nodded in response.

"Now about McBride, yes, he's definitely gone missing. We're pretty sure he hasn't even tried to check his messages, and we've told his secretary to document them and certainly not to erase anything. She's also been instructed to let us know, immediately, if he calls in. We've got a copy of his schedule and, Ed, I'd appreciate it if you would give the customers on it a call and reschedule the meetings he's missed. His secretary has already confirmed that he did miss the meetings and didn't contact them to reschedule. You undoubtedly have some damage control to do." Bradly handed him the list Gloria prepared.

"And Gloria has no idea where he is?"

"That's what she says."

"We may have to look into that a little further," Carenza responded. "Would appreciate it if, when offering to pick up the ball with the customers, you also take some time to pump them a little to see if they know anything. Also, a couple of his pet names are on the list. I know you're familiar with them by now. I'd really be interested in your take on their reaction to McBride missing the meetings he had scheduled with them. If they show the least bit of concern about an upcoming transaction, I'd really like to know that. In the meantime, my guys are checking the names against recent transactions with the bank, and we'll see what we can match up."

"Sure, no problem. Those customers should be called anyway. Gloria's probably heard from them, and I'll double check with her again. She's already referred some of his calls over to me where the customer seemed agitated. Do you want those names as well?"

"Yeah, just add them to the list. Get as much done between now and noon tomorrow. At this point, that's probably when we file our first suspicious transaction report and place a call to the US Attorney's office...if that's what our attorneys recommend." He hesitated, looking at Bradley. "And senior management agrees."

"So it is what we expected?" Ed leaned slightly forward in his chair and looked straight at Carenza.

"That's one of the questions we have: What, actually, is it that you suspect? The report outlines questionable behavior but doesn't really make any accusations."

Jim noticed that Tony Carenza had clearly taken charge of the meeting while Bradley just sat back and let him run.

Jim pegged him as being light on the small talk side. A bit intense. Tony had a mission, and it looked as though once he had his teeth into something he was not likely to let go. He hardly said a word since they first entered the room except for that brief interchange, but Jim could feel his eyes on him—just sitting there and watching. *May have to be careful here,* Jim thought.

"That's the difficult part," Jim said. "I had no idea what was really going on. All I did know, especially when I looked at the wire transfer traffic, was that it was very suspicious. Moving money around, marshaling cash, controlled disbursement, credit and collection, these things I know something about, and some of

the funds movements were extremely cumbersome and very inefficient. We don't need intermediaries to send funds directly to
Europe or the Caribbean. We do it all the time, besides, when we
do, we get credit for it with our correspondent bank. Why go
through Chase or Bank One—or anybody else, for that matter?
Why incur additional charges? It didn't make sense. Larry was
close to the companies and didn't seem to see the opportunity but
then—maybe he did. The point is I saw something that looked
funny but, in itself…well, could be nothing." He made a point of
looking directly at Carenza as he spoke. "However, when Ed
started coming up with the file hoarding issue—"

"Before we get to that part," Carenza interrupted, "could you
just step back a bit and give us some idea as to where your suspicions originated?"

Jim moved slightly forward in his chair. "Sure. I know I've
mentioned to Robert just yesterday about the book sale and the
invoice I found, and that was really the trigger—"

Carenza interrupted again. "I've heard about this from Robert,
and I'm havin' trouble making the leap from your finding that
invoice to everything else that went on."

"Fair enough. I suppose it's one of those things where you
had to be there to appreciate it. Look, to me, Larry McBride was
a guy who just exuded confidence. I didn't know him that well,
but whatever contact I ever did have with him was one where he
was always in complete control—had it all together. When I met
him at the door to the book sale, he was upset and agitated, which
to me, seemed a bit out of character. Again, my exposure to him
was limited so seeing him popping off at a charity event volunteer just seemed strange. I probably would have taken notice, no
matter who it was. I mean, why pick on a volunteer like that first
thing on a Saturday morning? It caught my attention. She knew
we were acquainted, and McBride was being rude to her, which
made the scene all the more impressive. So then, later on, I saw
this all-together person crawling around on his hands and knees
under a table, pulling apart boxes of books. That definitely caught
my attention. My first reaction was that he, inadvertently, put one
of his valuable first editions in a box of books to be donated to
the book sale—I actually did that myself once—and suddenly
realized what he had done. But then he apparently found what he

was looking for, made an excuse as a cover-up, and left. I mean, it was real strange to watch."

"So how did you find the invoice?" Carenza prompted.

"Well, I mean, with all McBride was doing, I was curious. I went over to where he was crawling around on the floor to see what he was doing and found it in a box that came from his place."

"How did you know it was his?"

"I just assumed it was. The books in the box were his. Or at least, they were until he donated them."

"It never occurred to you that it could have been someone else's?"

Where is this line of questioning going? Jim mused. *What's he after?* He shot a look at Robert Bradley who just sat there quietly, leaning back in his chair and letting Carenza continue to take the lead. "No, it didn't. I mean, it was in a box of his books that had his library mark."

"So why didn't you just go after him and give it back?'

"I couldn't do that. I'd be—"

"Embarrassed?" Carenza said with that wry smile.

"Excuse me?"

Bradley, seeing a certain tension brewing, stepped in. "That seems understandable, under the circumstances." He moved forward in his chair and now had his elbows on the desk.

"No," Jim said. "I don't have a problem answering questions. I want to get to the bottom of this as much as anyone, and I'm willing to help in any way that I can, but whatever personal reactions I have to something or someone shouldn't be an issue."

"Jim, we appreciate that. It's just that we have to fully understand what's going on and the motivations involved."

"What do you mean *motivations*?"

Carenza jumped in. "Motivations! Look, you admit there was a certain hostility between you both. Could it have influenced your actions in some way?"

"You mean am I out to get McBride? I hardly even know him. That makes no sense. I've been to his home, attended his parties, worked with him on bank projects, been an advocate for his expertise with the bank's clients, and I have a professional working relationship with him."

"Look, to be frank, there's something very fishy going on

here, and McBride's in the middle of it," Carenza shot back. "This isn't the first suspicion that I've heard. Jane Moran and I have had a couple of conversations over the past few weeks, where she has suggested our next audit strengthen the recommendations on file handling."

"Jane did that?" Ed asked, surprised, looking at Carenza and then Bradley.

"It's not uncommon," Bradley said. "You should know that, Ed, from your operating background elsewhere. It's no different here. If you want to tighten up something that makes you uncomfortable and you're pretty sure the boss isn't going to go along for any number of reasons, the auditors can be your best friend. We can *discover* it during an audit and make a recommendation. You just, off the record, put an idea into our heads, and we become the bad guys. That's what we're supposed to be anyway. But first, we have to make sure we're not a pawn in some kind of internal office personality problem. Jim, all I want to do is clear the air from the beginning with regard to you and McBride. The whole idea of you snooping around after him, initially, didn't smell right."

"Wait a minute. There was no snooping." Jim jumped in with his back obviously up. "There was curiosity. It wouldn't have made a damn bit of difference who was crawling around on the floor, I would have done the same. It's a natural instinct. My first priority is always to protect the bank. Have you guys figured out something or not? To my way of thinking, McBride has been doing an end run on bank procedure—procedures you guys are supposed to enforce.

"And that's exactly what we're doing," responded Bradley. "This is part of the process. We also believe McBride has been doing an end run on procedure. We're looking to make sure your views aren't colored by anything other than fact. This is an informal discussion here. We want to know what you think, what you thought was happening to give us a head start on the review. I know we have the report you filed, but you and I both know that was intentionally bland. Now, as we discussed in your office, I'm looking for a gut reaction. What is it you really thought was going on? And stay with the domestic side. We'll let Ed handle the international."

The sharpness of Bradley's reply took Jim back. Auditors were political animals. They didn't ruffle feathers. They danced around subjects and issues. Jim was getting a sense that there might be some fallout from the McBride issue that could be career threatening for Bradley and possibly for everyone else in the room. "Okay, but I want to assure you there's no ulterior motive behind anything I've said. My objective here is to protect the bank—nothing more,"

"Jim, that's not an issue. I just want to completely satisfy myself that nothing else has crept into your reasoning, and you're not holding anything back that might be brought out later on."

"All right. I'll buy that."

"So I guess I'm back to the same question, what did you think was going on?"

"To be perfectly honest, I still don't really know." Jim sat back a bit and gave his reply as much to Carenza as to Bradley. "Again, I know a bit about effective cash management and those wire transfers didn't make any sense. Obviously, I thought of money laundering, but the individual amounts weren't overwhelming, and they were all tied into commercial transactions. Actually, that's why I brought Ed into the picture, to see if he could spot anything."

Carenza tossed his hat into the ring, "But when did you really decide something fishy was going on?"

"Well, I don't know. I suppose..." Jim paused, thinking. "I suppose it was the seminar. McBride ran an international sales-awareness seminar for non-international people. It's where I met Ed for the first time. There was a section that dealt with invoices. Actually, it had to do with the substituting of one shipping invoice for another. It just triggered something, so I asked a few questions, and when I found out that banks aren't supposed to have blank customer invoices hanging around...well, I started to get suspicious again. Until then I had just dropped the whole thing."

"But we're still back in early September, right?"

"Yes, we are but, at this point, I still don't know what I'm looking at."

"But you decided to play cop?"

"No, well...yes. But that's not really the way it was. I was curious. My gut was telling me something wasn't right."

"So you decided to go your own way."

"No, that's not really true either."

Bradley gave Carenza a simple nod. "Jim, I think what we're trying to do is determine why it took so long to hear about this."

"Robert, believe me, if I thought I had something to bring to you sooner, I would have been in here a long time ago. There was just no other way to do it."

"I'm sure you feel that way, but you know as well as I do, there will be an issue of damage control. Hind sight will always be an issue with the press, who we hope will not have to be involved. We have to anticipate every possible question, and the most common one is why didn't we do something sooner? Why didn't we spot this before it got out of hand?"

"Is it out of hand?"

"That's what Tony believes. But, in view of McBride's absence, I have to assume *he* thinks there's something for us to find, and we're looking to you for a head start. Naturally, we wish we were having this discussion some time ago but let's focus on a few things that could get us on track."

At this point, Bradley began to analyze the conversation on the wire transfers and why they looked suspicious. Carenza quieted down and spent a lot of time taking notes. Jim, at one point, opened his briefcase and pulled copies of the account statements of K E N Automotive with the suspect transactions circled, which Bradley looked at and then passed to Carenza. Tony looked at them without comment but shook his head from side to side the whole time.

Ed never said a word.

"Jim," Bradley said, "I don't know what to say. I certainly would have loved to have this before McBride disappeared."

"Amen," chimed in Carenza.

Ed finally spoke. "I think you're all making an assumption that may not be valid. I mean, McBride may still not know the purpose of the audit and certainly may not know that either Jim or I suspected there was something funny going on in international."

"Explain," Carenza grunted.

"Look, if we're looking at either money laundering or asset flight, and I don't know if it's either or both, there are other people involved. From what I've been able to piece together, there are no less than four companies involved in the US, which means there are at least that many abroad. We may be looking at just the tip of an iceberg here."

"That's what I'm afraid of," Carenza said. "Which leads me to you. I can buy off on Fairmont not quite recognizing what he was looking at but, if anyone should be able to spot an international scam, I figure you should be the one."

"I thought I did."

"Yeah, but you sat on it."

"Oh, no I didn't. Besides, you're still making an assumption that something is wrong because McBride has skipped. Asset flight from a foreign country to the US may be a crime in the country where the money comes from, but not here. From what I can tell, the bank doesn't even have any rules against soliciting asset-flight accounts.

Carenza looked at Bradley who said, "Technically, that's true, but if McBride is involved in encouraging it, he's in clear violation of a whole series of ethical behavior rules."

"I'll agree with that."

"Maybe I'm missing something," Jim said, directing his comment to Bradley and doing his best to ignore Carenza. "Asset flight is not illegal?"

"Not here."

"So if McBride was involved in helping foreign companies get restricted funds out of their countries, he really hasn't done anything wrong?"

"Technically, no."

"What do you mean technically? Are you saying that I could be wrong about the whole thing? I mean, is McBride a threat to the bank or not?"

"That's what we need to find out."

"No, no. There's something screwy going on here, now. Look at the pattern of those money transfers. Are you telling me that you don't see something suspicious there?"

"No, I'm not. Those transfers are definitely suspect. That's why the bank will file a suspicious transaction report."

"I think I'm getting something, Jim," Ed responded. "It's finally starting to sink in. If the report to the feds can be limited to those funny transfers through New York banks and others that end up in Antigua, then the focus of any investigation can be placed on the companies in the US that assisted in the asset flight scheme. The bank can be kept out of it."

"As long as McBride stays hidden," Jim interjected.

They both looked at Bradley and then Carenza.

"Did somebody at the bank tell McBride to disappear?" Jim asked.

"Jim, you know that's something we wouldn't do."

"Maybe so, but let's play devil's advocate for a moment from a public relations aspect. McBride's internal management quirks can be tossed off to just that—a personal management style. In fact, I'll bet someone could almost make a case that he was watching those files to make sure the companies didn't step over the line. It could be made to look like he's in the clear. He could get off with being chided for not notifying his superiors about an asset-flight scheme. If nothing can be proven against McBride or it can be shown that he was unaware of what his customers were doing, the bank is in the clear."

"Not even that," said Ed. "Remember, asset flight is not a crime. It may be poor judgement and lousy public relations but not illegal. As Mr. Carenza has already accused me of being able to spot an international scam, as he called it, you can be sure the feds will do the same with McBride, or at least assume that he knew. No, I think there's a bigger problem in front of us that we haven't yet considered."

The room was quiet. Finally, Carenza spoke. "Don't stop now. If you see something we don't, let's have it."

Ed hesitated. "What if some of the money being moved abroad belonged to McBride? What if there were some hidden fees involved? Something on the side? It's not an unknown practice. And then there's another matter that relates to a credit exposure to the bank. I spotted one broken back-to-back that was ignored. What if there are others out there that are treated as back-to-backs that really aren't? A blank invoice that could be fabricated might come in very handy. In my experience, First State, for its size, seems to have a bigger share of such credits than I would have expected."

Carenza wrote on a small notepad as Ed talked. "Now you've really got my interest. We need to have a talk with McBride."

"Trouble is he's not here."

"And if he's not here, where is he?"

CHAPTER 32

The Problem Expands

Jim had no desire to go back to the office after the meeting with Bradley and Carenza. The whole discussion left a bad taste in his mouth. He was irritated and spent a good deal of the trip back to his office talking to himself.

It was what one did in cars on highways. There was a sense of being alone, of being in a room by yourself, except that everyone out there could see you making a fool of yourself—singing or, in this case, talking away in a car with no passengers.

Jim went over the conversation, time and time again, and it just seemed to get worse after each review. He knew the bank would try to protect itself—that was only natural—but Bradley's handling of the meeting bothered Jim and left a feeling that, if he had made his suspicions known earlier, someone would have warned McBride, confidentially. Nothing formal, just a suggestion that he clean up his act and follow bank procedures in the future. Protecting the business and the revenue had always been a priority, but the new predatory nature of the banking industry reinforced it to the extreme. Employees were expendable work units, unless the employee was the CEO.

Ian had warned Jim that this would probably be a no-win situation. Should he have left it alone? Should he have looked the other way? Why did he have to think of it as his responsibility? He was an employee, a stockholder, it wasn't his bank—regardless of what the stock certificate said. But whose was it? The shareholders had no real say in what went on. The directors? He supposed a good case could be made for them as the legally elected representatives of the shareholders.

The real truth was that there was probably was no real ownership, in the common understanding of the word, which was why the term "stake holder" had come into vogue. A great buzzword for senior management to kick around at an annual meeting to show they cared about the employees—past and present—customers, suppliers, and just about anyone else who relies on the company in any way, other than ownership of a stock certificate. In effect, senior executive management ran the company as though it was a sole proprietorship or partnership but, unlike a real ownership situation, they could still walk away and move on to something else.

Jim kept arguing with himself over whom to blame, over why he should care, but he did, and there was nothing he could do about it. It was the way he was raised—you did something because it was right, because you believed in it.

The drive back from West Patterson was just a blur. He kept mulling over the meeting in his mind and had no recollection of the trip. By the time he realized where he was, he had already passed the exit to his office and was continuing south on I-287.

He knew where his instincts were taking him: to Marian. That was where he would naturally go, where he would want to be. She was his safe harbor, the only one he felt he could really talk with. But that had always been the case. He knew that was why they'd been married so long when others had fallen by the wayside. They were best friends.

Some men had their college buddies for best friends, and women always seemed to have more friends than they knew what to do with, but, for Jim, it was Marian. She was his confidant. She was the one he told his secrets to, his dreams. She was the one he could unload on.

So it was really no surprise to him when he realized that he had just passed the exit to the office and kept heading down the road to Marian.

It was because of the anger and distress over the meeting with Bradley that he didn't notice the blue Mercury that had been following him, but then why would he? Why would anyone want to follow him? He was just a run of the mill banker—just an ordinary person who had no reason for anyone to be following him.

His focus now was on Marian and, with that, he punched up her number on his car phone and auto-dialed it. When her voice came on the line, an enormous weight seemed to lift from his shoulders. He was not alone.

"Glad you're there."

"Jim, how did everything go?"

"I'll be there in a few minutes and tell you. Is the store busy?"

"On a Wednesday afternoon with a threat of rain? I don't think so. It doesn't sound like you had a good time."

"Just stay there, and I'll tell you all about it."

"Okay. Love you."

"Love you too, hon. See you in a couple of minutes."

Jim ended the connection and, for the first time all day, he had a smile on his face. He could put up with just about anything as long as he had her.

The New Vernon exit was just up ahead and, as he put on his turn signal, he glanced into the rear view mirror and noticed that the car behind him had turned on its signal as well.

❦

After Bradley walked Ed and Jim to the elevator—all the while making every effort to assure them that his primary objective was to make sure the bank was safe—he returned to his office and Tony Carenza.

"So, Tony, what do you think?"

"I think you've got some work ahead of you. Fairmont will be more of a problem for the bank than Campbell. I know you don't want any of this to hit the press, especially if the guys upstairs are looking at another merger. I know you haven't said they are, but let's face it. Greenspan has opened the floodgates by not resisting the moves to deregulate all the banks. Sometimes I actually think he really believes that no CEO would ever, consciously, do anything that would damage his company for personal benefit. I guess that's what living in an idealistic ivory tower will do for you. Right now, there isn't a bank in the country that isn't looking over its shoulder to see if someone's creeping up on them, while they do the best to scout out someone for them to creep up on. My feeling is that, if Fairmont sees any attempt to give McBride a pass, he won't stay quiet. And, in all honesty, I'll be on *his* side."

Bradley walked around his office as he spoke, "I understand all of that. It's why I hired you, but I still want to keep as low a profile as possible, and that's the challenge here. So how do we control Jim Fairmont—or maybe guide is a better word?"

Carenza was back in his chair, moving around was not his strong point. "The problem, as I see it, is that he feels he has a true vested interest in the bank being up front on the problem. Feels his own reputation is linked to it."

"But wouldn't keeping the profile of everything low also feed into his own desire to protect the bank?"

"Not if it smacks of something unethical. Believe me, I know where he's coming from. Remember, I've been there. He's trying to promote ethical conduct in an unethical world. He's definitely the more idealistic of the two of them. Probably the best approach would be to have Campbell keep explaining that the object is to fix the problem and not to assess blame and punishment. It looks like they really trust one another. I think Campbell's a realist. He knows that, to do business internationally, you have to be trustworthy, but he also knows that when things get tough, you don't screw your family. Although everyone else is up for grabs. What you have to do is assure him that the bank sees him as family. The bad apple is out of the barrel and steps have been taken to prevent other bad apples from appearing. Do that and Campbell will be happy. He won't question the motivation behind selling the product in the first place or how it really got into the product offering catalogue, only that it's fixed, and it's time to mend fences and move on. The guy's definitely senior management material." Tony chuckled over his last comment.

Bradley smiled and stopped his pacing. "Okay, you're the expert on people, so I'm making it your problem. Where do we go from here with McBride? What are we looking at?"

"Asset flight, tax evasion, and maybe some money laundering. What I don't have my finger on yet is McBride's piece of the pie. What's he getting out of this? I have to believe he wasn't doing this just to make the department look good at senior management meetings. He's been taking some sizeable risks with fudging credit policy on back-to-back credits. Nothing's gone wrong yet, but there's definitely a time bomb ticking out there. The key is to neutralize it before the bank gets seriously hurt. What worries me is his apparent disappearance. If he stays missing, it's probable he took something with him."

"How?"

"Those weird transfers of proceeds from the credits. Definitely something going on there."

"Any possibility of pushing the blame onto the US companies that are helping the foreigners get capital out of their home countries? Focus on them. Make it seem as though there was no overt involvement on the part of the bank."

"That may be hard to do without McBride to explain away his actions."

"Maybe yes, maybe no. If he stays away and no one can prove that he's taken bank funds as opposed to a side cut for himself…"

"But he's still missing." Bradley looked a bit nervous. Keeping the bank clean was looking more and more problematic. "Wouldn't it be better if he was here?"

"It would. He could add some innocent names to his pet list, so it would look like it was a list of companies that he really wanted to provide special attention to rather than cover a trail."

"How involved do you think he was?"

"Not sure, at this point. But I'll bet he's up to his neck."

"What have your people come up with, so far? I know you've had them working on it all night."

"We did find a couple of the missing files in his office—another real bad sign. It looks like the transactions have been manipulated—under shipping of merchandise, inflated pricing. Standard asset flight stuff. On the face of it, McBride definitely knew what was going on. What we don't know is the extent of his involvement. Whether it's active or passive."

"Any chance he was soliciting the asset-flight business?"

"Can't tell. But I'll bet if pressure is put on any of the US companies involved, and McBride stays missing, they'll tag him with it as being his idea."

"Could the charge stick?"

"That's *charge* in the non-legal sense. Remember, our handling the accounts is not a crime, but without McBride to defend himself, the press would love it."

"So the bank gets a black eye, no matter what?"

"Right on. And that's where Fairmont has to be kept out of the way. If someone from the press were to ask him what he thought, he just might tell them."

"Tell them what?"

"Well, almost whatever he would tell them would probably

make it seem that the bank was hungry for profits and didn't look too closely at where they were coming from. We didn't provide the kind of supervision that we should have and gave McBride too much leeway because he was being successful. The press would have fun with that. The rest of us know that's the way the game is played today. Get that bottom line up and reward, like hell, the guy who gets it there without causing the company embarrassment. That last part's the key. Ask the boy wonder if he's following company policy, and, if he says yes, you don't look any further. If what he's doing does cause a stink…well, that's cast-him-or-her-loose-as-an-outsider time and start the damage control."

"So should we be doing something about Fairmont?"

"I would say no. Keep him out of it as much as possible. He did his job, now we do ours. Act like he didn't have anything to do with it in the first place."

"But we said we wanted to keep him in to help with the wire transfer investigation."

"We can handle that. That's what the wire transfer department is for. Campbell, on the other hand, will be needed. It all started long before he came on board. Besides, he has a specific knowledge base that can help us and can present a good cooperative face to the feds when they come snooping around."

"Okay. Keep at it, but try not to ruffle too many feathers."

"Me? Come on, Robert, we've known one another for a long time. I don't ruffle feathers. I pluck 'um."

"I know, Tony, but also keep in mind that the reason I wanted you here is to take a hard look at the people and the acquisitions we've made and the ones coming down the road. Find out for sure what we're getting, but also keep in mind that most of us are bubble people around here. We live in nice suburban settings. Poor people, working people, crooks, and drug addicts are people you see on the evening news. They don't live down the street. Police give tickets and direct traffic. They don't shoot up your street, looking for bad guys."

"Okay, so old habits are hard to break. I'll do my best,"

෴

It was twenty minutes before Marian suddenly realized that

Jim never showed up as promised. He said he was only a few minutes away. She became distracted with a phone call after hearing from him and just realized that he still hadn't come into The Walk.

A police car went by with its lights and siren going, and she looked out the window. It was heading north up 202. She remembered hearing another one while she was on the call after Jim, but this sound was different, and she was pretty sure it was an ambulance. The local volunteer fire and rescue squad was just down the street. *How do they do that?* she wondered. *Make themselves available day and night on a volunteer basis to respond to fires and medical emergencies.* Why they hadn't gone the route of paid professionals like pretty much every other large metropolitan area in the country she couldn't understand? Although she was sure it was a money issue. Nobody wanted their taxes to go up and, by all estimates, it would sky rocket if they went to a paid system.

Tragedy always happened to someone else. Oh, well. She moved away from the window and headed back to her desk to call Jim on his car phone.

CHAPTER 33

An Understanding

When the light went green, Jim made a right turn instead of a left and pulled over to the side of the road. The Mercury followed him. Tony Carenza had flashed his headlights at him along the exit ramp and waved his arm to have him pull over. Jim's first instincts were that he ran a speed trap, but when he slowed down, he could see Tony behind the wheel.

Carenza jumped out of his car first and, given his size, surprised Jim with the agility and speed with which he reached him. Jim rolled down his window on the passenger side where Carenza headed.

"Jim, had to catch you before you got home. We need to talk. Lemme in," Carenza said, motioning for Jim to unlock the door.

"What's this all about?" Jim asked, watching Tony slide in beside him.

"McBride."

"He's back?"

"No, and that's the point. The last time anyone saw or heard from him was on Friday, five days ago. His secretary filed a missing employee report just after noon today. Copies went to bank security as well as auditing and some other places as required by bank policy. Security then filed a report with the state police."

"Yeah, I figured that would be next step on the list."

"After our meeting earlier, I learned that local cops were at McBride's last night. Apparently, there was a break in and some kind of disturbance that ended up in a shoving match between a neighbor and someone who apparently trashed the place. The neighbor ended up getting himself punched in the face for his trouble."

"So that's what that was."

"What?"

"Marian, my wife, and I went for a ride around the neighborhood last night after dinner and happened to see an ambulance and some police cars in the complex where McBride lives. We live about a half mile away and usually cut through the park next to where his place is when we go driving around."

"You didn't see anything?"

"No."

"Look, there's something really nasty going on here. I don't know what it is, but I'll bet it's tied into our audit. The cops said the guy who was in McBride's was reported to be completely out of control. I don't mean to scare you, but be careful. White collar crime usually doesn't have a violent component, but there's definitely something else going on here. Just be careful. I had to make a choice between chasing after you or Campbell and chose you for another reason."

"Tony, this is crazy. What could McBride be involved with?"

"Don't know. Just remember this is New Jersey, and there are a lot of things going on in the background that some people would just as soon stayed there." Tony stopped and gave Jim a long, hard stare. "Look, there's another reason I need to talk with you. Robert Bradley is a nice guy, and I've known him for a long time. He's a straight shooter, but he's under a lot of pressure. He talked me into coming on board here because he's worried about the direction the bank is going. Yeah, he's another of you dinosaurs that puts the bank first, and he's trying to do his best to keep doing it. Right now, my job is to play bad cop to his good guy insider image with senior management. I'm not your enemy. I'm not anybody's enemy. My job is to make sure the bank's rules are kept. I'm on your side. I'm on the bank's side. I've made it clear to Bradley that I intend to follow this wherever it goes. I don't do witch hunts. I do fact hunts. I'm not out to pin anything on anyone. As I said, my job is to verify compliance with the bank's standards, policies, and procedures and, where non-compliance is found, point it out and document it. I especially need your help as well as Campbell's because I think the two of you have stumbled onto something that goes beyond policies and procedures and borders on the edge of criminal behavior. I don't have anything to prove that—yet. And that's not my job, anyway. The incident at McBride's place worries me and, yes, I've run into this sort of thing in the past with a money laundering scheme at a bank in New York. It can get nasty, which is why I want you to be careful. If you suspect something, say something. Don't try to *do* something. I intend to give this same speech to Campbell."

"Tony, I appreciate your frankness. You haven't said anything to Ed yet?"

"No, I decided to go after you first, and I'll get Ed later. I have to go back to Newark anyway and, besides, I'm convinced Ed is in the same place I am on this, only he understands the potential for manipulation more than I do. I think he also understands the risk and where the loose cannons might be."

"Do you really think we might be in danger?"

"Can't say, but given the way the guy at McBride's acted…well, all I can say is that it's better to be safe than sorry. You have any idea who could be that upset with McBride?"

"Not really. I don't know what goes on at his office in Newark. Any possibility it could be one of his special customers? You know, the files he's been protecting."

"Thought of that. Have a feeling his secretary is the one who knows who the most volatile ones are. Will get together with her later this afternoon after I talk with Ed Campbell. Anything else you can think of? Secretaries sometimes tend to be somewhat protective of their bosses, especially if they've been together for a long time."

"I understand you've had some contact with Jane Moran. She's been with us a long time. Probably should have McBride's job except for the bank's past gender practices, but her loyalty's still to the bank and not McBride."

"Good point. She suspected something before you did. Questioned the length of time some of the files were missing from the bins. Yeah, she could be the key for us here."

The two of them continued discussing options by the side of the road, and Jim acquired a respect for Carenza he didn't think possible after the earlier meeting. After another five minutes, they shook hands, Tony got into his car, and they headed off in different directions. Jim immediately autodialed Marion on the car phone.

"Sorry, I'm running late."

"I was wondering where you were."

"Got stopped by Tony Carenza."

"The auditor? You're kidding."

"No. That commotion at McBride's last night has triggered a whole bunch of stuff. Tell you about it in a few minutes."

જજ

Ed Campbell kept driving toward Newark but not very fast. He started out on Route I-80 East and then dropped down to US Route 46 where traffic backed up in both directions. His next attempt, hopping down to NJ 23 proved to be even worse, so he decided to try the streets and made his way over to Bloomfield Avenue, but that didn't prove to be any better. He noticed the cars in front and behind him were trying the same traffic avoidance maneuvers and, obviously, weren't having any luck either.

Finally giving up, he used his car phone to call the office, and Gloria Martinez answered. "Ed, where are you?"

"Stuck in traffic. Thought it might be easier along the streets, but I think it's worse."

"Bloomfield Avenue?"

"How'd you guess?"

"Newcomer mistake. Jane waited for you as long as she could and then had to head off to another meeting. Said she'd stop by again about five and see if you'd made it back."

"It's about four-thirty, now but I have no idea how long it will take to get there."

"Where are you? Did you pass the Garden State yet?"

"No."

"Get on it, going south. Get off onto I-Two-Eighty East and take it to Broad Street."

"Won't it be backed up as well?"

"It's a toll road. It always moves faster. Everybody's too cheap to use it. Traffic should be moving okay east. Nobody comes *toward* Newark at this time of day. You'll make it just fine."

"Okay. Any news on Larry?"

"Nothing. Got some phone calls for him and took the names down for you. Also a couple of strange ones. Wouldn't identify themselves or leave a number. One guy called at least twice. I could tell from his voice. Also asked for you and then hung up. I think I recognized his voice but can't be sure."

"Okay. I see a sign for the Garden State up ahead. Be there as soon as I can.'

Ed hung up the phone with Gloria and concentrated on moving over to the right lane. Looking in his rear view mirror, he could see the three cars immediately behind him switch on their right turn signals just after he did. Everyone seemed to be taking the same route.

The entry ramp seemed to go on forever as it stayed parallel with the parkway for about a half mile before he could see the merge up ahead.

Traffic moved at about twenty miles per hour. The Garden State seemed to be moving around forty or fifty, even though the cars were bumper to bumper. He checked the rear view mirror, and a black GMC SUV continued to track just behind him. He was sure it had been there ever since he left Route 46 for Bloomfield Avenue.

The merge lane approached, and the line of cars entering began to pick up speed as they searched for an opening in the adjacent lane. He did the same—although the black SUV dropped back a bit—and picked his spot, concentrating intensely as he did.

Suddenly, the car behind rammed him in the right side of his rear bumper. Ed's Ford jumped forward before he could take his foot off the accelerator and entered the adjacent lane right in front of a white Toyota Highlander, which tried to break and swerved to the left. It hit Ed's car on the left side just ahead of the driver's door. The car behind it unsuccessfully tried to break and gave the Highlander a glancing blow in the rear just before slamming into the rear of Ed's rear. A third car bounced off the two in front of it and was hit by a car in the adjacent lane. The last thing Ed saw was a flash of white as his air bag exploded in his face.

After the black SUV rammed Ed, it braked and took a hard right onto the shoulder. The driver then gunned it and took off down the parkway.

☙❧

Gloria and Jane waited until six. Gloria tried his car phone, but no one answered. It went directly to voice mail.

They had no idea he was in an ambulance being actively worked on by two paramedics as they raced toward East Orange General Hospital.

CHAPTER 34

The Accident

Hope you don't mind our not going out?" Jim said as he and Marian cleared off the kitchen table of the remains of two take out dinners.

"No, it's perfectly fine. You can take me to the Black Horse Inn another time."

"But I hadn't planned on the Black Horse. Actually, I was originally thinking more of Willie's Tavern."

"I know," she said with a smile, "but that's where you're going to take me to make up for the Dinner for Two."

"Actually, I was going to suggest Pierre's Bistro for dinner but since you have your heart set on the Horse—"

"Yeah, right."

"Anyway," he continued, going back to the afternoon meeting, "it was just the way Carenza presented everything. He really thinks there's a danger factor to what's happened, and we just need to be prudent until some things are sorted out. He said we should expect the state police to be in touch."

"I just don't believe this. All because of a blank invoice?"

"Well, it's more than that. As I found out, Jane Moran already made some informal noises with auditing before I ever became involved. The invoice thing led to the funny transfers, and then everything took on a life of its own."

"But McBride wanting to do us harm—"

"He didn't say that. I think he believes McBride is on the run."

"But why? Who?"

Just then the phone rang. Marian walked across the kitchen and picked it up. "Oh, yes, Ms. Fredericks. He's right here." She walked the handset, which had a fifteen foot curl cord, across the room. "Jim, it's Grace Fredericks."

Jim took the phone. "Hello, Grace. Boy, they've got you working late." He looked at his watch. "It's after seven."

"Oh, I'm not at the office, I'm at home. I'm sorry to bother you. I know you've been working a lot with Mr. Campbell, and I thought you might want to know."

"Know what?"

"He's been in a terrible car accident. Gloria, Mr. McBride's secretary, told me a few minutes ago."

"Is he all right?"

"We don't know. The police called on his office line. They got it from one of his business cards. Gloria was still in the office at the time. She's been working late ever since Mr. McBride disappeared."

"Have they contacted his family?"

Marian, at this point, got the sense of something being seriously the matter and sat down across from Jim. She mouthed the words "What's going on?"

Jim held his hand up and then used it to cover the mouthpiece part of the handset. He whispered, "Ed's been in an accident." Then he held up his hand to her again as he listened to Grace.

"Gloria said that seems to be a problem," Grace said. "She asked me to cover for her tomorrow, early, as she and Jane Moran are heading for a meeting in personnel. She said that, with his being relatively new, no one really knows much about his family. Anyway, I thought you might want to know."

"I appreciate that, Grace. If I remember right, his wife is in Chicago. If you get a chance, ask Gloria to give me a call. I'll tell her all I know."

"Okay, Mr. Fairmont, I will."

"And, Grace, thanks for calling."

"What happened?" Marian asked immediately.

"Ed's been in an accident. Must have been on his way back to the office from the meeting this afternoon."

"Is he all right?"

"She doesn't know. Gloria told her to come in early tomorrow morning as she and Jane Moran have to go to personnel for a meeting. I'd better hang this up," he said, indicating the hand set he still held on to.

"I'll take it. Do you think it's on the news?" she asked while walking across the room and gathering up the cord as she went.

"It's after seven so all the local news casts are over until ten or eleven. Local radio might have something, especially a Newark station, although we don't know where it happened."

"You try the radio," she said. It sat on the kitchen table. "I'll try the PC and the internet. *The Newark Star Ledger* might have something on-line. Should you call someone at the bank? How about your new friend, Tony Carenza?"

"Let's see what we can find out from the radio and the internet first."

As Jim turned on the radio, Marian headed upstairs to the office they'd made out of one of the spare bedrooms. After trying both AM and FM stations for about fifteen minutes, Jim gave up. Marian did the same, after surfing the internet unsuccessfully, then came back downstairs, and joined him at the kitchen table. "Any luck," she said.

"No. The next news break will probably be on the hour at eight."

"I drew a blank too. I think WPIX does a ten o'clock news broadcast on Channel Eleven. That might be our best bet until tomorrow morning. Do you think this is a real accident or is this what Carenza was afraid of?"

"I have no idea. It's all a bit scary. We'll just have to wait until tomorrow. Find out what the official report is. I hope Ed's okay."

They both sat quiet for a minute and then, as Marian finally got up to clear the table of what dinner dishes were left, Jim cleared his throat. "You know, what bothers me is this whole thing with McBride's pet customers. There seem to be a couple of them that are really volatile. Like that whole dispute over documents that went on with Rayburn and then the guy who was making the stink ends up being killed in a car crash just up the road. Ed mentioned a guy by the name of Field, Charlie Field, I think it was, as being a real hothead."

"Field?" Marian looked at Jim questioningly. "Why does that name ring a bell? I'm sure I've heard it just recently. Let me think. Wait—the store. He was in the store."

"Seriously? Field was in The Garden Walk?"

"Yes. Just this morning. He was the first customer. All

dressed up in a business suit and everything. Just wandered around. Didn't say anything until I saw him peeking into the office. I asked if I could help—answer any questions for him. He said no and then picked up one of the ceramic cardinals and, I think, a bluebird, and came over to the register. He looked like he was going to say something when another customer came in, so he just said 'These will be fine.' He took out his wallet and seemed to be about to pay cash but didn't have the twenty-two fifty-something so he used a credit card. That's why I remember the name."

"And you don't remember him ever coming in before?"

"No."

"I don't like this. His company is over the Jersey City. Journal Square, I think. That's…what?…twenty-five maybe thirty miles from here?"

"Coincidence? Had some business in Bernardsville and just stopped by?"

"Not bloody likely," Jim commented as concern spread over his whole body like a blanket. "I think there are two things we should do right now. One, I *will* call Carenza, and two, you should call the Fordstown police. Who's your contact over there?"

"Charlie, the cop."

"Excuse me?"

"What can I say, that's what everyone calls him. His job is to keep track of the local retail places. Has a bicycle. Checks the parking lots, stops in to say hello at the store, helps out with traffic control at peak times. Basically stays visible. Really nice guy."

"I didn't know that. Anyway, why not give him a call and say you had some suspicious types in the store and see if he can make himself more visible around the place over the next couple of days. You know, a little pro-active shoplifting control."

CHAPTER 35

Estimating the Damage

T ony, come on in," Robert Bradley directed when he spotted Carenza enter the outer office. "What brings you here so early?"

"You hear about Campbell?"

"Don't tell me he's gone missing too?" Bradley's posture immediately stiffened. "Take a seat."

"I better close this first," Carenza said, indicating the open door he passed, entering Bradly's office. "No, he's been in an accident. A bad one."

"Really."

Taking his seat, Carenza continued. "Got a call from Jim Fairmont last night a little after eight. He heard it from someone in international."

"Is he going to be all right?"

"They don't know yet. We need to do some anticipation planning."

Bradley leaned forward. "Are you saying it wasn't an accident?"

"Not yet. No one's saying anything."

"How would it involve us? The audit? McBride?"

"Let me tell you what I've learned so far." Carenza leaned back in his chair and settled in. Leaning forward was not a particularly comfortable position when you had a fifty-inch-plus waistline to try to fold. "When Fairmont called me last night, and I should preface this by saying I encouraged him to call me anytime he felt it necessary. I met with him later in the afternoon yesterday after our meeting here, as I felt he came away with a negative impression of how the McBride problem would be handled. I again wanted to assure him that our objective is the protection of the bank, and we were not trying to fix blame anywhere. We just needed a sense of where everyone was coming from."

Bradley nodded his head in agreement.

"As I started to say," Carenza continued, "when Fairmont called, he had two issues to tell me about, one being Campbell's accident and the other being a visit from Charlie Field."

"Charlie Field? I don't recall that name. Is he an employee?"

"Afraid not. A customer of McBride's. You recall the original report mentioned McBride's pet names, well, Field's company, Alliance Automotive Export, is one of them. It was one of his invoices that triggered the whole inquiry. Field also has a reputation for having a short fuse. There was a disturbance at McBride's house the other day, and the description of the person causing the ruckus matches Field's. Also, a person identified as Charles Field showed up at Marian Fairmont's local retail business yesterday morning. He didn't identify himself and didn't create a problem. But Mrs. Fairmont thought he acted a bit strange—like he came in to look the place over. He seemed to be checking out the physical layout more than looking at merchandise. When he did finally buy something, he used a credit card, which is how she got his name.

"The second part relates to the Campbell accident, and I did some independent checking with some National Guard friends who are with the New Jersey State Police—"

"So there's some question of its being an accident?" Bradley said.

"It's still being sorted out, but there are questions, and they're looking for what they think is a black SUV. It's entirely possible it's just coincidental, and the guy in the SUV just panicked—when he saw what he caused—and took off. It happens. The point is, the state cops are pretty smart and will check everything. Right now, they have a vice president of First State in the hospital because of a suspicious accident, a group vice president of First State on a missing bank officer report, and, a break-in and altercation at the home of the same group vice president. Trust me, someone will be on the phone to Gene Fasbach before the day is out and, once bank security is involved, this could go anywhere."

Bradley sat back, looked at Carenza, and said nothing, but the wheels upstairs were turning fast and furious. Finally, he sighed. "And you think all of this can be laid at the feet of McBride?"

❧❧❧

As Jim pulled into the parking lot of The Garden Walk, he spotted a uniformed policeman on a bicycle, leaving. *Good,* he thought and sighed with relief. The visit from Field, Ed's accident, and the call from Carenza mid-morning had put him on edge. He grabbed his briefcase and headed for the shop and Marian.

"I see your friend Charlie the cop's been here."

"Yes, I confess, Charlie and I have a special relationship."

"Oh, really?"

"Yes. I point them out, and he shoots 'em."

"Kinda dangerous for customers, isn't it?"

"Well, not all of them, just the non-paying types."

"Speaking of non-paying, I believe it's your turn today."

"Hmmm…where's Charlie when I need him. Okay, how about The Velvet Turtle?"

"Perfect. It's just down Two-Oh-Two a ways. But before we go anywhere, I've got something for you."

"What caliber is it?"

He gave her a chastising look, put his briefcase on the sales counter, and opened it. "Yeah, right. Like I'd trust you with a gun," he said, while removing two boxes from his case.

"How about two Revolutionary War cannons that actually work? I could put them out front aimed at the parking lot."

"Marian—"

"Just trying to ease the tension. Actually, a diamond studded tennis bracelet would really take the pressure off."

"Don't get your hopes up," he replied, while removing two cell phones from their boxes.

Oh, neat," she said, seeing the black phones. "We've been talking about getting those for the last six months. Did I just say *neat*?"

"Yes, ma'am, you're as hip as they come in Mayberry."

"Is there a cell tower in Mayberry?"

"Don't know, but I'll bet the AT and T headquarters in Basking Ridge has one. They're just down the road, and the president of Bell Atlantic lives over in New Vernon—a short distance in the other direction—so I have a feeling reception should be pretty good. Jim picked up one of the phones.

"Which one is mine?"

"This one. They're already activated." He handed her a sheet of paper with two phone numbers on it. "You're on top." He immediately looked at her and spotted the grin on her face. "Oh, shut up, and let's have lunch. And bring the folder you made up with all the material we've collected on McBride."

ɛ✺ɔ

Jim asked for his favorite table in the back corner, the one they called the *gunfighter's table*. It sat positioned so two people would always have their backs to a wall and be provided with a clear view of the entire room, including the two exits, the door to the kitchen, and hallway to the restrooms. Also, the people at the table could not be seen from outside as a planter blocked the nearby window.

"Let's take a look at that file before the food comes."

Marian removed it from her bag and put it on the table between them.

"That's really thick."

"I put everything into it. Not just from the day you and Ed were passing messages back and forth but everything else as well: all the emails, phone messages, and anything that impacted McBride in any way. The original blank invoice is in there."

"Good job." Jim picked up one of the emails that Ed sent with letter of credit information on it, looked it over, and then waved it at Marian. "I hope he's all right. Ed, that is. Actually, I really wouldn't like anything to happen to McBride either. I guess I'm not built that way. But I just have this bad feeling about Ed's accident. I know there are coincidences that happen, but...I don't know."

"You haven't heard anything more?"

"No. I'll check later, though, if someone doesn't give me a call." He put the email back in the folder. "I have a feeling that Tony is on the right track, and the key to all this has to be the payment instructions on every one of these questionable credits. We can forget the merchandise and even the countries involved.

The feds and the state people can look into all that stuff but, for the bank, it's all about McBride. Tony thinks he came up with the whole scheme before he ever came to First State. What he needed was a bank with a basic international presence but no real focus on it, other than as an accommodation for local customers. A bank that treated international as an orphan business line they never intended to emphasize until congress, and the Fed started to play hands-off-the-financial-services-industry. Then they found themselves caught up in merger mania, while trying to play offence and defense at the same time and suddenly discovering they had acquired all these international assets and liabilities and had no real expertise to manage it. First State became the perfect vehicle for McBride when we acquired the two banks in Essex County that also had the largest books of international business in the State of New Jersey. Tony Carenza believes that McBride probably had something going at the last place he worked, but it was risky. Every mid-west and west coast bank that opened an international branch in New York under congress's Edge Act hired serious, experienced international staff. So his options for manipulation were limited. He needed a vulnerable bank with an internationally clueless senior management and—" The sound of a telephone ringing interrupted him. "Is that a phone? Your purse is ringing."

Marian became flustered, a condition that rarely affected her. "My goodness, it's the phone you gave me."

"Well, answer it."

Some fumbling ensued while she tried to figure out how the phone worked. "Hello?...Florence?...No, no, that's all right. Who was it?...Ah, yes, I'll tell him...No, no, I'm sure he has it...Thanks, Florence." Marian looked at Jim while she figured out how to end the connection.

"Who was it?" he asked when she hung up.

"Florence. I gave her the number before we left in case an emergency came up."

"And it did?"

"Tony Carenza called The Walk, looking for you. Said he needed to speak with you right away. He's at his office."

Jim shook his head in disbelief. "I haven't even had a chance to store any numbers in my phone yet." He pulled a pocket address book from the inside of his suit jacket and quickly began to thumb through it. "Ah—here it is." He took his new cell phone from his briefcase and dialed Tony's number. "Tony, Jim Fairmont. You tried to reach me?…Hmmm…Yeah…Not a problem…Be there by three-thirty…Okay."

"You have to go?" Marian inquired just as lunch arrived.

"He needs me to be at a meeting in Newark at three-thirty this afternoon and to bring everything I have on McBride. Jane Moran and some people from the state banking authority and the state police will be there."

"So you have to leave?"

"Let's finish lunch first. I've got time. It's only a little after one. Besides, there's something we need to talk about. Remember when we were getting ready for the Hansens' dinner party, I mentioned that we might think about retiring at sixty-two and not waiting any longer, figuring we'd still have five years to decide what to do?"

Marian thought a moment. So much had gone on since that dinner it seemed a lifetime ago. "Yeah, we thought we might start exploring some place to retire to along the Atlantic coast and mentioned taking a few extra days over Easter week next year to do some exploring."

"I think we need to get serious about it. United Jersey Banks just announced their intention to acquire Summit Bank. It's obviously a defensive move to make themselves too pricy for the new super regional banks that are developing. Could even be planning to become a regional themselves. But it leaves First State wide open. It wouldn't surprise me if Fleet, Regions, First Union, NCNB, and Wychovia have already been in touch with us."

"Do you really think First State is that vulnerable?"

"Absolutely. It's not Carl Hansen's bank anymore. It belongs to the Paressis of this world. They'll take what they can and run. Besides, given what's been going on, I'm sure the board will be presented with an over-priced offer they can't refuse. Besides, there's going to be an awful lot of bankers looking for work in the next few years, and I'd rather go out standing up."

Marian looked at him in silence. She'd stopped eating when he raised the subject and didn't restart.

Jim, on the other hand, merely picked at his own salad, as though it had suddenly spoiled.

Marian finally gave up and put down her fork. "How long do you think we have?

Jim sighed, his cheeks ballooning as he released the air. "One and a half, maybe two years, at the outside."

"And you still don't think we can stay here?"

"Oh, I could probably push for a deal to stay on, but I'd spend my whole time looking over my shoulder or reporting to someone a quarter of my age. Besides, if this whole thing with McBride turns ugly, I'll be tainted by it. The new management will want to make the case that it was a First State problem, and all the people involved are no longer part of the new bank. It makes sense when you think about it."

"Well—" Marian picked up her fork again and toyed with her salad. "—we always agreed we would move south, once you retired. Just do it a little sooner, that's all."

Jim could see her disappointment—everything from the way she held her fork to the now-slouching shoulders. She had agreed that it was what they would do, but now that it faced her...well, reality check time.

"We'll still keep the summer place." He reached out and took her hand. They needed to touch at this moment—to be unified, to let the energy flow between them. "It'll be okay. I've always wanted to teach, and we'll find another Garden Walk."

CHAPTER 36

The Fall Out

When Jim was about a third of the way to Newark on I-78 after lunch, Marian called him on his car phone. "Jim, you forgot the file. You left it on the table."

"Oh, shit!"

"Don't worry. I'm already on my way behind you. You keep heading for the meeting. I'll get there fifteen or twenty minutes after you."

"Where are you now?'

"In the car. On that fancy new cell phone you bought me. It'll go really well with the new Coach purse I'm going to buy to hold it. If I remember, there's a Macy's not far from the Newark office where I can shop until your meeting is over. Then you can buy me dinner at that Portuguese restaurant in the Ironbound section of Newark."

Jim laughed. "Did you have this all planned? Hide the file from me on purpose?"

"I don't need help. You're your own worst enemy."

"You're too much. Okay, it's a deal."

They both hung up, smiling.

Driving the rest of the way to Newark proved to be a concentration challenge for Jim. He really didn't want to retire, and the idea of moving away from Fordstown left a bad feeling in his stomach. Luckily, being early afternoon, traffic moved evenly in all directions, so when he missed his turn, it wasn't the disaster it normally would have been during rush hour.

Changing jobs was never easy on anyone and, in the financial services world at this point in time, it didn't make a lot of sense—especially if you were doing it voluntarily. Well, he had a few years to work it out. Or, at least, he hoped he did. In reality, his major concern would be the effect it would have on Marian. She loved The Garden Walk. She made it her success story, her pride and joy. He didn't want to see her hurt, physically or mentally, as a casualty of the upheaval in the banking world. Hopefully, they would have a few years to properly plan together for their next step, but they had to get started soon and do their homework.

Daydreaming again, now he found himself in the wrong lane. The exit coming up would be from the left lane. *Got to get my head on straight. Gonna need it for the meeting.*

ᴄᴢᴇᴢ

A local East Rutherford police car pulled up to the entrance to the employee parking lot of Meadowlands Optical Products, Inc. The officer looked over the row of parked cars not far from the entrance.

Earlier, one of the employees had reported a car without an employee decal parked in the wrong place in the lot and notified the security desk attendant in the lobby. Security went out to take a look at the car later in the morning when the lobby traffic eased. As a United States Defense Department sub-contractor, security procedures were well defined, and any activity that deviated from the norm had to be addressed.

The company security employee noted the license plate number and the make and model of the vehicle and then went back to reception to check out the visitor log. The procedure called for determining if a visitor had just parked in an employee slot as there was no room in the visitor parking area. Not an uncommon problem. Normally, if an employee changed cars for any reason, they were instructed to obtain a temporary decal from security to avoid any identification problems. The security employee could not find a match for the improperly parked black, GMC SUV.

The security manager at the lobby desk made a number of other inquiries and then waited until after the lunch rush to give the East Rutherford police a call.

The officer eased her cruiser into the parking lot and slowly drove past the black SUV. She continued down to the end of the row, turned, and headed back the way she came, again driving slowly past the SUV and, this time, noting some damage to the left front of the car. Continuing on, she made her way back to her starting position, where she called in what she observed and followed instructions to go back to the entrance of the parking lot and wait for assistance.

It took no more than five minutes for the second police cruiser to show up, and it pulled alongside its mate back to front so the two officers could talk without exiting their vehicles. It also gave them a 360 degree viewing area.

"All quiet?" the new officer asked.

"Yeah. I drove around a bit. Looks okay. Is it the one we've been looking for?"

"Reported stolen from a corporate lot in Verona some time yesterday. Owner said he parked it going to work about seven a.m., and it was gone when he went to get it at four-thirty. Dispatch is sending more backup. Have a feeling it's definitely the one the state police have been looking for. You know, the one that took off after that nasty accident on the GSP yesterday."

"May get a break on this one. With all the government work Meadowlands Optical does, they got cameras everywhere."

"Yeah. I'm gonna go inside and talk to the rent-a-cops. You better pull up in front of the SUV and put your lights on. Keep anyone from accidently approaching it and messing something up. Just heard one of the guys in the crash died an hour ago."

ඏ

On his way to the conference room, Jim stopped at Gloria's desk and asked about Ed Campbell. She told him that Ed's wife and one of his daughters flew in from Chicago and were with him. There wasn't much else she could find out, as hospital regulations prohibited the release of any medical information to anyone but family members.

Jim thanked her and then went across to the meeting room, where the door stood in an orderly, efficient, but unwelcoming closed position. Inside, the opposite prevailed. Files and papers were spread across the conference room table. At the far end, away from the door, letter of credit files were neatly stacked, presumably no longer needed for the ongoing review. Around the rest of the table, the files and papers were spread out but carefully organized and being scrutinized by three people in shirt sleeves, their jackets draped over the backs of their chairs. At the head of the table, where Jim entered, another four were standing and huddled together in conversation. He recognized only two of them: Tony Carenza and Jane Moran,

"Jim, come on over. Glad you're here," Carenza said. "You know Jane, of course, but let me introduce you to John Ponzurac and Rob Kenny, both from the state banking authority."

Jim shook hands with John—tall, dark hair, military bearing, brush cut—and Rob—medium height, thinning brown hair, jacketless, white shirt with sleeves rolled up—and polite greetings were exchanged by all with a more informal acknowledgement between Jim and Jane Moran.

"There are two more people missing from the room," Carenza continued. "They're from the Newark Police Department. I'll introduce you when they come back. First, let me bring you up to date. Grab a seat."

Everyone sat down.

Carenza explained that another team of auditors set up an analysis area in the wire transfer department on the third floor. It seemed that McBride arranged to have an account established with the bank even before he became employed by First State. It was done in the name of Export Import Consulting Group with an address in Antigua but with special mailing instructions to send all statements and transaction advices to a New Yok law firm, which also had signing authority for the account. McBride's name, L. A. McBride, showed up as one of the officers of the company in Antigua, although he didn't have signing authority over the account.

"Activity in the account started to drop off after he joined First State," John Ponzurac explained. "Prior to that, it was pretty active as a regular deposit location for proceeds of letters of credit paid by a variety of New York banks, including the one he used to work for."

∽∾

While Carenza and the others brought Jim up to date on the activities of McBride—some clearly against banking credit policy, some ethically suspect, some highly risky, and some mysterious as to their purpose—and then had him go over what he and

Ed Campbell had developed, the police combed Meadowlands Optical Products from top to bottom. One team worked all around the black SUV and another in the company's security control room, viewing tapes from the previous day. The driver of the car was clearly visible from three different cameras.

"Run that last one back. I think I know him," said the tall detective now seated next to the operator of the equipment and carefully watching the images on the monitor. A uniformed officer moved closer and looked over the detective's shoulder. "Yeah," the detective said, "that's it. Hold it right there. Wadda ya think, Leo?" he said to the officer.

"Buddy Sands?"

"Bingo!"

"I thought he was still inside from when we grabbed him for breaking into cars at Giant's Stadium?"

"Obviously not. Know where he hangs out?"

"Yeah."

"Pick 'im up."

かかか

"I personally think the people in wire transfer will be the key to everything." Jane Moran sat back in her chair. "You know, in every transaction we've identified so far, I don't see anything that's outside of his authority. He made sure to get the account officers for a customer like Alliance Automotive to issue standing authorizations in his favor to make payment decisions. Larry brought the accounts into the bank, but the account officer's profit plan got credit for the revenue. Don't mess with success. I have authority over a whole bunch of accounts where the account officer wouldn't know what to do with an *authority to pay* request any more than I would know how to evaluate the risk in a controlled disbursement account. Come on, Jim, you know that to be true. One of the reasons Ed Campbell's international seminar for domestic bankers is such a success is because it's really needed."

"I thought that was McBride's idea?"

"No. Ed came up with it, and Larry took the credit. Said no one would know who Ed was since he was new to the bank, so Larry put everything out under his name. Larry actually argued against it, at first, but Ed made the point that educating the contact staff on international products and services would be a great transaction producer for international. Larry had to agree."

"Well, now we know why he wanted to keep the domestic side of the bank in the dark," Carenza said, "and senior management is so focused on mergers and acquisitions, they're just leaving everybody alone down below."

As they continued to discuss various theories as to why everything seemed to go wrong, Jim kept looking at his watch. "I think I'd better call Marian. She said she was about twenty minutes behind me and it's already almost forty-five."

"Yeah, I think we need a break anyway." Carenza stood up and stretched, and everyone followed suit.

Some just leaned back in their chairs, others headed for the coffee maker.

Jim made his way to the telephone on the far end of the table and dialed Marian's cell phone. The clock on the wall announced the time as a quarter to five. The call went in to her voicemail, but he couldn't leave a return phone number as he left his cell phone in his briefcase and didn't know its number or the extension for the conference room. He went back to get his briefcase, and it started to ring just as he reached it.

"Marian?"

"How many other women have you given this number to?"

"Oh, good. I was worried. Where are you?"

"Not far now. Nasty accident on the off ramp from I-Seventy-Eight to downtown. Got stuck in traffic. Taking the back streets in. Should be there in another ten minutes."

"Good, we're taking a break now. Park in McBride's reserved space in the lot next door. I cleared it with security. See you in a few minutes."

"Okay."

eჰეჰ

Jim leaned back in his chair and thumbed through the folder that Marian prepared while she took a seat two spaces down from him. "You know, as I looked through all the material Ed gathered from the suspect letter of credit files and the resulting wire transfers, Ed's comments are really interesting. He was sure that what we touched on is just the tip of the iceberg."

"Give all that to Jane," Carenza said. "It'll probably reinforce some of the ideas she's already come up with." He then turned to John Ponzurac next to him. "You're probably gonna want a copy of this as well for your international guys. Hey, Peter," he called, referring to one of the young shirt-sleeved examiners working down the table. "Make us five copies of this stuff, will ya?"

"Sure. Just take a couple of minutes. Copier room is just the next door over."

"Thanks."

Jim thought a moment. "Jane, you said something a little while ago that intrigued me. You said McBride had the authority to do the manipulating he did."

"Well, we're right on the edge. The account officers gave him blanket authority to approve documents and, basically, make all decisions about their customer's transactions. They, essentially, transferred their credit authority to him. I'm sure you've done the same thing from time to time. Difference with McBride is he got them to give blanket authority. He argued the accounts were high volume and having to chase down the account office on every little problem, when the account officer had no idea what he was approving anyway, could result in a delay that might lose a customer money and, possibly, the bank a customer."

"Another point," Ponzurac added, "the instructions relating to the movement of the proceeds were originated by the bank's customer and were part of the letter of credit itself. At least the ones reviewed so far. The fact that McBride dictated to the customer how the instructions should read is another matter. Chalk that up to ethical lapse, I suppose. In any event, there is no indication that McBride changed a customer's instruction without authority."

"So McBride could be in the clear?"

Marian sat quietly, not wanting to interrupt, absorbing everything she heard. Somewhat out of her element, she still grasped the net effect of what they were struggling with.

"Well, I wouldn't go that far," Carenza said. "He made a number of mistakes. One big one has to do with the Hudson River: it's the state line between New York and New Jersey, and the feds have a big opening to be all over this."

ⵀⵀⵀ

While Marian had been weaving her way around the streets of Newark earlier, the tall, sandy-haired detective sat in the passenger side of the police cruiser in the parking lot of the optical company and spoke with the arresting office in Secaucus. "So what's the story?"

"Said he was hired by a guy to follow Campbell. Accidently got too close, bumped him in traffic, Campbell panicked, and Buddy has no idea what happened after that, as he took off before anything happened."

"So he's blaming Campbell for the accident?" The detective laughed. "You gotta be kidding. Did he give you the name of the guy he's working for?"

"Doesn't know it. Never mentioned names. Only second time he met him. Both times at a bank in Newark."

"Really?"

"Yeah, followed another guy for him a few weeks back."

"So he can pick him out for us?"

"Definitely. Says his pretty sure he works at the bank."

CHAPTER 37

No Place to Hide

Gloria had had enough for the day. It was bad enough that everyone wanted Larry McBride and her phone wouldn't stop ringing, but now she'd been instructed to record and document everything possible she could for auditing and whoever showed up with a badge.

She used to be able to pass off inquires to Ed Campbell, but that didn't work anymore, so now Jane Moran was the person to chase down. It was either that or tell the customer to call their account officer. In many cases, the caller said they thought McBride was their account officer.

The calls Gloria didn't get went to international customer inquiry, where Grace and her knowledge of the domestic side of the bank proved to be really useful.

At this point, the whole bank was on edge.

The United Jersey Banks' Summit Bank announcement of their planned merger shocked the staff on both the domestic and international sides. Summit, just slightly smaller than First State, looked to be safe by historical standards. UJB and Summit had too much of a business overlap for a merger to get the Fed nod.

But this was a new Federal Reserve. This was the hands-off Fed that decided that the market, left to its own devices, should decide. Besides, they were convinced that every CEO of a financial institution recognized his fiduciary responsibility to depositors and that would never be undermined by a vision of personal gain. The end result left every staff member at both banks facing the possibility of being let go. Senior management rationalized that the banking consolidation was necessary and came at the right time.

The recession brought on by the Reagan years had eased and

was finally put under control by George H. W. Bush's policies, and now Clinton claimed credit for Bush's success, as the economy expanded at a record clip. So what if a bunch of banking people were on the street? There were plenty of other jobs being created.

Gloria had enough. Time to quit for the day. Normally, she would hang around until the meeting in the conference room finished, but it looked like they were a long way from shutting down for the evening. After notifying Jane Moran, Gloria packed her desk, changed her shoes, grabbed her purse, and headed for the elevator.

Back in the conference room, Jane, Jim, and Carenza developed a list of all the corporate names that showed involvement with a letter of credit where McBride actually exercised his authority as the person who brought the account into the bank or obtained transaction approval from the account officer. Jim focused on the names based in the United States and Jane the foreign ones.

Marian—after assuring Carenza that she would abide by the rule of confidentially that governed her being able to stay in the room—worked on developing a chart showing the common links among the various corporate names as each transaction was outlined, a task not unknown to her from twenty years earlier when she worked as a credit analyst in New York analyzing interlocking corporate structures and related liabilities.

Carenza would then take a few of the names and go over them with his two examiners and the two state banking people. They would concentrate on the actual letter of credit transactions to see where banking policy had been circumvented in any way.

The overall plan they worked out involved assembling all the material and then getting together with the examiners working in the wire transfer area tomorrow morning. Each area would review what they developed, the pattern that resulted from the most common links.

Around the same time Gloria left, the group in the conference room took another break. Jim and Marian stepped out into the hallway by the copier room.

"Glad we had a decent lunch. I think we're going to be here a while yet," Jim offered. "All of this is going back a lot farther than I thought it would. Can't believe he's been at this since the day he arrived. Some of those transactions actually pre-date his time with First State. Jane Moran has been pulling files that go back more than five years."

Marian switched subjects. "Didn't get a chance to ask you earlier but have you heard anything more about Ed?"

"No, haven't heard anything. Hospital can't tell us anything as he's not a relative, and nobody wants to press his family, which is the right approach. Apparently, before I got here there were two Newark police detectives in the room that were investigating the accident but left for some reason. They were supposed to come back but never did. I had hoped they would be able to find out about Ed for us. The hospital *will* talk to them."

"There wasn't anything on the local news, which isn't surprising since New Jersey doesn't have a TV channel and the only news, except for NJPBS, comes from New York and Philadelphia. Traffic accidents in New Jersey aren't exactly a high priority for them. Guess we'll have to wait for *The Star Ledger* tomorrow. So, did you learn anything new about McBride? Do you think my folder has been helpful?"

"Oh, yeah. On both accounts. The building consensus now seems to indicate he may have been at this for almost ten years. As you now know, the trail heads back across the Hudson to where he worked before he came to us. Tony has the theory that the emerging confusion in the banking industry in New Jersey was perfect for exploiting and he actually sought employment at a couple of banks he targeted. Lucky First State won out."

Marian stared at him with her mouth agape. "Wow. I thought you were nuts to make a big thing about the invoice, especially when it looked like he was just bending the rules a bit, an ethical lapse here and there."

"I guess I'm that dinosaur they talk about. Still think ethics and character count, even when they injure the bottom line."

"Speaking about bottom lines, I've been looking at places to our south to explore after our First State adventure is over."

"Good. I've got a bad feeling about all that's going on here. Keep in mind that most of the corporate names we're looking at come under my jurisdiction in some way and everything pre-dates Paressi. In a merger, I'd be a tempting target for new management to focus on and use the excuse of merging business lines. Get rid of the old guy who didn't see it coming." He now paced up and down in the hallway. "Might think about bailing out while we're still in an upright position with no bruises showing."

Marian did not respond right away. Then she sighed. "You really think it's that bad?"

"If Tony's right and this involves banks on both sides of the river, yeah, it's going to get very messy."

✑✑✑

The sandy-haired police detective walked behind the long, dark marble reception counter that ran twenty feet along the matching marbled wall of the entrance to First State's Newark main office. There he joined the two police detectives who were in the conference room earlier in the day, the uniformed officer he spoke to earlier in Secaucus, and an animated Buddy Sands.

"Connor, you gotta believe me," Buddy said, addressing the sandy-haired detective, "I didn't do nothin' wrong. All I did was follow him. I didn't know he was gonna panic."

"Save it, Buddy." The sandy-haired detective then introduced himself to the other two cops. "Pat Connor."

"George Britt."

"Pete Carty."

They shook hands. "Any luck yet," Connor asked. "Understand you've got something else working that the GSP accident might tie into."

"We've got one banker from here that's in the hospital and another that's gone missing," Britt answered. "Buddy here says that the guy that hired him is an older guy, late fifties early sixties, about five eight, on the heavy side. Doesn't match the guy who's missing—"

"Yeah, but he works here. I know he does," Buddy interrupted.

"Well, we're gonna see if you can spot him." Britt turned to the other policemen. "It's a long shot, but with the guy in the second car dying earlier today, and Buddy here being so cooperative, had to give it a go."

"Not just bankers in here," Carty added, "bunch of law firms, accountants, insurance, and some doctors and dentists. Been here since just past five. Almost an hour. We'll give it a little more time. Already made a request of bank security to get a copy of their ID photo files. We'll work on that while we see what we can get from the other tenants."

～～～

Gloria exited the elevator at the far end of the bank of six that lined up three on each side of the corridor. She walked a few steps and then moved to the side letting the other passengers pass her. She then stopped to retrieve her bus pass from the wallet in her purse. Opening a purse on a street corner while waiting at a bus stop was something a savvy commuter didn't do. Finally ready, she headed for the lobby.

At the end of the elevator bank, an arm reached out and grabbed her just above the elbow.

She jumped, startled.

"Over here, Gloria."

"Mr. Field! Let go of me. What're you doing?"

Field didn't let go but increased his grip and pulled her toward him and a large potted ficus plant near the entrance to the elevators. "You gotta tell me where McBride is."

"Let me go!" She raised her voice. "I have no idea where he is." Louder this time, she yelled, "Let go of me!"

Across the lobby near a newsstand, a plain-clothes police officer spotted Field and Gloria and gave a wave to another officer standing behind the reception counter across from him. That officer gave Pete Carty a nudge with his elbow.

When Carty looked up so did Buddy Sands who immediately pointed. "That's him! That's the guy!"

They all now looked toward where Field struggled with a now very frightened and unhappy Gloria.

"You sure?" said Carty.

"Yeah, that's him."

Carty then looked at Britt. "Isn't that McBride's secretary from upstairs?"

At the same time, one of the building security guards saw the struggle going on between Gloria and Field. "Hey!" he yelled at Field.

The plain-clothes officer, on a signal from Carty, started toward the commotion, as did Britt and Connor.

Gloria was now frantic, "Leave me alone!" She broke free of his grip and swung her bag at him.

"I gotta—" Field looked up and saw the security guard coming his way. "Shit."

He gave Gloria a shove, and she lost her balance, falling to the floor in front of the guard, while Field headed for an empty elevator. The door closed just as Britt got to it.

"Shut down each of the elevators on the bank," he yelled.

At the reception desk, Carty called for back-up. He had previously arranged for a patrol car with two uniformed officers to be stationed down the street from the bank, just in case Buddy did point someone out. Britt stepped back from the closed elevator door and watched the floor indicator light above him. Gloria was helped to her feet by two men who just came out of another elevator nearby.

Two more elevators opened their doors. Another security guard started directing traffic from the other elevators and shut them down as the people exited. Field's elevator continued going up. All the other elevators in the bank were now at ground level and being shut down.

Britt continued to watch the indicator light. "He's all the way up. Seven. The international floor." A guard at the reception desk then remotely shut down the elevator Field was on.

A call was also placed to the international conference room to lock the door from the inside and stay put.

Being a building constructed in the 1920s, the emergency stairway had windows that overlooked a rear alleyway. The stairway went up in two stages with a landing containing a window halfway between floors. A one-foot space separated the railings as it went from floor to landing to floor, which allowed the plain-clothes officer to position himself in the stairway so he could tell if anyone on the upper floors touched the railing.

Field, in a rush, exited the elevator as the doors began to open, squeezing sideways just as the lights behind him went out. The only exit way from the elevator bank on the seventh floor led to the right where a floor directory announced the location of McBride's office, Campbell's office, the conference room, the international inquiry section, and the international collection department.

All arrows pointed to the left where two large wooden doors

announced the location of the international group. To the right, an illuminated *EXIT* sign indicated the direction of the emergency stairway, which was next to the restrooms.

He headed for the wooden doors, all the while chastising himself for panicking. He knew he shouldn't have grabbed Gloria the way he did but he had to find McBride. The response of the guard and those other people yelling just spooked him. *Who were they? What the hell's going on?*

Detectives Carty and Connor, along with two uniformed officers entered an elevator on the ground floor, along with the security guard from the reception desk, who activated the elevator with the fire emergency key.

Detective Britt and another officer quietly started up the stairway listening for sounds above them while looking up the gap in the center of the stairwell and watching for motion on the railing. Some of the windows on the landings above were open, and they could hear the siren sounds of arriving police vehicles.

Although the conference room door had been locked after being notified by the reception desk and making sure everyone was in the room, Carenza braced some chairs against it and called back the security line at the lobby reception counter. "This is the conference room on ten. Can you tell me what's going on?"

"Mr. Carenza?"

"Yes. This Sam?"

"Yeah. Is everything okay there?"

Tony explained the door and told him who was in the room. Sam wrote down the names and said, "I just got here, so I don't have much information. There was an assault on a woman in the lobby, and the guy took an elevator to seven. No idea if he's armed or what his intensions are. Luckily, we happen to have some police on hand looking for someone, and they're headed your way. I think you know what to do."

Sam, the security director for the building and a first sergeant in a Newark-based national guard unit, and Tony Carenza, a captain in a national guard transportation unit in New York, often had lunch together discussing security issues. Both knew that the lock on the door was useless against a forceful kick.

"As far as I know, there's no one else in the office here, everyone's gone, including Gloria Martinez, McBride's secretary. In fact, she just left."

"I think that's who was attacked."

"Really? Okay, we'll keep this line open just in case." Tony then turned to Jane Moran, who, with two of the auditors stood at the far end of the room. "Sam said Gloria was attacked in the lobby and the guy's on his way up here."

"Is she all right?" Marian asked.

"He didn't say. I'm sure the EMS people are on their way, no matter what. But he did say we need to secure this place," Carenza said, looking primarily at Jim and John Ponzurac. "Was that the elevator?" he asked, hearing the chime that announced an arriving car?

Jim eyed the size of the table, which almost filled the rectangular shape of the room. "That comes apart, doesn't it?" he whispered.

"Has to. Only way they could get in in here," Tony whispered back.

Now everyone was speaking and moving as quietly as possible.

"Okay," Jim said. "Kenny, this looks like the one we have in Morristown. There should be a pair of release catches holding the two halves together. Take a look."

"They'll be at the outside edges of each half," Marian instructed.

The state banking examiner, who stood at the midpoint of the two halves of the table, dropped to his knees and looked at the underside of the table. "You're right. It comes apart where you said."

"Good," Jim said. "Release the catches that hold the two parts together. We'll turn it into a 'T' with one end horizontal to the door and the other perpendicular to it. Jane, check the supply closet. There should be some projectors in it. Grab them and the extension cords that go with them. We'll definitely need them. Kill the light."

A few moments later, Field burst through the double doors into the executive area. Having been here on numerous occasions, he knew exactly which office belonged to McBride.

Looking first to his left at the closed conference room door as he entered, and then to his right where Gloria's desk stood guard over McBride's office and sitting room, he did not see the light from the conference room showing under the door go out, although he sensed something changed.

He looked again to his left to the conference room door and the copier room.

No, nothing had changed.

He turned his attention back to McBride's office. The open door surprised him. It was always kept closed. Was someone in there? He looked around the space. Empty. No movement. No Gloria. No Campbell. No secretary. Other staff desks empty. Lights on for the cleaning crew. Normal.

He headed straight for McBride's office.

Tony listened at the conference room door and knew, as did everyone else, when the intruder burst through the entry doors and then stopped just as Jane turned off the lights. He held up his hand to make sure everyone stayed quiet. He listened. Nothing.

"McBride, you bastard, where are you?" Field yelled, and Tony could tell he was heading away from them.

"He's in the office," Carenza whispered. "Jim, tell the desk. Bob, John, let's get the first section of the table against the door. Everyone else, bring the other section around."

Marion, Jane, and the two other auditors started to move the other section around and then Jim, finished with the phone, helped. "Jane, bring over the projectors and the extension cords. Slow and quiet."

Field looked into the sitting room as he went past. Lights on. Empty. Next McBride's office. He slammed his hand against the half open door. It swung back and bounced against the wall, coming back at him. He grabbed it. The room, empty. Field lost it. He pushed over chairs and swept everything off McBride's desk. He tried to open the closet near the window that looked the seven stories down onto Broad Street, all the while yelling, "McBride, where are you, you bastard?" He stopped. "You screwed me. You said no one would ever know. You set me up. My business is toast." He ran his fingers through his hair. "The tax liability will kill me. You moved everything I have out of Panama." He flopped down into McBride's chair and put his head in his hands.

The elevator with the Newark police and building security stopped on six.

Everyone came out cautiously.

Carty, Connor, and one of the uniformed policemen headed

for the door to the emergency stairway then Carty looked at the security guard operating the elevator. "Go back down. Should be more uniforms there. Make sure fire and rescue have been notified. I got a bad feeling about this." Then he turned to the other uniformed policeman. "Check the floor. It's supposed to be empty but make sure. Okay, let's meet up with Britt and make the seventh floor."

Inside the conference room, Jim had his back to the wall about two feet from the door. Tony held a similar position on the other side but with his ear to the wall. Ponzurac, the other examiners, and Marian pushed the second half of the table perpendicular to the first.

Jim motioned for Jane to switch on the small light in the supply closet so there would be enough visibility in the room for them to see but not be seen under the now blocked entry door. The barricade now consisted of two halves of the table braced against the door with about a foot of room between the end of the second table and the opposite wall.

Tony whispered to Ponzurac to position the backs of two chairs so the space would be filled. Jim then whispered to Jane and Marian to bring the two slide projectors and the overhead projector to the table and position them so the lenses would face the door.

Marian then immediately began plugging all three into the same extension cord. Jane had to add a second cord in order for it to reach the outlet they would use. Marian knew the procedure as they had practiced it before. She waved to Jane not to plug the cord in but to just lay in on the floor near the outlet. She then turned on all the projectors and made sure they were aimed head height at the door.

Tony watched it all and then whispered to Jim, "Neat idea. Who came up with that one?"

"Marian. Read it in a mystery novel someplace. Local police liked the idea, so we set up one of the interior rooms of her business as a safe room. Bought a table that would fit just right."

Entering the stairwell, Connor looked down the staircase and spotted Britt and the other officers three levels below them. Carty, Connor, and one officer started, cautiously, up to the landing between the sixth and seventh floors.

The stairway between the seventh and eighth floors had more

lighting because it served as a shortcut to the other international operations floor above.

Another team of police would eventually secure eight. They stopped on the landing. There was no sound and no movement above them. They continued up with weapons drawn. At the metal emergency door, which was propped open for easy access, they waited for Britt.

They listened quietly. Someone yelled, but it was a muffled sound a distance away.

They began to move out into the area in front of the restrooms. A uniformed officer checked the men's room first.

Connor and Carty moved on to the edge of the wall where the elevator bank started. Connor peeked around the corner while Carty looked straight ahead toward the large wooden doors of the international group. The officer cleared the women's room next.

Carty moved into the open.

The elevator bank was empty. He motioned for the officer to now check the elevator Field came up in, then he and Connor headed for the wooden doors.

They froze as the yelling rant started and stopped again. It had definitely been coming from inside the doors but not near them.

Carty, having been up on the floor earlier related a full description of the seventh floor so they would all know where the conference room and offices were in relation to the door. Britt and two more uniformed officers now joined them.

In the conference room, all was quiet. They had been listening to the ranting by Field about McBride. Jane recognized Field's voice and told Tony and Jim who it was. From the sounds in addition to the yelling, they could tell Field was trashing some part of the office.

They were all frightened. No one moved or made a sound.

They could hear one another breathing.

Field tried to pull himself together. *There's got to be an address book and calendar here someplace.* "But where?"

He started opening the drawers and ripping them out of McBride's desk. Pulling papers out, giving them a quick look, and them tossing them, he went from drawer to drawer.

Carty and two of the uniformed officers moved slowly toward the sitting room, while Britt moved toward the conference room door.

"Carenza, Ponzurac, it's Detective Britt," he whispered

"Here," Tony replied softly.

"Everybody okay?"

"We're good."

"Stay put—on the ground, as far away from the door as possible. We've got it now."

"Will do."

Britt gave a wave to Connor and then started moving toward Campbell's office. One officer stayed behind near the copy room to secure the area around the doors to the outside and the elevator bank and stairs.

Field kept ravaging McBride's desk, throwing drawers, and muttering to himself. He was hot, sweaty, frantic.

He turned to the large window behind McBride's chair and threw it open—one of the pluses and minuses of old buildings, the window's still worked.

He felt the fresh breeze as it hit his face. "Gloria! You idiot, the secretary. She's got it. She's got his calendar, everything. Shit!" He immediately headed for her desk, kicking debris on the floor out of his way, and rushed out the door, focusing only on Gloria's workspace.

"Police!" Carty called as Field came rushing out.

Field looked up, immediately reversed course, and jumped back into McBride's office, grabbing the edge of the door and slamming it behind him.

Carty, Britt, and two uniformed officers rushed the door.

They heard a loud noise and then a crash of glass.

Field yelled.

The police charged McBride's office.

Empty.

Drapes were half out the window.

The sash was gone, and so was Field.

CHAPTER 38

The Aftermath

T he seventh floor finally started to calm down.
While the paramedics checked out everyone in the conference room, two detectives discreetly questioned them. Police were everywhere. Some talked in groups and pointed to various locations around the larger open space while others, wearing protective clothing, carefully sifted through the debris in McBride's office. Photographers took pictures of everything.

After a while, Jim, Marian, Tony, and John Ponzurac stood outside the conference room. They learned some of what happened from the police and paramedics and needed to get cleared further by the police before any of them would be allowed to leave. Jim figured it would be another half hour.

"So he definitely went out the window on his own?" Jim asked Tony, who always seemed to have the inside track when it came to finding out information when no one else could.

Tony's position as director of audit operations gave him a status as "one of them" in any investigation. He not only gathered information for his own use but also provided insight for others as well. Marian and John Ponzurac quietly talked with one of the paramedics.

"Yeah," said Tony. "Nothing official. They sealed off McBride's office immediately. It's a real mess. Carty said that's what got him."

Marian and John then joined them. "Gloria's okay," John said. "Has some nasty bruises on her arm and a skinned knee. Really shook up, though. She said Field looked crazy. What's the story here?"

Jim looked at Tony. "What did you mean, 'that's what got him'?"

"The office. The mess. Field trashed the office. Papers all over the place. Ripped the drawers out of the desk and threw them on the floor. When he rushed back into the office, he stepped into one of the empty drawers on the floor and took a header out the window. They said it was already open. That's all I got from Carty. All unofficial. I'm sure they'll piece it all together. All sorts of people saw him go out the window. Everyone was looking up from the street. Not sure I want to know any more."

They were all silent for a moment, then Marian asked, "What was he looking for?"

"McBride," said Ponzurac.

"Well, yes, but he knew McBride wasn't here. It was his location he wanted." Tony looked over at some of the papers that blew out of McBride's office from the door and window being open. "That's why he went after Gloria downstairs and, after trashing the office, started to go after Gloria's desk, looking for information."

Marian covered her mouth. "What a tragedy."

They stood talking for a while among themselves and occasionally someone would come over and say a few words.

The two young auditors and Rob Kenny from state banking tried fixing up the conference room table but were told to just leave everything alone. Some pictures were taken of the room as well as the area outside of it.

The press had not arrived on the floor yet but were already assembled in the lobby. A TV crew parked their mobile unit a block away and shot long distanced views of the entrance to the building.

The street was closed to traffic as Field hit the sidewalk right in front of the walk-up ATM to the right of the entrance. Some people were working late on the sixth floor and saw him go by their windows. They eventually told their stories to the waiting reporters, as did the people who were walking by when Field hit the pavement. Two of them were in shock and were attended to by paramedics. It was all madness and pandemonium.

When Jim and Marian were finally permitted to leave, they decided to let Marian's car stay in McBride's parking spot and take Jim's car home. They told detective Carty and gave him Marian's keys in case the car needed to be moved for any reason.

Field had parked his car next to McBride's occupied space, which may have given Field the impression that McBride was in the building someplace.

Connor and the two uniformed police officers from East Rutherford turned Buddy Sands over to the Newark police who, as they learned more of the background story, needed to get a more comprehensive picture of everything. The FBI was also invited in, and they would all figure out who would take the lead going forward. It being Thursday, all employees who worked on the seventh floor were told not to come in on Friday.

The newspapers and TV news programs covered everything on Friday, but by Monday they had moved on. *The Newark Star Ledger* would continue to follow the story as would *The New York Times* as they could smell a larger story unfolding.

Cable and local news would drop it and only return when the *Star Ledger* started to report on the on-going investigation.

The main picture that went with the original story was one of Field, but now a photograph of Larry McBride accompanied the follow up newspaper story. Field's death was reported as an unfortunate dramatic accident, the culmination of a banking dispute between First State and a distraught small business owner. The larger story evolved to be about some form of mundane white collar crime not suitable for prime time. The reverse of the old adage seemed to apply: *If it doesn't bleed, it doesn't lead.*

On Monday The Garden Walk opened for business as usual, well, not quite as usual. Marian stayed away over the weekend. She and Jim were mentioned in the newspaper article but avoided the TV cameras. Tony Carenza was the only one interviewed and appeared on air for about fifteen seconds, although he actually answered questions for fifteen minutes. He didn't see anything, was in a conference room attending a meeting with others when it all happened

Jim went to the office in Morristown. He had some telephone conversations with John Paressi, the executive vice president he reported to, as well as Robert Bradley, the head of auditing to whom Tony Carenza had given a verbal report. Adam Turner also called, and they discussed both Alliance Automotive and Rayburn. He also heard form Carl Hansen.

Before the day ended, Tony called to say a meeting was being put together for the following Friday at the head office to review the preliminary audit finding and they wanted him there.

Ed Campbell came out of intensive care on Friday morning. The FBI spoke with him briefly and would speak with him again. They didn't expect Ed to be there for the Friday meeting, but the FBI promised to relay any information to the bank that would be relevant to the preliminary bank audit.

By Tuesday afternoon, the world returned to normal. Paula rescheduled all Jim's Friday and Monday missed meetings and tried to get as much as possible into Wednesday and Thursday, as the upcoming Friday audit meeting blocked out that whole day. Tuesday had been all make-up, changes, and answer phone calls.

He took a late lunch at his desk on Tuesday and called the hospital for the third day in a row to see if Ed could take calls yet. Late Wednesday Gloria managed to reach Ed's wife, Susan, who gave her a rundown on his condition.

They exchanged calls on a daily basis after that, and Gloria agreed to be the go-between for bank acquaintances and that way controlled the number of people trying to find out about Ed. Gloria would relay information to three or four other people at the bank, and they became the local point people for information. Jane Moran and Paula were two of the people on Gloria's list, which is how Jim had Ed's room number and called it on Wednesday afternoon.

"Hello?" came a soft quiet voice answering Ed's hospital room phone.

"This is Jim Fairmont at First State."

"Oh, yes Jim. Ed's mentioned you and your wife Marian a number of times. I'm Susan, Ed's wife."

"I heard from Gloria Martinez earlier today that Ed might be well enough to take some calls, and I thought I'd give it a try."

They talked quietly for a while, two strangers with common friends becoming acquainted. Each had a piece of a relationship the other was either unfamiliar with or knew a version of a story the other didn't recognize.

Susan knew of Marian, and she told Jim how embarrassed Ed felt. Ed, at one point, considered resigning and taking an offer from First Union that a head hunter continued to dangle in front of him. She also explained how their marriage came to an impasse over his agreeing to take the First State position and not trying to find something in Chicago, as she didn't want to move and interrupt the girls' last year in high school. But once the whole business with Larry McBride surfaced, they began to talk almost every evening and started planning all over again.

Jim listened politely and quietly. It seemed as though she needed someone to talk with that wasn't family or a close friend. She felt comfortable talking to Jim as she had heard so much about him. Ed trusted him and looked upon the two of them as aging dinosaurs trying to fight off a newly evolving predator that was younger, faster, and willing to risk the safety of the whole species for his own personal benefit. Jim reciprocated the analogy, which was why they felt comfortable with one another, regardless of any unfortunate history.

The conversation continued against the backdrop of Ed Campbell sitting up in his hospital bed while two nurses poked and prodded him. They checked blood pressure, recorded fluid levels, adjusted pillows and the angle of the bed, as well as other hourly maintenance chores.

Finally finished, the taller of the two waved at Susan, "We're all done, Mrs. Campbell. He's doing really well. If you need anything, just check with the nurses' station."

"Thank you." She turned to Ed. "It's Jim Fairmont. Want to say hello?"

He perked up, waved her over, and took the phone in his right hand. His left side took the brunt of the punishment in the accident and was immobilized from shoulder to thigh. There were bandages on his head from bouncing around inside the car and the effects of the air bags exploding.

They were both relieved at hearing each another's voice. A bond had developed over the past month, born out of shared stress, fear, anger, suspicion, and mystery. Jim asked how he was doing and what the future looked like for him. Ed asked about what happened the week before with Field—having heard some of the basics from Susan—and the audit and now criminal investigation. They then began to discuss the upcoming Friday audit meeting.

"I don't want to tire you out too much."

"No, no. I've still got one good arm left. We have some time yet. Susan will shut me down when she sees me going overboard. Besides, it's good physical and mental therapy. So there's still nothing on McBride?"

"No. Been talking with Tony Carenza almost daily since Field died. FBI has been over at Alliance Automotive going through all their international transactions. They've also been huddling with Jane Moran. Have they been in to see you yet?"

"They were here yesterday but didn't stay long. Was still heavy with pain medication so I wasn't thinking too straight. They said they'd be back. Newark police will still be the lead on my accident."

"I've been trying to put some notes together for the Friday meeting. If you don't mind, Marian and I would like to come by tomorrow, probably about noon."

Ed laughed. "I don't think I'm going anywhere. I'll mention it to Susan."

"How's the hip?"

"Looks like that's going to be my problem side. Already said I would need another surgery to make some additional repairs. Susan knows more than I do. I just sleep a lot."

"Well, at least they haven't cut the medical plan yet so you should be okay." After the last merger, the bank had decided to adopt the industry trend—switch to the plan of the bank that was the cheapest, regardless of the benefit cuts. "That won't kick in until the first of the year."

"This industry is going nuts," Ed said with a sigh.

"Hey, I don't want to keep you. And if tomorrow is too much, please let me know."

"No, no. I'll be fine. Could use some mental stimulation."

"Okay. Well, for starters, think about Panama."

"Panama?"

"Yeah, something Field said while he rampaged around the office. Have a feeling it will come up on Friday. Think about it, and we'll talk tomorrow. Get some rest and put Susan back on the phone."

Jim told Susan that he and Marian would be in the following day and offered to be of help in any way. Anything they needed, he would welcome her calling on them. Jim knew Susan and her daughter were staying in Ed's apartment in The Hills, which was a short ride down I-287 from Fordstown.

They chatted for a few more minutes before ending the call.

✑✑✑

The FBI seemed to be everywhere Tuesday and Wednesday. About an hour after Jim called, they were in to see Ed again. Jane Moran, in Newark, spent her time explaining the operations and procedures in the international department and also explained the bank's foreign exchange trading policy and how customer trades were handled when First State did not have direct access to a currency needed.

Gloria provided McBride's calendar for the past three years, to see who his meetings were with, and overseas travel itineraries and the companies and banks visited. They developed a list of all his international contacts as well as his domestic ones.

A separate group of agents were combing through the wire transfer department and generating paper trails for proceeds of letter of credit payments. A systematic list of contact priorities continued to grow as each new name came to light.

The agents in charge could smell something larger looming out there, as the investigation expanded across the river to New York. The antennae were now up at the Federal Reserve and the relevant US Attorney's Offices.

The visit to Ed at the hospital on Thursday proved to be one of those events that created life long bonds. Susan and Marian hit it off immediately, and after an hour of just sitting around and chatting, the two of them decided to go to lunch together.

Jim and Ed continued their discussion about Field and McBride. Ed admitted he missed quite a few warning signs with McBride while trying to fit in and make a place for himself at First State. Being the new kid on the block, he followed the time-tested job saver of shut up, keep your head down, and don't rock the boat. Jim told him it wasn't his responsibility but senior management's. They were the ones responsible for asking the questions when they didn't understand something.

Ed also brought up Panama. He said the FBI questioned him yesterday on the subject along with a whole lot of names and transactions that related to activities he knew nothing about as they occurred long before he arrived. Having had time to think about Panama, he remembered seeing some notations McBride made on a couple of the letters of credit he reviewed back when he was sending information to Marian. He didn't remember the exact transactions, but they would be on the list that would be in Marian's file, which the FBI already had.

Jim said he had to leave for a meeting in Somerville, which he and Marian anticipated by having driven to the hospital in separate cars. Ed's daughter arrived as Jim left and stayed with Ed while Marian and Susan went to lunch in the hospital cafeteria.

They all expressed a sense of relief, now that everything was out in the open, but there continued to be a sense of foreboding about the Friday audit meeting. Would this be a point the finger get together or one of discovery, revelation, and shock? Only Friday would tell.

CHAPTER 39

The Friday Audit Meeting

Jim arrived a half hour early for the Friday meeting with the hope of getting together with Tony Carenza beforehand only to find out that no one had any intention of being late and he ended being next to last to arrive. Only Mary Wilson, the senior agent assigned by the FBI, came in after him.

The usual coffee and Danish sat on a cart provided by food services. Jim never did get a chance to chat privately with Carenza, who spent his time schmoozing with the three auditors and two of the FBI agents working for Mary Wilson. He ended up spending his time with Jane Moran and Robert Bradley.

Ten minutes prior to the start of meeting, Wilson came into the room along with John Paressi, who the chairman had designated his personal representative to oversee the investigation. He would not participate or even stay for the meeting, but he was there to show how important the bank considered the subject of the meeting. In fact, he gave the opening remarks and introduced Mary Wilson to the group and encouraged everyone to work diligently in an effort to resolve this most important task before them, indicating it had the highest possible priority.

He also went on to provide a quick update on Ed Campbell saying how personally pleased he was to learn of Ed's progress and that he should be released from the hospital fairly soon. Jim knew Paressi never spoke to Ed—as Ed never mentioned it—but received all his information from others.

"Finally, let me again emphasize that we want to get to the bottom of this very serious breach of trust. The management of First State will support following this matter where ever it leads and we look to the expertise of all of you in this room to bring everything out into the open, so that the proper corrections and adjustments can be made for the future of First State, its customers and shareholders. And now let me turn you over to Robert Bradley." Paressi then shook hands with Bradley, went over and did the same with Wilson and left the room.

"Thank you, John," Bradley said as Paressi left the room. "Well, Tony, the floor and the agenda are all yours. I'll be in and out as the meeting progresses. Tony."

"Well, let's get started then." Carenza took over. "The agenda is a pretty simple one, in that it's not too detailed. So let's start with Jane Moran to explore what we have discovered thus far. Jane."

Jane shifted some of the papers in front of her, opened two file folders and removed the handouts she brought with her for the meeting.

Her career with First State, and its predecessors, spanned twenty-seven years. However, her pay slip during that time contained a continual succession of six different banking companies, even though she worked in the same building on Broad Street the whole time.

She began as a secretary to the commercial banking officer handling the port of Newark district. Not having gone to college, the bank officer she reported to advised her to take whatever courses she could at the American Institute of Banking—even though she had to travel to the Woolworth Building in New York where the classes were given—as the bank would reimburse all her expenses. She jumped at the chance.

When the bank decided to open a special import/export customer support unit she was chosen as its head. Her employer then sent her off to classes in banking administration and international trade sponsored by the Bank Administration Institute and the American Bankers Association.

With the subsequent growth of container shipping out of the Port of Newark, her section was upgraded to a department. Although women were not permitted to be officers of the bank at the time, she was considered the equal—if not more so—of all the other (male) department managers. With the last merger, which created First State, international trade business tripled, and Larry McBride was brought in. Not wanting to lose her, he bargained for her to get an official title.

"Before I get into specifics of various classes of transactions, let me provide you a few documents on international group background." She took out the papers from her folder and passed them around the table. "The top sheet is an organizational chart of the International Group. The second is a flow chart of a traditional export letter of credit transaction as it would make its way through the Letter of Credit Department. The third is a similar flow chart of a domestic letter of credit transaction. The fourth page is the same for a back-to-back transaction. The fifth page is the numbering protocol for all letter of credit transactions. You will note there are three categories with prefixes: zero-zero for domestic letters of credit. Zero-one to zero-nine is for export letters of credit, with each prefix designating a county or region of origin. The prefix ten is for import letters of credit. Since everything that goes on in the world of letters of credit involves varying degrees of risk, the numbering system also becomes a risk exposure management tool. Any questions so far?"

Everyone around the table continued to receive the papers as they were distributed. No one made a comment.

Finally, Mary Wilson said, "No, this is very helpful. Very helpful."

"Good. Okay. Let me just mention that much of what I will present has been the combined work and input not just from me and the various section managers in the Letter of Credit Department, but also from Ed Campbell, who, as Mr. Paressi mentioned, is expected to be released from the hospital next week, and Jim Fairmont, who aided Ed in assembling some of the data.

"Now, the next two sheets of paper represent a typical problematical transaction we've uncovered."

Jane then went on to document the activity related to a letter of credit sent to First State from a bank in Venezuela on behalf of an automotive group in Caracas. The bank requested the letter of credit be confirmed—thereby substituting First State's liability for the payment from that of the Venezuelan Bank's—and sent on to Alliance Automotive Export, Charlie Field's company. Next, she directed their attention to a second letter of credit, a domestic one, opened by First State on behalf of Alliance Automotive Export.

"The establishment of both these transactions complied with all of First State's policies and procedures. However," she pointed out, "the way they achieved that compliance and the handling of the documents and the subsequent payment, is where everything fell apart—"

At this point, the young auditor sitting next to Carenza interrupted. "I should point out that this is one of the first transaction's I flagged."

Jane gave him a stern look for interrupting, which was echoed by Carenza, and then continued her presentation, which—as agreed to by Jane and Tony—was supposed to be factually neutral. Nobody took credit for anything, and no one pointed fingers.

"The files for both of these transactions were initially unavailable to the auditors and subsequently found in a locked cabinet in McBride's office. The next problem uncovered involved the Venezuelan credit, in that the two-hundred-fifty-thousand-dollar liability exceeded the Venezuelan global country limit of three million dollars by just over two hundred thousand dollars. It turns out that McBride authorized the issuance of the credit and later— a full week later after the credit was issued and all parties notified—sought and received credit committee approval. The file reflects the formal bank approval of the excess, but the records were adjusted to show it occurred before issuance—"

"Really?" Jim interrupted. "The credit committee agreed to back date the approval?"

"Yes and no. McBride made a special, private presentation to the committee, arguing for the approval but not the back dating of the official record."

Tony, looking exasperated, said, "Frankly, as auditors, we would simply have made sure the approval was there and not verified the dates unless there was a clear reason to do so. It's not the credit committee's job to verify the dates, so they just moved on. Since there was no record in the file of an invalid credit approval, we wouldn't have had any reason to flag anything and certainly not to write up McBride."

Jane, seeing that Carenza had finished his comment, continued her analysis. "The approval to issue the domestic letter of credit and incur a contingent liability for Alliance Automotive Export was not approved by the account officer but by McBride. However, we found a memo from the account officer, giving McBride blanket credit authority over the account. The credit officer denied he gave such authority but admitted it was his signature on the memo."

Carenza looked irritated as he leaned forward in his chair and picked up the pencil lying on the pad in front of him. He did not look happy. "This is still under review and seems to be a pattern with a lot of what has been referred to as McBride's pet names. They're all domestic corporate names brought into the bank by McBride." He shot a quick look at Jim, which didn't go unnoticed. "The business relationships were strictly international related: letter of credit, import and export collections, foreign drafts, and foreign exchange. McBride made a practice of telling the account officer that the customer had special needs that only his international group staff could service. He apparently explained that all the profitability for the relationship would still be theirs but that his people had to be in control, or the relationship would flounder, and the bank's overall profit would be impacted."

"Which is how they flew under the radar of corporate banking," Jim offered defensively. "We didn't know any of the accounts. They were deemed to be unsuitable for typical cash management services like lock-box, disbursement, payroll, and so on. Sorry to interrupt. Trying to bring in the wider scope of the problem that developed. Can certainly see why McBride was taken back when Ed Campbell wanted to establish a program to acquaint domestic bankers with the international side of the bank."

"Not a problem," said Jane. "Our job in international operations is just to make sure the transactions are processed properly and accurately in a timely manner, in accordance with bank policies and procedures."

"Agreed."

Carenza could tell that Jim had his back up and decided to soften his tone. "If a good many of these names are a mystery to you, Jim, and the rest of us, it was because none of these accounts were reported on the weekly new account report that is circulated around the bank. Well, actually it's not circulated anymore because it's more efficient to eliminate paper—or so they say—it's posted on the Deposit Services Information Report for access by interested parties. Gloria Martinez says she was instructed not to bother to mark it for posting as they were all international names, and no one else in the bank would care."

Jim just shook his head.

Jane then continued on and outlined the establishment of the domestic letter of credit and the classifying of it as a back-to-back tied to the original Venezuela credit. Everyone at this point was taking notes, and Robert Bradley decided not to leave when his secretary came in to interrupt him. He told her to reschedule.

When Jane started to go over the procedure for checking for the domestic side of the back-to-back, she raised the proper but questionable practice that McBride instituted, whereby standing instructions at the document window required that deliveries relating to certain letters of credit were to be hand carried to Gloria Martinez for McBride to review first.

Here Mary Wilson interrupted. "Jane, there are a couple of points to bring up that we learned from Ed Campbell during our interviews with him in the hospital that are probably germane to your policy review. McBride made a practice of combing the files of all transactions to or from any country where exchange restrictions were in place or there was a threat they might be. He checked the names of the principals abroad and did research on them in the US. When traveling abroad, he made a point of making contact with them and actively soliciting their US-dollar accounts. Now, as you know, this is not an illegal activity, but I know there are guidelines out there, endorsed by the ABA, recommending that such solicitation not be engaged in, and First State has endorsed that recommendation. Also, some weeks ago, we understand there was a major disagreement over a transaction with Rayburn Corporation, which McBride made into a major incident. Mr. Campbell determined that McBride just signed up a principal with Rayburn's Argentinian importer for an account with First State, and this was the first transaction going through First State."

"I thought you said it wasn't illegal for foreign nationals to have US-dollar accounts in the US but just not a good idea from the US Government's point of view," said Jim.

"Technical point. Not illegal for the US bank to accept such accounts but illegal in the country abroad for the foreign national to have it. State department and treasury find it a bit embarrassing in discussions with a number of countries around the world when a US bank is found, overtly, helping foreign nationals avoid taxes and currency restrictions, while, at the same time, we're trying to get their help with money laundering and tax evasion activities of US citizens. The pressure being put on US banks is a contributing factor in why many internationally focused law firms serve as fronts for foreign business executives. But that's something we can discuss later."

Jane then took back control of the meeting and began to review the payments made under the letters of credit. "Here again changes were made to the distribution of the funds by McBride, but, in every case we've found so far, McBride had obtained written instructions from the account party in Venezuela, or Charlie Field on behalf of Alliance Automotive Export, to take the actions he did."

"There's another place we would like to investigate further," Mary Wilson said while looking directly at Tony Carenza, "and that's McBride's expense reports. His most recent trip to Central America has not been filed yet, but his secretary had the documentation on her desk."

Wilson then explained that McBride usually had an extra leg added to his trips that was not recorded as part of his official itinerary. It showed up in his expense reports, but no customer reports were ever filed. "Miss Martinez said the extra leg always managed to be added to his trips at the last minute and often on the spur of the moment, after he had already left. However, there seems to be a pattern, in that Antigua and Panama were consistent stopovers. His passport travel records are being requested from state."

Jane continued on with her review of the payment process and how McBride tightly controlled just about everything that went on with his pet names. The only time she became involved was when he was away on a trip, and Gloria always kept him informed of anything that came up during that time. He always left very specific instructions for her with regard to which special names might have activity while he was away. Jane then concluded her remarks and provided copies of her presentation to Carenza and Wilson

Next, it would be Tony's turn, and his main focus would be to pick up on the wire transfers where Jane left off and follow them through the wire transfer department, following not just the transfers in question but similar ones as well. As Tony spoke, Bradley seemed even more intense and again waved off an interruption by his secretary.

When Carenza brought up Antigua as a destination for a

number of funds distributions, Jim clearly saw Bradley flinch.

The meeting lasted two hours and not much of a discussion followed.

Everyone continued their cooperative and cordial demeanor but knew there was a whole closet full of shoes just waiting to drop.

Jim could see his group would be under immediate fire for delegating too much, and Jane Moran had a deep sinking feeling about her future.

The one big question still unanswered hung over the whole room: where was McBride?

cɔcɔ

Jim stopped at The Garden Walk after the meeting. He had no intention of going back to the office and notified Paula she could reach him on his new cell phone if necessary.

"You look awful," said Marian, seeing her very tired and dejected looking husband come through the front door. "Was it really that bad?"

"Yeah, it was. I really feel like a fool. I've had people—" He shook his head and took a deep breath. "Can we get out of here? Maybe go over to The Store and grab a cup of coffee or something. I need to sort some things out."

"Sure. Florence is here. Not a problem."

Jim remained silent during the five minute drive to the restaurant, and Marian didn't push him to talk, just let him drive while her stomach churned wondering what happened. She thought of all sorts of scenarios, and none of them were very encouraging.

Finally, after parking on the street in front of The Store and getting out of the car, he spoke. "It hasn't been a good day."

"I kind of figured that."

"Yeah, I need to talk it out." They walked up the street to the corner, turned it, and headed toward the back entrance, which was actually its main entrance, off the rear parking lot. "I wonder how long that's going to be there."

"The Store?

"No. The bank across the street." He motioned toward the Midlantic local branch bank on the opposite corner. "None of them are going to be around much longer."

"That bad, eh?"

"I think so. Technology is catching up with everyone, and it's expensive, contrary to what's advertised." They made their way up the brick steps to the entry door. "Banks can't afford to be small neighborhood businesses, anymore. Need size to make the technology affordable. Need volume to cover the costs. Need to cut costs to increase profits. Fixed costs keep rising."

"I guess you *have* had a bad morning."

"Yeah. Let's sit down, and I'll tell you about it."

They got a table on the porch where they ate with the Ryans a few days ago and ordered drinks.

Lunch time was over but, it being Friday, it tended to last a lot longer, so there were a number of groups still around, mostly women. The way you could always tell a good restaurant was if the tables were regularly filled with women having lunch together. Forget the restaurant ratings and the "Best of…" awards run by the chamber of commerce or the local newspaper. Just peek in at lunch, and if the room wasn't dominated by four female friends having lunch or daughters taking their mothers out at noon, the food wouldn't be good, place wouldn't be pleasant, and the bathroom definitely wouldn't be clean.

"So what's the bad news?"

Jim, taking a sip of his iced tea, leaned forward and told Marian about Jane Moran's presentation, Mary Wilson's comments, and Tony and his auditor's findings.

He spoke for a full fifteen minutes without interruption from Marian, which may have been a record for her but she could see the intensity in his commentary. He finally stopped as he got to the wire transfer part. He never touched his iced tea again as he spoke.

"So do they actually have anything on McBride?"

"That's the crazy part. The only thing they seem to be able to pin on him is the procedures stuff. He broke the rules, but the bank didn't lose anything. In fact, it generated tons of business revenue in the areas of fees and commissions, expanded international relationships and greatly increased deposits. The people on the hook are the account officers who agreed to delegate their authority to him along with the credit committee members that continued to go along with his requests and never made a formal objection. Apparently, he came to them a lot on an exception basis, and they always went along. Larry just continually used Harrigan's name when he wanted something, and no one seemed to want to go to the CEO and complain, especially as the international group reported directly to him. Guys like Paressi really didn't understand the business and made the case that Harrigan himself should watch over it until it grew large enough to have a special EVP watching it, like Paressi does with domestic banking. I mean, he's basically right. We have Joe Taylor for the trust division, there's Pete Raymond for branch banking, and so on."

"So he's scot free?"

"Possibly, as far as the bank is concerned, but the FBI and US Attorney are still putting some things together. Wire transfers are taking center stage right now. The stuff Ian mentioned the other night about the transfers to Antigua and some of the other movements are really suspicious. I talked with Tony afterward, before he had to run off and huddle with Bradley, and he said McBride's equity interest in an import/export company in Antigua seems to be a real red flag, although—as usual—not strictly prohibited. Apparently, the FBI is looking at a money trail that tracks funds from letters of credit that go to Antigua and then are split into transfers to Panama, Cayman, and New Jersey. Some other transfers take a different route from us to New York to Delaware and then Panama and Antigua, and another that goes to Miami to Panama and then on to Delaware. There's also another mix that involves law firms in New York, Delaware, and Panama that specialize in managing the financial affairs for foreign nationals and operate US-dollar accounts in their names. Don't ask me how they know all of this, but it would appear they have special arrangements with all sorts of points around the Caribbean."

"Who knew? So McBride isn't in the clear yet?"

"Not really, but there's a practicality problem. He's an interesting fish to the FBI but, as yet, not a large, high profile, dangerous one. Everything will be documented to the last degree, but how actively he will be pursued over a long period of time is any one's guess."

"What does that mean?"

"It means he may not take the fall, as far as the bank is concerned."

"Then who?"

"I run domestic corporate banking, so I'm, technically, responsible."

"But so is Harrigan. McBride reports to him. And what about personal banking?"

"I think we can forget about anything sticking to Harrigan. He'll probably have someone appointed right away to be a buffer between him and international. This is going to be a complete nightmare. Scuttlebutt has it that we're in preliminary discussions with a large, unnamed regional that is looking to establish itself as a dominant player from Maine to Florida with the Appalachian Mountains as its Western border."

"So they're bigger than First State?"

"Yeah, they've been bulking up over the past five years."

During the last few minutes, Marian had stopped sipping her iced tea. Jim, on the other hand, revived and started working on his. He felt better having unburdened himself on Marian, and it appeared, from the look on his face, he'd made a decision.

Marian put down her glass. "I have a feeling you've made up your mind."

He stopped eating and took a sip of his iced tea before answering. "I think so. Gave it a lot of thought on the drive home."

"And…"

"Put everything in gear for getting out. We've talked about it. Even done some planning."

"I know."

"I don't think First State will be a survivor this time, and one of those growing regionals to our south will be the winner. I think we hold out until the announcement comes, and I'll try to get the best deal I can. We put the house up and get out of town."

"When?"

"No more than a year."

"What about McBride?"

"From what I can tell, as long as they can show that First State has not been impacted negatively, from a financial standpoint, he and what he's been doing won't matter. All the three regionals on the hunt have bigger international footprints than we do. They'll rationalize that their checks and balances are better and more sophisticated than ours and will just absorb everything without a problem."

"Well...I knew this was coming, and I've already mapped out a trip for us just after Thanksgiving. There's a dead spot in there re The Garden Walk. Florence can handle everything, and I've decided to get a new part timer."

Jim smiled. "You're amazing."

"Of course, I am."

"Where are we going?"

"South Carolina lowcountry. I've got my eye on a small, quaint, coastal college town called Morgan."

"Not related to J. P. I hope?"

CHAPTER 40

Three Years Later

July 1996, Morgan, South Carolina:

So, have you become natives yet?" Ian Ryan pushed his chair back from the breakfast table set nicely by Marian on the screened porch of their rented house.

"I don't think that will come until we get our own place." Jim took a sip of his coffee and also pushed back a bit. "Now that Marian has started up The Garden Walk again, and I've been invited to join the local Rotary Club, at least we've become more visible to the community around us. Actually, my joining the club is probably more a result of my new job at Coastal Rivers Community Bank than anything else."

"That's right, you're a banker again."

"Yes, but it's quite a bit different this time. Reviewing financial statements that have six figures for total assets rather than nine or ten certainly takes the pressure off. Although, I must admit the personal nature of the banking relationship does present a different kind of pressure: the businesses are those of hard working friends and neighbors rather than the nameless and faceless millionaire executives and investors."

Marian looked up. "Jim would be the only one to care. Can't change the old leopard's spots—"

"You two aren't talking banking again, are you?" Doris interrupted.

"Who us? With Jim and I having a combined sixty-plus years of banking experience between us and no other life to speak of—except golf, of course—why would you think that?"

"Oh, well, if it's between golf and banking, please, don't let me interrupt the banking conversation."

"I'll switch anyway. Marian, Jim says you've started up The Garden Walk again."

"Well, yes and no," she answered while getting up to begin removing the breakfast dishes. "I've changed the name to A Southern Garden Walk. It's the same business and, actually, I planned to call it The New Garden Walk but learned the word *New* is not a *positive* expression for the locals of Morgan. It gives it an 'outsider' connotation. I mean, why would anyone in such an ideal place want anything new? That's not intended as a negative comment, but just a realistic observation from the perspective of people who have been happy living here for a few hundred years and truly believe that if it ain't broke, don't change it."

"Ah, trouble in paradise?"

"Not at all, Ian. The people here are delightful. They're just under attack from us northern invaders, trying to change their world into ours."

Doris got up to help clear the dishes. "So, Marian, what have you planned for us for today?"

"The grand tour. Since the two of you have decided to settle down, finally having completed your plan of visiting every capital city in the European Union and playing golf at one course in each country, I thought I'd give you a tour of the lowcountry of South Carolina. Besides, there are probably more golf courses here than there are in all of Europe. You can call it a scouting trip."

"What we saw of it coming in from Charleston was very pretty. I've seen Kiawah Island on television, and that Ocean Course has my antenna up." Ian made a putting motion as he got up from his chair."

"My plan is to show you some of the island areas between here and Hilton Head, and we'll do lunch at a plantation outside of Beaufort along the way. Jim arranged that. Coastal Rivers Community Bank financed their new clubhouse. It's a beautiful place."

"One of the new perks of being a community banker, Jim?" Ian stopped his putting and looked up.

"Hah, as senior loan officer of the bank, it gives me an opportunity to monitor one of our assets."

"Very good. By the way, is there anyone left back at your old bank? Do you keep in touch at all?"

"I did for a while." Jim got up. "Actually, since United Jersey Banks took over, the only one left is my old secretary, Paula. We old guys were all expendable as expected. Technically retired— whether you wanted to be or not. It's all about the numbers. The young and inexperienced are cheaper than the old and experienced. Technology is supposed to make the difference. Harrigan, the CEO, got the usual golden parachute. Bradley held on as director of auditing for northern New Jersey, although I think that was a three year contract so he may be gone now too. Paressi ended up at the new headquarters in Princeton. No idea what happened to him after that. Wonder how he's making out now that PNC has United Jersey in its sights."

"He always impressed me as the ultimate survivor type."

"I think you have that right."

"That fellow Carenza seemed to fall into that category as well."

"He landed at First Fidelity. Those national guard connections continue to work for him, although with First Union making a run at them, who knows."

"And Ed Campbell?"

"Ah, Marian and Susan Campbell became good friends and stay in touch regularly. By the time he came back to work—six months later—UJB was already in the picture. They couldn't let him go. Bad image firing someone just out of the hospital, so he stayed on, but he knew he had no future."

Marian came back from the kitchen with Doris. "Talked with Susan last week. Not a good career path in banking now days. When Ed and Susan looked at the offer from First Union—that reappeared on the table as he got out of the hospital—it disappeared almost immediately when First Union picked up another bank which turned out to have the personnel with international expertise they were looking for. So, he took an offer from Nations Bank in Charlotte, North Carolina. That's where they are now. Ed heads up a group dedicated to developing international business from US corporations. The reason Susan called is it looks like Nations and Bank of America are coming together and, with the wealth of international talent B of A has in San Francisco and New York, it looks like its retirement time for them. They're coming down from Charlotte in two weeks to look around."

Ian just shook his head. "And now Chemical Bank has Chase and is keeping the Chase name. Unbelievable. Congress and the Fed have to be nuts."

⌘

The luncheon appointment of one o'clock grew near as Jim turned onto the causeway leading to the gate house for River Island Plantation.

As they passed the ruins of an old seventeenth-century sugar mill, that sill had some bars in place in the windows of one of the out buildings, Ian looked at it long and hard. "That reminds me, what ever happened to that McBride guy and the whole mess he created?"

Jim slowed down as there were two cars in line awaiting clearance to enter the island. "Not entirely sure. McBride never surfaced. Carenza said he might be wearing cement overshoes somewhere in New Jersey—given the company he was keeping. The FBI and the US Attorney's office are still putting the case together. Apparently, they found that McBride has two other partners that were working similar operations in Miami and Chicago dealing with flight money. They did determine that he was taking a twenty-five percent cut for his services. The money went everywhere and was controlled by law firms in Miami, Delaware, and Panama City, Panama. The guy who hit Ed's car was also convicted of doing the same to Sam Kramer, the export manager at Rayburn who figured out what McBride and Field were doing. It's a real can of worms. No one else has been convicted of anything. They're still trying, though."

As the car pulled up to the barrier, Marian noticed that the uniformed guards, one on the right side of the car and the two in the guard house were carrying side arms, and she could see two rifles in a rack on the wall.

"Good afternoon, sir. How can I help you?"

"Jim Fairmont. We have a reservation for lunch at the club."

The guard looked at his clip-board. "Yes, sir. Party of four." He looked inside the car and confirmed the number of passengers. "Luncheon at one p.m. May I see your ID, please?"

"Yes."

As Jim continued to speak with the guard, a black limousine

pulled up on the exit side of the guard house. The driver handed his temporary vehicle pass to the guard and engaged him in conversation. Marian, in the backseat behind Jim, watched the exchange while Jim provided his driver's license and waited for the entry pass to be completed. The rear dark frosted window suddenly came down, and a man in the rear seat leaned out the window to receive a one-foot-square cardboard box from the guard. Both windows then closed and the car drove off.

"It's him," yelled Marian as Jim put the car in gear and moved forward.

"Who?"

"In the limo. McBride.

"McBride. Are you sure?"

"Positive. It's Larry McBride."

END

ACKNOWLEDGMENTS

When writing a piece of fiction that has an historical base to it there are times when the history gets in the way of the story. A number of the events in the book did not occur exactly within the tight timeframe of the story. There were so many acquisitions and mergers going on in the country at the time, it was somewhat of a challenge to keep them in a tight chronological order. Yes Chemical Bank did acquire Chase and NCNB did become Nations Bank and then acquired Bank of America and they both adopted the names of the acquired bank. First State Bank is completely fictional as are all the characters and events.

Any story with the kind of technical transactional information that it contains requires a good deal of research and I'm indebted to a number of sources with some of the main ones being: *Export-Import Banking—The Documents and Financial Operations of Foreign Trade* by William S. Shaterian, *Practical Aspects of Commercial Letters of Credit* by Ernest D. Shaw and *Offshore Lending by US Commercial Banks* F. John Mathis Editor.

I have to give a special thanks to my critique group who waded through all of the writing and rewriting. A big thanks to: Peter Stype, Pat Ryther, Elizabeth Brown and Cynthia Fridgen. A big special thanks goes to my wife, Carol Holland, who not only edited every page I wrote, but also made it consistently better with her analysis and suggestions. She also served as one of my first full text readers and my final editor. Mystery lover and good friend Phyllis Leigh is also due for a thank you for being the final full text reader. I don't know where I would be without all of their help. And to the people at Black Opal Book, who I'm sure I seemed to be a bit of a pest at times, thanks for putting up with me again.

And lastly a thanks you to the people at Growth Enterprises. They run the best independent restaurants in the State of New Jersey and I'll always be a fan. Also to the Carl Sandburg Museum and Sarah Perschall who put me on the right track with one of my favorite poets.

ACKNOWLEDGMENTS

About the Author

With a background in international banking, author Tim Holland's financial articles have appeared in banking and financial trade magazines. Book reviews and literary criticism have appeared in publications of *The Recorder Publishing Co*, New Jersey; *The Brontë Society*, Haworth, England; and political commentary and general interest in a variety of newspapers and other publications around the country. He has given speeches and presentations in twenty-two states and twelve countries to large and small groups alike and loves to talk to book groups.